'Gibson's eye for comedy is keen, especially her satirical take on the thorny "coming out to the parents" debate' *Gay Times*

'Gibson has written a series of unputdownable thrillers . . . [she has] cornered the market in tooth-and-claw business practice salted with romance . . . The important thing is the story, and this just keeps rocketing on from climax to farcical climax' *Books Ireland*

'Gibson has a rare insight into what it's like to be caught in matrimonial misery' *Ireland on Sunday*

'In a tale of deception, confusion and danger Maggie Gibson draws on her own experience of growing up, marriage and divorce to create a comical story that leaves you wanting more' *Birmingham Post*

'For anyone who wants a light-hearted, comical read, this novel will be a joy' *South London Press*

Maggie Gibson lives in the west of Ireland with her dog.

By Maggie Gibson

Deadly Serious
The Longest Fraud
Grace, the Hooker, the Hardman and the Kid
The Flight of Lucy Spoon
Alice Little and the Big Girl's Blouse
First Holy Chameleon
Blah Blah Black Sheep

Blah Blah Black Sheep

Maggie Gibson

ORION

An Orion paperback

First published in Great Britain in 2001
by Orion
This paperback edition published in 2001
by Orion Books Ltd,
Orion House, 5 Upper St Martin's Lane,
London WC2H 9EA

Second impression 2002

A CIP catalogue record for this book
is available from the British Library.

ISBN 0 75284 389 3

Printed and bound in Great Britain by
Clays Ltd, St Ives plc

For Beau

With thanks to Claire Grady, Michael Kenny, Katy Egan, Kirsty Fowkes and George Capel

Chapter One

'But it wasn't my fault!'

'Of course it was your bloody fault! You got yourself thrown off the set, for God's sake!' A look of exasperation knotted his face. 'What the hell's wrong with you?'

She saw red. '*Me?* ... What's wrong with *me* ...? Nothing's wrong with me. I can't help it if they're totally unreasonable. It was an honest mistake.'

Kerrigan glared down at her, fighting a strong urge for violence, his fists stiffly balled by his sides. He drew in a breath, contemplated a further rant, then, frustrated, shook his head and stalked off to his office, slamming the door. She noticed Marty Green cast an enquiring glance in her direction but, not feeling up to his usual caustic banter, fled to the kitchen.

It was shaping up to be one of those days. Yet another of those days. She seemed to be having a lot of them lately. It had started on an iffy note when she'd slept through the alarm. It had descended a further few notches on the bastard-day metre when the milk had oozed out of the carton in a glutinous mass and disintegrated into tiny globs of goo floating on the surface of her coffee. And it had gone steadily down hill ever since.

She rooted in the fridge, found a yoghurt drink only a couple of days past its sell-by date and wallowed in self-pity. Drew Looney was not by nature a negative personality; usually she was an up-beat, think positive kind of person. But in the last nine months it seemed that her life had started to unravel. That she was a constant source of disappointment to her mother was a given – principally because, at the age of thirty-one, she, Drew Looney, had failed miserably in Barbara Looney's eyes. Unlike her younger brother Justin (arch high-achiever, blue-eyed boy, chief executive of his own gazillion-pound computer software company, and he not yet thirty *and* almost engaged), she was still very definitely of the single persuasion and only a couple of rungs from the bottom of her chosen career ladder. Not that her mother considered journalism any kind of *career*. Her eldest child was not chief political correspondent of *The Irish Times*, nor was she sharing the nine o'clock news slot with that nice Ann Doyle on the TV; she was only a staff reporter on *The Daily Record* with little prospect of advancement, due to her singular lack of ambition.

Drew could argue with her mother's assessment on the grounds that her lack of motivation was more to do with the fact that after eleven years in her chosen profession she was not altogether certain that journalism was what she really wanted to do. The problem was, she had no idea what else she *could* do. In truth, Drew Looney was bored. Bored to the back teeth. Ever since Brendan Kerrigan had taken over as news editor nine months previously, he had made it quite clear that he had little respect for her ability. This was unfair. Drew was a good, methodical, bread and butter reporter. She had thrown herself into the two-year journalism course at the Rathmines College of Commerce, now upgraded to an Institute of Technology, with gusto, after which she had done the statutory schlep around all the established dailies and Sundays, looking for freelance work. Still fired up with the idealistic zeal of the cub reporter she had gratefully accepted anything offered. After two-and-a-half years of fairly steady work with *The Record*, Jack Higgs, then news editor, had offered her a staff job.

She'd been sorry to see Jack retire. Not least because she liked and respected him, but also because from day one at *The Record* she and Kerrigan had not hit it off. It was a clash of personalities, to put it mildly. In her opinion Kerrigan was an anally retentive misogynist, clearly holding the view that women were best kept pregnant, barefoot and chained to the kitchen sink and other sundry cleaning appliances – all the better to keep his orderly life both pristine and germ-free. This view didn't add to their relationship; neither did it help that it was no secret that she had even less respect for his skills as a news editor than he had for her journalistic prowess. And because diplomacy was not one of Drew's more obvious skills, it had soon become apparent that she was not going to be included in Kerrigan's fast-track advancement scheme. Increasingly he had relegated her to the more mundane, less challenging assignments, giving the higher profile work to colleagues with half her experience who, in her opinion, were not always up to the job in hand, and who often turned in sloppy, ill-researched pieces. Worse still they got away with it, largely due to some skilful editing by Marty Green, super sub.

At ten fifteen that morning she had sidled into the newsroom hoping that Kerrigan hadn't noticed her absence. She was wet, having missed her bus and been caught in a downpour, hungry because she had skipped breakfast, and miserable in anticipation of Kerrigan's inevitable lecture, with her standing mutely in front of his desk like a ten year old who had forgotten to get her mother to sign her homework book. He was picky about time keeping. So too was she, once upon a time. Couldn't bear to be late. Her friends used to slag her about the Looney family gene which had programmed her to arrive at least an hour early when catching planes or trains. But lately it was all falling apart. Lately, the thought of work, of going into the office, of having her pieces either spiked or completely rewritten, had shaken her confidence to the core. Maybe that was the problem. Maybe Kerrigan was right. Maybe she just wasn't cut out to be a journalist.

She could see him through the glass partition that

separated his office from the newsroom floor. He was talking on the phone and she thought she was home free, but he looked up just as she reached the first vacant desk and beckoned to her. He had a sour look on his face.

'Sorry, had to stop off on the way in to do some research for a follow-up to that story about the dwarves,' she said, plonking herself down on the sofa. Bluffing it out.

Kerrigan waved a dismissive hand. 'Never mind that. I want you to . . .' His eyebrows knitted together. 'What dwarves?'

She had been hoping he wouldn't ask. 'You know? The dwarves in the panto. You sent me to do the human interest story about whether they preferred to be called "dwarves", the more PC "people of small stature", or "vertically challenged".' (This was the general calibre of Drew's assignments of late.)

'Oh.' He sounded genuinely interested. 'So what was the verdict? I bet they went for "people of small stature".' As if acting independently of his brain, his hands automatically straightened his blotter and carefully adjusted the letter opener so that both were perfectly aligned.

'Actually they prefer to be referred to as "dwarves". Said they found the other terms both demeaning and patronising.'

'Really?' He sounded surprised. 'Oh well. Anyway, where was I? Oh yes, I want you to go down to the studios at Ringsend to interview Bruce Gold.'

'Who?'

'Bruce Gold – remember the Aussie glam rocker? He was big back in the seventies. Shaved head? The guy with the trademark black leather catsuits with the fibreglass codpieces? Six-inch platforms?'

Drew vaguely remembered. 'So what's he doing here?'

'Fronting an ad campaign for some kind of chicken fast-food product.' He sniggered. 'Should be doing fishfingers really.' Drew stared blankly at him. 'Fishfingers . . . fish . . . codpieces? Geddit?'

Drew gave a polite smile. 'Very good.'

Serious again, he shook his head then looked her directly in the eye. 'Oh how the mighty have fallen.'

The subtext of the remark wasn't lost on her. It occurred to her briefly that maybe she was being paranoid, but then she remembered the old chestnut, 'Just because you're paranoid, it doesn't mean they're not out to get you.'

She headed out to Ringsend.

Gold was unavailable for interview as the first shot was all but set up and they were going through a final rehearsal. On the brightly lit set he looked much the same as he had back in his heyday, if a tad chunkier. The black leather catsuit with obligatory codpiece, the shaved head, the make-up, the platforms – all were present, but out of context he looked bloody ridiculous. It occurred to her what a fickle thing is fashion, considering that at the peak of the glam rock era he had appeared quite normal, and no doubt, to some pre-pubescent girls, quite sexy.

Drew had done dozens of interviews like this one in the past six months. It should have been routine. It should have been a walk in the park, and at the end of the day she did feel that the food stylist had completely over-reacted.

Later, as she hid in the office kitchen licking her wounds, Scarlett O'Hara put her head around the door. 'So what's the story?'

Drew hadn't heard her approach and visibly jumped in fright. 'Jesus, Scarlett! Do you have to creep around like a fucking phantom?'

Scarlett ignored her attempt to deflect the question. 'So what got Kerrigan so pissed off then?'

'Don't ask.'

Marty Green shambled in at that point. 'You're no craic,' he said as he opened the fridge, his beady eyes searching for anything edible. Then he smirked, and winked at Scarlett. 'I thought our mighty leader sent you out to interview that elderly has-been fella. What's his name? You know . . . yer man, the Aussie singer?'

'Bruce Gold?' Scarlett said.

Marty picked out the remains of a dry-looking sausage roll, turned it over, inspecting it for any traces of living organisms, then popped it into his mouth. 'The very man,' he said, spraying them with crumbs. 'So how is ol' Bruce these days, Drew?'

'Piss off, Marty.' Still sensitive and stinging somewhat after her ejection from the set, she folded her arms and glared at him.

'Suit yerself,' he said. 'Not my fault if you've no friggin' sense of humour.' He stomped out of the room, scattering stale pastry crumbs in his wake.

Scarlett waited until he was out of earshot. 'So what *did* happen?'

Drew moaned, then relented. 'Oh all right. But you've to keep it to yourself, OK?'

Scarlett drew an imaginary zip across her lips. 'My gob is sealed.'

'Well it all started off OK,' Drew said. 'I was waiting for yer man, and this girl Sarah, the copy writer, comes over . . . "Hi, I'm Sarah Keogh. I'm the copy writer," she says. "You must be the reporter from *The Record*." So I asked when I could talk to our Bruce and she tells me after the first shot. So then she points me in the direction of the refreshments, so seeing as I'd missed breakfast I got myself a coffee. Anyway, the next table was all set out with food, so I helped myself to this chicken snacky thing.'

'Chicken snacky thing?'

'Yes, it was one of those grommet things shaped like a chicken drumstick. You know, covered in crumbs?'

Scarlett had an idea and her stomach heaved at the thought. 'Go on.'

'Well, I took one bite and it was vile. The coating was the consistency of sand and definitely hazardous to tooth enamel. The taste was indescribable, but there was no bin so I had to swallow it. How I kept it down I've no idea. Anyway, that was when the director called for the Hero Chicken.'

'The *Hero* Chicken?'

'Yes. That's what they call the cosmetically enhanced food they use for the shoot. Would you believe they have Hero Chicken *and* Rehearsal Chicken? Something to do with the lights wilting the product—'

'Cut to the chase, Drew.'

'I'm getting there, I'm getting there. As I said, that was the point at which the director yelled, "OK. Bring on the Hero Chicken." Then suddenly there was this wail from behind me, followed by a string of profanities, followed by, "Where the fuck's my Hero Chicken?"'

Scarlett caught on quickly. 'Shit! Yeh ate the friggin' Hero Chicken.'

'It's a wonder I got off the set alive. They had to physically drag the food stylist off me.'

Scarlett was doubled up now, close to hysteria. Holding onto the kitchen counter for support, tears streaming down her face, she said, 'Yeh ate the Hero Chicken?' Gasp, gasp. 'Yeh ate the friggin' star of the show.'

'It was an understandable mistake.' Drew tried to sound irate, but even she could see the funny side.

Still laughing, Scarlett shook the kettle to check for water and plugged it in. 'By the way, Kerrigan's lookin' for yeh again,' she said. 'I think he wants yeh to cover a deportation story.'

Drew was stunned. 'Are you serious? What's gotten into him? Has everyone else been mowed down by a runaway juggernaut or something?' A moment of paranoia. 'Why didn't he send you?'

'I'm chasin' up a reclusive Lotto winner . . . Anyway, I

don't know what your problem is. It'll beat the human interest crap he usually gives yeh.'

Scarlett had a point, but Drew was still wary. There must be some sort of catch. It was months since Kerrigan had given her a decent 'real news' assignment.

He was in quite a civilised humour when she walked into his office. Jolly almost. 'Ah, Drew. Need you to go out to the airport with Lenny. The Department of Justice bods are deporting that Romanian guy, Nicolae . . .' He looked down at a press release on his desk. '. . . Nicolae Illescu. Today.'

'Nicolae Illescu? The guy who was up for GBH?'

'That's the one.'

Drew remembered him as a swarthy, serious-looking man in his early thirties. Eight months before, he had been involved in an incident in O'Connell Street. Drew had covered the court hearing. The Guards had charged him with grevious bodily harm because he had bottled a man, causing him to require fifty-three stitches to a head wound. Illescu had claimed that he'd been set upon by racist thugs as he was walking with his black girlfriend. He said that before attacking him they had shouted offensive remarks at them. He had grabbed a bottle from one of the yobs to defend himself, resulting in the injury to his attacker. The prosecution wheeled in seven witnesses, friends of the victim, who swore that the Romanian had launched an unprovoked attack on their friend with the bottle. Illescu was sentenced to a year and six months in Mountjoy, but was out on bail pending an appeal. Now he was being deported.

At the time, Drew was inclined to believe the Romanian. She felt it highly unlikely that whilst walking with his girlfriend he would have set upon eight men for no apparent reason. It would have been bordering on suicidal, but as well as the seven witnesses, the prosecution also trundled in a character witness who stated that the magnificent seven plus one were model citizens, involved in youth work and currently participating in a drug rehabilitation programme.

'What time are they taking him out?' Drew asked.

'Three-thirty Aer Lingus to Paris.' Kerrigan shoved his glasses up the bridge of his nose and handed her the press release to signify that their meeting was at an end. 'And try not to get chucked out of the airport before you get the story.' His voice was jaded and Drew's hackles rose, but she just couldn't think of a suitably clever or cutting remark.

'You right?' Lenny was standing in the doorway, camera bag slung over his shoulder. They walked out to his car which was parked in the Jervis Centre. It was raining heavily as they stepped out of *The Daily Record* building onto Middle Abbey Street, so they cut through the Marks & Spencer food hall on Liffey Street. 'What's with Kerrigan?' Lenny asked.

'Let's just say I'm not flavour of the month at the moment,' Drew said. 'I was supposed to interview Bruce Gold this morning and I got thrown off the set before I had the chance.'

Lenny stopped by the sandwich display and picked up a BLT. 'Want one? We could be a while at the airport.' Drew nodded, her stomach rumbling to beat the band, and reached in to grab a smoked salmon and cream cheese bagel. They made their way to the checkout. 'Don't know why you put up with it,' he said. 'That gobshite's been dissin' you for months.'

Drew sighed. 'Me neither. But you know, Lenny, at the end of the day I'm past caring. In fact, I'm not sure I even want to do the job any more.'

'Don't let him get to you, kiddo. You were doin' fine til he got shunted up the ladder. Why don't you look for somethin' else?'

That solution hadn't actually occurred to Drew. Kerrigan's attitude had insidiously undermined her confidence to the point where she was seriously doubting her own ability. He'd taken the fun out of the job. It was unfamiliar territory to her. If she'd analysed it, she would have realised that for most of her adult life she had looked forward to going to work. Now, in the space of only nine months, every day was a chore to be endured until knocking off time.

They walked on in silence across the central concourse of the Jervis Centre towards the lifts, stopping on the way to pick up take-away cartons of coffee at the Bewley's stand. The shops were putting up the first of the Christmas decorations even though it was only early November. 'I hear *The Irish Times* is lookin' for a staffer,' he said out of the blue. 'Right up your street.'

Drew smiled. She could only imagine her mother's pleasure if she was in a position to tell her bridge buddies that her daughter had just landed a *big* job at *The Irish Times*. She would be bound to exaggerate Drew's importance in the general scheme of things.

Lenny wasn't going to let it go. 'You should apply, kiddo. You're wasted on this crummy paper.'

'So why do you stay?' she asked, on the defensive.

'Because I'm just a hairy aul' gobshite photographer.' He smiled and gave her a shove. 'At this stage all I want is a bit of beer money, a few bob to put on the gee gees and a press pass for Lansdowne Road and Croker. Come on, kid, you're better than that. You know it's only a matter of time before he gets rid of you, one way or another. Why don't you jump before you're pushed?'

'You really think he'll sack me?' The possibility hadn't entered Drew's head. 'What about the union? Surely the NUJ wouldn't wear that?'

'Well he probably won't sack you, but he's doin' a pretty good number on you at the moment. If he keeps it up, knowin' you, you'll tell him to stuff his feckin' job.'

'So if I'm in a no win situation, why should I give him the satisfaction?'

'All I'm sayin' is, think about it. From where I'm standin' it looks as if you're just ploddin' on from day to day takin' all he can throw at you. It's not on. And listen to you! A year ago you'd never have thought of quittin' the job. You loved it. And you're good at it, make no mistake, Looney, you're good at the job.'

It was uncharacteristic for Lenny to be so outspoken, so irate. World-weary cynical repartee was his usual style, so his words of support and encouragement warmed her.

'It's nice of you to say so, Lenny, but I don't know. I'll think about it.'

'You should, kiddo. You'd be useless at anythin' else. It's the only job you're qualified for.' They reached the car and he unlocked the tailgate then slung in his camera bag. 'So how are you goin' to earn a crust if you get the push?'

Back down to earth with a bump. 'Thanks for the vote of confidence.'

On the way out to the airport Drew ate her bagel ravenously, and with some food in her stomach and the kick of the caffeine her spirits lifted. Reading the press release she ascertained that Illescu's deportation was on the grounds that he left the jurisdiction whilst waiting for his case to be decided. He had been stopped in Dublin Port leaving the Liverpool ferry on the way back in. The Department of Justice was also invoking the Dublin Convention which stated that an asylum seeker or refugee must declare himself as such in the first EU member country in which he lands, and in Illescu's case he had landed in France.

'Poor sod,' she said aloud.

'Who?'

'This Romanian guy. He was caught getting off the Liverpool ferry, so they're slinging him out for leaving the jurisdiction before his case was decided.'

'Rules is rules,' said Lenny, speeding up to catch an amber light before it turned red. 'Anyway, there's too many of them. Them an' all the blacks. Milkin' the system they are.'

Drew was gobsmacked. She had never thought of Lenny as a racist. 'Oh come on, Lenny. How can you say that?'

'Jeasus, you can't walk down Mount Street, the place is

only crawlin' with them. Eeek-oh-nomic refugees the lot of them. We should look after our own first.'

Drew snorted. 'And how many economic refugees did we export over the years, illegally I might add, to the States, for God's sake? How many to England? Jesus! In the seventies and eighties it was the government's *policy* regarding unemployment. They actively *encouraged* whole generations to emigrate. Come on, Lenny. It's pay back time. We're in the middle of an economic boom ... the ubiquitous Celtic Tiger. The government doesn't know what to do with the budget surplus.'

Lenny pursed his lips. 'Well I don't want them spendin' my tax money on bleedin' foreigners. That was then. This is now. I tell you, it'll end in tears all this lettin' people in willy-nilly. Before we know it we'll have more of them Mooslums than we have decent Catholics.'

Drew guffawed. 'And when did you last go to Mass?'

Lenny was well into his stride and his ire was reflected in the speed at which he whizzed, almost on two wheels, around the roundabout on the airport approach. Drew was flung against the passenger door. 'Not the point, kiddo, and you know it. Mark my words, blood will be spilt.' He tapped the side of his nose and pushed his tongue into his cheek to make the point. Drew just shook her head and let the matter drop. Lenny and his ilk weren't open to reasonable argument.

They arrived at the airport just before two. She was determined to be in plenty of time in case the Department of Justice officers tried to spirit Nicolae Illescu to the departure lounge, thus evading the media. Deportations were a touchy subject at the moment. Lenny dropped her off at the entrance to departures and went off to park the car.

The check-in area was crowded with people toting luggage, queuing at the various desks. Drew scanned the bays until she recognised the Aer Lingus logo. Then she picked out the Paris queue. A straggle of passengers lined up. None of them was Nicolae Illescu. She recognised a staffer from *The Irish Times* and nodded a greeting. 'Bit harsh, chucking him out because he left the jurisdiction.'

'More so when he went to see his mother who's apparently in London and dying of cancer as we speak,' the journalist muttered.

'Are you serious?' Drew was appalled. She scribbled a note. That should keep Kerrigan happy on the human interest side.

Lenny sauntered up at that point. 'No sign then?'

'Not yet,' Drew replied.

He opened his bag and started to sort out his equipment. Other media people were assembling in a huddle now. 'I'll meet you over at the departure gate,' Lenny said, then walked off with *The Irish Times* photographer.

Drew scanned the crowd. About twenty feet away she recognised Patricia Dever heading towards the Aer Lingus check-in. She was with a beautiful, elegantly tall black girl, and they were deep in conversation. Patricia and Drew had been in the same class at Kylemore Abbey and she was now a social worker with The Eastern Health Board. Putting two and two together, Drew hurried over. 'Patricia, hi!'

Her former classmate looked startled for a moment. 'Oh, Drew. It's you. I suppose you're here because of Nicolae.'

'Yes. How are you involved?'

'I'm with the Refugee Unit now, and I tell you, this whole business is a disgrace. They're deporting him before they've properly looked at his case.' She was visibly angry.

'I suppose the conviction didn't help matters,' Drew said.

The girl with Patricia looked outraged. 'That was not justice! We were attacked. Those men they attacked us.'

Patricia put her arm around the Somalian girl's shoulder. 'It's OK, Iman.' Then to Drew, 'This is Iman Dirie. She's Nicolae's partner.'

'You were with him? I didn't see you in court. Why didn't you give evidence?'

'Defence cock up.' Patricia almost spat the words out. 'I tell you, it's been one thing after another. That was our grounds for the appeal, but it's all academic now.'

'That's awful. But why the rush? It all seems very harsh, particularly considering the circumstances with his mother. Even by the usual Department of Justice standards it qualifies as undue haste.'

'I think they're trying to make a point and poor Nicolae's it,' Patricia said.

Iman grabbed Drew's sleeve. 'You are a journalist? You work in the media?'

'Drew works for *The Daily Record*, Iman. We were at school together.'

'Then you will help us. My Nicolae, he had to go to London to see his mother. She is dying. What is so bad that your government, they send him back to Romania? In Romania he will be arrested. He will be persecuted.'

'Why? Is he political?' Surprised, Drew had assumed, like Lenny, that in common with many Romanians he was an economic refugee, choosing Ireland as having better social welfare than most other European countries.

Iman gave a frantic nod. 'He is monarchist. The government they treat the monarchists very badly. My Nicolae cannot go back there.' She was visibly distressed now. Patricia, who still had a comforting arm around the girl's shoulder, gave Drew a pained look.

'So why did they turn him down?' Drew asked.

Iman dug into her pocket, pulling out a bundle of soggy tissues, then blew her nose and dabbed her eyes. 'They don't believe him. They say he is economic refugee. But what do they know? The police they beat him up. He cannot get work because he is a monarchist. They say he is trouble maker.'

Patricia nodded confirmation. 'It's true. It was political persecution that drove him from Romania. It's so unfair. He's a qualified chef.'

Over Patricia's shoulder Drew noticed the media rabble making a surge towards the entrance. She took their cue and followed hastily. 'Come on, guys, show time.' Patricia and Iman were hot on her heels.

Nicolae and a man whom Drew took to be Department of Justice were surrounded by four burly Gardai who headed straight for the departure gate at a hefty rate of knots. The Romanian looked pale and bewildered under his five o'clock shadow. His collar-length curly hair was matted at the crown as if he hadn't seen a comb for a couple of days, and his clothes were creased.

Journalists were roaring questions at Nicolae and the official. 'Isn't it true that Mr Illescu will be persecuted when he returns to Romania?' Drew shouted, on the trot, to the official. He stared straight ahead, one hand firmly propelling Nicolae towards the gate. 'What about his mother?' someone shouted. 'What's the rush? Why can't he stay on humanitarian grounds?'

Ahead, baying for blood, was a small refugee support group. They had unfolded banners denouncing government policy on refugees and asylum seekers. The cops executed a nifty turn and hustled their charge past at an increased pace. Reporters were still throwing questions at the pair but getting no answers. Drew heard Iman call Nicolae's name, but her voice was lost in the general melee and they didn't even manage to make eye contact.

Approaching the departure gate, Drew saw Lenny lining up his camera. Even without a quote from the stony-faced official she was sure that the pictures would be the foundation of a good story, especially when she got the real human interest background from the girlfriend. Divided lovers. The Department of Foreign Affairs penalising a man for visiting the death bed of his mother; there were any number of angles.

At the other side of the gate another official was waiting, holding the boarding passes and a scruffy Nike sports bag which Drew assumed must be Nicolae's. She remembered seeing the man earlier at the check-in. There was a scuffle as the momentum of the pursuing media and the protesters propelled those at the front into the two airport police who were presumably there to prevent them from stampeding through the departure gate. Cameras flashed away, then suddenly it was all over. The gaggle of reporters dispersed. Standing ten feet away, with her back to the departure gate, Drew saw Una Halloran, the RTE legal affairs correspondent, doing her piece to camera, and a little to her right a crew from TV3.

She glanced around, looking for Iman, but she was nowhere to be seen. Cursing quietly to herself for letting the girl get away before she'd pumped her for the full background, Drew consoled herself with the fact that she could always give Patricia a call. She'd be bound to have Iman's address.

'Got some great shots,' Lenny said, packing his camera in its case.

'Did you see where the black girl went?'

'What black girl?'

Just then she caught a glimpse of Patricia at the end of the concourse. 'Wait for me, Lenny, there's someone I have to talk to.'

Lenny looked at his watch. 'Will you be long? I need to get this lot processed.'

Drew sighed impatiently. 'Oh, never mind. I'll find my own way back. I wouldn't want to *keep* you.'

'Keep your bleedin' hair on. I'll see you in the bar.'

'Thanks, Lenny.' She grinned at him then dashed off after Patricia.

Chapter Two

Georgina Fitz-Simons stood by the luggage carousel waiting for her bag to make an appearance. It was not looking good: only a cruddy black chain-store hold-all with a twist of pink wool tied to the strap was making its third circuit, along with a cardboard carton held together with duct tape. Even more worryingly, the label on the carton announced that its destination was Glasgow. She was hot, sweaty and in need of a strong drink. A very cold, very dry martini. It had slipped her mind that Aerfungus didn't serve martinis to steerage passengers.

She hadn't had a drink in four weeks. No cigarettes and no drugs – or at least no class A drugs. But then that was the object of the exercise. At enormous expense she had submitted herself to the spartan regime of the Hermitage Clinic in order to kick a serious cocaine habit. The flaw in the plan was that because the clinic treated diverse dependency problems, all alcohol and cigarettes were banned and all prescription drugs were doled out to patients as directed.

It had been a tough four weeks. The rehab involved a lot of group therapy. It was the baring of souls that George found particularly difficult. Georgina Fitz-Simons had not been brought up to share her feelings, particularly with the disparate crowd in her group, which included a middle-aged corporate wife and a rotund union official, both kicking alcoholism, and a guy who looked too young to shave yet had just sold his computer software company to a Japanese conglomerate for an obscene amount of cash and stock

17

options, also kicking the demon drink; a policeman and an ageing rock star, both attempting to kick drink and class A drugs, and an *IT* girl, who like George had a serious coke habit. But it had to be done.

George's life was going down the toilet, or rather up her nose, and it was time to call a halt and get her life back. And tough though it had been, she felt she had succeeded. She was determined to stay clean. She had left the clinic feeling strong, confident and full of hope. An epic train journey from Leicestershire to London had sapped her spirits, however. Flooding on the line, a catalogue of broken rails and storm-vanquished trees across the tracks had caused the two-hour journey to Paddington to last for six hours, with no dining car or bar facilities. She had arrived at Heathrow tired, grumpy, and bordering on paranoid, then had to practically run to catch her flight. All the more ironic then that on the London–Dublin flight, the over-large man stuffed into the seat next to her had upended his red wine all over her cream Joseph cashmere trousers, then insisted on dousing her in white wine to kill the stain. By that time she was past caring about the trousers, but she wasn't in the mood to have his fat hands dabbing self-consciously at her thighs, however apologetic he was. She was feeling too fragile.

To all outward appearances George Fitz-Simons was a beautiful, upwardly mobile career woman. At the age of thirty-five she owned her own apartment in Dublin 4, drove a new Golf GTI Cabriolet, dressed expensively and ran her own corporate events and entertainment company. She seemed to have it all. And this would have been an accurate assessment only a year previously, but in the space of twelve months George Fitz-Simons had fallen behind with the mortgage, owed four payments on the Golf and was close to financial ruin. It was a classic Catch-22 situation. The pressures of running a successful business has caused her manageable recreational coke habit to escalate. From the occasional snort at an event or party she was, at the height of her habit, hoovering up four to five grams a week. The greater the pressure the more she snorted. Soon it became a necessity to have a hit before she could start the day. She felt as if she was running the wrong way up a greased escalator.

Scraping together enough for Grillo's payment was taking up all her time these days. He knew this, of course. She felt that he was playing her like a salmon, reeling her in only to let her swim away so far, before he'd yank at the line again. He was a cruel bastard. He knew how strapped for cash she was and that she could sense he was basking in the power. She had never intended to get in this deep, but one thing had led to another. She wondered if Grillo had engineered the whole sorry business. Knowing him as she did now, it wouldn't have surprised her.

'Will passengers from flight EI 105 from London Heathrow still awaiting baggage, please go to the customer service desk.' George groaned inwardly. Her left thigh was still damp and the sour smell of the stale wine offended her. The fat guy was standing close by, sweating. He gave her a shy smile and picked up the tatty hold-all from the moving belt. She hoped that he wouldn't try to strike up a conversation again. She didn't feel capable of even rudimentary civility.

The woman at the customer service desk took her baggage check, scanned the barcode, then peered at her computer terminal. It didn't cheer George up any to overhear another clerk advising a gesticulating Italian woman that he had no idea where her luggage was, and if it didn't turn up in seven working days she could put in a claim.

'Sorry, no sign of it yet,' her clerk said cheerfully. She handed George a card. 'If you fill this in with your address and phone number and leave it with me, then ring this number in a couple of hours, we should have a trace on it by then. Everything's computerised, so we'll soon find it.'

'If everything's so bloody electronic, how come yer woman's luggage has disappeared off the face of the earth then?' George asked as she scribbled her address and phone number on the card, nodding in the direction of the disgruntled signora.

The customer service clerk gave her a frozen smile that didn't reach her eyes. Like George, she didn't need this. The Heathrow baggage handlers had cocked up again. There was a line of passengers snaking around the wall, all waiting to give her hell. As if it was her fault. How hard could it be to read a label for God's sake?

'I'm sorry, madam, it rarely happens that we can't trace a bag. Just bear with me.' She tapped at the computer again, then her face brightened. 'Oh, looks like it's shown up in Paris.'

'Fine.' George shoved the card aggressively across the counter. 'Just get it couriered to me as soon as it gets here.' As she stomped off towards the blue channel the Italian matron was still ranting at her clerk and doing vigorous semaphore.

The cold hit George as soon as the automatic doors opened. She pulled up her jacket collar and waited for a break in the traffic.

Drew thundered down the concourse. Patricia and Iman had disappeared again. She stopped by the escalators and looked frantically in every direction. Thankfully she spied Iman's lissom figure at the foot of the escalator, gliding towards the exit. Drew set off after her at a belt, apologetically shoving her way past the stationary passengers enjoying the effortless ride to the bottom. She couldn't understand people who stood on a *down* escalator. What was the point? Had they lost the use of their legs? The same went for moving walkways. No wonder half the country was overweight.

As she reached the foot of the stairway, she could see Iman and Patricia on the other side of the automatic exit doors, waiting to cross the road. They were heading towards the car park. She leapt off the end of the escalator and sped after them. An elderly woman pushing her infirm husband in a wheelchair abruptly changed direction and lurched into Drew's path. She tried to side step the obstacle – it was her only option bar leaping over them – but her general momentum caused her to skid on the wet floor and career through the exit doors into the back of a woman in a cream trouser suit who was standing directly outside. The woman gave a shriek, the kinetic energy causing her to cannon into the road like a snookerball. There was a screech of brakes. The taxi stuck to the road. The driver roared a string of abuse, more in fright than anything else, at the startled woman plastered across the bonnet of his Toyota.

Drew tried to help her up. 'I'm sorry. I'm sooo sorry. I slipped on the . . . Are you OK? It was the . . . Sorry, I couldn't . . .' Aware that she sounded like a babbling half wit, she shut up and attempted to drag the traumatised woman into a standing position.

George gradually came to her senses and shook the lunatic's arm away. 'I'm all right. Get your bloody hands off me.'

The taxi driver, in a calmer state of mind now that it was clear that the accident was not his fault, picked up George's handbag from where it had fallen in the road. A small crowd had gathered.

'You OK, love?' Then to Drew, 'You stupid bitch. You could've killed her.'

'It was an accident. I'm sorry.'

The taxi driver turned his back on Drew and, dazzled by the beautiful blonde creature whom fate had hurled into his path, took her arm. 'You sure you're OK, love?' he asked. 'Can I buy yez a drink t' settle the aul' nerves?' He was practically salivating now.

George, in no mood for niceties, snatched her bag from the cabby and shrugged his arm away.

'Fuck off!'

She stomped across the road. As she got to the other side she heard him snarl to anyone who would listen, 'Well that's *very* nice. Pluck someone from the jaws a' death an' . . .' The end of the sentence was drowned out by the horns of the backed-up traffic, impatient to get by. Could the day *get* any worse? As she reached the ticket machine she rummaged in her bag for the parking ticket. It was then that she realised that she had lost her wallet. She closed her eyes and banged her head slowly against the machine. Thump, thump, thump.

'Know how you feel.'

George turned around wearily. 'I doubt it,' she sighed. 'I very much doubt it.'

'I found this on the road. I assumed it must be yours.' Drew held out the leather wallet. 'And I'm really sorry about before. I was in a rush and this geriatric death racer cut me up.'

George stared at her, at a complete loss.

Sensing the lack of recognition, Drew explained, 'I was the one who was responsible, well, to a degree, for your brush with death.'

George recognised her now. She reached out and took the wallet, embarrassed by her ungraciousness towards the cabby. 'Don't worry about it. It's been one of those days.' She flipped open the wallet and drew out the parking ticket along with a twenty and fed them into the machine. The machine immediately spat out the note. She threw her hands in the air. 'Wouldn't you fucking know it.'

Drew picked up the money from where it had fluttered to the floor. 'Here, let me.' She folded the note lengthways and fed it through the slot. The machine accepted it and after a bit of whirring and clicking disgorged both the ticket and the change. 'It's a knack,' she explained. 'Anyway . . . sorry again for before. I hope you didn't get too much of a fright.'

George held up the wallet. 'Call us even,' she said, and made her way to the lifts.

Realising that it was fruitless to search for Patricia and Iman, who could be anywhere in the labyrinth of the car park, Drew headed back to find Lenny, planning to call Patricia at her office and hook up somehow with Iman later. The woman was anxious to get publicity for her lover. That and the whole angle of the dying mother would make for great copy. It occurred to Drew that she could also possibly get a handle on how the Romanians were getting into the country. There must be some sort of network. There could be a good story there as well. If she managed to track her down by six at the latest she'd have plenty of time to file her piece.

Lenny was sitting up at the bar on the mezzanine level with a half finished pint of the black stuff in front of him, reading the racing page of *The Irish Mirror*.

'So where's your brand loyalty?' she asked, digging him in his podgy midriff as she slid up onto the high stool next to him.

'A man's gotta do what a man's gotta do,' he said, looking at her over the top of the page. 'Yer man Eugene McKenna doesn't know the first fuckin' thing about racin'.'

Drew felt in need of a stimulant. 'I'll have one of those,' she said, nodding in the direction of Lenny's glass. He raised an eyebrow at the bartender, lifted his glass to his lips and emptied it, then held up two fingers and pointed at Drew. The barman nodded and topped up a couple of half settled pints.

'Did you get the business done?' he asked as the barman slid the two pints across the counter. Drew picked hers up and took a long, comforting velvety swallow of Guinness. She licked the corners of her mouth then ran her tongue along her top lip to catch any lingering traces of the creamy head.

'No, didn't catch her, but no panic. I can call her at her office after lunch.'

'Grand so,' Lenny said, lighting up a cigarette. 'We'll finish these then head back to the factory.'

Chapter Three

She recognised his car the moment she nosed the Golf into the car park. She could clearly see him sitting behind the wheel, reading the paper, slap bang in the middle of the No Parking area outside the front entrance. She wasn't up to facing him yet. Not without the aid of alcohol anyway. Four weeks and not a drop had passed her lips. She thought this could be some sort of record. Not that she had a drink problem, but under the circumstances she was in need of a substitute stimulant.

George eased the car into reverse and backed out of the gate, certain he hadn't seen her, then did a U-turn and drove back down Waterloo Road, taking a right into Pembroke Lane. She took another right into Wellington Road and parked about half way up. Locking the car, she trotted back up through Pembroke Lane and took a left into Heitsbury Lane. She felt like a fugitive. Damn Grillo for doing this to her.

Halfway down the lane she slipped through an open gateway and scurried past the tiny mews house, her eyes scanning the yard for some means of climbing over the back wall and reaching her apartment building. A stout green plastic wheelie bin caught her eye so she dragged it over, jammed the lid on tight, then clambered up and onto the wall. A scruffy ginger moggy eyed her imperiously, then hissed at her as she swung her legs over. George hissed back and the startled cat arched its back, its fur standing on end. That was shen she lost her balance and half slithered, half fell down the wall into a large rosemary bush.

The fall winded her. She sat for a moment, gasping for breath, then surveyed the damage. The wall had grazed the heel of her left hand, and there was a green moss stain on the sleeve of her jacket, but otherwise she was unscathed. Under the circumstances, landing in the middle of a fragrant shrubbery with only minor injuries was a small price to pay if it meant postponing her meeting with Mr Broylan Grillo. She shivered. She was cold now. Hungry, tired, cold and in dire need of a bath. She rummaged in her bag and, taking out her keys, headed for the back door. Grillo would just have to wait until she was ready to see him.

Suddenly she was depressed. What had her life come to? Scraping to pay Grillo a debt that she should never have been responsible for in the first place. She'd been doing him a favour, for God's sake. Where was the justice in that?

Once safely inside, she sidled along the wall towards the stairwell, making sure that she kept out of direct line of the glass panelled front door. The last thing she needed was for Grillo to casually look up and see her skulking about. That would be too humiliating. Then, as she pushed the door to the stairs, she heard the lift trundle open and in the mirror on the opposite wall caught a glimpse of Grillo's reflection. He had obviously gone up to check out her apartment whilst she had been entering via the scenic route. She ducked inside the stairwell and quietly closed the door, pressing her ear against the jamb to listen. A rhythmic thumping sound made it difficult to hear clearly and she realised that it was her own heartbeat. Not wanting to take the risk of opening the door and coming face to face with him standing in the hallway, she allowed herself to assume that he had left the building, and crept up the stairs. Her legs were shaking now; she hoped it was from the fatigue of close on ten hours in transit. She hated the thought that Grillo could be the cause, but deep down, despite her whistle-in-the-dark bravado, she had to admit that he frightened the shit out of her.

At the top of the second flight of stairs she gingerly opened the door a crack and peeked through. The landing was clear. She realised that she was holding her breath and exhaled, then scooted across to her door. She heard the lift rumbling and anxiously fought with her keys, hands shaking, struggling with the lock. The lift doors rattled open and her heart stopped for an instant, until she recognised the weird thin guy who was sub-letting the apartment across the hall from the couple who worked for the Bank of Ireland, and who were on a two-year leave of absence, backpacking around the world. He gave her the creeps. He had the shifty look of someone who probably stored dismembered body parts in his freezer. Either that or he was an accountant. He gave her a covert glance before scuttling inside. The lift doors closed again and the lift descended. She looked at her keys, selected the right one, and hands still shaking, jammed it in the lock.

Once she was inside, in her own space, her panic receded. She double locked the door and slid the chain on. Then, without pausing, she hurried to the kitchen, retrieved the vodka from the freezer and set about making a large jug of martini. The answering machine was blinking but she ignored it.

Thirty minutes later, hair clean, manky clothes discarded, knotted muscles unravelled in a hot lavender bath, she finally relaxed. The martini jug was three-quarters empty now and for the first time in four weeks she felt relaxed, really relaxed.

Patricia was a hard woman to pin down. Drew had phoned her office three times already, only to be told that the social worker was out. Drew had left two messages on her mobile but Patricia still hadn't been in contact. It was almost five and she was getting edgy. The last thing she wanted was to blow what promised to be the first good story she had worked on for months.

She needn't have worried. She set about putting the bones of the piece together using the information about Nicolae Illescu from her own court file and the Department of Justice press release, adding the facts about his political affiliations, his appeal against the GBH conviction, and mentioning his dying mother in London, intending to fill that paragraph out after she had spoken to the girlfriend. The piece was taking shape.

At five-fifteen Patricia finally called her back. 'Drew, sorry for not getting back to you sooner. How can I help?'

'I need to contact Illescu's girlfriend for some background,' Drew said, dispensing with the usual pleasantries. Time was marching on.

'You're going to do a story?' Patricia sounded surprised.

'Of course,' Drew replied. 'It's a good human interest piece.' She cringed as the words 'human interest' came out of her mouth. It sounded so Kerrigan. So naff. 'I mean, the whole refugee thing. The deportations without appeal. The whole system's a mess.'

'You can say that again,' Patricia agreed. 'Completely arbitrary. Anyway, Iman lives in Rathmines. I have her phone number. It would be terrific if you could give the case some publicity.'

Drew took down the address and phone number, thanked Patricia and, after an enquiry about her family's health for shame's sake, terminated the call. She immediately dialled Iman's number but the phone just rang out. Undaunted, she finished the piece about the events at the airport, planning to do a follow-up with more detail when she spoke to Iman. Things were looking up.

Twenty minutes later they took a sharp downturn when her phone rang.

'You haven't forgotten about tomorrow night have you, dear?' It was her mother. 'You haven't forgotten about Justin's party?'

As if.

'No, Mother,' she replied, heart plummeting. 'How could I forget Justin's party?'

'Don't be like that, dear.' Barbara could smell reluctance at two hundred paces. 'I understand that under the circumstances you might be a little . . . shall we be charitable and say, *jealous*, of your brother, but the least you can do is have the good grace to be pleased for him.'

'I am not jealous of Justin!' Drew kicked herself mentally for rising to Barbara's bait. 'Why would I be jealous of Justin?'

Barbara made a humphing sound on the other end of the line. 'It's all right, dear. I can understand that it might make you feel a little . . .' She paused, searching for a word, then gave up and sighed 'Well, anyway, just be happy for your brother. On a lighter note, Mona Harrison's boy Cian's just home from Australia. You remember Cian?' Without waiting for a reply Barbara pushed on. 'He's the surgeon – livers, I think, or kidneys maybe. Remember him?'

Drew did vaguely, but the fact that her mother was trying to set her up was enough to put her off. 'So?'

'Mona says he's just got a big job with The Mater Hospital. A consultant, no less.' Barbara continued, ignoring her daughter's pointed lack of enthusiasm. 'I was thinking of asking him to the wedding as your partner, seeing as you'll be on your own.'

'That won't be necessary,' Drew lied. 'I, um . . . I already have a partner for the wedding.' There was a shocked silence. 'Are you still there, Mother?'

Barbara cleared her throat. 'A partner? Really? Who?'

Drew felt that her mother could have had the decency to sound less shocked. 'Um . . . no one you know, Mother. Just someone I met through work.'

'Oh.' It was a disappointed Oh. A resigned, my daughter's never going to meet a *suitable* man type of Oh. Never going to get a husband type of Oh. It never ceased to amaze Drew how her mother could fill one tiny word with so much meaning. 'Well, if it falls through,' – subtext, if he stands you up or dumps you – 'I could always ask Mona to have a word with Cian.'

Oh, the ignominy. 'That won't be necessary, Mother.'

'Well,' Barbara said, with a touch of martyrly huff, 'just bear it in mind. Remember eligible surgeons don't grow on trees.' A surreal image flashed across Drew's consciousness. 'And remember,' Barbara continued, 'be pleased for your brother. Come with a good spirit, however jeal— Em, just come in good spirit and be happy for him.'

'Don't worry, Mother, I'll be there,' she said, stiff lipped. 'I wouldn't miss my little brother's engagement party for the world.'

Scarlett wandered over and perched herself on the corner of Drew's desk. She had her coat on and a couple of large take-away lattes in her hand. She plonked one in front of Drew. 'How's it goin'?'

Drew pointed to the receiver and mouthed 'Mother.' Scarlett held up her two index fingers in the shape of a cross.

'Well I'm glad to hear that, dear,' Barbara said. 'See you tomorrow.' There was a pause, then she added, 'And *do* make an effort. Wear something *nice*.'

'Goodbye, Mother.' Drew dropped the phone back to its cradle and picked up the tall disposable cup. A tiny hint of foam was oozing up through the little gap at the edge of the plastic lid. She licked it away. 'Things are great,' she said to Scarlett. 'At least, they were until five minutes ago.'

'She never lets yeh down, does she,' Scarlett commented. 'What was it this time?'

'Oh, she was just reminding me about Justin's engagement party tomorrow night, and trying to set me up with the son of one of her bridge buddies seeing as I don't have a partner for the wedding of the year. Usual subject.' She mimicked her mother's voice. 'Remember, dear, surgeons don't grow on trees.'

'So how did yeh get outta that one?'

'I lied. I told her I was bringing someone.'

Scarlett laughed. 'Well, I could always set yeh up. There's me cousin Vinnie.'

'Sod off, Scarlett. I've been down that road,' Drew said, chucking a post-it pad at her friend. 'And I haven't forgotten the last time you tried to set me up either. It was a disaster.'

'Only cos yer not into bikes. Marlon's a sweetie.'

Drew laughed. 'It wasn't the bikes. It was the body piercing.'

Despite Barbara's untimely call, Drew was feeling fundamentally good. In fact she hadn't felt this good in a long time. She realised it was the almost forgotten satisfaction that came with a worthwhile job well done. She sucked some more foam through the lid. 'Moving swiftly on, did you find your reclusive Lotto winner?'

'Yeah. He's a bakery worker livin' out in Tallaght, and get this,' she cast her eyes up to the ceiling, 'he's not goin' to let it change his life. He's keepin' the day job, tradin' in his 1988 Nissan for a newer – mark you, new-*er* – model, and buyin' his wife a new set of false teeth. I mean, what's the point in that? There should be some kinda law against it. What's the point in winnin' two-and-a-half-million squid if yer not goin' to let it change your bleedin' life for fuck's sake?'

Drew laughed. 'Beats me. But I bet he'll have relatives coming out of the woodwork now.'

Over Scarlett's shoulder she was suddenly conscious of Kerrigan storming up the newsroom like a white tornado. His face was puce, his usually well-groomed hair was standing on end, his tie was askew, and even from a distance of twenty feet and closing she could see the purple veins standing out on his temples.

'That man is going to have a stroke one of these days,' she muttered, idly wondering where he was heading in such a squiff and what had rattled his cage so violently at this time of the afternoon. She was confident that for once she wouldn't be the butt of his ire.

Bad call.

Abruptly he turned on his heel and stalked down the line of desks, stopping directly beside Scarlett. He had a tattered copy of *The Herald* in his fist and was shaking in fury, seemingly speechless. Scarlett leapt off the desk. Drew just gaped at him, at a complete loss. She hadn't even filed her story yet. What was his problem? He flung the paper on the desk and stabbed at it with his index finger. Then, with what appeared to be a monumental effort to regain the use of his vocal cords, he spluttered, 'An exclusive! A fucking exclusive and you fucking missed it! You fucked up again! Big time! What class of a fucking amateur are you for fuck's sake?'

The whole newsroom was stunned, not by Kerrigan's outburst, of late they had increased in frequency, but by the fact that Kerrigan had never been known to use the F word under any circumstances. Rant and rave he may, but the worst he usually came up with was the odd feck, a namby-pamby damn or two and the odd bloody, but never the F word. Now, in the space of a few sentences, he had used it five times. The room was completely silent for the first time in history. You could have heard a speck of dust drop, never mind a pin.

Drew, who like all of her colleagues wasn't averse to the use of invective from time to time as circumstances demanded, or indeed all the time if you were Marty, was convinced that Kerrigan's shortcoming in this direction was the cause of his almost continuous truculence. Of course, she also suspected that anyone who tucked his shirt tails in his nylon Y fronts and still lived with his mother at the age of forty, had to be repressed anyway.

'What are you talking about?' She was still at a loss.

Kerrigan struggled with the crumpled evening paper,

smoothing it out in an ineffective fashion, then stabbed at the headline. Drew's eyes scanned the bold type:

SEVENTIES POP IDOL ON TEEN RAPE CHARGE.

Beside the copy was a half-page photo of Bruce Gold, a blur of shiny black leather, as the Guards hustled him into the back of a patrol car. She skimmed the article. Bruce Gold, seventies glam rocker, blah blah blah, dramatically arrested this morning at the Ringsend studios (here she cringed) after an unnamed Dublin teenager, blah blah blah.

Kerrigan swiped the paper away before she could finish the piece. 'And where the fuck was our intrepid reporter while those hacks from *The Herald* were getting their exclusive?' he asked the silent assembly, all with gobs agape. He cast a withering glance in Drew's direction. 'I'll fucking tell you where she was. She was on her way back to the office with her fucking tail between her legs, without even so much as an interview with the . . . the . . . the fucking pervert!'

Again, it was Kerrigan's frequent use of the Anglo Saxon that was holding everyone's attention. That, and the vein in his temple, which was now pulsating like an independent entity. Drew couldn't take her eyes off it and mentally readied herself to duck should it blow. The room was hushed for a moment longer before she gathered her wits.

'But Brendan, they'd have the story before us anyway. They're an *evening* paper for God's sake. They go to press twelve hours before us.'

Kerrigan's facial muscles went into spasm at this point. 'That's not the fucking point,' he rasped. He was almost dancing a jig with frustration now. 'Call yourself a fucking journalist.'

'Hey man, chill out,' Scarlett said. 'Ye'll have a stroke if yeh carry on like that. We can do a follow-up for the first edition, there's plenty of time.' The news editor stared blankly at Scarlett. Something about his eyes disturbed her. She placed a reassuring hand lightly on his shoulder and softened her tone. 'I'll get on to it now, boss, no sweat.'

Kerrigan's eyes darted around the newsroom, and without further warning he put his hands to his face and crumpled to his knees, sobbing.

In the absence of Joe Mulloy, the deputy news editor, Marty put the paper to bed that night. Kerrigan had been discreetly carted off by Alec Munroe to see a consultant psychiatrist. Later, the editor-in-chief was non-committal, only stating that Kerrigan was indisposed and that, until his return, Joe would take over as acting news editor.

In the confusion that had followed Kerrigan going off the deep end, Drew had been unable to contact Iman. She tried a number of times but got either the engaged signal or no reply. However, the information she already had made for a good, solid, factual report. She filed the story and headed off to the Palace with Scarlett and Lenny.

It was plain to see that Kerrigan had had some sort of mental breakdown, or at least that was the speculation in the pub.

'Yeah,' Scarlett commented over a pint, 'he was a break-down waitin' to happen all right.'

Lenny shook his head with mock gravity. 'An' yer woman here just . . .' he looked in Drew's direction and mimed a shoving motion, '. . . *tipped* him over the edge.'

'Sod off, Lenny. The man was so screwed up it's a wonder he didn't disappear up his own orifice.'

Though Scarlett was well aware that Lenny was joking, she was harbouring the odd twinge of guilt herself. Regretting perhaps her habit of removing the pages from the news editor's page-a-day calendar and randomly shuffling them up, before theading them back into place. Or sliding his blotter three inches forward on his desk in the knowl-edge that it drove him nuts if he got as much as a finger mark on the highly polished desk top. 'D'yeh think we should send him some flowers or grapes or somethin'?' she asked lamely, as if a few scabby blooms and a bag of fruit would return his overloaded brain to a state of equilibrium.

'Good one, Scarlett,' Drew said, then knocked back the last of her pint. 'Have you forgotten about his terminal sinus trouble?' She handed her empty glass to Lenny. 'Your shout, I think.'

Chapter Four

It had started as a social habit. A couple of lines at a party, or maybe before an important meeting or a big event, just to set her up. She hadn't been a big user. Maybe a gram max a week, sometimes nothing. But it had sort of crept up on her. Escalated. It was the pressure of life in the fast lane. She had thought she could stop any time she wanted. Thought that she didn't rely on it. She had never considered herself to be an addict. Funny that. People talked of heroin addiction, but always referred to a cocaine *habit*. It sounded somehow innocuous, polite, cool. She should have known better. She had seen what large amounts of cocaine could do. Seen friends with the lining of their noses in a handkerchief. Nonetheless, within a relatively short space of time she was routinely doing five grams a week, effectively shoving four hundred quid up her nose. And although the business had been doing well, it couldn't support her lifestyle, her twenty grand a year habit *and* her payments to Grillo. Something had to give. The mortgage, the car payment, the VAT. Paying bills became a robbing-Peter-to-pay-Paul exercise. The business was suffering. Her credit rating was rubbish and some people wanted money up front now. Worst of all, she was still in hock to Grillo.

George sighed and poured herself a gin and tonic. After a long soak in the bath she felt that she had washed away the accumulated grunge of her journey. After that she had tackled her mail, then made some calls. She needed to finalise arrangements for the big engagement bash she had organised for the following night. Thank God that would bring in some much needed cash flow. There was a slight hiccup when the florist tried to get her to pay in advance, but she charmed her way out of it with copious compliments and the promise of a credit in the *VIP* magazine photo spread. After that she confirmed the piper and the string quartet, then ordered in a pizza. A surge of relief flooded through her body. All set. The party would be a triumph with A-list guests and would cost Justin practically nothing because of the magazine deal that she had brokered. Not that he was short of a few bob, but George had long ago learned that the very rich were generally canny about their cash.

Grillo would want his money. The man gave her the creeps. Even though on the face of it he was still as charming and charismatic as ever, there was no mistaking the edge of menace. The implied threat of violence. She wished that she had never set eyes on him. But how was she to know that the charming mysterious foreign businessman whom she had met at charity functions was also a ruthless drug dealer? She wished she had never taken up his offer of help. It was all down to him. She stopped herself.

'No, not down to him,' she thought. 'Down to me. I have to take responsibility. I let it happen.' The therapy had shown her that. Even though he was always there with a ready supply, a gram here, a couple of grams there, she had allowed it to happen. Of course, as soon as he realised he wasn't going to get into her knickers, the debt started to mount and it was a case of business is business. It depressed her to feel so out of control, so dependent on the drugs, on Grillo.

That was when she realised that something had to be done, and she'd booked into the clinic. Step one, kill the habit. Step two, pay off the debts. Step three, get my life back. That was the plan. It had required organisation. Her brother had loaned her the cash, though she'd had to come clean and tell him why she needed it. He was judgmental, of course, but she had expected that. He had always been an arrogant tosser. He'd been reluctant until she had threatened to go to her mother. It was humiliating, especially as he'd refused to give her a cheque, opting to have her send him the clinic invoice instead. Still, no one said it would be easy, least of all her therapist, and God knows she had been pulled inside out emotionally during the rehab.

She took another gulp of her gin and tonic and sat on the edge of the sofa. Grillo was due any minute. She placed her glass on the coffee table beside the two champagne flutes and picked up the envelope. Four thousand. Four thousand she could ill afford, but it was important to pay him off and get him out of her life, once and for all. It was part of the plan. Step two, pay off debts. Easier said than done. She'd cobbled the money together by selling a watercolour that her grand-mother had left her, and an antique Art Deco diamond brooch, a present from her mother. She felt bad about selling the brooch, but it was a means to an end. Only two grand left to pay Grillo, and the other debts she could whittle away within six months now that she wasn't chucking away four hundred quid a week on drugs. She smiled, proud of herself. She was in control for the first time in an age.

She heard the intercom buzzer and stiffened. 'Relax,' she said aloud. 'You're in control. Relax.' She didn't bother to speak, just pressed the door release, waited, and as soon as she heard the lift, opened the door.

'My, but you're looking well, sweetness,' he said, kissing her on both cheeks. His lips were moist and she felt repelled, but didn't show it. He was inclined to spit when he spoke, though he had quite a charming, some would say sexy, Eastern European accent. He was a small man and on the heavy side, but he dressed well. Always Armani or Versace, and hand-made shoes and shirts. She had never seen him dressed casually or with a hair out of place. He was a vain little man. 'You've been away?' There was a question in the statement.

'Just got back this afternoon,' George said, leading him in to the sitting room. 'Had a nightmare journey. It was the storms. Broken railways lines, trees down, you name it. Only made my flight by the skin of my teeth.'

He handed her the obligatory bottle of Bolly. It was cold and the glass of the bottle misted up in the warm room. George took the bottle from him and opened it, pouring it into the two champagne flutes ready on the coffee table. It was a ritual: the champagne, the pretence of civility. Grillo sat on the sofa and patted the seat beside him. 'Come. Sit. Tell me about your holiday.'

'It wasn't a holiday,' George said. 'My brother sent me to a rehab clinic so I could kick my cocaine habit.' She felt the urge to giggle and quelled it, but couldn't hide the self-satisfied, proud smile.

Grillo's bushy eyebrows shot up to his hairline. 'I see. Well, that's a shame.' He slid his hand into his pocket, drew out a small ziplock bag full of white powder, at least two grams, and dropped it on the table. 'I brought you a little gift,' he said, smiling back at her.

George felt it was a challenge. Bastard. She pointedly shoved the bag back across the table. 'Thanks, but I don't use it any more,' she said, then slid the envelope towards him. 'Four,' she said. 'I can't manage the other two just yet. I've bills to pay.'

Grillo pursed his lips, gave a quiet tut tut, then shook his head. He always went through this ceremony. Always had to wring the last ounce out of it. 'How much is it you've paid me to date?'

As if he didn't know to the penny. 'With this I've paid you twenty-three,' she said. 'You know very well I've paid you twenty-three.'

'Correct.' He beamed at her. 'So that leaves another two and then there's the matter of the interest.'

'Interest? You never said anything about interest.' George's heart lurched.

'Of course, sweetness. I'm a businessman. What did you expect? But cheer up. The interest is only five thousand. You'll have paid that off before you know it.'

'Five grand? Are you out of your mind. The original debt was only twenty-five. That's outrageous! That's downright extortion.'

Grillo smiled. 'Business is business, sweetness. You snorted some of it and lost the rest. You pay for it.'

George was appalled. 'But I didn't lose it . . . It was stolen. It wasn't my fault.' She felt helpless again and it angered her. 'I'll pay the debt, but I won't pay interest. It's exorbitant.'

Grillo shrugged. 'Up to you, sweetness. You can take that route, but, well . . . let me put it this way, the consequences of such an action could be catastrophic for you.'

George's guts danced a jig. She'd heard stories about drug dealers. Hard to equate the stereotypical image of a seedy inner-city drug dealer with the suave and polished image Grillo favoured. But then he had a very upmarket clientele. She felt a trickle of cold sweat running down her back and her hackles rose. 'Are you threatening me?' she snarled. Tough talk.

A look of mild surprise flashed across Grillo's face, then he smiled again. Chillingly, the smile was warm and friendly. He reached over and patted the back of her hand. 'Of course, sweetness. Of course I'm threatening you.' He opened his briefcase, drew out a manila envelope, emptied out half a dozen eight-by-ten black and white photos and handed them to her. They were pictures of a familiar middle-aged naked man and a younger woman, obviously taken covertly. The man and the woman were on a bed, having sex. She recognised him immediately and her heart lurched again.

'Pretty, isn't she? One of my best girls.'

George felt heat rising up her neck. She threw the photos on the table. 'One of your *girls*?' She was in a state of shock.

It took a moment for her to catch on. 'You mean she's a hooker? You're a *pimp*?'

Grillo raised his hands in mock horror. 'Please. My girls are professionals. They provide executive recreational services. I'm just their agent.' He gathered the pictures together, then laid them out neatly in chronological order.

'Where did you get these?' she demanded, averting her eyes.

Grillo laughed. 'Don't be naïve, sweetness. Where do you think? Information is power. And you never know when it will come in useful. I mention this, just so you're aware of the consequences.'

George's heart was pounding. 'The consequences?' Her eyes wandered involuntarily to the images on the table. Her father, the late Judge Maurice Fitz-Simons and a young woman. She dragged her eyes away again. 'He's dead. You can't hurt him.'

Grillo gave a regretful shrug. 'I know, but you wouldn't want your mother, his still grieving widow, to see them, would you?'

She grabbed the pictures and tried to rip them to shreds, but her hands were shaking too much. 'Bastard!'

He laughed. 'I can print more.'

Her knee jerk reaction was to pick up the phone and call the cops, but what could she say? My drug dealer's black-mailing me because I lost twenty grand's worth of his charlie and snorted another five grand's worth that I can't pay for?

Grillo stood up. 'I'll see myself out, sweetness. I can expect a payment from you soon?'

George glared up at him with hate and contempt in her eyes, but he was impervious. He nodded, then picked up his briefcase and left.

They left the Palace a little the worse for wear at closing time and as they were waiting in the taxi queue, Scarlett expressed a preference for a Chinese take-away. Drew didn't need any persuasion. One pint of Guinness and she could eat for Ireland. That she'd had three, followed by a good few vodka shots, increased her appetite in direct proportion to the amount of alcohol in her system. She'd heard this phenomenon referred to as the limbic response. Limbic, as in limbic brain, the lower part of the brain which deals with basic human emotions and is known to be less evolved than that of a lizard. Excess alcohol in the bloodstream apparently banjaxes the neuro-receptors of the higher brain, whereby all willpower and inhibiting responses fly out of the window. At this point of the evening Drew was marginally running on her limbic system – enough to disregard the knowledge that Chinese take-aways should not be eaten after midnight, but not sufficiently so that she wasn't aware that every mouthful would land directly on her hips and bum, but she just didn't care.

When they reached Rathmines they paid off the cab and ordered sweet and sour chicken and chicken in black bean sauce with fried rice, prawn crackers and two diet Cokes (well, a girl's got to watch her fat intake), then headed back on foot to Scarlett's flat in Castlewood Avenue. It was a cold night and not many people were lingering outside the pubs. The aroma wafting from the take-away carrier was tantalising. Scarlett dug her hand into the bag and grabbed a prawn cracker. 'God I'm bleedin' starved,' she said. Not that she had anything to worry about. She was as thin as a rail with a speed-of-light metabolism.

Ahead of them at the corner of Leinster Road Drew noticed that a small knot of people were arguing loudly. Instinctively, she and Scarlett crossed the road to avoid the fall-out. Drew glanced across. There were two men and a tall black woman, whom she immediately recognised as Iman Dirie. Iman was screaming at one of the men, and the other was trying to restrain her, holding her back by the arm. He appeared to be trying to placate her, but she kept pushing him away. Drew slowed her pace and watched. She couldn't make out what the argument was about as Iman was yelling in French and Drew's knowledge of the language was sketchy to say the least, but it was obvious that the Somalian woman was incandescent with rage. Her companion was still holding her back and now had a grip on both of her arms. Drew saw the other man throw his arms in the air in a gesture of frustration and stalk off down Leinster Road, Iman still screaming abuse after him. At the corner of Castlewood Avenue, Drew looked back again, half thinking of going over to talk to Iman, but she had gone. In her drink-befuddled state she couldn't cope with asking meaningful questions anyway, so decided to go and talk to her in the morning.

The cold night air, her underlying discontent and the spectacle of her boss in the process of losing his mind, had heightened Drew's need for comfort food. They headed at an increased pace to Scarlett's flat. Drew ate most of the sweet and sour and a goodly portion of the chicken in black bean sauce and fried rice, washing it down with the diet Coke.

She had known Scarlett O'Hara for five years, ever since she had joined *The Record* from the *The Sunday World*. Scarlett was a one-off. Her mother, who'd given birth to Scarlett on the wrong side of forty, had been a life-long fan of Clark Gable, and of *Gone With The Wind* in particular. She had named her children in homage. Scarlett had two older brothers, Ashley and Rhett, and a younger sister Melanie.

Scarlett was tall and pale, black haired and skinny and dressed in a sort of gothic-meets-biker-girl style. She always wore basic black, favouring leather and zips, but with a twist, generally in the form of dayglo Doc Martens and lace tops over which she always wore an ankle-length black wool overcoat and fingerless gloves. She was a scary looking woman, exuding confidence. Even she speculated that the main reason she was taken on as a staffer was because Jack

Higgs had been afraid to say no when she approached him about the job. Drew and Scarlett's friendship had survived way longer than their various romantic entanglements.

After they had taken their noses out of the trough, they pushed the take-away debris aside, sat on the floor in front of the gas fire and talked about the usual subject. Men. Or lack thereof.

Drew looked over at Scarlett. 'Why is it that women find it so hard to find men that are caring, sensitive and cute?' she said.

Scarlett took a swig of Coke. 'Dunno. You tell me.'

Drew grinned. 'Because they've all got boyfriends.' Though the joke was old as the hills they both howled with laughter.

Then Scarlett said, 'OK, what's the difference between a man and a catfish?'

Drew thought about it, then shook her head. 'Tell me.'

'One's a bottom feedin' scum sucker, the other's a fish.'

More laughter, then Drew groaned. 'OK, but why *are* all the best men either married or gay?'

'Fact of life,' Scarlett said. 'Of course, me cousin Vinnie's single again. Between relationships as they say . . .'

'So?' Drew had been here before.

'Soooo, he's a nice fella.'

'Yeah, I know. I did go out with him briefly, if you remember. But he's a cop, and I don't go out with cops.' Drew's last, in fact only long-term relationship had been with a police officer whom she had met at the Four Courts. It had lasted only six months. Vinnie didn't count. Their brief relationship had occurred before he had joined the force.

'What's wrong with cops?' Scarlett asked, affronted that Drew was casting aspersions.

Drew gave her a leery look. 'Have you forgotten about Wil?'

44

'There was nothin' wrong with big Willie,' Scarlett said, sniggering.

'Except the fact that he failed to mention that he was married,' Drew reminded her. 'What a pig.'

'What's the difference between men and pigs?' Scarlett asked, then before Drew could answer, told her, 'Pigs don't turn into men when they get jarred.' They both fell about again. After she recovered Scarlett said, 'Seriously though, yeh should let me fix yeh up with Vinnie. You know him and he's a darlin'. Not married. No drink problem. Not gay, one hundred percent hetero.'

'No cops. I'd never go out with a cop again. All that macho testosterone competitive shit when they get together. No thanks.'

'Our Vinnie's not like that,' Scarlett said, then paused. 'Yeh should ask him to your Justin's party . . . I know he fancies yeh.'

'He does not,' Drew scoffed.

Scarlett ignored her objections. 'In fact, I'll ask him,' she said, innocently examining her fingernails.

Drew had forgotten about the party. 'Don't you dare.' She gave Scarlett a dig in the ribs with her elbow. 'Not a chance.'

'Ah, Drew. Do yeh not want to make yer ma a happy woman?' she said, with mock seriousness. 'There'll be Justin showin' off his intended, and you there on yer ownsome.'

'Thanks for sharing that with me.' Drew sighed. 'But a cop wouldn't do. Barbara has her heart set on someone in the medical profession for a son-in-law. And the thought of spending the evening with Mother in full hostess and occasional martyr mode's daunting enough without having to endure my darling brother's intended and the family Grimm.'

Scarlett reached for the grease-soaked bag of prawn crackers and retrieved the last one. 'Aw, come on, she can't be that bad.'

'Not that bad? Are you kidding? We are talking about Madeline Reibheinn here, the Posh Spice of Foxrock?'

'Is that her name? Raven?'

'Yes. But they changed the spelling to the Irish. R-e-i-b-h-e-i-n-n. That's *just* marginally less pretentious than pronouncing Bucket, *Boo-khaay*.'

Scarlett laughed. 'Well, Justin must love her and that's what counts.'

Drew grabbed at the prawn cracker bag and groped inside in the hope of one final artery-clogging morsel. 'Shut up. You're supposed to be on my side.'

'I just think you're over-reactin', that's all. What's so awful about her?'

'Apart from the fact that she's a perfect size eight? Or that she's thick as a brick and, apart from playing at being a model as the fancy takes her, has never had to work a day in her life because Daddy and now Justin keep her in the manner to which we all aspire? Or maybe it's the way she wraps my brother around her little finger and makes a complete eejit out of him . . . Or all of the above. Take your pick.'

'So you don't really like her then.' Scarlett cast her eyes to the ceiling. 'Give it a rest, Drew. It's no skin off your nose whether Justin makes an eejit out of himself or not. Personally, I think they sound well suited. I think yeh should do the decent thing an' be nice to her. Anyway, look at it this way, at least it gets your ma off your back. With this weddin' to organise, which will no doubt be a bleedin' triumph and most probably reported in livin' colour in *VIP* magazine, she'll forget all about your failed love life, an' in the eyes of all the Rathgar matrons she'll have redeemed herself.'

It was a mildly encouraging thought, though Drew was in no doubt that the only way she would get her mother off her back was to bring home a fiancé, or better still a husband, preferably a consultant heart surgeon. Drew poked Scarlett's arm. 'Will you come with me?' she asked.

'Me?'

'Yes, you. I could do with the moral support.'

'Am I invited?'

'You are now,' Drew said.

Scarlett looked reluctant, then thought again. She shrugged. 'Ah, sure, why not. It should be good for the laugh.'

Chapter Five

The phone woke George with a start the following morning. She was groggy after an uneasy night's sleep and it took her a moment to get her bearings.

'All set for tonight?' Justin asked.

She pulled herself up onto her elbow and squinted at the clock. Ten thirty-five. She lurched fully awake. 'Tonight . . .? Oh yes . . . um . . . no problem. Everything's sorted.' She was half out of bed now.

'You got Carla's message about the final numbers?'

'Yes . . . Yes. No problem.'

'Are you all right? You sound a bit stressed?' His voice was concerned. 'Nothing's wrong is it?'

You mean apart from the fact that my life's in danger of going down the toilet again? she thought. You mean apart from the fact that I have to pay that bastard Grillo an extra five grand or he'll destroy my mother? It left her with a bad taste in her mouth, the fact that he had power over her again. Half of her wanted to tell him to go to hell, but the photos had knocked the stuffing out of her.

'No, no. I'm fine,' she said to Justin, consciously lightening her tone. 'Just a bit travel weary. Everything's on track. See you later.' But she was sick to her stomach.

'Did you manage to get the piper?'

George cringed. ''Fraid so.'

Justin laughed. 'I know. I know. My mother has a thing about pipers and I have to keep her happy. You know how it is?'

She had an idea. Keeping people happy was second nature to her these days.

After the call she padded out to the sitting room and checked the answering machine. There was a message from her mother which she had avoided listening to the previous afternoon. She had listened to all the others, but saved her mother for another day. She needed to be in a strong frame of mind to listen to her mother. She pressed the play button. 'Darling. Where *are* you? I thought you'd be home at the weekend . . .' There was a pause and an almost imperceptible sniff, then she carried on. 'Still, I know you have a life of your own.' She was using the whiney *'Don't worry about me. You go out and enjoy yourself and I'll just sit here in the dark'* voice that drove George crazy. 'Anyway,' sniff, sniff, 'you know how I love to see you . . . eh . . . Ring me . . . Bye, bye, darling.'

George picked up the phone, then replaced the receiver. She wasn't able for her mother yet. Though she loved her dearly, the woman drove her to distraction. And it had been worse since her father died a year ago. Her mother had been completely dependent on her husband for everything, and George knew that she hadn't forgiven him for dying and leaving her. Come to that, neither had she. She still missed him just as much as on day one. People said it would get easier with time, but that wasn't true. She knew it must be even harder for her mother. She knew she should make allowances, but it was hard sometimes, especially when she whinged. Having always been self-sufficient and independent herself, her mother's inability to stand on her own two feet was anathema to her. She assuaged her guilt by resolving to send her mother flowers. Emily Fitz-Simons loved flowers. She picked up the phone again and called the florist.

After a restorative shower she dressed and got into work mode. Time to be positive. So Grillo thought he had power over her. Only up to a point. She had kicked her cocaine habit, now she would get him out of her life once and for all. 'I can do this,' she said aloud. 'I can get through this. I can beat it.'

Lots to do. She made some calls, rechecking the final details of Justin Looney's engagement party, then checked her mail. She placed the bills in order of urgency. A payment on the car was imperative; the finance company were threatenting to snatch it back. She was three payments behind with the mortgage. Thankfully, Justin's party fee should see to that. As a priority that left the phone bills for the land line and her mobile. She'd have to take care of that on her credit card. She couldn't do without her mobile. She flipped through the remainder of the bills and made a mental calculation, juggling the figures in her head. She was still way short, even with her fee from Justin Looney.

Next, she scanned the pages of her diary. Work was thin on the ground, mainly because she'd been away for four weeks. Only a small hair products promotion and a CD launch for an up-and-coming boy band. But not to worry. With her new positive attitude she felt she could tackle anything and planned to phone around all her contacts to advise them that she was back and ready and available. No contract too small. She leafed through her Filofax and made a list.

The atmosphere in the newsroom was subdued. Even though Kerrigan was not universally loved by any stretch of the imagination, nonetheless, witnessing his meltdown had had a salutary effect on everyone. Alec Munroe dropped down from the top floor to let it be known that the news editor was still under sedation.

After the morning editorial conference, Joe sent Drew out to cover an illegal picket by a group of animal rights protesters at the Department of Agriculture, who were demonstrating about live cattle exports and had apparently driven a dozen live sheep into the lobby. She was glad to be out of the office as it took her mind off Kerrigan, and she was considerably cheered when she witnessed the Minister of Agriculture slithering on sheep droppings as he made a hasty exit to his waiting Merc. Lenny got a great picture of the esteemed politician as he tried to salvage what was left of his dignity – not an easy task when you've sheep shit all over the back of your cashmere overcoat. When she got back to the office there was a message on her voice mail from her mother, reminding her about Justin's party (as if she could forget), and reiterating her warning to 'make an effort'. In fear of the 'Wrath of Barbara', Drew phoned the hairdressers and made an appointment for a cut and blow dry in her lunch break. After that, she started on her animal protest piece. However, as she was working, Iman Dirie kept impinging on her thoughts. She wondered what the previous night's argument had been about. It had looked pretty serious. She picked up the phone and dialled Iman's number. Once again there was no reply, so she hung up and finished her animal piece, deciding to pay Iman a visit after her hair appointment.

Scarlett wandered over a little later and perched herself on the corner of the desk. 'So what are *you* wearin' to the event of the minellium then?' she asked.

Drew hadn't given it much thought, but as her wardrobe wasn't exactly bulging with formal party attire, there wasn't a lot of choice. 'The old reliable little black number, I guess.'

'Black? Good. That's what I'm wearin'.' She picked up a clump of Drew's fringe. 'Yeh should go for a bit of colour, yeh know? A few copper streaks or somethin'.'

Drew ran a self-conscious hand through her hair. True, it was a rather non-descript brown at the moment and in need of a trim, but it wasn't that bad. Scarlett's remark made her dither, however. 'You think so? You don't think it'd be too much?'

'Naa, go on. A bit of colour'd set off the black. And your ma did say to make an effort.' She had a wicked gleam in her eye.

Drew was dubious. 'I don't know . . . Anyway, I've only booked for a cut and blow dry. They'd never have time for colour.'

Scarlett smiled. 'Never fear.' She picked up the phone. 'I've a friend who works in a salon in Temple Bar. I'll give him a call.'

'What do you mean, you need the cash up front? What are you talking about?' George was dumbfounded.

Conor Kenny shrugged. 'I'm sorry. But you know how it is . . .' He plunged his hands deep into his pockets and stared at the granite worktop.

'What the hell are you talking about? I never pay cash up front. No one pays cash up front.' George picked up the coffee pot and refilled her cup. Conor was still avoiding eye contact, and his body language said that he would rather be anywhere other than in George's kitchen.

George was on the edge of panic. This couldn't be happening. The caterer demanding cash up front, not a sign of the food, and only five hours until guests started to arrive. The day was going from bad to worse. It was only by pure luck and fast talking that she had avoided having the Golf repossessed. She'd batted her eyelashes and pleaded bank error. She'd been out of the country and the bank had messed up all her standing orders. She'd squeezed a tear out of the corner of her eye and looked helpless. The bailiff was a sweet, apologetic man pushing sixty, who looked totally unsuitable for the job. She had waved her chequebook and promised to pay the arrears on the spot. Fat chance. The account was nine hundred above her overdraft limit as it was. She had blathered on about how embarrassed she was, and how she was never in debt, and how inefficient the bank was, and so on. He had taken pity on her, probably mortified by the couple of passing pedestrians who had stopped to watch, and said that if she promised to pay the arrears, he would lose the paper work for a week, and that he was sorry if he'd upset her, and not to worry.

Now this gobshite was trying to rain on her parade.

'If it was up to me . . .' he bleated.

'Bollox! Of course it's bloody up to you. How long have I been dealing with you?' she asked. She was a good head and shoulders taller than the chef, and she used her height to its full intimidating advantage. She could see a thin film of sweat glistening on the bald patch on the crown of his head.

He shrugged again. 'Well, um . . . that's not really the point. The thing is, um . . . You see your last cheque—'

'Not the point? Not the point? Who was it gave you your first break, Conor?'

'Well, um . . . it was you, George, but you see, well, I've overheads and your outstanding—'

'Overheads? Everyone has overheads, for God's sake. If you couldn't handle the job, you shouldn't have taken it on. Now is *not* the time to tell me that you can't handle it. How professional is that?' She had her arms folded now and was impatiently tapping the toe of her two hundred and fifty quid Patrick Cox stiletto. Her belligerent stance belied the fact that her heart was dancing a hornpipe.

'Of course I can fucking handle it!' Equally belligerent. 'I've catered for four hundred.'

'And who gave you that contract, Conor? Who was it, eh?' He visibly cringed. She gave an exaggerated sigh. 'Who had faith in you when you started out? Of course, if I'd known that you were going to prove so fucking unrelia-ble . . .' She was calling his bluff, confident that the food must be ready at this late stage. Hoping that he was chancing his arm with an idle threat. He was shifting from foot to foot now. He was wavering. She seized the moment. Half to herself she said, 'I suppose I could call in a favour and get Sean Branagh to do it. He owes me one. I know it's late in the day, but I'm sure he could pull it off.'

Mention of his arch rival made the caterer cave in. He threw up his hands in submission. 'OK. OK. I'll get the lads to set up. But I'll need a cheque.'

George gave him a ten kilowatt smile and reached for her chequebook. 'No problem, Conor. I knew you wouldn't let me down.'

Drew was edgy. She glanced at her watch. Six thirty-five and she was still sitting with a head full of tin foil envelopes. If she'd had even an inkling that it would take this long she would have made do with just the trim and blow dry. So far she'd been sitting on her bum for four interminable hours. Why did the colourist think it necessary to colour each individual strand separately? She'd never get to see Iman Dirie now, let alone make it to Justin's bash on time. The salon was a hive of activity, with every chair full. She tried to catch Warren's eye, but he was engrossed in his current client, a tall leggy creature with a long mane of red hair. He was snipping minute amounts off the ends, and stopping between snips to listen some more.

Drew glanced at her watch again anxiously. Had the man no sense of urgency? He inadvertently caught her eye, so she seized the opportunity and waved at him like a moron, pointing alternately at her hair and then at her watch. What was it about trendy hair salons that was so intimidating? Perhaps it was the stick-thin black-clad staff, or the equally stick-thin designer-clad clientele that left her, although a regular size twelve, feeling fat, painfully plain and inadequate, and prompted her to lose all of her social skills.

Warren smiled at her and nodded, then beckoned to Tanya, the colour technician, who was standing chatting to the receptionist. Tanya looked alarmed for a moment. An *Oh fuck!* expression briefly flashed across her thin, pointy face, but she recovered well and hobbled over on her impossibly high platform boots.

'Like to take a seat at the basin now? You should be cooked.'

Drew followed her over and sat back gratefully, mentally calculating, six-forty, another half hour for the blow dry, she'd forgo the cut. Grab a cab, get home by quarter to eight. Just time to shower, change, slap on some make-up and back into town by nine.

Ten minutes later she was gaping mutely at her reflection, whilst the magenta-haired Tanya beamed at her in the mirror, waiting for a reaction. Warren rushed over, full of enthusiasm, and terms such as vibrant, translucent and lively were bandied about. The truth was, Drew's request for 'a few subtle copper highlights' had been translated into alternate orange and mahogany stripes. Hardly subtle. Or on second thoughts, maybe it was in hairdresser speak. 'I'd go for the colour slices,' Tanya had advised. 'With your colouring, they're yer only man.'

'I can't go out like this,' she wailed. 'I look hideous.'

Warren tried to calm her down. 'No you don't. You look sensational. Trust me. Slices are *sooo* now.'

'But all I wanted was a few subtle copper highlights.'

The stylist gave her a piteous look. 'But highlights are so eighteen months ago, petal. Trust me, you look wonderful.' He said it with all the sincerity of a politician looking for votes.

'You said you wanted the slices,' Tanya grunted accusingly.

'No. *You* said I wanted the slices. *I* asked for subtle highlights,' Drew snarled, poking at a particularly psyche-delic clump of orange in the middle of her fringe. 'Warren, I can't go out like this. You have to *do* something.'

Warren looked helplessly at Tanya. Tanya looked thoroughly pissed off.

'Well, I could bring it down a few shades,' she said peevishly, truculently examining the red stained remains of her bitten down fingernails.

'How long will that take?'

Tanya shrugged. ' 'Bout another hour and a half.'

Drew's heart sank. 'But I have to be somewhere by nine and I still have to go home to change.'

Warren placed a placating hand on her shoulder. 'Look, you just need time to get used to it. By tomorrow you'll *love* it. Trust me.'

She wished he wouldn't keep telling her to trust him. She had long ago learned that one should never trust Greeks bearing gifts, or hairdressers wielding scissors and tint brushes. Why did she always forget this maxim between hair appointments?

Warren soothed her as he did the blow dry, and almost convinced her that she looked good. Granted, when dried her hair was glossy and straight and didn't look quite so startling, or maybe that was just because she *was* getting used to it. Sundry members of staff stopped by her chair as Warren's brush stretched and straightened, and enthused about Tanya's handy work. Again plenty of *vibrants* and *livelys* and *translucents* were thrown about, along with a couple of *iridescents*. At the reception desk she meekly paid up the seventy quid lulled by Warren's hypnotic assurances that she looked gorgeous, and that if she still wasn't happy in a few days, Tanya would tone it down the following Monday. Drew left the salon feeling drained.

She had to wait twenty minutes for a cab on the Dame Street rank. It was drizzling and she had no umbrella. She was further tortured by a chatty cab driver who insisted on giving her chapter and verse on the stupidity of Dublin Corpo's current plan to deregulate taxis and issue a zillion new taxi licences. His argument was that Dublin had enough taxis and that if they brought more on to the road, no one would make a decent living. She couldn't be bothered to argue.

As soon as she got in she phoned and ordered a Hackney cab for nine o'clock, then ran upstairs and had a quick shower, after which she rooted in her wardrobe for the trusty little black number. Thankfully it still fitted, if a touch snugly. She pulled it down and sucked in her stomach. The up side of the tight fit was that it gave her a magnificent cleavage. She stood in front of the mirror and then turned sideways. The satin fabric had a goodly proportion of Lycra but it still wasn't winning the battle of the Chinese take-away. She hoped that the voluptuous boobs would draw attention away from her little pot belly. The misty rain had frizzed out her lustrous locks into big hair mode, and her fringe had crinkled up into a sort of Margaret Thatcher quiff. With the added effect of the colour she looked a bit like Ronald McDonald in drag, but by this time she was past caring. She made a half hearted attempt to blow dry the fringe straight and was halfway through applying her make-up when the taxi arrived. She told the driver to wait and speedily finished the paint job. On the drive into town she felt far from party mode, in fact she was beginning to feel distinctly evil.

Chapter Six

In the foyer the piper was well into his stride, playing traditional airs. Waiters were hovering, proffering champagne to the arriving guests. Everything was going well. Inside the function room the cold buffet looked spectacular: lobster, poached wild salmon and fillet of beef. The hot food selection included honey roast ham, duckling, roast suckling pig and various vegetarian dishes. Waitresses were circulating with the dim sum and sushi appetisers.

George sighed with relief in the knowledge that Justin's bank draft was nestling comfortably in her handbag. The only slight annoyance was that the wail of the pipes, a sound she wasn't partial to at the best of times, was intruding into the main function room and drowning out the string quartet, who were valiantly doing their best. She made her way through the crowd towards the foyer. Justin and his fiancée were greeting their guests at the door. George had never seen the fiancée before but was not in any way surprised that she was tall, supermodel skinny, blonde and beautiful.

As she approached, Justin caught her eye. 'George. Have you met Maddie?'

'Delighted to meet you,' George enthused, offering her hand.

'This is Georgina Fitz-Simons, darling, the party organiser.' He glanced over George's shoulder. 'Oh . . . Would you two excuse me a moment? I see Ronan Keating and Louis Walsh over there and I need to have a quick word.' He hurried off to chat to the singer and his manager leaving George with Madeline.

Maddie gave her a limp handshake. 'The party organiser? Oh. How nice.' The response was polite but unenthusiastic, and a little aloof, as if she wasn't sure why Justin had left her to talk to the hired help.

George filled the ensuing awkward silence. 'You look wonderful,' she said, which was true. Maddie was wearing a slinky black number with spaghetti straps that looked very Donna Karan. Around her neck on a white gold chain hung a diamond pendant the size of a large pea, and on her lips she wore a vibrant red lipstick which none but the intensely brave or seriously beautiful could carry off. And without a doubt Maddie Reibheinn qualified in the latter category. Then the light caught the ring: an obscenely large pear-shaped diamond, which made the pea-sized bauble look positively puny. George was momentarily dazzled. 'Fabulous ring.'

Maddie raised her hand and glanced at it. 'Justin had it specially made,' she simpered. 'It was almost impossible to find *just* the right stone, but in the end a friend of mine managed to locate this one in South Africa.'

'You do a little modelling I hear,' George said after a further uncomfortable lull.

Maddie's face brightened. 'Well, only for charity these days. My agent is very upset about that. He says it's a downright waste of talent. They wanted me for a *Vogue* cover you know, but . . .' She gave a little shrug. 'But I'm going to concentrate on looking after my Justin now. I'm going to be just an ordinary housewife.'

It took effort to prevent a gaffaw escaping. Maddie Reibheinn would never be an *ordinary* anything, let alone a housewife. Just as this thought was forming in her mind she saw, waddling through the foyer, the familiar figure of Broylan Grillo. Maddie saw him at the same moment and gave a little gasp of delight, then half raised her arm in one of those little girly waves, flapping her fingers against the palm of her hand. Grillo caught her eye and, capped teeth flashing through his neatly trimmed beard in a beaming smile, made a beeline for her.

'Broy! Wonderful to see you.' She met him in the doorway, bent down and gave him a hug. 'Super of you to come.'

'Oh well, must get on,' George said. 'Things to . . .' But Maddie's attention was on Grillo and she scarcely heard. Or maybe, after deigning to speak with the peasantry at all, she felt she had done her duty. George wondered in what capacity Grillo had been invited. Was he a business associate of Justin Looney's, or was he one of Maddie's friends? Considering her extensive charity work, either option was a possibility. Their eyes met and he gave her a little nod. She gave a curt nod in reply then hurried through to the foyer to disembowel the piper.

Drew searched the crowd for Scarlett. She felt in need of moral support and had already gulped down a few large G&Ts, not to mention quaffing three glasses of bubbly in the time it took her to cross the foyer. In the far corner, Barbara was holding forth to Aíne Reibheinn, Maddie's mother. No doubt they were talking weddings. She knew that this was going to be a contentious issue. Although she had only met her once, Drew had formed the opinion that, unlike her daughter who had been weaned in Baby Prada, Aíne had only acquired the lifestyle due to the resounding success of her husband Eddie's printing business, and still couldn't quite hack it in the style department. Her taste was definitely on the flashy, ostentatious, no good if it doesn't have a label side, whereas Barbara Looney favoured the more traditional chintzy Laura Ashley approach. As far as wedding arrangements were concerned, Drew knew that there would be wailing and gnashing of teeth before bedtime. And in her present foul humour this gave her a certain feeling of smugness. Pipers, little Irish dancers and chintz notwithstanding, she was firmly on Barbara's side, blood being thicker than water – particularly as far as the whole Reibheinn/Raven family was concerned. This attitude had been reinforced shortly after her arrival, her mood descending to Beelzebub level, when Maddie had greeted her with the usual air kiss, then stood back and stared at her hair.

'You're *soooo* lucky that you can carry off that hair colour,' she'd cooed. Then her eyes had travelled down, briefly stopping at Drew's cleavage then her stomach, which she was sucking in as if her life depended on it. 'I think *big* women look wonderful with outrageous hair and clothes. I could *never* wear that in a million years . . . You're *sooooo* lucky.' Then she shrieked and ran off to greet a similarly screeching bulimic blonde clothes hanger.

As Drew handed her empty glass to the barman and ordered the same again, she was relieved to see Scarlett pushing her way through the crowd. She looked amazing. She was wearing a vintage, circa 1950s, halter-necked black taffeta cocktail dress with a full skirt, long, marabou-trimmed black satin gloves to the elbow, and the leopard-skin Docs with fishnet tights. Around her neck she wore a diamanté choker which sparkled against her white skin, and her jet black hair stood up in a spiky ponytail on the crown of her head. Drew noticed her mother glance over and shudder. In her now base state of mind, this further brightened her evening.

'Great hair,' Scarlett said. 'I told yeh Warren an' Tanya wouldn't let yeh down.'

Drew scowled. 'Hmm. The bride-to-be said I was *soooo* lucky. That only *big* woman can carry off hair like this. Cow!'

Scarlett's eyebrows shot up to her hairline. 'Fuckin' scrawny bitch! Take no notice, it's fab. And truth be told, she'd only die for tits like yours . . .' Her eyes scanned the room. 'So where is the flat-chested, scraggy shrew?'

'Over there with the rest of the coven.' Drew indicated a cluster of chattering skeletal women. Just then, above the sound of the musicians, they heard Maddie's high-pitched giggle. Drew took a hefty gulp of her drink. 'Bitch!'

'So aren't yeh goin' to introduce me?'

'Sure. Why not.' Drew knocked back the rest of her drink and grabbed a couple of glasses of bubbly from a passing waiter. She handed one to Scarlett. 'Come on. Let's have a bit of fun.'

Maddie was still prattling to her chums as they approached. One of them cast a wary glance at Scarlett, and Drew saw the other eye her from head to toe, then stifle a snigger. Her expression read, 'Beep! Beep! Beep! Embarrassing relative alert!'

Drew gave the three women a dazzling smile. 'Maddie, I'd like you to meet my *dearest* friend, Scarlett O'Hara.'

Maddie paused in mid-sentence and glanced around. 'Oh!' Almost a yelp. 'How lovely to meet you.' She offered her hand, and Scarlett enthusiastically pumped it. 'You know my sister-in-law-to-be?' Maddie asked the witches of Eastwick, nodding in Drew's direction. 'This is Drew. Justin's sister.' The two women nodded, lips twitching.

Scarlett raised her glass. 'Good to meet yeh. So, will yeh be givin' up the day job when yer married then?'

'Well . . . Um . . . I'll still be doing my charity work, of course,' Maddie said, pleased to be talking about herself. 'And I'll be playing hostess for my husband.' At the mention of the word 'husband' she looked almost coy.

'And will you be taking Justin's name?' Drew asked, dead pan.

'No,' Maddie said. 'I'll be keeping my own name. With me being an only child Daddy said he'd like me to keep the family name alive. But of course, our children will carry both of our names. Hyphenated.'

Drew glanced at Scarlett, a malevolent glint in her eye. '*Hyphenated?* . . . Right, so let's see . . . that would make your kids the Raven-Looneys then,' she spluttered. Hysteria overtook her at this point and she cracked up, but the three social X-rays just stood staring, uncomprehending.

'Would that be the *Munster* Raven-Looneys?' Scarlett gasped.

Maddie shook her head in bewilderment. 'No, my family's from Leinster. Why do you ask?'

Drew, close to a convulsion, was clinging onto Scarlett now, who was braying like a donkey. Suddenly the joke dawned on Maddie. Her face turned crimson with rage and with a 'Well really!' she stalked off towards Justin, leaving her two less cerebrally endowed chums gaping at the Embarrassing Relative and Gothic Biker Girl.

Mid-way through the evening, after a small glitch with the rock band (their manager was also looking for money up front, but George managed to play the righteous indignation card to full effect again, thus averting another crisis), she felt in need of a break from the melee and headed for the sanctuary of the Ladies' loo. She was surprised to find Maddie stooping over the vanity unit with a rolled-up twenty about to snort a line of coke. She washed her hands and fixed her hair, ignoring the hostess. She heard Maddie inhale, then watched her through the mirror as she stood up and rubbed the residue on her gums.

'God, I needed that,' she said to her reflection. 'Fucking-in-laws!'

'You OK?' George asked.

Maddie gave a little start, as if she had been unaware of George's existence. 'I'm fine. Fine . . .' Her eyes narrowed. 'You're the caterer, right?'

'Corporate party organiser, actually.'

'Whatever.' Maddie took her lipstick out of her bag and reapplied. 'Lovely food by the way. Pity about the piper.'

'Nothing to do with me. I understand the piper's down to Justin's mother.'

'God! I'd better warn Mummy about that. There's no way I'm having a fucking piper at my wedding. That woman has about as much taste as . . . as . . .' Unable to think of a suitable noun, she shook her head. 'Well, the woman's no taste.'

George was inclined to agree, but having taken an irrational dislike to Justin's fiancée, she felt a sudden surge of annoyance and the words 'pot' and 'kettle' came to mind as she remembered the hideously glitzy, sequinned Moschino number that Maddie's mother was wearing. Also, she felt it was bad form for the woman to be mouthing off about her future mother-in-law to a relative stranger. George swiftly changed the subject. 'Um . . . So how do you know Broylan Grillo?' she asked.

'Broy? Oh, isn't he just the sweetest?' she gushed, mother-in-law from hell forgotten.

'Indeed. So how did you two meet? Is he a friend of Justin's?'

'No, no. I did a charity fashion show for him once and we've been pals ever since.' She leaned forward conspiratorially. 'You know if you ever need anything . . . you know . . . *charlie* . . .' She mouthed the word then winked. 'Broy can get it for you. He knows absolutely *everyone*.' She opened her bag and George spied a clear plastic ziplock bag three-quarters full of white powder. 'He gave me this tonight as a little gift. Isn't he just the sweetest man?'

George nodded. 'A regular honey,' she said drily, idly wondering about his agenda as far as Madeline Reibheinn was concerned. She was well aware that the brave Mr Broylan Grillo gave nothing away for nothing.

Maddie flicked her hair and took a last look at her reflection, smiling in satisfaction at what she saw. 'Well, better get out and circulate,' she said. 'Nice meeting you.'

'My pleasure,' George replied, without so much as a shred of sincerity. It occurred to her that there had been at least five grams of coke in the bag. Grillo had started off by giving her the odd little gift like that, but that was while he was trying to get into her knickers. Surely he didn't seriously think he had any chance with Maddie. Even if she wasn't engaged to the indecently rich Justin Looney, she was a trust fund kid. She was way out of Grillo's league. But then she realised that Grillo wouldn't even consider that possibility. Such was his ego, the thought wouldn't even cross his mind. She gave a mental shrug. Not her problem. She finished fixing her hair then headed out to check on the buffet. She was in good spirits now. The party was going well and everyone seemed to be enjoying themselves. The lobster looked particularly good, so she picked up a plate and helped herself, then settled at a table to enjoy it.

'Excellent party.' Grillo's voice came from behind her. 'Mind if I join you?'

'Be my guest,' she said stiffly. 'Glad you're enjoying yourself.'

He had a huge platter piled high with a gross amount of food. He'd chosen the roast suckling pig (an appropriate choice in her estimation), and every square centimetre of the plate was jammed with steaming vegetables, slices of pig and cold fillet of beef. He sat in the chair next to her, his thigh brushing against hers. She inched away. A waiter came over then with a bottle of champagne and two glasses. 'Perhaps you'd join me in our usual bottle?' he said. 'I think champagne is particularly good with . . . well . . . anything, don't you?' He laughed at his joke.

George nodded and took the proffered glass, smiling politely. 'Absolutely.'

Grillo then proceeded to scoff a goodly amount of the food in his trough. When he came up for air he patted the back of her hand. 'I suppose you pulled in a large amount for organising this?' he said, indicating the roomful of guests. 'I have to say, my dear, no one can organise a party like you.'

'Thank you,' George said, confident that talk of money

would lead on to the subject of her next payment. She was not disappointed.

'About your little debt,' he continued predictably. 'I have thought of a plan which would alleviate the need for you to make any further payments. Your debt would be completely cleared and the negatives destroyed.'

'Are you serious?' Suddenly George was elated. 'Completely cleared? You'll give me the negatives and the prints?' Suddenly she caught the distinct whiff of rodent. She frowned. 'What's the catch?'

Grillo smiled. 'So cynical for one so young,' he said. 'No catch. Are you interested?'

It hadn't been Drew's intention to get smashed. In fact she had gone along to Justin's party with the best of intentions, intending to make an effort for his sake. But after Maddie's initial broadside, Barbara had cornered Drew (literally) up against a large potted palm where escape was impossible, and started on her.

'What in God's name did you do to your hair?'

After a bucket of gin Drew was cruising on her limbic system again and, throwing caution to the wind, countered with, 'I'm fine thanks, Mother, and how are you?'

Barbara's eyes narrowed and her mouth became pinched. She leaned towards her daughter and lowered her voice to a fierce rasp. 'Don't you take that tone with me, my girl!' She drew herself up to her full height and, puffing out her bosom like a turkey hen about to get the chop, hissed, 'Lord only knows I don't ask much of you, but was it *too* much to expect that you'd make a *proper* effort for your brother's sake?'

Drew briefly considered explaining that she had asked for a few subtle highlights. That it honestly hadn't been her intention to end up looking like a cast member for the *Rocky Horror Show*, but Barbara edged in closer still, hissing like a cobra, 'What is the *matter* with you? Just because you're not capable of making a success of your own life, there's no need to go spoiling things for your little brother.'

'Spoiling things? How the hell am I spoiling things? You asked me to make an effort and I did. I got my hair done and even rooted out my bloody party frock.'

'Pity but you wouldn't, Drew. He is your brother. Pity but you wouldn't. The two of you look like a *freak* show for God's sake. It's bad enough having the likes of Aíne Reibheinn looking down at her nose at us, and her only one generation away from a council house, without the two of *you* making a holy show of us.'

Drew blinked back a tear. Just as she never failed to irritate her mother, however hard she tried, Barbara never failed to dig the knife in where it really hurt. She was doubly annoyed that she felt so upset by her mother's tirade. Scarlett put things into perspective to some extent when she commented, 'So what's new?' Later Drew put it down to the depressive effects of the gin, but why was she so surprised?

'Well, I'm sorry if I'm such a trial to you, Mother, but believe it or not, I did my best. I did make an effort for Justin.' The tear escaped from the corner of her eye and she swiped it away. 'I'm sorry if I haven't reached the same resounding levels of attainment as my sainted brother. Perhaps you'd like to consider putting me up for adoption.'

Barbara's eyebrows knitted together over the bridge of her nose. Over her shoulder Drew noticed Aíne Reibheinn approaching, sequins a-flashing. Barbara who was in the process of inhaling a lungful of breath in preparation for another assault, was cut off at the pass as Aíne's high-pitched voice with the carefully affected South County Dublin accent (or *Syth Kyne-ty*, if you were Aíne) blasted them with one hundred and seventy decibels.

'Eau! Drew's here. Hi lavely.' She eyed Scarlett. 'And who's this?'

Barbara's face immediately broke into a stiff smile. 'This is Scarlett O'Hara, Aíne, a colleague of Drew's.' Aíne shook Scarlett's hand.

'Eau! Do I kneau yew? The name's very familiar.'

Scarlett shook her head. 'Eh, no . . . I think I'd have remembered if we'd met.'

Aíne furrowed her brow. 'Quite seau . . . Eau well, I'm sure it'll come back to me. I must say yew both look lavely. Your memmy and I were jast discassing the wedding yew kneau, and we, Maddie's Daddy and I, would lav it if yew would be a bridesmaid, Drew. What with Maddie being an eaunly child.'

Drew was about to snarl, 'Over my dead body,' when Barbara vice-gripped her arm and gushed, 'She'd be delighted, Aíne.' Then, with a warning glance at her prodigal daughter, 'Wouldn't you, Drew?'

Thirteen years of convent-indoctrinated politeness kicked in and Drew smiled sweetly through gritted teeth. 'Love to.'

Thankfully Aíne then dragged Barbara off to meet some distant cousins. Drew and Scarlett took the opportunity to escape, but bumped into Justin half way to the bar. 'Well, if it's not Claris and Cora direct from *Gormenghast*,' he sneered. 'Just where do you get off upsetting Maddie like that, Drew? You can be such a bitch sometimes.'

Drew had had enough. 'Oh, wake up and smell the manure, Justin. She's making a complete eejit out of you. I can't believe you can't see it.'

'Maddie is the sweetest girl I've ever met,' he said. 'She hasn't a mean bone in her body, unlike the pair of you. Just leave her alone, right?' He had his hands on his hips and looked faintly ridiculous.

'Or what?' Scarlett snarled, like a six year old facing off the big kid in the playground. At this, Drew and Scarlett's eyes met and both women convulsed again.

Justin stared at them, mystified, shook his head and stomped away muttering, 'I give up.'

Half an hour later, as they were sitting on high stools at the bar knocking back vodka shots, Scarlett said, 'Of course yeh know why the walkin' bean pole wants yeh to be the bridesmaid, don't yeh?'

Drew shook her head. 'Haven't the vaguest notion.'

'Revenge.'

'What?'

Scarlett lined up the two shot glasses on the bar, stood up, then bent from the waist and closed her mouth around the top of the small glass. Drew followed suit, then they both threw their heads back and swallowed. The fiery liquid burnt its way down the back of Drew's throat and she shuddered. 'What?' she demanded again once her vocal cords had unseized.

'Revenge,' Scarlett repeated. 'I bet she'll make yeh wear a really naff girly frock with puffy sleeves an' a bow.'

Drew thought about that. 'Naaa. She'll be aiming for *VIP* magazine, or better still, *Hello!* My guess is she'll have a couple of her size six buddies and me. But she'll choose some clingy satiny number in a colour and style that makes me look both jaundiced and like the Michelin man.'

This observation made them both crack up again. Scarlett caught the barman's attention and pointed at the two empty shot glasses. 'Time for a toast.'

The barman slid the bottle of vodka across the bar. 'Help yourselves,' he said, watching them with mild amusement. The two women stood and bent over the bar, hands behind their backs.

'A curse on all bony-arsed socialities,' Scarlett declared.

'I'll drink to that,' Drew agreed. And they did.

Chapter Seven

A favour he'd said. It had sounded like nothing. A friendly arrangement. Really he was doing *her* a favour. Deliver a package. He'd promised her two grand. With hindsight she knew she'd been thoroughly stupid to believe he'd pay her two grand just to deliver a package, but she'd been desperate. She was into her dealer for nearly five grand and the situation was getting nasty as she was strapped for cash. At that time she'd been unaware that Grillo was actually her dealer, and that she'd been getting her gear from one of his runners. He had played on her fear, pointing out that the *dealer* knew where she lived. Under any other circumstances she would never have agreed, but he was a persuasive man.

In her frantic state she hadn't even asked what was in the package, but she had a fair idea it must be drugs. The parcel only weighed about a pound. Around half a kilo. It fitted easily into her bag. It had to be valuable for Grillo to pay her two grand for merely delivering it, so it had to be drugs. He had turned up at her apartment, handed over the package and given her instructions for the delivery. She would be picked up and driven to the hotel. She would then go up to a specific suite and hand it over. Wallop. Two grand. Easy peasy. And the promise of more.

She was the ideal candidate. No reason for the cops to suspect her. It was the first time that it had occurred to her that Grillo was actively involved in the drug trade. He would disagree with this assumption. His rationale was that it was business. He was supplying his contacts. It was a service. A sweetener. A necessary inducement to oil the wheels of commerce. But she didn't believe him. People didn't give away twenty grand's worth of cocaine as a sweetener. Until then she had assumed he was just a recreational user like herself. He always seemed to have a ready supply, but only small amounts – one, maybe two grams.

His driver had collected her as per the arrangement and then driven her to the city centre hotel. He had parked at the bottom of a dark side street. George had been unhappy about this, but the driver told her he was only following instructions and refused to go any further. It was a miserable rainy night. She'd pulled up her coat collar against the unseasonably cold April air and hugged her bag to her chest. At the end of the street she could see the welcoming bright lights of O'Connell Street.

The man must have been hiding in a dark cavern of an alleyway running behind the hotel because she didn't see him until he jumped out at her. He terrified her. He had a blade. He stank of sweat. His filthy hands were on her body. Her throat muscles seized up so she couldn't scream. He'd wrestled the bag from her, then shoved her roughly against the wall. She'd cracked her head and for a moment saw stars. By the time she came to her senses he had vanished around the corner into the broad avenue. What could she do? She could hardly call the cops. She was incensed that the driver had made no move to help her.

'Nothing to do with me, love. I'm just paid to drive. That fella could've had a syringe full of contaminated blood for all I know. Just give him the bag.'

Easy for him to say.

He'd driven her home, advising her to put some Dettol on the graze on her forehead, then buggered off without even waiting to see her safely indoors. When she got in she was jumpy and hyper. She'd tried to call Grillo, but his mobile was switched off. In her state of heightened anxiety it hadn't crossed her mind that it could be a set-up. It hadn't occurred to her that it was all too convenient that a mugger just happened to be waiting in an alleyway as she was passing by with twenty thousand pounds' worth of class A drugs about her person.

Now she could see the bigger picture. Grillo was a manipulator. He had set her up from the word go. Now she knew why. He was paying her back for refusing his rather crass attempt to get her into bed. She thought he'd been OK about it. And even though the situation had been embarrassing and awkward, she had tried to be as diplomatic as possible at the time. What kind of ego did this man have to go to these lengths? She shuddered at the thought of what he was asking her to do.

'What the hell do you think I am?' she said, full of indignation when he had laid out his offer.

His lizard eyes smiled at her. 'Time will tell,' he said. 'Time will tell.'

Scarlett O'Hara was enjoying herself. Not that her outward appearance would have given a casual observer any clue. She was sitting up at the bar with her best friend, looking miserable if anything. But actually she was having the best time. Scarlett O'Hara's hobby was people watching. She loved to observe the human race interacting with one another in their usual habitats. That was why she had chosen to do the part-time degree course in Psychology. She was in her final year now, and it had taken her all of five years, studying nights. Also, observing the dysfunctional relationships of the so-called great and the good reminded her how lucky she was to belong to her own close-knit family. Both parents still alive and two brothers and one sister she thought the world of, not to mention mad Auntie Lulu. Tonight she wanted to give Barbara Looney a hard kick up the backside for the way she treated Drew. Oedipus eat your heart out, or what?

A not-too-shabby rock band was playing and all the oldies

were strutting their stuff on the dance floor in the usual embarrassing middle-aged way. She could see Barbara dancing with Justin. She was shifting from one foot to the other, in time to the music, arms bent at the elbow, hands as if on a steering wheel, rocking from side to side. She had about as much rhythm as a Thunderbird puppet. Maddie was dancing with a short, fat, bearded little man wearing Versace. His head only came up to where her boobs would be if she had any. Surprisingly, he was a passably good dancer. He was jiving, and evidently leading extremely well because Maddie was following without a problem. Drew was slouching over the bar, her head resting on her folded arms, nodding gently in time to the music. The band was playing a version of David Bowie's 'Heroes'. Scarlett nudged her friend. 'Fancy another?'

Drew leaned over and grabbed the vodka bottle. 'Don't mind if I do.' She carefully refilled the shot glasses to the brim.

George eased herself up onto the barstool beside Drew. 'Mind if I join you two?' she asked. 'You look as if you want to get thoroughly wasted, and the way I feel right now, I could do with the company.'

'Help yerself,' Scarlett said. 'The more the bleedin' merrier,' and signalled to the barman for another glass.

Drew squinted at the woman sitting next to her. 'Don't I know you from somewhere?' she asked, rummaging through her memory.

George shrugged. 'Don't think so.' Who could forget that hair? 'So why are you two seeking oblivion?'

Drew set up her shot then held up her hand for silence. In unison, she and Scarlett carefully slid off their stools and leaned over their glasses, hands behind their backs. George watched, uncomprehending for a moment, then copped on and assumed the starting position.

'To getting completely rat arsed,' Scarlett declared.

'Rat arsed!' the other two repeated solemnly, then swooped over their glasses and tossed back the burning, slightly viscous, deliciously cold, clear fluid.

'So, I know why I want to get twisted, but what about you two?' George repeated when they were safely reinstalled on their respective barstools.

'Family dos always have this effect on me,' Drew said. She was slouching over the bar again, and everything was slightly out of focus. She'd been OK until that last shot, then it was as if the get-you-pissed fairy had suddenly waved her magic wand and said, 'You're drunk.'

Scarlett, who was faring better having omitted the pre-confrontation gin and tonics, signalled to the barman for another bottle, then commented, 'I only came to give her moral support.' She shifted on her stool, trying to get more comfortable. 'I usually like family dos, but then I suppose it depends on the family.'

George took a sip of her vodka and nudged Drew. 'Which side do you belong to?'

'I'm Justin's prodigal sister.' She ran her index finger around the rim of the shot glass and licked it. 'I'm the black sheep of the family. The proverbial skeleton in the cupboard. Though my prospective sister-in-law would query the description . . . what with me being such a *big girl* and all.'

'I suppose compared to Miss Anorexia, y'are,' Scarlett commented, and Drew gave her a dig. She was getting maudlin now.

'I'm a continual source of despair to my mother and my *darling* brother.'

Scarlett nodded. 'That's true. But then I don't think yeh could ever please yer ma. As far as she's concerned yer a failure 'cause yer not married to some rich wanker an' droppin' a grandchild every couple've years.'

Drew looked over at George. 'My mother's got the "Irish Mother" fixation on her son. Of course, the fact that he's made a fucking tanker full of dosh and is about to marry that bony-arsed rich-bitch probably helps.'

'Mothers are like that about sons,' George observed. 'But then I was a daddy's girl, so I suppose I can't criticise.'

Drew looked up. 'Was? Is he dead?'

George nodded. 'Just over a year now.'

Drew laid her head on the bar. 'Mine too. And I still miss him.' She dipped her finger in the vodka and licked again. 'He died when I was away at school. We were pals. He used to take me to the races and I'd caddy for him in the holidays.' She paused and stared into space. 'I really miss him. He was only forty-two.'

'That's tough,' George said. 'At least my father made it to sixty-four.'

'Heart was it?' Drew asked.

George shook her head. 'Brain haemorrhage. I think most daughters love their daddies.'

'Ah, come on lads. Get a grip will ye. Ye're bleedin' depressin' me. What we need is to give our Seratonin levels a bit of a kick start.' Scarlett slid off her stool. 'So who's up for a Chinese take-away and a shitload of chocolate for the endorphin rush?'

The taxi dropped them off in Waterloo Road and the three women made their way unsteadily up to George's apartment. Together they somehow managed to dole out the food without causing themselves or the carpet injury, and Scarlett prepared a hefty jug of her award-winning Sea Breeze. After they had demolished their cholesterol fest and a goodly measure of the jug of cocktail, George said, 'God! It's an age since I got this smashed on drink.' She drained her glass.

'Yeah? So what do yeh normally do for oblivion?' Scarlett asked as she gathered the empty glasses and set about recharging them with vodka, cranberry and grapefruit juice.

George didn't reply for a moment, then sighed and said,

'Sod it,' under her breath. Then, 'I've just been in rehab. Four weeks. I was kicking a cocaine habit.'

'No shit?' Drew said. 'Good for you. Was it hard?'

'The hardest part was not having a drink or a cigarette,' George said, making light of it. 'Everything was bloody well banned in that place. No chocolate either, because they treated compulsive eating disorders too. I tell you, I'd have killed for a Mars bar.'

'Ooooh, Maaaars baaaars,' Drew said, doing a very passable Homer Simpson impersonation. George staggered to her feet and weaved her way to the kitchen, returning moments later with three king-sized Mars bars, cold from the fridge.

'Now yer talkin', sister,' Scarlett said, grabbing one and ripping off the wrapper. 'Who needs men when there's chocolate?'

'Ain't that the truth,' Drew agreed, taking a bite.

George laughed. 'Do I detect a slight note of bitterness in your tones, ladies?'

Drew swallowed. 'Not bitterness exactly. Suffice to say I've never been exactly successful in the choosing a nice man stakes. Always seem to go for the bastard type.'

'It's a common affliction,' George said. 'The good ones are all married—'

'I know,' Drew cut in. 'Or gay.'

They all laughed. 'What's the quickest way to a man's heart?' George said, after their laughter subsided. Scarlett and Drew both shook their heads. 'Through his chest with a knife.' More drunken laughter.

'So have you never been tempted to step up to the altar, George?' Drew asked.

'I think, therefore I am single,' George replied, then smiled. 'Well, that's not strictly true. I guess I just never met the right man. I got close a couple of times, but in the last three years I haven't had a relationship, and only the odd date. Haven't really had the time. Work's been crazy.' She paused in thought. 'I think I intimidate men . . . Don't know why . . . How about you two?'

'Much the same,' Drew said. 'Though I don't think I intimidate them, I just seem to go for the ones with Nean-derthal tendencies. You know the type?'

'Only too well,' George agreed.

'Well I'm not ready to settle down anyway,' Scarlett said. 'I like me independence. Play the field, I say. Have a bit of fun. Yer a long time dead.' She started to giggle. 'Hey . . . Why do men find it difficult to make eye contact?'

George and Drew both shook their heads and gave a collective drunken 'Dunno.'

Scarlett dissolved into hysteria, and between gasps squawked, 'Because breasts don't have eyes.'

'I've got one, I've got one,' Drew said, grabbing George's arm. 'What's the definition of making love?'

'I know this,' George squealed. 'It's what women do while men are shagging them.'

'How many men does it take to screw in a light bulb?' It was Scarlett's turn. Neither George nor Drew were capable of speech by this point, in the grips of drunken hysteria. 'One.' Gasp, gasp. 'Men will screw anything.'

They howled like a crowd of banshees.

For a moment Drew hadn't the first idea where she was when she awoke the following morning. And when she opened her eyes and saw the mound of another figure in the bed beside her, she inwardly groaned, but relaxed when she recognised the spiky black ponytail spilling from under the duvet, onto the pillow. Her head was thumping and her mouth felt as if someone had covertly emptied the contents of a cat litter tray into it during the night. She staggered to the bathroom and rooted in the medicine cabinet for some pain killers, focusing hard on not throwing up, then cleaned her teeth with her index finger and a dollop of toothpaste. Her reflection was pretty grotesque. Bags the size of grapes under her bloodshot eyes, not to mention the black panda circles. It was fortunate that the image was still fairly blurry as her brain would have been unable to cope with the full horror of the scary hair standing on end. She mentally told her reflected image that she would never drink alcohol again.

No change there then.

She saw Scarlett's reflection appear in the mirror. Through the haze she didn't look much different from normal.

'How're yer feelin'?' Scarlett asked.

'How do I look?'

'Like shite. Want a coffee?' She sounded distinctly perky. How did she do that? The woman seemed impervious to the effects of alcohol and sleep deprivation.

George was collecting up the empty take-away cartons, plates and glasses when Drew ventured into the sitting room. She looked on the fragile side too. She raised a hand in greeting then pointed vaguely towards the kitchen. 'Eh . . . Scarlett's making . . . um . . . stuff.'

After three double espressos from George's nifty state-of-the-art designer espresso machine, Drew was halfway between feeling wired for action, and intermittently wanting to barf. George looked a tad green in the face too. She took her coffee back to bed with a request that they pull the front door closed behind them.

Drew took a cab home to Sandymount to wash and change. The hot shower helped considerably. With her wet hair dragged back in a ponytail, she dressed then headed into work, early for once, but that could have been due to the fact that she hadn't even considered breakfast as an option. Only Marty was at his desk, flipping through the first edition of *The Record* when she wandered in. He feigned (or not) shock at the sight of her. 'Jesus! Is it that late?'

'Fuck off, Marty, I'm not in the mood,' she snarled and,

dumping her bag and coat under her desk, headed for the kitchen to replenish her caffeine overload. It occurred to her as she glugged down yet another cup, that at this stage of the morning her bloodstream must be completely toxic. For certain, despite cleaning her teeth yet again, her breath was bordering on radioactive. Joe displayed the same surprise at her early attendance as had Marty, which marginally annoyed her, but she let it go and settled herself down at her usual desk to check her E-mail and messages. Her brain snapped into gear when she heard Iman Dirie on her voice-mail. She sounded very agitated.

'I have to talk to you. There are things I have to tell you.'

There was something about her tone. An air of desperation maybe. Or was it fear?

The pain killers of earlier were wearing off now and the dull kerthud at the back of her head was increasing in intensity in direct relation to the noise level of the newsroom. Also, her stomach was rebelling against all the coffee and she was experiencing waves of nausea once more. She couldn't face the morning editorial meeting. She needed air. So after clearing it with Joe, Drew headed out to Rathmines to see Iman.

As it was a bright, dry morning she decided to walk. At a crisp lick she made it over to Rathmines in twenty-five minutes. She was slightly breathless but felt much better for the air and exercise. It even left her feeling peckish, so she stopped off at the bakery and bought a jam doughnut, recalling the well-known fact that the best treatment for a hangover is a sudden intake of fat and salt. Well, one out of two ain't bad. She ate it on the hoof. It was fresh and still slightly warm, and the jam oozed over her tongue. As she licked her fingers and wiped the remnants of the sugar from around her mouth, it occurred to her that Maddie Reibheinn and her cronies would never allow themselves to experience the sensual pleasure of eating a really fresh jam doughnut, especially not in the street. She smiled to herself in satisfaction and dumped the grease-spotted paper bag in a litter bin.

The Kenilworth Road house looked well maintained and respectable from the outside, and the only sign that it contained bed-sits was the tell-tale row of doorbells. There were no names attached to distinguish which bell belonged to which room, so Drew took a chance and pressed the fifth one down. After a moment she heard the buzz of the door lock being released. She shoved the door and walked in. It was on a spring and glided shut behind her. The hallway was a surprise. It was dingy and dank with a large dusty mahogany sideboard against one wall, piled high with junk-mail and letters to past residents long forgotten. An evil-looking stuffed ferret glared at her with vitreous eyes from a glass case hanging on the wall above it, and the sickly sweet smell of stewed mutton mixed with the stench of boiled cabbage pervaded the air. The reek of the mutton and cabbage reminded Drew of childhood visits to her paternal grandparents' farm down in Mayo and reactivated her queasiness. Her mouth filled with saliva. She swallowed hard and tried not to breathe.

A young black woman struggled down the stairs with a baby in a buggy. She was dressed in a long colourful traditional African gown covered by a knee-length wool coat. A long hand-knitted woollen Dr Who scarf was wrapped a number of times around the woman's neck, and Drew caught a flash of pink trainers under the gown. She looked frozen. Only the baby's nose peeked out from under the blankets in the buggy. Drew gave her a hand with the last few stairs and asked on which floor number five was situated. The woman directed her to the floor above. She had a strong accent which Drew found quite difficult to understand.

Iman was waiting for her, the door opened only a crack, when she reached the first landing. She looked haunted and apprehensive, but her face brightened up when she recognised the journalist. She pulled the door open. 'Please, come in. Thank you for coming.'

Drew followed her into the room. It was quite large and airy, situated as it was at the front of the house. The windows reached almost from floor to ceiling and most of the original Georgian ornamental plasterwork was intact, except for a bit of crumbling damp damage in the corner near the chimney breast. Iman had done her best with the room. It was sparsely furnished and, although it could have done with a fresh coat of paint, it was clean and orderly. A colourful African throw covered the bed and between the two front windows sat a desk piled with books and papers. Two old leather-look armchairs were drawn up near an elderly gas fire which was bubbling in front of the white marble mantelpiece. A seen-better-days steel kitchen sink and drainer lurked in the alcove to the left of the fireplace along with an ancient gas cooker, on top of which a whistling kettle hissed over a lit ring. Apart from a battered wardrobe behind the door, a veneered plywood drop-leaf table, two hard chairs and a row of books and ring-binder files marching in a line along the scuffed skirting board, that was it.

'I'm not sure what I can do for you,' Drew said. 'I mean, your boyfriend's on French soil now. Maybe he'll fare better in France than he did here.'

'It is not to do with Nicolae,' she said. 'Not directly.'

Drew shrugged. 'So what is it?'

Iman sat on the end of her bed. 'There are things you need to know.' Drew waited. The woman bit her lip. 'I'm not sure if I should tell you this. It could be dangerous. These people don't value life.'

'What people? What are you talking about?'

Iman stood up and walked over to the window. Her shoulders were stooped in contrast to the first time Drew had met her, when she stood tall and erect. She looked scared. Drew wondered if she too was in fear of imminent deportation back to Somalia. 'Are you going to be deported? Is that it?'

Iman shook her head. 'No, I am a student. I have a visa.'

Drew was mystified. 'So what's your problem? They can't throw you out if you've a valid visa.'

'It is not for myself I am afraid. There are men, you see.' She turned back from the window and her eyes were fearful. 'These people, they prey on refugees and asylum seekers. They exploit their own.'

'What men? What are you talking about?' Drew asked, intrigued.

The insistent whistle of the kettle intruded. Without waiting for a reply, Iman hurried over to the stove and lifted the kettle from the gas flame. 'You would like some tea?' she asked.

'What men?' Drew repeated, impatient for answers. Iman poured the boiling water into two mugs that were sitting on the drainer and added milk. 'They bring people in illegally. Then they exploit them.' She handed Drew a steaming mug and they both sat on either side of the fire. 'When people are desperate, they will pay.'

'So how do they exploit the refugees? Did Nicolae come in with these people?'

Iman shook her head. 'No. He came with others like them. He paid them to bring him to Ireland, but they bring him only to France and leave him there. Nicolae had to find his own way here. He thought that his mother was here, you see. They told him that his mother was here.' She was getting agitated.

'So who are these people? How else do they exploit the refugees?'

Iman took a sip of her tea, then wrapped her hands around the cup for warmth. 'I know of one man. He is Serb. He has contacts who bring people with little money in. The people are grateful to get away and they go, but when they get here, they have to work to pay off the debt.'

The black woman fell silent. Drew waited. After a moment she prompted, 'But how do they work if they're illegals?'

Iman took another sip of tea. 'This man, he does not let these people register as refugees. He has their papers. Officially they do not exist. He has friends, business contacts. The refugees, they work there like slaves in a factory sewing clothes. A sweat shop I think you call it. He pays them very little, he just gives them shelter and feeds them.'

'But that's outrageous. Why don't they just go to the cops?'

Iman gave an ironic shrug. 'Because they are afraid. Many refugees, they do not trust the police. In their own countries . . . well, you know what I am talking about. They don't trust the police. They don't know who to trust. Many don't speak English.'

'But who are these people? Can you give me names?'

Iman shook her head. 'I don't know the names. But I know it's true. Nicolae told me and I know a girl who ran away from them. She told me what it was like.'

Drew felt the excitement in the pit of her stomach. 'Where is this girl? Could you set up a meeting with her? I'd like to talk to her.'

The Somali shook her head again. 'I don't think she will talk to you. She is afraid.'

'Afraid of what? If what you say is true she needs to tell her story. These people have to be stopped. She has to go to the Guards.'

Iman was emphatic. 'No police! She won't talk to police!'

Frustrated, Drew wanted to shake her. 'Then I don't know what you think I can do, Iman. If you don't give me some more concrete information I've no story. I can't help you.' She was bluffing. Hoping Iman would relent.

Iman was sitting very still now, staring down at her mug of tea, her shoulders stooped. She looked angry, or perhaps she was just as frustrated as the journalist. The fire hissed. Drew was conscious of the sound of passing traffic outside. After a pause she said, 'Look, I know a cop. I could talk to him unofficially. Test the water, so to speak. How about that?' Iman made no reply. Drew pressed on. 'Look, Iman, all you've given me is an unsubstantiated rumour. Until I've more information, there's no story. Talk to your friend. I promise I won't mention her name or identify her in any way. She'll be perfectly safe. In the meantime, I'll talk to my friend the cop . . . How about that?'

'And if she will talk to you, you won't report her to immigration.'

'Of course not! I wouldn't dream of doing that, I promise.' She could see that the African woman was still unsure. 'Look. Couldn't you just talk to her. Tell her she's nothing to fear from me, and that I'll sound out my cop friend without mentioning her specifically. I'll approach it as a hypothetical question . . . How about that?'

Suddenly Iman jumped up from her chair and hurried for the door, grabbing her coat as she passed the bed. 'Wait here,' she said, and disappeared. Startled, Drew heard her running down the stairs. She moved over to the window and looked out. The front door banged and she saw Iman running out of the gate, taking a sharp turn to the right. She watched as the woman hurried down the road, pulling her coat on, nervously looking over her shoulder every now and then. Four doors down she turned into a gateway and scurried to the front door, disappearing inside. Drew stood waiting by the window. A couple of minutes later Iman and a tall black man came out of the house and stood talking on the path. Drew was sure she had seen him with Iman the night she witnessed the argument at the corner of Leinster Road, but she couldn't recall if he had been the object of her aggression or the man trying to hold her back. A moment later a small, thin, pale-skinned girl hurried from the house carrying a sagging hold-all. She was looking around nervously. Then she grabbed the man's sleeve. After a few seconds they all walked briskly down the path and up Kenilworth Road. Drew felt a tug of expectation in her gut, believing that Iman had managed to talk the girl into meeting with her, if indeed this was the girl in question. Seconds later, however, she was disappointed as Iman turned into her own gateway and the other two headed off towards Grosvenor Road at a hectic pace. Then she heard the front door bang and Iman returning.

'Was that her? Was that the girl?' she asked as soon as Iman walked into the room.

'You were spying on me?'

Drew was surprised by the accusatory nature of her tone. 'I was looking out of the window,' she said defensively. 'What's wrong with that?'

Iman glared at her for a moment then shook her head and slumped down on the end of the bed. 'I am sorry. Forgive me. In my country it makes you very . . .' She searched for a word. 'It makes you *careful*. Your life can depend on it.'

'Don't worry about it.' Drew pulled one of the hard chairs from under the table and sat on it, facing Iman. 'So was that the girl?'

Iman nodded. 'But she is afraid. She wants to think about it for a while. I tried to reassure her, and Gregory will talk to her.'

'Who's Gregory? Is he illegal too? Did he come in with the people you were talking about?'

'Gregory is my cousin. But he is here as a refugee on a programme. We look out for each other.'

'Where's the girl from?'

'Romania. She came in from Romania six months back. Nicolae knew her. That is why she came to him when she got away. She had his address. She was staying in his room.'

Drew was surprised. 'But wasn't that risky? Wasn't she afraid that the immigration hit squad would find her?'

Iman shook her head. 'She was in Gregory's room until Nicolae was taken. Gregory is safe. He has refugee status.'

'So where have they gone now?'

'I make Gregory move her to another place. It is not safe for her to stay in one room too long. Those people, they are looking for her.'

Drew shook her head. 'Poor girl. Being chased by gangsters *and* the Department of Justice. Hard to know which consequence is the worst.' She rummaged in her bag for a pen and scribbled her mobile number on the back of a till receipt. 'Look. Here's my number. Call me day or night if she agrees to talk to me. OK?'

Iman nodded. 'I will. I promise. And we will try to persuade her.'

'Good. I'll talk to my friend the cop and see how the land lies as far as immigration goes.'

Drew stood up and headed for the door. Iman followed. 'Thank you for doing this,' the black girl said. 'She needs help, and we can do nothing.'

Drew stopped by the door. 'What's her name, by the way?'

Iman hesitated, then said, 'Nadia. Just call her Nadia.'

Drew paused before leaving. 'I saw you the other night. On the corner. You were arguing.'

Iman nodded. 'Some people won't help. They make me angry. And Nadia has no one.'

As she walked back towards the city centre, Drew was both excited and horrified by what Iman had told her. The notion of slavery was appalling, but in reality, if what Iman said was true, poor unfortunate desperate souls were being held in sweat-shop slavery in twenty-first century Ireland. And God knows what would become of them. They were in the classic rock and hard place situation. Work to pay off a debt that would most probably never be repaid, with no rights whatsoever, or go to the cops and risk deportation. She remembered reading an article in *Marie Claire* about impoverished Filipino women being recruited ostensibly for office work in London and Rome, only to end up being held against their will in brothels and sweat shops. It was an appalling vista that maybe the same could be going on in Dublin. Appalling, though not inconceivable.

She couldn't get Nadia's haunted, frightened face out of her mind. She quickened her pace as she reached the end of Rathmines Road and crossed over the canal at Portobello Bridge. She had rashly promised to talk to a cop, but the only cop she knew well enough to ask a favour of, apart from the slimebag Wil, was Vinnie Hogan, Scarlett's famed cousin. She was on Adelaide Road now, only a stone's throw from Harcourt Terrace. Making rash promises was one thing, but bumping into Wil, who also worked out of Harcourt Terrace, was entirely another. It would be too embarrassing. She dithered. Their last meeting had been anything but cordial. He couldn't see what she was so worked up about. So he was married – so what? She had been so angry with him, mainly because she liked him and felt a fool that she'd been so taken in. The resulting confrontation had ended with her looking a complete spa, ranting and raving, whilst he just stood there looking bewildered. Of the firm belief that discretion is the better part of valour, she stepped into a shop doorway and took out her mobile.

Naturally Vinnie was surprised to hear from her. They hadn't met for a good six months. As Kerrigan's promotion had coincided with the débâcle of her break up with Wil, they'd had no occasion to bump into each other since the news editor had removed her from court reporting and reassigned her.

'Hi, Vinnie. It's Drew. Drew Looney.'

'Drew!' Surprised. 'How are you? It's been a while.'

'Yeah, well. Um . . . I was wondering . . . could we meet? I need to run something by you. Sort of unofficially.'

'Run something by me?'

'Yes. It's to do with a story I'm working on.'

'Oh . . . OK then. I'm in the office right now. Where are you?'

'I'm in Adelaide Road, but I'm not really comfortable coming into the station . . . You know how it is?'

'Oh! . . . Right.' He paused. 'Look, meet me outside. I'll be right down.'

Vinnie was waiting by the entrance for her. 'Good to see you,' he said. 'Come on. Let's walk up to the Green.'

On the way Vinnie picked up a couple of take-away coffees, then they crossed the road and wandered through the gates of the city centre gardens.

'So what's this thing you want to run by me?' he asked as they reached a convenient bench.

Drew was guarded about how much she should tell him. At the end of the day, Scarlett's cousin or not, on or off the record, a cop is a cop is a cop. She paused and collected her thoughts. 'OK . . . Hypothetically speaking, what if a person was an illegal immigrant? And what if they knew of a crime, but were afraid to report it because of the fear of deportation? Is there any way that they could remain anonymous? Or that the law would turn a blind eye?'

Vinnie took a gulp of his coffee, then exhaled loudly. 'Tough one. Do you know this hypothetical person by any chance?'

'No,' Drew answered, almost truthfully. 'But I know *of* them.'

The cop nodded. 'OK. So are we talking serious crime here?'

'Would that make a difference to the informant's situation?'

'Might do. Are they a refugee or asylum seeker in the true sense, or are they just an economic?'

'I don't know yet . . . I'm trying to set up a meeting.'

Vinnie took another gulp of coffee. Drew only sipped at hers. It was scalding hot. It occurred to her that Vinnie must have an asbestos gullet. He remained silent, staring into his now empty coffee carton, mulling the problem over in his mind. Eventually he screwed up the cup and tossed it at a rubbish bin, scoring a direct hit. 'Let's assume that the informant, although an illegal, *would* qualify under the refugee act. That being the case, if some agency acted on their behalf to regularise their situation, it's unlikely they'd be deported until their case was properly looked at.'

'That doesn't help, Vinnie. I think what they had in mind was just giving the information and disappearing.'

Vinnie sighed. 'That's not very sensible, is it?'

Drew agreed. 'I know. You can understand how difficult it is for them, though. They're afraid they'll be chucked out and sent back to God knows what.'

Vinnie nodded. 'Hmmm . . . So, you didn't tell me. Are we talking serious crime here?'

'Exploitation. Sweat shops. They smuggle people in then get them to work like slaves.'

Vinnie nodded. 'And this friend, are they illegal too?'

'No, she's legal, she has a visa.'

'So why doesn't *she* report the crime? The illegal doesn't need to be involved at all.'

Drew bit her lip. That hadn't occurred to her and she felt stupid for not having suggested it to Iman. But then she realised that it wasn't an option either. If Iman reported the gangsters, and the factory or whatever was raided, it was probable that all the refugees would be caught in the middle and chucked out of the country anyway, which would compound their victim status even further. 'I'm not sure she feels able to without the consent of the other parties. It's they who are being exploited. And I don't think she knows all the details anyway.'

'Look, try and get some more specific details and I'll see what I can do,' he said. 'But at the end of the day they'd be better off coming forward and reporting it themselves. It would look better for them than if they're caught as illegal labour.'

Drew finished her coffee and tossed the cup at the bin but missed. Hand–eye co-ordination had never been her strong point. She walked over and picked it up then deposited it in the bin. Vinnie stood up. 'Look, thanks for your help, Vinnie. I appreciate it.'

He smiled. 'No problem. Get back to me if you get a result,' he said. 'But you should try and talk this person into sorting out their situation. As an illegal they've no future. You know yourself.'

Familiar with the true situation, Drew agreed more than Vinnie could ever realise. 'I'll see what I can do,' she said as they parted company.

Scarlett had to hang around for nearly two hours before Bruce Gold's bail hearing was called. It was par for the course, and she sat through half a dozen other cases taking shorthand notes. One drink driving, one driving without tax and insurance, and two taking and driving away without the owner's consent. Two shoplifters, one of whom was a Spanish student who had somehow expected to get away with pinching goods to the value of one hundred and twenty-nine pounds from Penny's. Taking into account that the previous Saturday Scarlett's sister Melanie had bought an entire five-piece outfit from Penny's, including a pair of shoes, for under thirty pounds, she immediately had a mental image of the girl dragging a body bag stuffed with merchandise towards the exit. Hardly surprising then that she was nicked. She was given three weeks in Mountjoy and a fine for her trouble, on the understanding that she was to return home to Spain after her release.

After she was taken down, sobbing uncontrollably, Gold was brought up from the cells. His solicitor, one Mervyn Drury, had evidently brought him in fresh clothes because he was sporting a well-cut black suit, shirt and tie. The bail hearing was straightforward. Drury undertook to surrender his client's passport and the star was required to remain in the State and report to the Irishtown Garda station every week. She was unable to get any information about the teenage complainant, due to the fact that she was under age and so her identity was protected by the court.

Afterwards, outside the court building, the lawyer read out a prepared press release stating that his client would strenuously defend himself against the rape allegation, maintaining that intercourse never took place.

'My client did not have sexual relations with this girl and was horrified when he discovered that she was only fifteen. Mr Gold would never under any circumstances knowingly consider having intimate relations with an under-age girl and is appalled that he has been so erroneously accused.' As the statement was being read, and cameras were flashing, Gold stood by looking haunted and wretched. He was driven off at speed in a Beemer with blacked out windows.

As Scarlett was checking her messages on the mobile she felt a light tap on her shoulder. She looked around to find Vinnie grinning at her.

'How's it going?'

She'd always had a lot of time for Vinnie. His mother was her father's sister and they had played together as kids and only really drifted apart when he went away to Templemore Garda College. She hadn't seen him for an age. 'Vinnie! How are yeh?'

He looked well. A little leaner maybe. He smiled. 'Good . . . I'm good. How's yourself? How's the family?'

'Great.' She paused. 'I heard you finished with that Kyla wan.'

'Yes, a while back.' Vinnie plunged his hands into his pockets and grinned down at her. 'Was my ma complaining to your ma or something? I know she'd the grandchildren's names already picked out!'

Scarlett laughed. 'Somethin' like that. Listen, we must get together some time. Catch up on things . . . You and me and Drew.'

Vinnie looked surprised. 'Drew?'

'Yeah,' Scarlett said with an air of innocence. 'Me and Drew. Go on. Yeh know yeh like her.'

Vinnie laughed. 'Sod off, Scarlett. You're getting as bad as Ma with your matchmaking.'

Undaunted, Scarlett said, 'I am not matchmakin'. I was only talkin' about a quiet drink to catch up on old times.'

'Yeah, right!'

She grinned back at him. 'Don't flatter yourself, Mister. You're no bleedin' catch.' Though now, after having broken the ice, she was quietly plotting.

On her way back into *The Daily Record* office Scarlett met Drew in the lobby. 'So how was your mornin'?' she asked as they climbed the stairs together to the newsroom.

'Got a good lead on a refugee story,' Drew said, 'but I'm not sure it'll go anywhere. I'm relying on a reluctant source.'

'No,' she sniggered. 'I mean did yer ma catch up with yeh yet?'

'Not so far.' Drew grinned. 'I think I'll keep a low profile for a couple of days. No doubt Justin, prompted by his beloved stick insect, reported back.'

'She's no sense of humour, that wan,' Scarlett complained.

'Oh, I dunno,' Drew said. 'She is changing her name to Maddie Raven-Looney isn't she?' They both laughed, remembering the incident the previous night.

'Guess who I met at the district court,' Scarlett said.

'Who?'

'Vinnie.'

Drew glared at her. 'Don't start,' she warned.

'Ah, come on Drew. It can't hurt.'

Drew decided against mentioning that she had seen Vinnie herself that morning in case Scarlett got the wrong idea. It would only encourage her. 'Don't even think about it.'

Marty met them at the door on his way out of the newsroom. 'Susie found that archive stuff you asked her to check out about yer man Gold,' he said to Scarlett. 'She was lookin' for you.'

'Thanks Marty.'

'What's that about?' Drew asked.

Scarlett waved at Susie, a young graduate who was free-lancing, to attract her attention. 'Marty said he remembered yer man had a bit of trouble way back. I'm just checkin' it out.' As she hurried over to get the dope on Gold, she called over her shoulder to her friend, 'Think about it. About Vinnie. From where I'm standin' there isn't actually a queue.'

Drew gave her the finger then settled herself at her usual desk and checked her messages. The expected harangue from her mother still hadn't materialised. It left her a bit edgy. Barbara Looney had a habit of lulling her daughter into a false sense of security then zapping her with both barrels when she least expected it.

Just then the phone rang, making her jump sky high. She stared at it for a couple of seconds before gingerly picking it up with a very tentative, 'Newsroom. Drew Looney.'

It was not Barbara. There was a little yelp at the other end of the line, then 'Eau! Drew? Is that yew, Drew?'

'Hello, Mrs Reibheinn.'

'Eau! Drew, please . . . call me Aíne. Anyway, I was just talking with your memmy . . .' Drew flinched, but Aíne

93

continued, 'We feel it's time to make a start on the brides-maids' gowns.'

Only Aíne Reibheinn would have bridesmaids' *gowns*, when every other normal mortal had *dresses*. Did she say normal mortal?

'Um . . . are you sure Maddie still wants me to be bridesmaid, Mrs Reibheinn?'

'Drew, Drew, pleee-ase, it's Aíne, call me Aíne.'

'Um . . . OK, *Aíne*, but are you sure . . .'

'But of course. Why, eaunly this morning she expressed a particular wish that we get it all sorted ite. She's such a talented gel my Maddie, you kneau.'

'Um . . . yes.'

The words revenge, satin, clingy, and especially designed to make me look like a fat dog crossed Drew's mind.

'Well, the thing is . . . You see I'm not sure . . .'

'Nonsense! Now don't be silly, dear. We'll expect you ite at Raven's Court tonight at around nine. And don't bother to eat. We're going to make it a bit of a girlies' soiree. All girls together. We've given the boys strict instractions to geau ite.'

Drew cringed. 'Well, the thing is . . . You see . . .'

'Good,' Aíne said. 'That's settled. We'll look forward to seeing you and your memmy at Raven's Court at nine then.' The line went dead.

How to get out of this one? Difficult considering Barbara was part of the equation, and as far as her mother was concerned she was deep enough in the mucky stuff as it was. However, she had to put the problem to one side as Joe called her into the office to check on the progress of her refugee story. She filled him in with all the information she had to date.

'The trouble is, I checked with a cop friend of mine and he can't give any guarantees. And if the girl talks to me and the sweat shops are raided, then the poor sods will probably be chucked out anyway.'

Joe scratched his head and sighed. 'Sure, but are they any better off as they are? In fact, they're probably worse off. It sounds to me like slavery.'

'I know, but isn't that their decision?'

Joe shook his head. 'Not really. They're illegals. They shouldn't be here in the first place unless they apply for refugee status or asylum. Are they economics do you know?'

'I don't know. I think they might be or Nadia wouldn't be so iffy about talking to the immigration bods. And as far as the others, well, who knows. The gangsters have their papers. They won't let them register. But if I get to talk to Nadia, I'm going to try and persuade her. I've a friend in The Eastern Health Board Refugee Unit.'

Joe nodded. 'OK, Drew, good work, keep me posted.'

It was a pleasant change to hear words of encouragement. The concept was alien to Kerrigan, as far as she was concerned anyway.

Scarlett was working away at her terminal as Drew sauntered over. She was getting peckish as it was long past her normal break. 'Are you going for lunch?' she asked her friend.

Scarlett looked up. 'Sure.' She saved what she had written and clicked off the monitor. 'Turns out our Bruce was arrested for under-age sex fifteen years back, dirty bastard, but the case never came to trial. The parents dropped the charges in the end.'

Marty, who was passing her desk, piped up, 'Word has it he paid them off to make it go away. His publicity people leaked the notion that he'd been set up.'

'Are yeh serious?' Scarlett said. 'Do yeh think he was?'

Marty shrugged. 'Hard to say. But why else would they drop the charges? I mean, what kind of parent would take money and drop the charges if their kid was really bein' messed with?'

'Yeah,' Scarlett agreed. 'True for yeh.'

The phone on Scarlett's desk rang and she picked it up.

'Newsroom.' There was a pause and she glanced up at Drew. 'Oh hello, Mrs Looney.' Drew shook her head vigorously and waved her hand in a *definitely no-way* motion. Scarlett grinned as she said, 'Em . . . no. Drew's out on a job I'm afraid.' Another pause. 'Yes, I'll tell her, Mrs Looney.' She was fighting hard to keep a straight face. 'I know, Mrs Looney, but I think she's *really* looking forward to it. She's never been a bridesmaid before, has she?' After a further pause Scarlett winked at Drew. 'I won't let her forget, Mrs Looney. Tonight at nine sharp at Raven's Court. No problemo . . . Yes, I'll tell her that you'll pick her up at eight-thirty. Bye, bye, Mrs Looney.' As she hung up she exploded into a fit of near hysteria. 'She's really doin' it. That cow Maddie's really goin' to dress yeh up like a bleedin' fairy.'

'Count on it,' Drew said dryly. 'Now are we going to lunch?'

Chapter Eight

Scarlett scanned the houses as she walked purposefully along Park Avenue. She was looking for a house called Shadowlands. At the DART level crossing she trotted across the road and walked back in the direction from which she had come, past St John's Church, scrutinising the gateposts for a name plate. After about thirty yards she spotted it. It was a tall three-storey Edwardian semi-detached set back from the road. It had a long narrow well-kept front lawn bordered by tired-looking shrubs. The curtains were all closed and there didn't appear to be any sign of life except for a tell-tale plume of smoke coming from the chimney. She checked the address again, even though she was certain that this was the place. She had phoned earlier but the woman who answered denied that Gold was staying there. Scarlett tried to reassure her by telling her that she wanted to get Gold's side of the story, but she continued to deny any knowledge of the Australian, eventually hanging up.

Scarlett didn't believe her for a minute. The Sandymount house was the contact address that *The Record* had been given for Gold when his publicity people had arranged the abortive interview at the chicken grommet shoot. Also, putting two and two together, Scarlett deduced that Park Avenue was in the Irishtown Garda station area where Gold had been ordered to sign on, so it made sense. She was anxious to talk to him, to see how he reacted when she brought up the previous incident, and if he would stick to the story of a set-up. Although she knew that as a journalist she should have an open mind, she felt ambivalent towards

Gold. It was hard to feel otherwise when the components of the story included a fifteen year old girl and the word rape.

Reluctant to risk being turned away at the door, she decided to hang around for a while, in the hope that she'd see some movement in the house, or other comings and goings. She crossed the road and sat on a low wall beside the bus stop to wait it out. She was familiar with the area. Drew's house, at least the house that Drew rented from Justin, was at the top of Park Avenue near to Sandymount Green. It was a tiny two-bedroom townhouse that Justin had bought for cash at the age of nineteen from the proceeds of his fledgling software business whilst he was still at college. At this stage of the game Scarlett was of the opinion that, considering the disparity in their respective incomes, Justin should let his sister live rent-free in order to give her the chance to save a few bob and maybe buy a place of her own. Come to that, it wouldn't hurt him to give her the house outright. God knows he was ultra-loaded and certainly didn't need the four hundred a month; in fact he probably paid out that much on his fiancée's hairdressing and beauty treatment bills without giving it a second thought.

An elderly lady towing a vile, smelly-looking terrier along on a leash eyed her suspiciously as she passed. She glanced back every time the decrepit canine stopped to pee, which was every couple of yards. Scarlett gave her a dazzling smile and a little wave. The woman, flustered that she'd been faced off, blushed and scuttled away, dragging the still urinating mutt in her wake. After about twenty minutes a number three bus pulled up at the stop and a couple of women with shopping bags got off. Scarlett felt tempted to jump on. Number threes were an endangered species, few and far between, so it seemed a shame to waste it. But she pulled herself together and let it drive away.

After a further twenty minutes, when there was still no sign of life in Shadowlands and the chilly dampness of the

November day was seeping into her bones, Scarlett took the bull by the horns and knocked on the door. At first there was no reply, though she was certain that she heard movements inside. She rang the bell. Eventually the door opened a crack and a small middle-aged woman peeped out. 'What do you want?'

'Sorry to bother yeh,' Scarlett said, in her most engaging, charming voice. 'I'm from *The Daily Record*, and I understand Mr Gold's stayin' here. I was wonderin''—'

'There's no one of that name here,' the woman snapped. 'Piss off.' She slammed the door.

Scarlett bent down and lifted the letterbox flap. 'Look, I just want to get his side of the story. He's denied the charges, so it's only fair that the public get to hear his side. It's in his own interests.'

There was a pause, then she heard the rattle of the chain, before the door opened again. Through the narrow slit the woman barked, 'If you don't go away I'll set the dog on you!' then slammed the door shut.

Scarlett jumped back to avoid getting her nose broken. 'Sorry to have bothered yeh,' she said to the brass letterbox, heavy on the sarcasm. She glanced quickly around but thankfully didn't see any evidence of a dog. She was cold *and* irritated now so she strode up to the Green with a view to getting some hot liquid refreshment. The coffee shop was quiet. She ordered a large hot chocolate, extra cream, and a toasted bun, then sat at a table by the window. She felt disgruntled. However many times she did the door-stepping routine, it always offended her when people were overtly rude. There was no call for it. She always endeavoured to be polite. And what did a little courtesy cost?

She was quietly mulling this over in her mind as she chomped on her bun, when she became aware of the man at the next table. He was slouching with his elbows on the table and his chin resting on his fist, wearing a fringed black leather biker jacket and a baseball cap with the peak pulled down low. There was an empty coffee cup in front of him and an ashtray full of cigarette butts. He reached into his pocket and pulled out a soft pack of Camel Lights. Scarlett covertly stared at him as he took out another cigarette and attempted, unsuccessfully, to light it with a Chrome Zippo. The lighter sparked but there was no flame. He snapped it closed and shook it, then tried again. As he lifted his head she recognised him. Bruce Gold.

She took out her lighter and offered it. 'Here, use mine,' she said.

Gold looked surprised for a second, then took the lighter and lit his cigarette, inhaling the smoke deep into his lungs. 'Thanks,' he said, handing it back.

'It's OK. Keep it. It's only a disposable.'

He hesitated, then nodded and laid the lighter down on the table next to the pack of cigarettes. 'Thanks. I get edgy if I can't have me smokes,' he said, half apologetically. He was softly spoken and the accent was definitely Antipodean.

Scarlett felt a rush of excitement. 'I know where you're comin' from,' she said. 'I used to be the same, but I'm tryin' to cut down.'

'Easier said than done.'

'Too right!' She paused. 'Do yeh mind if I join yeh?' Without waiting for his permission she picked up the remains of her hot chocolate and bun and slid into the chair opposite him. 'They do the best hot chocolate here.'

Close up his skin was pasty and very wrinkled, his eyes bloodshot, and she could see his eyebrows were almost invisible they were so blond and fine. 'Excuse me, but don't I know you?' she said. He stared at her without replying. She lowered her voice almost to a whisper. 'Aren't you Bruce Gold?'

He took a deep drag on his cigarette, squinting at her through the smoke, then exhaled through his nostrils. 'Yeah. So what?'

'Scarlett O'Hara, *Daily Record*,' she said, offering her

hand. Gold ignored the proffered hand and, leaning back in his chair, peered at her. She noticed that his eyes slanted up at the corners which gave him a faintly oriental look. 'I've been looking for you, Mr Gold. I wanted to get your side of the story.'

'Oh yeah?' he sneered. 'So you can crucify me?'

Scarlett shook her head. 'No, Mr Gold. I really want to get another perspective on this.'

Gold gave an ironic guffaw. 'Yeah. Right.'

'No, really. I know about that business fifteen years back and I was wonderin' if you'd any comment to make?'

He took another thoughtful puff. 'Such as?'

'Well, yeh claimed then yeh were set up.'

'I was.' His tone was curt and defensive.

'And this time? *Did* yeh rape her?' She knew it was a futile question as he would hardly admit to it if he was guilty, but it had to be asked.

'No.' He took another puff on the cigarette.

'OK. If you say so.' She paused. 'But did yeh *really* think this girl was eighteen?'

Gold stubbed the butt out aggressively in the ashtray and lit up another. Scarlett was afraid she'd blown it. He looked livid. After what seemed like an age he took off the baseball cap. This had the effect of ageing him twenty years. He looked like an old man, and to Scarlett's knowledge he was only about fifty-five or fifty-six. 'Look at me, Mizz ... whatever your name is.'

'Scarlett.'

'OK. Look at me, Scarlett. What do you see?' The journalist shrugged. She didn't know what to say. 'No, tell it like it is, Scarlett. Don't try and spare me feelin's.' He waited a beat then continued. 'OK, I'll tell you what you see. You see a fuckin' sad bastard. A has-been. That's what you see.' He picked up his coffee cup, then realising it was empty, put it down again. 'And you know what? I didn't bloody stop to think. I was *sooo* fuckin' grateful that a gorgeous young chick was throwin' herself at me. *Me.*' He stabbed at his chest to make the point. 'Well, you know what they say. There's no fool like an old fool.'

'So you knew how old she really was then?'

He shook his head vigorously. 'No . . . Not exactly. She looked . . .' He struggled for a word. '*Hot.* All woman. There's no way she looked under age. And the way she came on to me . . .'

'So she made all the runnin'?' Sceptical.

He nodded, then, turning in his chair, he signalled to the waitress. 'Another cappuccino please, Miss.' He glanced at Scarlett then gestured at her empty chocolate glass. 'Another of those?'

Scarlett was relieved that he hadn't stormed out. 'Please.'

'And a hot chocolate, love.' He turned back to the table. 'Yeah. She stitched me up good and proper. Like a bloody lamb to the slaughter.' He sat still then, staring at the table top and nodding his head ever so slightly, as if he was confirming the situation to himself. 'You know, I really missed it.'

'What?'

'The fame. The adulation.' He grinned, and suddenly looked twenty years younger. 'It was fuckin' great. Only lasted as long as I was at the top. But it was fuckin' great. Chicks on tap morning, noon and night. All the drugs and booze you could do. It was fuckin' A, man.' The waitress brought over the order and laid the bill on the table. Gold heaped three spoonfuls of sugar into his coffee and stirred it vigorously. 'Trouble is, I couldn't adjust to life after it was over. That's my problem. I hate real life. I prefer the fantasy. The whole bullshit of the fame thing.'

'So why do yeh reckon she shouted rape then?' Still sceptical.

Gold shrugged, then lit up another cigarette, even though he had one burning away in the ashtray. 'Set-up. It had to be.' He looked Scarlett square in the eyes. 'I never touched her.'

'If you say so.' She wasn't convinced. 'Where did yeh meet her?'

'In McDonald's. There I was eatin' me Big Mac, mindin' me own business, and her dad comes over and asks for an autograph. Well . . .' He gave an embarrassed grin, 'I was rapt. Doesn't happen often . . . well, *ever* really, these days. So he calls over Mandy, that's the girl, his daughter, and introduces me, and they sit down and he starts goin' on about how he went to all the gigs when he was a kid and was well into the band and stuff . . .' The sentence trailed off. Gold was staring at nothing again, off on some mental nostalgia trip.

'So what happened then? How did you and the Mandy wan get it together?'

Gold snapped back to the present and took a sip of his cappuccino. 'Sid, that's the father, asked me to a party at his house. Said it was his old lady's birthday and she'd be blown away if I showed up because she was a big fan too. Said he wanted it to be a surprise. Anyway, the party was really rockin'. Lots of booze. I was well tanked and then Mandy starts dancin' with me. You know, slow dancin', up close, and kisses me, tongues, the business, and one thing led to another and we ended up on the stairs . . .'

'In her parents' house! Were you mad?'

'Hey, gimme a break. It's years since a chick dragged *me* off to bed. I was tanked, I was randy. Anyway, we're halfway up the stairs an' I suddenly come to me senses. As you said, we were in her folks' house . . . I dunno, I had a bad feelin' about it. I tell her we can't. I tell her she's beautiful and I fancy her but we can't.'

Scarlett, despite her earlier mind set, was beginning to have second thoughts. 'And how did she react to that?'

Gold shrugged. 'She stuck her tongue down me throat

and grabbed hold of me, tryin' to change me mind. I tell you, even if I'd wanted to then, I couldn't have done anythin'. She frightened the shit outta me.'

'So what happened afterwards? Did she get upset?'

Gold shook his head. 'No. When she saw ... felt ... nothin' was about to happen, she laughed at me and we went back to the party and I got a cab home around three. The next thing I know the cops drag me off to the cop shop and I'm charged with rape.' He shook his head. 'Nightmare city.'

Scarlett took the last gulp of her hot chocolate and suddenly felt tremendously sorry for him. 'So what are you going to do?' she asked.

Gold picked up his cap and examined the peak, dusting a few grains of sugar from it. 'Not much I can do except tell it like it happened and hope the jury believes me.'

The call came at five-thirty. Drew had just clicked off her computer terminal and was getting ready to go home. She hesitated, debating whether to leave it to voicemail or take it, ever vigilant to the danger that it could be her mother in rant mode. Even though she knew it was inevitable at some point, she was putting it off as long as possible. She was banking on the hope that by the time Barbara picked her up to go out to Raven's Court, she'd be so geared up for talk of wedding arrangements that she'd have lost some of the head of steam that Justin and Maddie had built up.

Marty looked up from his desk. 'Aren't you goin' to answer that bleedin' thing?' he asked, then picked up his phone and punched the line button. 'Newsroom.'

Drew put her coat on and was heading for the door at speed when she heard Marty calling her. 'Drew ... There's an Iman Dirie on line two for you.'

Drew dropped her bag and ran to her desk, snatching up the receiver. 'Iman? This is Drew.'

'Nadia will talk to you.'

Drew's heart fluttered with excitement. 'When? Where?'

'She will come to my room at seven tonight. But she is very afraid. Do you promise that you won't to go immigration?'

Drew felt affronted that after her earlier assurances Iman would even ask. 'Of course I won't! I told you, I won't identify her in any way. But I *will* try and talk her into sorting out her situation. I have a friend who works for the Refugee Unit of The Eastern Health Board. If Nadia wants, I can talk to her.'

'But you won't force her?'

'Absolutely not.'

She heard Iman exhale with relief. 'Good. I agree with you that it would be better for her to get her situation sorted out, but I'm afraid if I tell her, she won't come, so I won't mention it.'

'Whatever you say, Iman. Whatever way you want to play it.'

She arrived home by ten past six, largely due to the fact that a number three was just pulling into the stop outside Cleary's as she was crossing the road at the GPO. She made a run for it and got there just before the doors closed. It's a good omen, she thought. First Nadia agrees to talk then a number three comes along. As soon as she got in she ordered a cab, then despite Aíne's invitation to eat, she stuck a frozen pizza under the grill as she was not partial to vol-au-vents, and she knew that these were the most likely offering. Aíne Reibheinn was the veritable vol-au-vent queen of Foxrock. Vol-au-vents with chicken in a gunky sauce; tuna vol-au-vents; salmon mousse vol-au-vents with a sprinkling of red fish eggs. You name the filling, Aíne would bung it in a pastry case, stick it on a paper doily and fling fish eggs at it. She considered phoning her mother to tell her that she was running a little late and to go on without her, but courage failed her. She decided to call Barbara from Iman's flat and ask to be collected from there if necessary. It was on her mother's way from Rathgar so it wouldn't put her out.

In any event, she changed her clothes and threw on a slap of make-up in readiness for Aíne's soiree, then bolted down the pizza. The molten cheese topping singed her tongue and welded itself to the roof of her mouth, and as the taxi headed over to Rathmines she could feel a blister forming on the tip of her tongue, but she didn't care. Nadia was going to talk to her, and if all went well it would be an exclusive.

It was a soft night, unseasonably mild and damp. The sort of rain which seeps under an umbrella, rendering it useless. Drew could feel her fringe frizzing up and was glad that at least the rest of her hair was still under control, dragged back in a ponytail. As she pulled up outside the house on Kenilworth Road at five past seven, she could see Iman's tall lissom figure silhouetted in the upstairs window watching out for her. She felt the excitement in the pit of her stomach.

The Somali opened the front door before she was halfway up the path. She glanced up and down the road apprehensively. 'Quickly! I don't want anyone to see you,' she urged as she pulled the reporter into the hall. Drew thought she was being overly cautious but didn't argue the point. Iman closed the door and hurried ahead of her up the stairs.

'Is she here yet?' Drew asked, labouring to keep up with the long-legged African. Iman turned, shook her head vigorously and put her finger to her lips. Again, Drew thought she was being over-dramatic but played along and waited until they reached Iman's room before speaking.

Iman closed the door and slid the bolt. 'She said seven. It's only just five past.' The kettle was bubbling on the stove and the gas fire lit, making the room oppressively hot. Iman resumed her station at the window. 'She is very afraid. We hear that they were looking for her.'

'Well, they would be, wouldn't they,' Drew commented. 'Did you find out any names for me?'

'Nadia will tell you everything when she comes,' Iman said. 'I know there is a Serb, but I don't know the names. She wouldn't tell me, she's so afraid.' She looked exhausted. She was wringing her hands and her face had a grey hue and a constant frown. Suddenly she darted over to the stove. 'I will make tea. She will be here soon. I will make tea.' Her hands were shaking.

In the interests of safety, Drew walked over to the stove. 'You sit down, I'll do it. You look stressed out. Chill a little. It'll be fine.'

Iman faltered, then appeared to relax. 'You're right. It will be fine. I'm just worried that something will happen to her. She is my Nicolae's friend, from his village. I don't want to let him down.'

'Have you heard from him?'

The change of subject appeared to relax Iman. The frown disappeared and her face lit up as she picked up a postcard from the mantelpiece. 'He sent me this from Paris. He has applied for asylum there.'

'Well, that's good,' Drew said, as she poured the boiling water into two of the three mugs set out ready with tea bags on the drainer. 'At least they didn't ship him straight back to Romania.'

Iman was by the window again. Drew joined her there and handed her a mug of steaming tea. Occasional traffic sped along Kenilworth Road and a few pedestrians walked by, but there was no sign of Nadia. Drew glanced at her watch. It was coming on for seven-fifteen.

By seven-thirty, when there was still no sign, Drew was getting as edgy as Iman. 'Where do you think she could be?' Stupid question.

It was Iman's turn to be calm. 'She will be here.'

A black Mercedes glided into the kerb and parked, engine idling. After a moment two men got out and strode purposefully up the path of the house four doors along. They were big and bulky and dressed in dark clothes. She felt Iman stiffen beside her, then she grabbed the journal-ist's arm.

'Do you know those men?' Drew asked, suddenly anxious.

Iman shook her head. 'No, but they are going to Gregory's house.'

'Hey,' Drew said, trying to lighten the atmosphere, 'lots of people live in that house. They could be going to see anyone.'

They watched as the men disappeared through the front door. Drew craned her neck to look up the road, hoping for any sign of Nadia. Even though she was trying to laugh off the strong feeling of paranoia that had come over her, she was still uncomfortable about the Mercedes and the two men. She glanced back at the car. As she did so, the back door opened and a squat little man got out. He was wearing a three-quarter-length sheepskin jacket and looked like a bookie or a football manager. As she watched, he took out a cigar and lit it up. The end glowed red as he puffed away. He looked familiar. A politician maybe. She scoured her brain, then remembered. She'd seen him at Justin's engage-ment party, dancing with Maddie. She relaxed. He probably owns the house and the men are collecting rent or some-thing, she told herself. Yes, that's it. They're collecting rent. She saw him take out a mobile phone and hold it to his ear. He was still talking into it when the two men hurried from the house a minute or so later. The fat man got back into the car along with the two burly guys, then the driver did a U-turn and drove away.

Scarlett had given her card to Bruce Gold with instructions to give her a call if there were any developments. She had a gut feeling that there was more to this story than met the eye. The ageing rocker had seemed so philosophical about the whole sorry business, but how this could be so, in light of the threat of a jail sentence, defied belief.

'Aren't you concerned?' she'd asked as they reached the house on Park Avenue after she had walked him back from the coffee shop.

He'd nodded. 'Of course I'm bloody worried. I could be lookin' at time here, and for somethin' I didn't do.'

'But you don't *seem* worried.' And he didn't. He was laid back. The epitome of the cool dude.

Gold shrugged. 'Different people stress out in different ways. Me, I go quiet. But inside me guts are twisted. It's déjà vu, remember. I've been through this before. I'm just hopin' it pans out like the last time.'

'You think they'll drop the charges?'

Gold shook his head. 'Not just like that. But they have to have some agenda. There's no way I raped that girl. Think about it. Who but a complete moron dag would rape a girl in her parents' house with them downstairs? I mean, come on! I may be over the hill but I haven't lost the use of me brain cells.'

Scarlett didn't need to be further convinced. She sat on the wall beside Gold as he lit up another cigarette. 'What's the girl's name?'

'Mandy. Mandy Cahill.' He pronounced it the American way, *Cay-hill.*

'And where does she live?'

Gold's brows furrowed as he tried to recall. 'Bally-something.'

'Ballymun? Ballyfermot? Ballyfingal?'

Gold nodded. 'Yeah, yeah, that's it. Ballyfingal. Why do you ask?'

'Just curious,' Scarlett replied.

Now she was on her way back to Sandymount to meet him again. He'd phoned not long after she got home in a state of high excitement. 'Sid Cahill called,' he said.

It took Scarlett a moment to place the name. 'The father?'

'Yeah. He wants to do a deal.'

'What kind of deal?'

'What do you think?' Gold said. 'They want money to make it go away.'

Scarlett was stunned. 'Are you serious?'

'You bet,' Gold said, with a note of triumph in his voice. 'See! That proves it. The bastards are settin' me up. Like the last time.' She could sense he was almost dancing at the other end of the line.

Scarlett's brain went into overdrive. 'So what's the plan?'

'I made an excuse and said I'd call him back. I wanted to talk to you first. I thought you could come along to the pay-off and we could tape him, or video him or somethin'. You guys do that kinda sting all the time, don't you?'

'Well, not all the time,' Scarlett qualified. 'But I see where you're comin' from. If you can get him to admit on the tape the whole thing's a set-up then we can take it to the cops.' After I've got my story, she added mentally.

This time she had no difficulty gaining admittance to Shadowlands. The obnoxiously rude woman of earlier in the afternoon greeted her like a long lost friend, and ushered her into the kitchen where Gold was sitting at the table with a mug of coffee and an almost demolished packet of Jaffa Cakes. 'Thanks for comin',' he said by way of greeting. 'This is me sister, Maisy.'

On second glance Scarlett could see the resemblance, except that the woman had hair and drawn on eyebrows. Maisy smiled at her then took another mug from the cupboard and poured her a coffee. 'Help yourself to the Jaffa Cakes,' she offered. She had a strong Aussie accent laced with a touch of the Celt. Scarlett sat at the table and added milk to her coffee, then grabbed a biscuit before Gold saw the whole packet off. Jaffa Cakes were her favourite.

'So can you do it?'

Scarlett nodded, her mouth full of the spongy biscuit. She swallowed. 'Shouldn't be a problem. But I'll have to talk to my editor and you'll probably need to wear a wire. Are you comfortable with that?'

'Whatever it takes,' Gold said. The pallid skin of earlier had been transformed and his face was glowing now like an excited kid. He looked years younger.

'Fine. Why don't you call him back and arrange a meeting?'

Gold glanced over at his sister. She gave him an almost imperceptible nod. He rummaged in his pocket and pulled out a scrap of paper with a number scrawled on it, then stood and walked over to the phone which was mounted on the wall near the door. 'Do you have an extension so I can listen in?' Scarlett asked.

Maisy took her through to the hall and Scarlett picked up the receiver after Bruce had dialled the number, being careful to engage the security button in case Sid sensed that someone was listening in. She was as excited as Gold. She'd never had the opportunity to do a deadly piece like this. The glib talk of wearing wires made her feel good. She was really warming to the part of Scarlett O'Hara, ace investigative reporter. She hoped Joe wouldn't attempt to put a halt to her gallop, but then why should he? It was a terrific story. Sid answered after six rings. Bruce started off with a tentative, 'Hello, Sid. Bruce Gold here.'

Sid said, 'You thought it over?'

'Yeah. How much do you want?'

'Ten grand should make it go away.'

'That's a lot.'

'Take it or leave it.' His tone was uncompromising.

There was a pause, then Bruce said, 'But how do I know you won't go back on the deal after I pay you the cash?'

Sid tut tutted at the other end of the line. 'Because I say so, Bruce. You have my word as a paid up member of the Bruce Gold fan club.' He chortled.

'I think I'll need some sort of assurance, mate. A paper or somethin' signed. Some sort of statement from you and Mandy that it was a mistake. I mean, ten grand's a lotta dough.'

'No problem,' Sid replied. 'I can do that.'

Scarlett was pleased with the way things were going. Under the circumstances it was looking good for Bruce being able to lead the conversation round to an admission for the tape whenever the pay-off took place. Sid and Gold then discussed details for the handover. Scarlett cursed when she heard Gold arrange it for the following night. That gave her no time to set things up. Also, the drop was to be out in Ballyfingal and she didn't know the sprawling West Dublin council estate that well. Still, what could go wrong? Better not to go there. As soon as the arrangements were discussed, Sid hung up. Scarlett returned to the kitchen to see the geriatric rocker beaming like an excited kid. 'How did I do?'

'You did fine, Bruce.' She didn't have the heart to burst his bubble by suggesting that it would have been better if he'd given her more time to set things up. 'You'll need to come into the office tomorrow to talk to my news editor, and to get wired up.'

'Sure.'

The meeting was scheduled for eight o'clock the following night at Sid's council house on Virtue Rise. She would have preferred somewhere more neutral and public. 'Do you have a car?' she asked the singer. Bruce, chomping on the last Jaffa Cake, nodded. 'Good.' Scarlett pushed her chair back and stood up. 'I'll give yeh a ring tomorrow as soon as I've talked to Joe, my editor.' They made their way through to the hall. 'In the meantime, if you're anyway religious, I suggest yeh start prayin' that yer man has a big mouth.'

Chapter Nine

By eight, when there was still no sign of Nadia, Drew and Iman were both feeling more than anxious and decided to go to her room themselves to check that she was all right. All the way up the road they reassured each other that she had just had an attack of cold feet, that she was fine. She was staying with a friend of Gregory's in a room in Charleston Road. At the end of the ten minutes it took them to walk over there, however, their reassurances sounded more and more hollow and they stood at the front door reluctant to go in for fear of what they might find.

Suddenly the door opened and two young women trotted out. They looked like students and spoke with Irish accents. Drew caught the door before it closed and held it open for Iman. 'Come on. Let's get this over with.'

'You think something has happened, don't you?' She was willing the journalist to reassure her again.

Drew obliged, as much for herself as for the African. 'No, no, not at all. She's probably just taken fright.'

Iman led her upstairs to the second floor and tapped on a door at the back of the house by the foot of the attic stairs. There was no response from within. She put her face against the door and called softly, 'Nadia, it's me, Iman. Are you all right?'

When there was still no sound from the other side of the door, Drew reached forward and turned the knob. She met with no resistance and the door swung open. The light was on but the room was empty. Drew stepped inside. Everything looked normal. The bed was made and a small camp bed sitting under the window had a neat pile of folded blankets and a pillow on top. The room was small in the first instance so the extra bed made it positively cramped. It was furnished in much the same fashion as Iman's but on a smaller scale. A double gas ring seemed to be the only means of cooking and a three-bar electric fire, of which two bars glowed red, the sole source of heat. The two women stood in the open doorway staring at the vacant room, not sure what to do next.

'She's not here,' Drew said, stating the obvious. She wasn't sure what she had expected to find. Blood-spattered walls perhaps? Furniture up-ended?

They heard the front door bang and then hurried footsteps on the stairs and a moment later Gregory bustled in, his expression serious. 'Where's Nadia?'

'You tell us,' Drew replied, shooting a worried glance at Iman. 'She was supposed to meet me at seven but she didn't show.'

'Why are you here?' Iman asked. 'What has happened?'

Gregory closed the door. He looked very shaken as he sat on the bed. He was a big man and the springs creaked under his weight. Iman and Drew remained standing. 'I was just at my place,' he said, rubbing his close-cropped hair nervously. 'Someone has broken the door and my room is trashed. I worry it was those people looking for Nadia.'

Drew caught Iman's eye. She was having the same thought. The Mercedes and the two heavies. There was a scuffling movement on the stairs and all three froze. Footsteps stopped outside the door and hesitated. Drew found she was holding her breath. She glanced at Iman who had visibly paled to a dusty shade of grey. The door swung open. All three were staring at it.

Gregory was halfway to standing, his hand braced on the mattress, then he let out an audible sigh of relief as a black woman in her early forties wearing a colourful headscarf,

Muslim style, poked her head nervously around the door. 'Suki! Thank God it's you. Where's Nadia Iacob?'

The nervous expression changed to one of puzzlement. 'I thought she was with you,' she said. She had a litre carton of milk in her hand. She looked at Iman. 'She went to see you nearly an hour ago.'

'We should call the police,' Drew said, reaching into her bag to retrieve her mobile.

Iman slapped her hand on Drew's arm. 'No! You cannot do this. It will bring trouble on us.'

'She's right,' Gregory said. 'What will the police do anyway? Nadia doesn't exist as far as they are concerned. She's an illegal. They will only deport her.'

'Only if they find her in one piece,' Drew commented ominously.

'But Gregory is right,' Suki added. 'If the cops suspect me of keeping an illegal it could harm my chances of staying here. I have the refugee status now.' She looked very anxious.

Drew was suddenly angry. 'But what about Nadia? What if something awful's happened to her?'

'Then it is the will of Allah.' The Muslim bowed her head in respect for the holy name.

Drew was horrified. 'So you're going to do nothing?'

'What can we do?' Suki said. 'If they have her, there is nothing we can do. We don't know where she is, and we cannot risk drawing attention to ourselves. We cannot do anything that would give the authorities cause to notice us.'

Drew was disgusted and couldn't hide her disdain. 'Well, you selfish so and sos.' She turned her attention to Iman. 'I thought you didn't want to let Nicolae down, and now you're just washing your hands of that poor girl.'

The three foreign nationals were standing staring at the floor, the ceiling, anywhere but at Drew. She hoped they were feeling bad. She hoped that she could shame them into doing something. After an uneasy silence Gregory cleared his throat. 'You don't understand,' he said. 'You don't know what we had to go through to get here. You don't know what it is like to be persecuted. To fear for your life. To go hungry. To see your family dragged off by the police to be tortured.'

'No. But that's still no excuse.' She was slightly shame-faced now.

'But what can we tell the cops anyway?' Gregory's voice was frustrated. 'Nadia is missing. So what? She's an illegal. Illegals go missing all the time for different reasons.'

'But you know there's a chance that some harm has come to her. What about those heavies? What about—'

'If they have her it is already too late,' Iman cut in.

Drew couldn't argue with that and her blood ran cold. She recalled the picture she had in her head of the girl. She had looked so young and vulnerable, but in many ways she was probably more streetwise than Drew would ever be.

'She could be hiding,' Suki said, on a more positive note. 'She could have taken fright and gone into hiding.'

'Where for God's sake? According to Iman her only friend was Nicolae, and you three now, I suppose. How has she had time to make any other friends?'

'We all look out for one another,' Gregory muttered defensively.

Drew snorted. 'Right! Like you're looking out for Nadia.'

'We looked out for her as much as we could. If it wasn't for Nicolae and me she wouldn't have had anywhere to stay. No one wanted to help. I fight with people to help her.' It was Iman's turn to be both irate and defensive. The scene on the corner of Leinster Road flashed through Drew's consciousness. Then her phone rang. She looked at the display and saw the word *Mother*. She glanced at her watch. It was after eight-thirty. 'Shit!' She punched the yes button.

'Drew! Where are you? I'm in Sandymount.' The tone was moderately stern.

'Sorry, Mother, I meant to call you. I'm delayed. I'm in Rathmines. Can you pick me up?' Iman, Suki and Gregory were staring at her resentfully.

'Rathmines! Oh really, Drew, you could have called earlier! Now I'll have to retrace my steps.'

'Well, if it's any trouble—'

A heavy resigned sigh. 'No, no. Can you be outside the Swan Centre in five minutes?'

'No problem. See you in—'

'Yes, yes!' Barbara rang off.

'I have to go,' Drew said. 'Call me if you hear from Nadia.' No one moved or made any reply as she left. She was both angry and frustrated. Frustrated that she couldn't do anything and angered by their resigned attitude.

The heat of her mood propelled her to the shopping centre in record time, so she had to fester by the kerb for a good five minutes before Barbara's black Polo screeched to a halt. Drew jumped in. Barbara sat po-faced behind the wheel staring straight ahead. Not a good sign. As soon as she slammed the passenger door her mother drove off like a bat out of hell. Drew fastened her seat belt and tried to take her mind off the drive. It was not one of life's more pleasurable experiences, driving with Barbara Looney, particularly if she happened to be in a bad humour. Barbara's driving was erratic to say the least; in fact she had to be the worst driver on the planet, but few if any had the courage to tell her so. And so daunting could Barbara Looney be that the general consensus amongst Drew and her friends was that the only reason she had passed her test at the first attempt was down to the traumatised examiner's fears that he may get her again.

After three minutes of icy silence Drew's anger had dissolved into a strong feeling of apprehension. Often, after one of Barbara's huffs had blown over, she would lecture herself in the bathroom mirror, pointing out that she was an adult and that buying into the whole rigmarole only

encouraged her mother. She told herself to pay no attention. To ignore her mother's disapproval and act as if
nothing was wrong. She had tried this tactic more than
once, but it was futile. At the end of the day, no matter
how much she told herself that she didn't care what her
mother thought of her, the truth was, she did. She needed
Barbara's approval but, perversely, life was conspiring
against her on that score. Scarlett had it right. She would
never manage to satisfy the wish-list her mother had
drawn up for her, unless she married a man like Justin
and presented her with two matching designer kids, preferably one of each sex.

'Sorry to mess you around,' she ventured, testing the
water. 'It was work. I'm researching a big story.'

The word 'researching' had a magical effect on Barbara
and she slowed the Bat-mobile to a legal speed. Her head
spun round and the car mounted the pavement for a brief
moment before bouncing back onto the road. 'Researching?'

Did Drew detect a note of grudging respect in the dragon
lady's tone? Flushed with success, she grasped the dashboard
for balance and went on. 'Yes. It's . . . um . . . a political
piece.'

'Politics?' Really impressed now. Drew's recent human
interest schlock had caused Barbara terminal embarrassment
at the golf club. Why did her daughter have to be doing
stories about dwarves and centenarians from Mullingar
when Miriam Stoney's girl was covering the serious issues
like the peace process and all those political scandals? She'd
even appeared on TV a couple of times on *Questions and
Answers*, when John Bowman had referred to her as a
political pundit. Drew could sense that Barbara was about
to inquire further, so she cut in. 'I can't say any more at the
moment, I'm afraid. It's very sensitive.'

Barbara nodded. She understood all about discretion. She
never subscribed to it herself, mind you. Someone only had
to warn her not to tell a soul about a salacious piece of

gossip to guarantee that it would spread like a rash. If asked, however, she would consider herself to be the soul of discretion. 'You can tell me, darling. I'm your mother.'

Drew realised, too late, that she had painted herself into a corner. 'Well . . . um . . . it's about refugees, but I really can't say any more at this point. It's a question of safety.'

'Safety? Whose safety?' She sounded slightly alarmed.

'Um . . . mine,' Drew blathered. 'It's rather delicate, you see. I'll fill you in as soon as I can.'

The hollow promise seemed to placate Barbara and the talk turned to weddings. The speed of the car had dropped in direct relation to her ire and was now fluctuating between twenty-five and thirty-five miles an hour.

'Now, Drew. I hope you will be gracious with Maddie. It's very good of her and Justin to think of you. I hope you realise that. I don't want you making a show of me tonight. I really couldn't stomach the likes of that Aíne Reibheinn looking down her nose at us again.'

Drew settled back in her seat and capitulated, resigned to the fact that for the sake of peace she was about to endure the evening from hell, and with vol-au-vents to boot.

Chapter Ten

Drew met Scarlett on the way in to work the following morning. It was their turn for the early shift. 'So how did the little *soiree* go?' her friend asked, sniggering.

'Surprisingly well,' Drew replied. 'Apart from the vol-au-vents. And Maddie was sweetness itself, would you believe? If I didn't know better I'd say she was on something.'

'Are yeh serious?' Utter incredulity while she took that in, then, after a pause, 'So what are ye wearin'?'

'Pale grey Armani.'

Scarlett gave her a shove. 'No, *really*.'

'Pale grey linen Armani,' Drew repeated. She wouldn't have believed it either if she hadn't seen the pictures and fabric samples with her own eyes. 'Straight, tailored, high slash neck, sleeveless, to just below the knee.'

Scarlett's jaw was slack. 'Are yeh sure she isn't just tryin' to lull yeh into a false sense of security?'

Drew laughed. 'Well if she is she went to a lot of trouble. The man from Armani was flown in especially to measure us all up.'

'Are yeh serious? Are yeh sure it wasn't the man from Del Monte?'

On that note, Drew went in to see Joe Mulloy. She wasn't looking forward to it, afraid that he'd judge her as Kerrigan had, but he was very understanding when she filled him in on her progress to date, which, in effect, was nil.

'Never mind,' he said. 'You can't win 'em all. The girl could just have gone to ground.'

Drew hoped so. She had woken up in the small hours of

the morning thinking about Nadia. She thought that was the end of it until Joe continued after a brief pause, 'Dig around a bit and see if you can get any other leads.' Drew was pleased by this development. She was so accustomed to Kerrigan's negative attitude that she had expected Joe to hold her personally responsible for the lack of progress and either kill the story stone dead or pass it on to someone else. In the meantime, however, it was her turn to check the Garda stations for overnight reported crime. She headed back to her desk with an unaccustomed spring in her step. Scarlett passed her in the doorway of the acting news editor's office.

'It's about the Bruce Gold story,' she said to Joe, getting straight to the point. 'There's been a development.'

Joe motioned her to sit. 'Such as? I thought it was straightforward and he got bail.'

'He did. But you know about the business fifteen years ago?'

'No, what business?'

'He was accused of having sex with a minor, but the charges were dropped. Rumour had it he paid the da off.'

Joe's eyebrows shot up. 'Really?' She had his full attention.

'Yeah. I went out to Sandymount to get a quote about that. Anyway, I have to say, I wasn't particularly impartial when I went out there, but to tell yeh the truth, after talkin' to him, I think he was set up.'

'Then? The last time?'

'Both times I'd say. I mean, what man would settle for money and drop the charges if his young wan was really messed with?'

'Depends on the man,' Joe commented, recalling a certain US mega star and his dubious association with little boys.

'Yeah, I suppose, but this fella phoned Gold and suggested cash would make it go away. Just like that. No messin'. If yeh ask me he knew about the business years back, thought it was a good little earner and set up the daughter to get Bruce into bed with a view to blackmailin' him. It was at their house while the parents were downstairs for feck's sake. What eejit would rape a fella's daughter in his own house with him down below in the sittin' room? Bruce said he never touched her.'

The fact that Scarlett was referring to Gold in the familiar wasn't lost on Joe. 'Or conversely, what father would set his fifteen year old daughter up to have sex, effectively, for money?'

'It's been done.'

Joe had to concede that point. 'OK. But how do you know Gold isn't stringing you along just to get sympathetic coverage?'

'Not the way he told it. Trust me, Joe, yeh had to be there. And I was there when Bruce called him back. Yer man Sid Cahill, the da, he sounded cool as yeh like. Anyway, I said I'd go with Bruce to the pay-off and put a wire on him to record the deal. Yeh know, get the da to admit it was a set-up. Then—'

'Hang on, hang on,' Joe said. 'What are you talking about, a *wire*?'

'A recordin' device,' Scarlett said impatiently. 'We can take the tape to the cops then and—'

Joe sat back in his chair. 'Scarlett, I know what a wire is, but we don't have such a thing,' he said. 'Now, the likes of *The Sunday World* might.' He had a grin on his face.

'Aw, come on, Joe. If we pull this off it'd be huge. Can't we hire it from one of them surveillance companies?'

'Jesus! You're serious, aren't you?' He sounded surprised and mildly amused.

True, *The Daily Record* was a very small, independent operation that didn't usually go in for the kind of investigative exposés that necessitated hidden recording devices, relying on exhaustive research and dogged digging over the facts, but she couldn't see what his problem was. It was a big story. 'DAILY RECORD JOURNALIST UNCOVERS BLACKMAIL PLOT'.

'And you're sure of your facts. This Sid Cahill's for real?'

'Absolutely. And the pay-off's set for tonight out in Ballyfingal.'

Joe was nodding now and swinging gently from side to side in his swivel chair. Scarlett felt he was at last taking her seriously. 'When you say you're going with him, do you mean to the actual pay-off or just out to Ballyfingal?'

'I thought I could pose as his PA or somethin',' the intrepid reporter replied. 'That way I can write the story first hand.' Joe looked as if he was going to object so she pressed on. 'It's no sweat, Joe. Yer man won't smell a rat. The likes of Gold always has a PA.'

Joe still looked reluctant. 'What do you know about this Sid Cahill?'

Scarlett shook her head. 'Nothin'. Why?'

'Well check him out. Give one of your Garda contacts a call, no need to be specific. If Cahill's into anything else of a dodgy nature we'll need to know about it, and in the meantime look up a reputable surveillance company in the Golden Pages.'

Scarlett didn't need to be told twice. She was on her feet and halfway to the door to ring her 'Garda contact' before Joe had finished the sentence. 'Deadly, Joe. Thanks.'

Drew sat bolt upright in her chair. Her heart was beating ten to the dozen and she could hear a faint ringing in her ears. 'Sorry, could you repeat that please.'

'A Romanian national, a woman of approximately eighteen years of age.'

'Are you certain?'

The sergeant sounded impatient at the other end of the line. 'Of course I'm certain. Isn't it my job to be certain?' He had a strong Cork accent and the intonation at the end of the sentence rose sky high with indignation.

'Sorry, Sergeant. When was she found did you say?'

'An hour ago by a woman walking her dog by the Grand Canal above Huband Bridge. The State pathologist's on his way to the scene.'

Drew thanked the sergeant and hung up. She was in a state of shock. Nadia? Could it be Nadia? Just because the victim fitted the age and nationality profile, it didn't mean to say it *was* her. Who was she kidding? Her gut feeling was telling her it had to be the girl.

She grabbed her coat and bag from where she had dumped them under her desk. 'I have to go out to follow something up,' she called to Marty and practically ran from the newsroom. She grabbed a cab on O'Connell Street and made it out to Huband Bridge in fifteen minutes. There was a gaggle of Guards, both uniformed and in plain clothes, and streams of blue and white Garda tape cordoning off the area of the Grand Canal above the bridge. A white tarpaulin erected over a frame about thirty feet along the bank signalled where the body was located. As she clipped the Press laminate onto her lapel she glanced around, looking for any familiar face with a view to getting some information. She vaguely recognised the uniformed Garda standing sentry by the side of the bridge so she gave him a warm smile and struggled for his name. He was standing impassively, looking bored to death as well as cold. Over his shoulder she could see the technical bods in their white coveralls examining the scene. As she reached him a name popped into her mouth. 'Dave! How are you?'

'Bleedin' freezin',' he said, stamping his feet. 'How's things?'

'Ah, you know yourself,' she said with a shrug. 'So what's the story?' He gave her a 'you know the score' look, so she added, 'Off the record, Dave, off the record.' Always a good ploy to be on first name terms with the cops at a time like this.

'Off the record, a woman found a young one a while ago. Looks like she was beaten to death by a punter.'

He was being very economical with his information, and talk of 'punters' surprised Drew for a moment until she realised that it was natural for the cop to assume that the girl was a hooker. The Grand Canal was a regular spot for clients cruising to pick up prostitutes, and a number of working girls in the past few years had met with a violent end above Huband Bridge.

'Is she Irish?' Fishing. 'Do you have a name?'

'As far as I know she had some identification on her, but I don't know the name. No doubt they'll release it in a while.'

Over Dave's shoulder she saw two detectives making their way from the scene. They stopped a little way short of the bridge and stood talking for a minute. She immediately recognised Vinnie, though she shouldn't have been surprised; Harcourt Terrace was only around the corner. The other detective, whom she didn't recognise, turned and walked back towards the crime scene and Vinnie carried on towards the bridge. Dave lifted the Garda tape and Scarlett's cousin stooped under it.

She took a deep breath. 'Hello, Vinnie.'

He nodded a greeting. 'How's the form?' His tone was neutral but not unfriendly.

'So what's the story with the victim?' No point in wasting time on awkward, meaningless pleasantries.

He looked over his shoulder towards the scene of the crime. 'Romanian national, refugee probably, about eighteen or so. May have been a working girl, though there's no obvious sign of sexual activity. Head injuries, probably beaten with a heavy blunt object. Dead about twelve hours.' Vinnie was succinct and to the point.

'What's her name?'

Vinnie took out his day book and flipped through the

pages. 'She had a letter on her. Nadia Iacob. I-A-C-O-B.' He mispronounced the surname but Drew didn't correct him. Her heart was beating wildly again at the confirmation of her suspicions and she had to fight to remain calm. He was staring at her. 'Are you OK? You look a bit seedy.'

Drew pulled herself together. 'Yes, yes. I'm grand, just a bit hung over.'

He nodded. 'Ah, the demon drink.'

She could feel a trickle of cold sweat running down the side of her face and she wanted to vomit, but her heart had slowed to a moderate gallop. She took a couple of deep breaths. 'Um . . . Have you any suspects?'

'No. Not at the minute. The lads are still doing the house to house.'

'And you've no idea of a motive?'

'Well, like I said, she could be a working girl. We've no clues at the minute. We'll know more after Doctor Yentob's done the post-mortem. There'll be the usual statement from the Press office later today.'

She felt very unwell now, dizzy and sick, and she was finding it hard to concentrate. It wasn't that she was squeamish. As a journalist she had learned to become detached from incidents, dispassionately reporting the facts and gathering background. She'd never previously experienced a problem like this, and she had covered a good deal of violent crime before, but then she had never known the murder victim. And though she had never actually met Nadia, she felt she did know her.

'Are you sure you're OK? You're white as a sheet.' There was concern in his voice. Drew reached out and put her hand on the bridge to steady herself and Vinnie grabbed her elbow. 'Come on, you need a hot, sweet drink, you look as if you're going to pass out.'

'No, really, I'm fine,' she said as her knees buckled.

There can be few more humiliating experiences than fainting in public. She came to, sitting on the ground with her back against the cold stone of the bridge. Someone was pushing her head down between her knees. She recognised Vinnie's shoes and pulled her head up. Her ears were ringing and she was sweating profusely. He had his arm around her shoulder supporting her, and Dave was down on his hunkers, for some reason holding a hanky out to her. Totally mortified, she pushed his hand away and tried to heave herself up. Bad idea. She experienced a sudden wave of nausea, then puked. Vinnie's shoes suffered minor splattering, but Dave got the brunt of it over his thighs. He was neither quick nor agile enough to jump out of the way. 'Ah feck!' he grunted, only managing to heave himself sideways in a vain attempt to avoid the full force of the vomit.

If the ground had opened and swallowed her at that moment, or Scotty had chosen that instant to beam her up to some parallel universe, she would have been well pleased. But no such luck. She had to suffer the ignominy of Vinnie hefting her into a standing position on her rubber legs. Dave was standing with his knees splayed and bent, holding the dark blue fabric in an attempt to keep his puke-sodden pants from sticking to his legs. All she could manage was an ineffectual, 'Sorry.' He looked completely disgusted.

She could feel the strength returning to her legs now and the faintness had passed. Vinnie looked into her face. 'You're getting a bit of colour back. I think I'd better take you up the road and get you a cup of tea.'

'Really . . . I'm fine.'

'Don't be an eejit. You look like shite. You need a hot, sweet drink.' He steered her up towards Percy Place. She didn't argue. What was the point? Anyway, she was anxious to get away from Dave.

By the time they reached the small café near the top of the quiet street she was feeling almost human. It briefly crossed her mind at that point that Aíne Reibheinn's vol-au-vents might have had something to do with the attack of projectile puking. She'd been feeling slightly queasy since she'd woken up that morning. For sure it wasn't a hangover. The only beverage on offer at Aíne's soirée was red wine, admittedly very good, expensive red wine, Chateau Margeux to her recollection, but red wine was inclined to make her evil, and Barbara, being well aware of this, had swiped the glass from her hand and replaced it with designer water, muttering dire warnings to '*be nice*'.

'Must have been some session last night,' he said as they sat down at a table in the corner. The steamy café was full of dusty building workers having their breakfast.

'Actually, I think it might be food poisoning,' she said huffily. He gave her a 'Yeah, right!' look which, because of her recent humiliation, made her hackles rise. She took a sip of her tea, already regretting that she hadn't just exited the scene with what was left of her dignity intact.

An uncomfortable silence hung between them. She felt his eyes on her. 'You look a bit better,' he said.

She took another sip of her tea. She felt better but still shaky. 'I'm so mortified. Poor Dave.'

Vinnie laughed. 'Don't worry about Dave. He'll be glad to get back in the warm.'

'I know, but all the same . . .'

'You changed your hair,' Vinnie said. Drew's hand involuntarily shot up to her luminous locks. 'It's nice.'

'Bit sudden.' She laughed self-consciously.

'No, it's nice.'

He looked very tasty sitting across the table from her; the years had improved him. She began to seriously reconsider Scarlett's suggestion.

'I met Scarlett the other day,' he said after a pause. 'She seems to think we should go out for a drink. Get back together. Can you believe that?' He was testing the water.

Drew felt herself redden. 'Shit! I warned her not to. I'm sorry.'

Vinnie laughed. 'Don't worry about it. Fixing people up

whether they like it or not is her mission in life,' he said, disappointed by her response. 'And it's generally a disaster.'

'Ain't that the truth,' Drew agreed, but she was more than slightly miffed that he hadn't jumped at the chance of a date with her, despite the fact that her reaction had been equally negative. Arrogant bastard.

'Dates from hell,' he said, shooting himself through the foot whilst it was still in his mouth.

Who the hell did he think he was? God's gift to women? 'Right,' she said huffily. Then she looked pointedly at her watch. 'Well, must go. Things to do. People to see.' He half rose from his seat and opened his mouth to say something but she headed swiftly for the door without giving him the chance, shouting a hasty, 'Thanks for the tea.' As she sped past the window she was aware of him staring after her through the corner of her eye. She made a mental note to rip Scarlett's ears off the next time she saw her.

Chapter Eleven

It hadn't even crossed her mind to admit to Vinnie that she knew Nadia Iacob. Maybe it was the embarrassment of Scarlett's clumsy attempts to pair them off and his singular lack of enthusiasm. Maybe it was guilt over Nadia. Though in fairness she knew that there was little if anything she could have done to help her. She was, however, determined to get to the bottom of the sweat-shop story. Bearing in mind that the little fat man she had seen outside Gregory's flat could well be involved, she made her way into town to Justin's Temple Bar penthouse. She needed to see Maddie to grill her about him. Failing that, she knew the only other option was to interrogate Iman to see if she really was as ignorant as she pretended to be about the whole sorry business. One way or another, it was a certainty that if either the Somalian woman, Suki or Gregory did know anything, the news of Nadia's murder would cause them all to have a sudden attack of amnesia.

Twenty-four hours previously she wouldn't have considered calling on her future sister-in-law, but after her unexpectedly civilised behaviour of the previous evening the thought wasn't too daunting. Besides, she wouldn't stay. As soon as she got the dope on the fat man, she'd make her excuses, as they say, and leave.

She jumped on a bus at Baggot Street and climbed to the top deck. The clouds had lifted now and Strumpet City looked splendid in the sunshine, even a watery November sunshine. She mentally rehearsed what she would say to Maddie. Start by enthusing about the bridesmaids' frocks, perhaps. Not too hard, they *were* Armani and absolutely gorgeous. Compliment her on the engagement party? Swing the conversation round to Fatty that way? Maybe not; that could bring to mind the incident with herself and Scarlett and might remind the stick insect how much she disliked yours truly. As she pondered the various scenarios, Vinnie kept intruding on her consciousness. It was disconcerting. True, he did look very tasty. What was that about? It was years since they'd dated. Shit, they'd been kids straight out of school. Her hand involuntarily touched her hair as she thought of him. What was *that* about? The check of him. 'Who the fuck does he think he is?' she muttered to herself as she crossed at the lights near the Central Bank on Dame Street. 'Arrogant bastard!'

In the end, unable to concentrate on planning a plausible approach for Maddie, she decided to wing it when she sussed what kind of humour the bride-to-be was in. It was still relatively early as she made her way down Crowe Street towards Justin's apartment, only just past ten-thirty. She hoped that Maddie would be up. The likes of Maddie Reibheinn operated on a different time frame to ordinary folk. Of course, there was always the possibility that she was out at a dance class or a yoga session, or having her legs waxed or a manicure or a reflexology treatment. All that beauty and grooming stuff must be very time consuming. God! Drew thought. What a trial it must be to be beautiful. All that maintenance. At least she would never have the trauma of lamenting her faded beauty. She chuckled to herself. No, all she would have to lament was her faded plainness.

She was surprised when there was no verbal answer to the buzzer, only the kerthunk of the automatic door lock release. She pushed the heavy oak door open and made for the lift. It shot up effortlessly to the top floor and the doors hissed open. Drew felt apprehensive. Just because Maddie had managed to maintain the persona of a human being the previous night didn't mean to say that she would be equally civilised now. The girl was moody to say the least, and Drew wasn't sure she was up to humouring her today. Unsure as to whether she'd be able to keep her temper long enough to get the low down on the fat man, she mentally instructed herself to focus, to be professional. But as she stepped from the lift, the penthouse door was flung open and Maddie's bestest buddie rushed into the lobby. She was wearing only a short T-shirt, a fuchsia G string and a wild, panicky expression. Her black hair was every which way and her waxy face streaked with the remnants of last night's make-up.

'I can't wake her up! She won't wake up!' she babbled, then grabbed Drew's arm and dragged her into the rooftop apartment. The sight of Maddie's mad coven mate had temporarily thrown the journalist and it took a moment for the words to register.

'How do you mean, you can't wake her up? Who? Maddie?'

They were in the master bedroom now and the answer became self-evident. Maddie was lying motionless, sprawled on the queen-sized bed in her pyjama top and knickers. Drew rushed over and felt for a pulse. There was barely a flutter and her lips were faintly blue. She shook Maddie's shoulder and slapped her cheek. 'Wake up, Maddie! Wake up.'

'I tried that! She's dead, she's dead!'

'Did you call an ambulance?'

When there was no reply she looked round at the girl. She was standing stock still, staring at the limp figure on the bed, her face ashen. Drew did the memory scouring trick again and dredged up a name. 'Tamzin, isn't it?' The girl nodded. 'Did you call an ambulance, Tamzin?' Tamzin shook her head. Tears were running down her cheeks. 'THEN FUCKING DO IT!' Drew yelled, yanking the terrified waif-woman back to reality. As Tamzin scuttled off to call the emergency services, Drew climbed on to the bed to feel Maddie's pulse again. Nothing. She wasn't breathing. 'Shit! Don't do this to me, Maddie. Don't do this.' She opened Maddie's mouth and checked her airway, then started mouth to mouth resuscitation. Come on, Maddie, breathe. Breathe. She shifted position and started CPR, mentally thanking the nuns at Kylemore Abbey for introducing first aid as an extracurricular activity. After half a minute she checked Maddie's pulse again. Still nothing. She recommenced the CPR.

She caught sight of Tamzin's reflection in the mirror, standing in the doorway. 'The ambulance is on its way,' the girl said in a tiny voice. Drew felt for a pulse again and her heart leapt as she felt a regular but faint beat. She put her ear to Maddie's chest. It was rising and falling now. She was breathing again. Drew rolled her over into the recovery position.

'What happened? Did she take something?'

Tamzin had pulled herself together at last and was dragging on her clothes. 'She was doing coke all last night after we got back, then when she wanted to go to bed she couldn't sleep so I think she took some downers.'

'Where's Justin?'

'He went off to New York on business yesterday. He's away for a couple of days, that's why I'm staying here.'

Drew rechecked Maddie's pulse. It was stronger now. Then, without warning, she suddenly coughed and vomited all over the quilt. Drew yanked her up, gripping her under her armpits, supporting her so she wouldn't choke. 'Good girl, Maddie. Puke up the tablets. That's the way.' Maddie threw up again. Drew struggled, one-handed, to wipe Maddie's mouth with the corner of her pyjama jacket. Her legs were aching with the strain of half standing, half crouching on the springy surface of the bed. In the distance she could hear the wail of a siren. She prayed it was the ambulance. For one so skinny Maddie Reibheinn weighed a ton.

Her prayer was answered. Tamzin, who had rushed to the window, yelled, 'It's the ambulance. I'll go down and show them the way up.' She ran from the room.

Maddie was still unconscious, but her breathing was regular now and her heartbeat fairly strong, if a little irregular. Drew lowered her back on to a clean portion of the quilt and felt her pulse at regular intervals. The sour stench of the vomit invaded her nostrils, and she of the weak stomach had to concentrate like hell to maintain her equilibrium. Moments later two paramedics bustled into the room.

'What's the story?' the first one asked.

'She took too many sleeping pills by accident, I think. She wasn't breathing so I gave her mouth to mouth and CPR. Then she threw up. Her heartbeat's still a bit irregular.'

'Good woman,' the older of the two ambulance men said as he checked the patient's pulse. 'Do you know what she took?'

Drew shook her head. 'I'll see if I can find any pill bottles.' She struggled backwards off the bed and made for the bathroom. At the door, she stopped. 'Um . . . and she might have done some coke.' She heard a grunt in response.

The bathroom was a mess. Wet towels had been dumped on the floor along with discarded clothing, and the basin was scarred with dollops of stale toothpaste. On the granite hand basin unit a platinum Visa card, a thin silver tube and a dull dusty residue was all that remained of the previous night's coke fest. Drew picked up a damp towel and wiped away the evidence. Then she slid open the drawer beneath the unit and swiped the card and snorting tube out of sight. There were three brown plastic pill containers in the drawer, two with Maddie's name on, one with Justin's. She picked up Maddie's and squinted at the labels. One was Prozac, the other had no information other than the dosage: 'One to be taken at night before sleep'. She shook it and pills rattled inside. Next door in the bedroom she could hear the paramedics talking to each other as they monitored Maddie's vital signs and prepared to cart her off to hospital.

Drew went with the patient in the ambulance and Tamzin followed by car. At St James's A&E, as Maddie was whisked off into resus', Drew gave in her details at reception, then went outside to phone Áine Reihbeinn. She stuck to the edited highlights. Maddie was in James's because of an attack of food poisoning. She explained that Maddie had vomited in her sleep and had choked, but that fortunately she (Drew) had called round at the opportune moment and had managed to revive her. As she said the words it occurred to Drew that Maddie probably had Áine's vile vol-au-vents to thank for ridding her of the excess pharmaceuticals in her digestive tract.

At first Áine's reaction consisted of, 'Eau my Gawd! Yew kneau, I was sick today too. It must have been the salmon mousse in the vol-au-vents. I'll kill thet fishmanger.' She didn't seem to grasp the seriousness of the matter until Drew spelt it out. 'She nearly died, Áine. Maddie nearly died. She's in the A&E resuscitation unit as we speak.'

That pulled Áine up short, but in the event she appeared to be more horrified by the fact that her daughter was in a public hospital than she was by her brush with death. She jabbered incoherently for a couple of minutes, words to the effect that she'd get the wheels in motion this minute and arrange for her darling daughter to be transferred to the Blackrock Clinic.

As Drew hung up, she spied Tamzin hurrying towards A&E from the car park. She had combed her hair and fixed her make-up somewhere between Temple Bar and the hospital. She caught sight of Drew seconds later and ran across the road. 'Is she all right?'

'I hope so, she's in resus'. I just called her mother.'

Tamzin glared at her accusingly. 'What did you tell her? I bet you dropped her in it.'

'As a matter of fact, you scrawny-arsed bitch,' Drew hissed, 'I told Aíne that Maddie was suffering from food poisoning. That she choked on her vomit and I revived her.' That took the wind temporarily out of Tamzin's sails. She blushed. 'So stick to the story, right?'

Tamzin nodded, shamefaced. 'Right.' Then there was a begrudging, 'Sorry.'

Drew accelerated away from her and headed for the reception counter. The plump, harassed-looking woman to whom she had given Maddie's details was talking on the phone. Drew waited patiently for her to finish, then Tamzin was at her elbow. 'Excuse me,' she said. The receptionist glanced up and raised a finger in silent request for her to wait. Tamzin was having none of it. 'EXCUSE ME!' she repeated, twenty decibels louder. The receptionist ignored her, eyebrows knitted together in annoyance. Drew heard Tamzin draw in a lungful of air, ready to register a protest, so she gave her a sturdy whack with her hip, sending her skidding sideways along the counter. The woman put down the phone.

'You'll have to excuse my friend,' Drew explained. 'She had a common-politeness bypass at birth.' The receptionist smirked. Tamzin scowled. 'I wonder if I could see the doctor treating Maddie Reibheinn?'

'Are you a relative?'

'She's my brother's fiancée,' Drew explained. 'I brought her in.'

The woman picked up the phone. 'If you'll take a seat over there, dear, I'll get someone to come and talk to you,' she replied, casting a withering look at the quietly fuming Tamzin.

A young doctor, who seemed barely old enough to legally buy a drink, let alone shave, came out a short time later and explained that Maddie was as well as could be expected. She had just had her stomach pumped (Drew felt nauseous at the mention of that) and she should be fine, but would be kept in overnight for observation.

The words 'over Aíne's dead body' crossed Drew's mind but she said nothing. 'Um . . . Maddie's medical details are confidential, aren't they?' she asked.

The doctor nodded, slightly puzzled by the question. 'Yes, of course.'

'Good. The thing is, you see, it's likely her mother will be along shortly and I know Maddie wouldn't want her to know about the drugs. I've already told her that Maddie had food poisoning, vomited in her sleep and choked, hence the reason for the resus'.'

'I see,' the doctor said. 'Well, OK. We'll stick to that story for now. If the patient, when she's able, chooses to tell her mother at a later date, that's up to her.'

'Exactly,' Drew agreed, relieved. The young doctor nodded, still looking like a schoolboy despite his gravitas, then scurried off.

Tamzin was at her elbow again. 'Why did you do that? I thought you couldn't stand the sight of Maddie.'

'Good grief, where did you get that idea?' Drew asked with mock surprise. 'My brother, for some misguided reason, loves her. That's why, and I don't want to see him upset, even if he does behave like a complete prat most of the time.'

As there was nothing else to be said, and safe in the knowledge that the love of her poor deluded brother's life had cheated extinction, she left Tamzin to it, explaining that she had to get back to work, but not before reminding her that when she saw Aíne she was to stick to the cover story.

With no possibility of Maddie being in a fit state to give her the dirt on the fat man, the only other alternative was to talk to Iman. On the way out she caught sight of Eddie Reibheinn's Roller as it pulled up by the 'No Parking – Ambulance Bay' sign. Aíne leapt out a nano-second later and dashed into the A&E entrance. Drew contemplated hanging round to see what bloodshed would ensue if Aíne didn't receive immediate attention, but she'd had enough trauma for one day and went to look for a taxi to take her over to Rathmines.

Chapter Twelve

George replaced the receiver with a sense of dread. It was all right in theory to consider it as just a means to an end, but in the cold light of day, the thought of having Grillo's podgy hands all over her revolted her. He was probably enjoying her humiliation as much as he was savouring the anticipation of the act of copulation. It was obviously a power thing. Like rape. Nothing to do with the actual sex. Well, maybe up to a point. She wondered if he would expect her to simulate pleasure, passion – God knows she was as good as the next woman at that – or if he would be satisfied just to take what he wanted and leave it there. Somehow she didn't think so. She had every confidence that he would wring the last ounce of delight out of her shame.

'Tonight,' he had said. 'I will be there tonight. Early. About seven. Wear something sexy. High shoes and silk stockings.' She could imagine him drooling at the other end of the line and felt violated. God! He wanted her to play games too. The thought made her angry, and the anger felt good; at least it was better than the strong sense of self-pity lurking close to the surface. The words 'don't get mad, get even' crossed her mind. How ironic. That was exactly what Grillo was doing. Getting even. What kind of evil bastard was he? As she was contemplating this, the phone rang, almost causing her heart failure. She snatched it up, determined to tell Grillo to go to hell if it was him.

'What?'

There was a hesitation at the other end of the line, then she heard Conor Kenny's voice. 'George, is that you?'

'Sorry, Conor, what can I do for you?'

The diminutive chef cleared his throat. 'It's about the cheque you gave me the other night, George . . .'

George cringed. She had fully intended to call on Conor, get the rubber cheque back and pay him in cash the previous day, but Grillo's little bombshell had put a stop on all normal activity. 'Oh, Conor, I'm so sorry. I meant to come round yesterday and give you cash, but I've been terribly busy and one thing just led to another and I clean forgot.'

He seemed to buy that but was insistent that he would call over in an hour to collect the money in person. In some ways she was glad. Her life was well tattered without losing her caterer to boot. She heaved herself off the sofa and padded into the bathroom. She was still in her comfy green fleece pyjamas even though it was almost mid-day. Her hair felt greasy too. She hadn't showered in two days. Hadn't done anything. She was too depressed. Her reflection didn't cheer her. Suddenly, as she gazed at her naked face and limp hair, she laughed out loud. Serve that manipulative bastard right if she presented herself as she was, unwashed in her mumsie nightwear. But that thought didn't last long. She knew it was a waste of time trying to get the better of him. No. Distasteful though it was, she knew that to rid herself of Grillo once and for all it would be better, more expedient, to just grin and bear it. To lie back and think of Ireland. With that thought in mind, she turned on the shower, stripped off her pyjamas and stood under the hot stream of water with the comforting thought that after tonight, after putting certain safeguards in place, she would be rid of Broylan Grillo for ever.

Scarlett met Vinnie for lunch in Hartigan's pub on Leeson Street. She was looking for a favour so lunch was on her. It would be true to say that pumping Vinnie about Sid Cahill wasn't the only reason she had called him, however. There were two or three cops she could have called, but since meeting him the other day outside the District Court, and unaware of his meeting with Drew that morning, she decided that it was time for phase two of her *Get Vinnie and Drew together* plan. But business first. After they collected their food they found a table in a quiet corner and sat down to eat.

'Is he from the Wild West?' Vinnie asked, using the colloquial name for the sprawling Ballyfingal council housing estate.

'Virtue Road or Rise or something?' Scarlett nodded, her mouth full of toasted ham and cheese.

Vinnie carefully put his pint down on the table. 'He hasn't any convictions barring the usual juvenile stuff, you know, shoplifting, a bit of joy riding, but he's well known to us. He calls himself a security consultant, the way they do. Does door work for one of the clubs in town. He's just a bouncer really.'

'So he's going straight now?'

'I didn't say that, I said he hasn't done time. He's had a couple of close calls, violence mainly, but the victims have always dropped the charges. What's your interest in him?'

'Oh, nothin' specific,' Scarlett lied. 'His name just came up and I wondered what he was into.'

Vinnie gave her a long, sceptical look. 'So you're buying me lunch because you were wondering, apropos of nothing in particular, what Sid Cahill's into?'

'Somethin' like that.' Scarlett smiled. 'Well, there was somethin' else.' Vinnie gave her a crooked, *I knew there was more to it* smile. 'It's about Drew.'

Vinnie frowned. 'Is she all right? I met her this morning at a crime scene and I thought she was acting a bit weird.'

'Weird? In what way?'

'Hard to put my finger on it,' Vinnie said. 'Like I said, I met her at a crime scene, and I suppose she was a bit squeamish and she threw up, so I took her for a cup of tea . . .'

Scarlett grinned. 'The way you do.'

Vinnie gave her an odd look. 'Um, yes . . . anyway, we were chatting away and suddenly, for no apparent reason, she just upped and left.'

'Musta been somethin' yeh said,' Scarlett said accusingly. 'What did yeh say?'

Vinnie shook his head. 'Nothing, really.' He took a thoughtful swallow of his beer.

'Well yeh musta said somethin',' Scarlett insisted. 'I know she fancies yeh.'

Vinnie, who had just taken another gulp of his beer, spluttered and almost choked. Then his phone rang and he fished it out of his pocket. Talk about saved by the bell, or in this case, the tinny jingle. 'Hello.' He listened for about half a minute. 'OK. I'll be right there.' He pushed his chair back from the table. 'Sorry. Have to go, duty calls. Talk to you again.'

Scarlett thought she caught a look of relief on his face. He obviously doesn't want to face up to the inevitable, she thought, as she watched him rush from the pub. What was it with men and their feelings?

When there was no reply to Iman's bell, Drew walked along the road to Gregory's. She got no joy there either, so she sat on the wall and waited, wondering if it would be worth her while to go around to Charleston Road to try the woman, Suki. As she was contemplating this she noticed a couple of burly foreign-looking men wearing heavy, dark overcoats, hands in pockets, walking down the footpath. They stopped outside Iman's house and stood looking up at the first floor window. She could only catch snatches of their conversation because of the intermittent traffic noise, but this was of little consequence because from the bits she did hear it was obvious they were speaking some foreign, probably Eastern European, language. She wondered if they were the same two heavies she had seen the night before. It was hard to tell.

As she was pondering this, a white Garda car skidded around the corner at speed, followed closely by a dark blue Renault. They screeched to a halt immediately in front of Gregory's house. Vinnie was driving the Renault, and sitting in the front passenger seat she recognised the detective she had seen him talking to that morning at the crime scene. Vinnie did a double take when he caught sight of her.

As the uniforms were heading up the path towards the house, the two detectives got out of the car. Vinnie stopped in front of her but his partner followed the uniforms, who had now disappeared inside. 'Hello again. Are you following me?' He sounded almost abrupt.

'Hardly, seeing as I've been waiting here ten minutes,' Drew replied defensively. She glanced up the road and saw the two heavies legging it towards Grosvenor Road.

'But how come you're here? Do you know something about the dead girl?'

His snotty attitude got her back up. 'I'm just waiting for a friend.' Anger changed to innocence personified. 'Have I missed something? Is this about the murdered girl?'

He stood staring down at her for a few moments, trying to decide if she was on the level or not, then nodded. 'Yeah. We think she lived here. The letter we found on her had this address.'

'Really?' Suddenly she appeared to be very interested. She made a show of taking her notebook out of her bag and scribbling a line of shorthand. 'And have you any motive yet? Any new leads? Any suspects? How long was she living here?'

Vinnie shook his head. 'Give us a break, it's only been a few hours.'

Drew looked at her watch. 'Well, I don't think my friend's going to show,' she said, getting up. 'See you around. Bye.'

Vinnie's eyes followed her as she trotted up the road. He didn't know what to make of her. If what Scarlett said was right, she was supposed to be attracted to him, but from where he was standing it certainly didn't look like it. He mentally slapped himself on the wrist for even listening to Scarlett. She was always doing this. Pity. Drew Looney was a fine-looking woman. And though there was no way he'd admit it, he did fancy the knickers off her. He shook his head and followed his colleagues into the house.

Drew could feel his eyes on her as she hurried away. She felt a tad guilty about not telling him that she knew Nadia, but then they'd found where she was living. Anyway, what could she tell him? All she had was a couple of vague bits of information about some men exploiting illegal immigrants, no names, no addresses. Granted, she could have told him about Iman, Gregory and Suki, but she'd promised them she wouldn't, hadn't she? As she was justifying all this to herself she was actually making her way round to Suki's to see if she had any idea where Iman or Gregory might be. Breaking the news of Nadia's murder would either shock them into spilling any information they did have, or conversely, as she had previously speculated, make them clam up as tight as a duck's behind. Still, she felt she had to try. Her mobile rang as she was crossing Rathmines Road.

It was Barbara.

'Hello, Mother.'

'Oh Drew! I'm so ill,' she moaned. 'I've been up all night vomiting.'

'You poor thing. How bad are you?'

'Terrible. Terrible. I think it was something I ate. I've got the most awful cramps.'

'I was sick this morning too. So was Maddie. I think it was Aíne's vol-au-vents.' Although she was feeling genuinely sorry for her mother, she couldn't help but rub in the fact that Barbara had almost force fed her the lethal finger food the previous night. Thankfully, she had managed to dispose of most of it and only ingested a small amount, unlike her mother who was partial to salmon mousse. 'Do you need anything? Did you call the doctor?'

'He's been. He came out last night.'

In the wee small hours no doubt, summoned to Barbara's bedside. 'So how are you now?' As Barbara launched into a detailed account of each and every symptom, ahead of her Drew glimpsed Iman coming out of a convenience store carrying a bulging plastic carrier bag. She turned right and hurried off up the road. As she watched, the Somali then took another abrupt right turn into Castlewood Avenue. Drew quickened her pace. Even money she was heading for Charleston Road to see Suki. She wondered if they had heard about Nadia. It was unlikely. She had caught a snippet of radio news in the taxi and Nadia had not been named, just referred to as 'a young woman found battered to death by the Grand Canal'.

'Drew? Drew? Are you still there?' Barbara had evidently finished her organ recital.

'Yes, Mother, I'm still here. You didn't say if you needed anything.'

'No, dear. I couldn't eat a thing. Ugh! The very thought of food sets me dry retching.'

She had reached the corner now. Iman was twenty yards ahead. She increased her pace. 'Look, Mother, I have to go now but I'll call over tonight to make sure you're OK, and maybe do you some soup or something if you're feeling up to it, OK?'

She heard her mother sigh. 'If it's not too much trouble, dear. If you have the time.' Uncharacteristically, Barbara was not being sarcastic, and Drew felt pangs of guilt for no discernible reason. Barbara always had that effect on her when she was being thoughtful or kind.

'OK. See you later, Mummy. Try to drink lots of water, and try to sleep. You'll feel better if you can get some sleep.' They said their goodbyes and Drew hung up.

Ahead of her Iman was turning into the gate of Suki's building. Drew broke into a run and caught up with her on the step before Suki answered the door. The running footsteps obviously frightened Iman because she spun around with an anxious expression, which only faded when she recognised the journalist. She put her hand to her chest in a gesture of relief. 'You scared me,' she said, embarrassed to have been caught.

It took a moment for Drew to get her breath back. 'We have to talk,' she gasped as Suki opened the door.

It took only half a minute to break the news of Nadia Iacob's murder to the two women, but a shocked silence hung in the air of the tiny, cramped room for a good two minutes afterwards. The news appeared to have rendered both women mute. Drew saw Iman swallow. Her complexion had taken on the same ashen grey hue of the night before. Suki's eyes bulged and she was chewing her lower lip.

Drew broke the hush. 'I was round at your flat looking for you a few minutes ago, Iman, and the cops were at Gregory's. Apparently they found a letter on Nadia with that address. Where is Gregory, by the way? Have you seen him?' Iman shook her head. She obviously didn't feel capable of speech yet. 'I'm sure I saw the two heavies that turned over his room last night,' Iman gave a little gasp, 'but they buggered off sharpish when the cops arrived. I don't think you should go back there. I don't think it's safe. They were looking up at your window. I'm sure they were looking for you.'

'But how would they know about me?' Iman's eyes were huge now and she looked horrified.

Drew shrugged. 'I don't know. But it's a bit of a coincidence that they were actually looking up at your window.

146

They must have found out about Nicolae. They must know he helped Nadia.' It was only then that the full implications struck Drew and she began to regret that she hadn't shared what she knew with Vinnie.

'You can stay here,' Suki said, casting a glance at Nadia's empty camp bed.

'Maybe you should go to the cops,' Drew said tentatively. 'Those guys might come back for you.'

Iman gave a frightened yelp. 'Why me? I know nothing.'

Drew shrugged. 'They don't know that. Maybe they found out you're Nicolae's partner and they're assuming that you do know something. Anyway, I'd rather you didn't take the chance. It would be safer if you went to the cops. They can't deport you. You've a valid visa . . . haven't you?'

Iman nodded, irritably. 'Yes, yes. I'm a student. I told you. But what can I say?'

'Just tell them about Gregory's room being turned over and that you saw these rough-looking men watching your house. It's probably no harm to say you knew Nadia through Nicolae. They're bound to find out at some stage. Better to have it come from you. You can pretend that you thought she was legal.'

Iman shook her head. 'I don't want to get involved. I think we have done enough.'

Suki nodded. 'She is right. It will only bring us to the attention of the authorities.'

'How can you say that?' Drew was shocked. 'Nadia's dead. It was probably those men who killed her. What about the others?'

'This is not our problem,' Suki said, sitting down abruptly on the end of the bed. 'We have our own troubles. Our own things to deal with.'

'She is right,' Iman said. 'I don't know anything about the men, anyway. And if I talk to the police, what if the men find out and come after me again?'

'So what are you going to do?' Drew asked. 'Hide here for ever?'

'The police will catch these people. Then I will be safe.'

'There's not much the cops can do without information. And if everyone's like you two they're not going to get much of that are they?' She was angry. She was standing with her feet planted apart and her hands on her hips. No mistaking the body language. It briefly occurred to her that she was as bad as they were in the withholding information stakes, but she didn't dwell on the point.

Iman was avoiding eye contact but Suki was up for confrontation. She sprang up from the bed, eyes flashing. 'How dare you judge us!' Drew was momentarily taken aback by the attack. 'What do you know about our situation? Have you ever had to fear for your life?'

'No, but—'

'Do you know what it is like to be in a strange country away from your home and family, with nothing?'

'Well no, but—'

Suki cut across her again. 'I do not know if my family are alive or dead. I came here to have some peace, to get away from the fear, the war. If we get involved, if we talk to the police, it will only bring trouble on us. Those men will come after us.'

'She is right, Drew. Those men will come after us.'

'But they're after you already, Iman. Don't you think you'd be safer if you talked to the cops? They'd keep you safe.'

'But I can tell them nothing. I have told you all I know.' She sounded desperate, frustrated that Drew didn't seem to understand. 'How can I tell them what I don't know? I wish I had said nothing in the first place.'

Drew didn't know what else to say. Iman had a point. If she knew nothing, what could she tell the cops? But still she was worried. The thought of the two heavies gave her the galloping butterflies in her gut. Well, it was either the thought of them or the remnants of Aíne's toxic vol-au-vents. She could see she was getting nowhere and capitulated. 'OK. But do you promise to stay out of sight for a couple of days? Not to go out at all?'

Iman nodded vigorously, indicating to Drew that she fully intended to stay out of circulation for as long as it took the cops to do their thing.

Suki said, 'I will bring her anything she needs. The police, they will catch these man.' She patted Iman on the arm. She sounded completely confident . . . certainly more confident than Drew.

Drew left a short time later. She knew it was pointless telling Vinnie about Iman – it could well put her in even more danger. It also crossed her mind that the only way the cops had of keeping her safe would be to put her into protective custody. And even if they had the resources it was unlikely that they'd give her a twenty-four-hour guard, which left only the option of Mountjoy Jail, which didn't bear thinking about. She hopped onto a bus and headed back into town.

Scarlett returned to the office at three o'clock. She had a small carton under her arm which contained two miniature cassette recorders with two tiny microphones. The guy at First Rate Security had instructed her enthusiastically on the best way to attach the hidden mike for the best sound quality. It involved a lot of feeding of wires under her clothing and he seemed to enjoy it. Scarlett, pumped for action, didn't even notice that he was taking an inordinately long time, or that he insisted on trying it a few different ways, she was just anxious that the recording devices should work without a hitch.

As she opened the newsroom door she spotted Bruce sitting in Joe's office, waiting for her. They were so deep in conversation that they didn't notice her approaching. She tapped on the half open door and walked straight in. 'Got the wires,' she said, nonchalantly, as if it was a procedure she was well accustomed to.

Bruce jumped up. 'Great!' He was as pumped as she was.

Joe was less so. 'Did you get the dirt on this Sid Cahill character?' he asked.

Scarlett nodded. 'Nothing much to tell. No convictions.' It was the short version. Joe nodded, satisfied. Scarlett put the carton on the desk and took out the cassettes. Each was the size of a small calculator and about half an inch thick.

Bruce picked one up and examined it. 'How do we, you know . . .?'

Scarlett took out a roll of micro-pore tape from the box. 'Taped to your body,' she said with the air of an expert. 'I'll wear one too to be on the safe side. In the event of an equipment failure it's better to be safe than sorry.'

'So what time's your meeting?' Joe asked.

'Eight o'clock,' Bruce replied. He was still examining the mini cassette. He picked up the tiny mike with its lead out of the carton and turned it every which way, examining the jack and the actual wire. 'This plugs in here I suppose?' he asked Scarlett, as he attempted to poke the jack into the earphone socket of the recording device.

Scarlett took it from his hand and inserted the jack in the adjacent socket. 'No, that's for headphones.'

'So do you two have a game plan?' Joe asked.

Scarlett handed the piece of equipment back to Bruce. 'Yeah. We go out there and Bruce gets him talkin'. He'll lead the conversation round in such a way so yer man admits he's settin' Bruce up.'

Joe guffawed. 'Just like that? Haven't you worked out some sort of script?'

'Well, not yet. But we will,' she replied, embarrassed that the need to do such a thing hadn't really occurred to her.

'Go on then,' Joe said, ending the meeting. 'Get out there to your desk and work out a cunning plan.' He was leaning back in his chair with a grin on his face, as if he wasn't really taking their cloak and dagger operation particularly seriously.

Bruce picked up the box of tricks and followed Scarlett out of the news editor's office. When they were out of earshot he said, 'Is your boss always that off-hand? This is serious, you know. Me liberty's at stake here.'

'Aw, Joe's OK,' Scarlett said, pulling over another chair for Bruce. 'Compared to the last guy he's a regular pussy cat.'

Chapter Thirteen

Broylan Grillo was a happy man. It was his sixty-third birthday. Not bad, considering that the odds against him reaching his tenth had been stacked. Wartime Poland was not a healthy place for any Jew. His family had survived Hitler only to fall victim to Josef Stalin, but he alone had escaped the Gulag and made it to America where his mother's uncle had taken him in until he was old enough to make his own way. Grillo stared into the fire and remembered that period of his life with fondness. After the privations of wartime and post-war Poland, existing hand to mouth in constant fear of discovery and deportation to the death camps or to Siberia, America was a paradise, brimming with opportunity. The uncle, a Rabbi, had constantly reminded him that he was lucky to be alive, but Broylan Grillo didn't believe in the concept of luck, despite the fact that he had more than once cheated certain death. Broylan Grillo believed in destiny. In this life, he gave credence to the concept, there were victims and there were survivors, and he was a survivor. That was his destiny. There had been too many coincidences, too many fortunate breaks to merely put it down to luck or to serendipity. He also had a strong belief in the notion of revenge, of retribution. At the age of fifteen, as he stood in line waiting for the US immigration officer to process his papers, Broylan Grillo had made a conscious decision that from then on *he* would call all the shots. *He* would take charge of his life, make something of himself, and that no one would get in his way again without paying the price.

A log slid into the hearth sending a shower of sparks up the chimney. Grillo reached for the poker and nudged it back into the grate. He loved watching the flames lapping the logs. Loved to feel the heat against his legs. Childhood memories of the biting cold and of the hollow ache of hunger in his belly haunted him still. He'd come a long way.

An import–export broker was how he described himself when asked. He enjoyed the irony. Happy birthday to me, happy birthday to me. Yes, this would be a birthday to remember. He stretched his legs out towards the comforting warmth of the fire and folded his hands across his belly, sighing contentedly. All in all, after an iffy start, it had been a good couple of weeks, barring the slight hiccup when the girl had gone AWOL. But that had been sorted, no thanks to those morons. And it had been a salutary lesson to the others. No fear of them following her example now. They were all terrified and that was the way to have them. They were victims, all of them, and he had no respect for victims.

It surprised him how quickly George had slotted into the victim mentality. Surprised and saddened him. He had expected her to have a bit of backbone, to be more street-wise, but streetwise she was not. He could hardly believe that she had fallen for it so readily. He laughed to himself as he recalled how grateful she had been. It was a pity. He had liked her, been attracted by her intellect as well as her obvious sensuality. He had desired a relationship; he had desired her. They had got on well. There seemed to be a certain chemistry and it was obvious that she enjoyed his company. He was so certain that she too was attracted that he was completely stunned when she had rejected him. The memory of it still rankled. Still burned, humiliated. How dare she?

In some respects he was almost sorry that this part of it was coming to an end now. He got as much pleasure out of the planning as he did of the successful execution of a strategy, and this one had been perfect. He had attained his goal, or was on the threshold, whilst at the same time he had the delicious satisfaction of knowing that he had so consummately destroyed her self-respect. It occurred to him then that she probably thought that this would make them even, pay off the debt. As if! He laughed out loud and despised her all the more. Yes. This would be a good birthday. A good birthday in more ways than one.

Drew had filed her copy by four o'clock. Just the bare factual bones of the story. The who, what, when and where. As for the 'why', she faithfully reported the current speculation that the victim may have been involved in prostitution and had become yet another casualty of the ever-increasing trend of violence towards women. Nadia's name had been released in the Garda press statement, as well as the fact that it was believed that she was an illegal immigrant. There was no new information, or at least if there was, the cops were keeping a lid on it. She had been tempted to ring Vinnie but chickened out, mainly because, despite her fears for their safety, she felt she hadn't the right to involve Iman, Suki and Gregory against their wishes, particularly as they claimed to know nothing.

As she was finishing up, Joe caught her eye and gestured to her to come to his office. Drew nodded and signalled 'Just a minute' as she ran a quick spell check. She filled him in on the day's events, starting with her visit to Maddie's and ending with Suki and Iman's refusal to go to the cops, or indeed get involved any further.

'Suppose you can't blame them,' Joe commented. 'Most of them have had bad experiences with the police in their own countries. The bottom line is they just don't trust cops.'

'Still, I'd be happier if she had protection,' Drew continued.

'She's an adult. It's up to her, Drew,' Joe said, leaning

back in his chair. 'Now, about this fat man? You said you think you know him?'

Drew nodded. 'I've seen him before. At my brother's engagement party. I'm hoping that his fiancée can tell me who he is. I'll call on her later and see if she's up to talking. Though she's a moody cow so she might just take a notion and blank me.'

'She ought not to,' Joe said. 'Sounds to me like you saved her life.'

The words 'More's the pity,' popped out of her mouth and she felt a surge of instant guilt. 'God! That was an awful thing to say.' She felt herself blush.

Joe just laughed. 'Give yourself a break,' he said. 'She sounds like a total spoilt brat.'

'That about covers it.' Through the glass partition Drew noticed Scarlett strolling up the newsroom with a middle-aged guy wearing a baseball hat and biker's jacket. They carried take-away cartons of coffee and were deep in conversation. He looked slightly familiar but she couldn't place him. 'Who's that with Scarlett?'

Joe glanced over towards Scarlett's desk where the pair were now getting settled. 'Oh, that's Bruce Gold. The Aussie glam rocker?'

'Are you serious?' Now she looked at him she could see it, despite the ridiculous leather get-up. He looked shorter though. Then she remembered the six-inch platforms.

'Thought you'd have recognised him, being as you were thrown off the set of what was supposed to be his big comeback.' Joe stifled a laugh.

Drew refused to rise to the bait. 'What's he doing here? I thought he was banged up for rape.'

'Your pal think she's uncovered a cunning plot to blackmail him. It looks as if he was set up. So she's setting up a sting.'

'Good grief. It's all go today, isn't it?' The phone rang

then so Drew drifted out to the main body of the newsroom while Joe took the call. Scarlett and Gold were in a huddle at her desk. As she approached, Scarlett looked up. 'So tell us about this sting thingy,' Drew said.

Gold's head shot up with a look of panic on his face. 'For fuck's sake! This deal's supposed to be bloody undercover,' he hissed to Scarlett.

'Chill out, Bruce. Yer secret's safe with Drew.'

Drew shot her hand towards the now flummoxed, rapidly ageing, rocker. 'I don't believe we've met,' she said. 'Drew Looney.'

Gold stared at her hand for a moment as if it was an electrified fence, then relaxed and grasped it. 'Sorry, bit uptight just now. A lot's riding on this gig.'

'Bruce was set up by this Sid Cahill fella, from Ballyfingal,' Scarlett explained. 'He got his young wan to yell rape. So we're hopin' to get an admission on these little suckers.' She tapped the carton. 'Bruce's goin' to get the bastard to spill his guts for the tape.'

'Yeah, we've worked out a script,' Bruce explained. 'We'll lead the conversation round. Make him brag about it. Hard cases like him love to brag.'

Drew thought they were being a tad optimistic, but not wishing to burst their bubble, didn't share the notion. 'Have you two time for a pint?'

Bruce's little eyes lit up. 'Now you're talking, girl,' he said pushing his chair back.

Scarlett was less enthused. 'OK. But just the one. We'll need clear heads if we want to pull this off.'

They headed out to the Palace and did indeed have just the one, before Scarlett and Bruce headed back to the office to wire themselves up. Drew, on the other hand, stayed for another. Strong drink was necessary before heading over to James's to see how her favourite sister-in-law-to-be was faring.

Chapter Fourteen

It was after six by the time Drew completed the schlep over to James's. She was not a happy bunny having been drenched by a passing bus, and was convinced that she had caught a malevolent glint in the driver's eye as he had deliberately veered into the side of the road so as not to miss the huge puddle. Of all the things in the world that Drew detested with a passion (Ryan Air and tinkly hold musak were high on the list), she hated to get her knees wet, and right now her knees, lower legs and thighs were dripping wet, so the news that Maddie Reibheinn had been transferred to the Blackrock Clinic didn't fill her with glee. That it took her quite some time to illicit this information from the harassed receptionist didn't enhance her mood any. Not a good idea to have sought it with a snarl rather than a smile, perhaps. Her mood lifted a little as she stood outside the hospital entrance, rummaging in her bag for her mobile to call a cab, when one disgorged a very pregnant girl and her partner, both of whom looked under eighteen. The boy was in a complete flap and as white as a sheet. The girl, on the other hand, was calmly paying the taxi driver. As Drew trotted across the road to claim the vacant cab, she said a silent prayer of thanks to the cab fairy.

Maddie was lying back against a mountain of pillows looking pale and wan. An enormous bouquet of long-stemmed red roses enveloped the bedside locker and a small table by the window was staggering under the weight of a huge hamper of exotic fruits. Drew felt slightly self-conscious proffering her paltry bunch of wilting garage flowers.

Maddie eyed the soggy arrangement then gave her a weak smile and fluttered her hand towards the sink. 'Just leave them there. The nurse will see to them.'

'So how are you feeling?' Drew asked as she abandoned the flowers to their fate.

'Like death,' Maddie gasped melodramatically. 'Like death.'

Drew sat on the side of the bed. 'I heard they pumped your stomach. That can't have been much fun.'

'It's the worst. Trust me. Stupid morons. There was no need to go that far,' she moaned. 'Bloody public hospitals.'

'I think they were afraid you'd overdosed. I suppose they had to be on the safe side.'

'Well you could have told them! You know it was the vol-au-vents. Why didn't you stop them?'

'Because you were unconscious, Maddie. You were out of it. And I wasn't sure what effect the bucketload of coke you did last night would have with the bloody Prozac or sleeping pills or whatever junk you took.'

That shut her up. Her face went rigid and for a moment Drew thought she was going to start screaming or something, but after a beat her features relaxed and she slumped down against the pillows. 'You won't tell Justin, will you? I'm going to tell him it was just food poisoning.'

Drew shrugged. 'Whatever.'

Maddie smiled, reached out and grabbed Drew's hand. 'Tamzin said you saved my life. Did that CRAP thing.'

'CPR,' Drew corrected. 'Yes, your heart had stopped. Really, Maddie, you should be careful taking sleeping pills with coke.'

'I know, I know. But I couldn't sleep.' Drew gave her a leery look. 'OK. So the coke didn't help. I'll be more careful, I promise. And if there's ever anything I can do for you . . .'

'Well, as you come to mention it, Maddie, there is something.' Maddie's face fell. She hadn't expected Drew to collect on the hollow promise quite so rapidly. 'I was wondering if you'd know that little fat guy that was at your engagement party. Short, sixtyish, fat, beard, flashy suit?' Maddie furrowed her perfect brows trying to recall. 'You were dancing with him,' Drew prompted.

More furrowing of brows and a nibble of a rosebud lip. Then ping! 'Oh . . . Broy. You mean Broy.'

'I do? So who is he?'

'But positively everyone knows Broy, dahling. Surely you know him. You must. He goes to all the openings, *everything*.'

'If I knew him, I wouldn't be asking, Maddie.' Drew was trying hard to hold on to her patience.

Maddie rocked her head from side to side and gave a little sigh. 'Broylan Grillo, I met him through my charity work.'

'And what does he do? Where does he live? Where's he from?'

Maddie flapped her hands agitatedly. 'Oh, I don't know. He's just Broy. He's a hoot.'

'A hoot?'

Maddie reached out and started to pick the petals off one of the long-stemmed roses, discarding them on to the floor. She was tired of this game. Drew made one final attempt. 'Look, Maddie. I need to speak to him. Are you sure you've no idea where I could contact him?'

Another little sigh. 'Weeell, you could try the caterer, or "party organiser" as she likes to be called.' Maddie did the quotes thing with the first two fingers of each hand. Her voice had a sneering quality to it. 'I think her name's Georgina something. Georgina Fitz-something.'

'Fitz-Simons,' Drew said.

Maddie did the hand flapping thing again. 'Whatever . . . But I don't know where she lives.'

'Well you wouldn't, would you.'

The door swung open and Aíne flustered in. 'Darling, darling. How are you feeling . . . Oh. Hello, Drew.'

Two Reibheinns in a confined space was too much for

this Looney. 'Hello, Aíne.' She made a break for the door after the obligatory air kiss. 'Well, must dash. Hope you feel better soon, Maddie.'

George was agitated. Before the clinic she'd have done a line or two to get her through the evening that stretched ahead, but that wasn't an option now. She settled for a tumblerful of martini instead. She was fidgety, uneasy. It was coming up for seven-thirty and she wasn't ready for it. Psychologically she was already feeling violated. As she took another hefty swig from the tumbler she heard the lift rumbling and her heart gave a lurch of dread. Earlier she had been OK with it. Well, to a degree. In the abstract the concept hadn't seemed so awful. An hour of her time. The debt paid off. She'd be rid of Grillo for ever. She argued with herself that it was no big deal. The trouble was, now that the time was drawing near, now that it was almost a reality, it was a different ball game altogether.

The lift stopped on her floor and she heard the doors hiss open. She held her breath. A moment later there was a familiar rap on the door. Tap, tap, taptap tap (pause) tap, tap. She took a deep breath, drained the dregs of the martini and headed for the hall.

He was almost dancing with excitement when she opened the door. Like a child about to see Santa. That sickened her even more. He had the customary bottle of Bolly in his chubby little hand, already misting up in the warmth of her apartment. In the other he carried his briefcase.

'Hello, sweetness,' he said, attempting to kiss her on the mouth, but she turned her head quickly and his slobbery lips landed on her cheek. She saw a flash of annoyance in his eyes. Then he smiled. 'Shall we do that again,' he said, 'but properly this time.'

Scarlett picked up her Big Mac and took a huge bite. She was starving. Between one thing and another she'd had little time to eat a proper lunch. Her slim figure belied the fact that she had an appetite that would defeat a Sumo wrestler.

Gold, on the other hand, was picking at his McChicken sandwich without enthusiasm. Since she'd wired him up back at the office he had gone quiet and thoughtful.

'Penny for them?' she said, trying to jolly him along.

He looked up. 'Sorry?'

'I said, penny for them. You were miles away.'

Gold sighed and absently picked up a thin salty fry. He dipped it in the ketchup then bit it in half. 'Sorry. It just brought me back to the last time, that's all. You've no idea . . .' He sighed again and suddenly Scarlett felt enormous sympathy for him.

'It must have been tough. I mean, knowin' that they could just up and attempt to destroy yeh like that.' She paused. 'Still, it worked out OK in the end, right?'

He shrugged. 'If you call bein' mugged for twenty bloody grand workin' out OK.' He took a bite of his sandwich and chewed pensively. Scarlett didn't know what else to say. Gold swallowed. 'And then there's the "no smoke without fire" crew. The only result I got was that I didn't get a conviction. Didn't have to do time. But there are still people, my ex-wife amongst them, who think I did it. I tell you . . . it hurts.' He took a glug of his Coca-Cola. 'Hell, I've got a kid of me own. I'd never . . .' He shook his head and gave up on the conversation.

Scarlett sighed. 'I can't understand how yer man Sid Cahill would set his own daughter up like that. I mean, it makes him no better than a pimp.'

'It never ceases to amaze me what people'll do for money,' Gold said. 'And believe me, I know what I'm talkin' about.' He paused. 'Oh, I was no angel. I had me fair share of groupies and chicks over the years, and who knows, some of 'em might have been on the young side, but I never went lookin' for it. Didn't have to. Jeez, I was high most of the time. It's all a fuckin' blur.'

Scarlett smiled. 'That's what they say, isn't it? If you can remember the sixties and seventies, you weren't livin' it.'

He laughed for the first time and his eyes lit up. He looked almost attractive. 'Amen to that, sister.'

They ate in silence. Scarlett helped herself to the remainder of Gold's fries after she had finished her own and rounded off the repast with a large vanilla milkshake. At seven-forty they headed for the car.

Drew picked up a cab outside the Blackrock Clinic and made her way over to Rathgar to see her mother. It was her night for visiting the sick it seemed. Thankfully her own guts had settled down, bar the occasional twinge of cramp, possibly due to the fact that, unlike Barbara, she had ingested only a small amount of the poisonous substances. It occurred to her again that had it not been for Aíne's virulent vol-au-vents causing her to up-chuck most of the sleeping pills, Maddie's situation could have been far worse and she could well have gone into a coma. How ironic was that? She was also pleased with herself for tracking the fat man down, or at least finding a reliable source, and she was sure that George Fitz-Simons would be reliable. But first things first. Time to play Florence Nightingale to her mother.

Barbara looked much the same as Maddie, lying back and looking wan on a sea of pillows. Her skin did have a slight tinge of green though, so Drew did feel genuinely sorry for her. Barbara was dozing when she arrived, so she crept downstairs and rummaged in the larder for a tin of soup. Amongst the lobster bisque, leek with mussels and coriander, and carrot with orange and cinnamon (ugh!), she found a lowly tin of good old-fashioned Heinz cream of chicken soup. She opened the can and poured it into a mug, then nuked it in the microwave. Whilst the soup was heating she toasted a couple of pieces of bread and set a tray.

'Is that you?' a feeble voice called from the top of the stairs.

Who? A burglar? A mad axe man? 'It's me, Mother,' Drew called back. 'I'll be up in a minute.'

Barbara had settled herself back in her bed of pain by the time Drew carried the tray upstairs. She left it on the dressing table and set about straightening the bed covers and fluffing up her mother's pillows. 'I called in to see Maddie earlier,' she said, making conversation.

'Call in where?'

'She's in the Blackrock Clinic,' Drew replied. 'She was sick as a dog too.' When Barbara looked alarmed, Drew hastily added, 'But she's fine now. They're only keeping her in for observation.'

Barbara put a limp hand to her forehead. 'I wonder if I should have been admitted. I did think Dr Paltry was a bit dismissive.'

'Oh, I'm sure you'll be fine, Mother. Maddie ate a lot more of the mousse than you did.'

'Did she? Really? I doubt that girl eats a pick, the size of her.'

'Trust me, Mother, you'll be fine. Now, why don't you try a bit of this soup.' Drew carried the tray over and placed it across Barbara's lap. Barbara eyed it unenthusiastically. 'I don't know if I could. A bite hasn't passed my lips since the soiree.'

Noticing the empty biscuit packet and the chocolate wrappers stuffed under the pillows, Drew doubted that. 'Well, just try, Mother. You need to keep your strength up, what with the wedding plans and all. You wouldn't want Aíne Reibheinn to steal a march on you.'

Talk of Aíne Reibheinn and wedding plans did the trick. Barbara made a sudden and miraculous recovery. 'Well, perhaps just a few spoonfuls,' she conceded. 'And maybe a couple of crumbs of the toast.'

Drew sat on the side of the bed and watched her mother eat. She felt obliged to stay a little and make conversation, but it wasn't easy. She'd had little to say to her mother for years. They might as well have been inhabiting different planets for all that they had in common. It was at times like this that Drew really missed her father. It gave her a physical ache in her chest to think of him. After he had died she had been unable to cry for him. This bothered her and loaded her with guilt. Barbara and even Justin had wept copiously, but she had shed not a tear. Some years later she awoke from a vivid dream, feeling joyous. She remembered the dream clearly. She was walking down Baggot Street and ahead of her, walking out of the Waterloo House, she saw him. Clear as day and equally real. She hugged him and he told her that he loved her. She heard his voice and it thrilled her because for years she had been unable to recall it. She hugged him back and asked him where he'd been. He said, 'Around. I keep my eye on you.' Sometimes when she felt low, Drew summoned up the memory of the dream and she still felt the same sensation of pure joy.

After Barbara had drained the last dregs of soup, she asked Drew to make her a cup of tea. She gladly obliged, then, after brushing the crumbs from the bed linen and making sure that the remote was in easy reach of her mother, Drew kissed her on the cheek and, with a promise to return the following day, left her to watch *Only Fools and Horses* in peace.

Outside there wasn't a sign of a taxi. It was just past eight o'clock, getting chilly, and drizzling slightly. Drew pulled up her coat collar and set off for Ballsbridge on foot.

They made it out to Ballyfingal just after eight, but by the time they found Virtue Rise it was after ten past. The place was like a rabbit warren of Virtue. There was a Virtue Avenue, a Virtue Crescent, a Virtue Chase and a Virtue Close, which they toured in turn before finally winding up on Virtue Rise. Scarlett would have been dubious about visiting the area in daylight, let alone on a cold, dark, late autumn night, and she certainly wouldn't have left a shiny new Beemer parked without taking the engine inside with her, or at least attaching the car to a convenient lamppost with a stout chain.

She scanned the houses as they cruised slowly along the road. 'What's the number again?' she asked.

Gold, who was peering at the houses too, said, 'Seventy-five. Must be up the other end, it's all low numbers here.' He accelerated and the car quietly surged ahead.

Scarlett was impressed. She had a thing about fast cars. The softly purring engine, the G force as Gold pressed the pedal, the soft luxury of the real leather armchair seats. I could get used to this, she thought.

Number seventy-five looked fairly respectable compared to the neighbouring houses, one of which sported a rusty washing machine in the front garden, whilst the other had one of the upstairs windows boarded up and a sheet of hardboard covering a hole in the front door panel. There were lights in the downstairs of Chez Cahill and a newish Jeep was parked outside. Scarlett unbuttoned her coat and hit the record button on her cassette. Gold was sitting bolt upright behind the wheel, staring at the house. 'Did yeh switch on yer tape?' she coaxed, trying to sound business-like, even though she had to really focus to keep her voice steady. She swallowed, and realising that her voice was three octaves higher than normal made a conscious effort to bring it down to an acceptable level.

Gold cleared his throat and fiddled inside his jacket. 'Yeah. Done it. Ready?'

'As I'll ever be.' Scarlett opened the car door. 'Let's do it.'

George was numb. As she sat on the end of the bed looking down at his bulging belly she felt dead inside. That she had come to this, that she had sunk so low. Suddenly she felt the urge to vomit and she rushed to the bathroom. She retched but brought nothing up. How could she? She hadn't eaten all day, sick at the prospect of giving herself to Grillo. The cold porcelain of the cistern cooled her brow. She wiped her mouth with a tissue, flushed, heaved herself onto her feet and walked over to the basin where she splashed her face with cold water. This can't be happening, she thought. I'll go back in there and he'll be gone. He won't be there.

She walked to the doorway and closed her eyes in the hope that when she opened them he really *would* be gone. In the hope that it was all some terrible nightmare. Slim chance. No chance. She had routinely done that as a kid if something ghastly happened and it had never worked then. Why should it work now, when the reality was that only ten minutes before he'd been . . . She shook her head in an effort to expunge the memory, then opened her eyes again. He was still there of course, larger than life and twice as ugly. A protruding purple varicose vein on the side of his calf caught her eye, and the silver appendix scar on his bulbous hairy abdomen. His tiny acorn penis was shrunken and purple now, like a little slug. The man was vile, truly vile. He'd wake up soon. Any minute now he'd wake up. She pulled her dressing gown tightly around her and shivered at the recollection of him lying against her pillows stark naked with one hand behind his head, the other on his penis. 'Strip for me,' he'd said. 'I want to see you strip.' Self-consciously she had lifted her sweater over her head. 'No, no,' he'd snapped, irritated. 'Not like that. I want sexy. I want erotic. You are my lover. I want you to show me how you want me.'

She wanted to stab him. He was basking in the power and she felt utterly humiliated, but she knew that in order to be rid of him she had to comply. The photos and the negs were snug in the floor safe in the bottom of her wardrobe. She smiled and started to sway her hips to imaginary music, then ran her hands up and down her body, kicking off her shoes. That he was impressed was instantly obvious as she slid her skirt off to reveal her stockings and lace panties. His breathing quickened and his eyes never left her. She sat on the side of the bed and rolled down her stockings. He was red in the face now. 'Dance,' he ordered. 'Dance for me.'

She'd stood up and swayed her hips and caressed her body, her eyes closed in counterfeit ecstasy so she wouldn't have to look at his face. She could hear him panting as she unhooked the clasp on her bra. As she let it drop to the floor he had gasped and given a strangled grunt.

She walked over to the bed, lifted her foot back and gave him a hefty kick in the side. He didn't stir. He was on the floor where he had rolled off the bed, lying on his back with his eyes open, like a beached whale on her Habitat rug. A small string of drool leaked from the corner of his blue lips. Jesus! He was dead! The bastard was really dead! For the first time the seriousness of the situation hit home and she started to laugh and cry at the same time. Hysterically. Uncontrollably.

Chapter Fifteen

As they walked up the path a security light snapped on, almost blinding them. On closer inspection Scarlett noted that the front door had a steel plate bolted to it. They could hear a canine of some description barking and growling and pawing at the back of it. Gold cast an anxious glance at Scarlett. She looked for a bell, and finding none, knocked on the panel. This caused the dog to go completely ballistic and the door shuddered as it flung its body against it in a futile attempt to reach them. They automatically took a step back and waited. After a moment, over the din of the dog, they heard a gruff voice shouting at the animal, then a yelp, then silence for a moment before the sound of a key turning in the lock and bolts being drawn back.

After her first impression of the house, Scarlett was not surprised by Sid Cahill. He was in his mid-forties, a big muscular man who looked as if he spent a goodly portion of each day in the gym. His head was shaved bald and he wore a Manchester United short-sleeved soccer shirt with black Adidas track-suit bottoms and spotless new Nike trainers. His forearms sported several tattoos. It struck Scarlett forcibly just how naïve Gold had been. Surely the steel door and the rabid dog should have been enough to signal caution, let alone the bald pate and the tattoos.

'Who's the mot?' Cahill asked, throwing a hostile glance in Scarlett's direction.

Gold coughed. 'Em . . . this is Scarlett. She's me assistant.'

'We never said nothin' about bringin' no assistant.'

'Um . . . I go everywhere with Mr Gold,' Scarlett said. 'I

am his assistant.' She was surprised that she sounded so cool and confident. Her guts were twisting at the sight of the hound of Satan crouching malevolently at the end of the hall, salivating in anticipation, a low growl rumbling in its throat.

'Yeah. Yer man said.' But he still didn't look happy.

Gold tried to smile, but his top lip stuck to his teeth giving him a manic look. He ran his tongue over his gums and relaxed. 'Ah, come on, mate. I needed a bit've moral support. You know ...' He grinned and winked at Cahill, tilting his head in Scarlett's direction.

The laddish agenda relieved the tension and Cahill grinned, then looked Scarlett up and down. 'Bit on the skinny side. I prefer 'em with a bit more meat on 'em, wha'?' He cupped his hands to his chest, mimicking breasts, and burst out laughing. 'Yez better come in.'

As they followed him up the hall, Scarlett glared at the Aussie but he refused to catch her eye. She tap-danced around the dog and side stepped into the front room. A mega sized, wide screen TV was on and one of those interior design makeover shows was playing. Laurence Llewelyn-Bowen was painting some poor sod's bathroom brothel red. Mandy was lounging on the sofa watching it. She was wearing the same Adidas track-suit bottoms and Nike trainers as her dad, with a Manchester United soccer shirt at least two sizes too small. It accentuated her ample (at least 38DD) bosoms and Scarlett could see how Gold had been reeled in. She looked nineteen going on thirty. It briefly occurred to her that the track-suit bottoms, Man-U shirts and trainers were probably part of a consignment stolen in a high-jacking the previous month. All of the estate were probably wearing them.

The room looked as if it could do with a makeover. The wallpaper was tattered at doggy height, as if the mutt got his jollies by chewing the walls if he couldn't find a convenient leg. The sofa was faux leather. It had several cigarette burns on the arms and the vinyl was cracked and grimy. A multicoloured nylon carpet curled away from the scuffed skirting boards. On the chimney breast a large studio portrait photo of Sid Cahill and a blonde woman with a Charlie's Angel hairdo smiled down at them. Sid looked no different with the exception of the 1970s clothes and sideburns.

Along the mantelpiece there were further framed photos, and a few loose ones propped against the wall, all various permutations of Sid, Mandy, Sid and Mandy, Sid, Mandy and Sid's wife, along with a couple of a young boy, the image of Sid, also wearing a Manchester United strip. Obviously the Cahills were big into football.

'Give us a minute, Mand,' Sid said to his daughter.

'I was watchin' this,' she moaned petulantly.

'Then friggin' tape it.' Cahill raised his arm as if to give her a clatter. She didn't flinch. Just scowled and slid off the sofa. She showed no sign of recognition or made any attempt to acknowledge Gold. She certainly wasn't showing any signs of trauma at being in such close proximity to her alleged violator. Whilst Sid's attention was on his daughter, Scarlett sidled over to the fireplace and, swiping a curly snapshot of Sid and the boy, surreptitiously pocketed it.

'So did yeh bring the dosh?' Cahill asked, smiling, in good humour once again. Scarlett noted that he had a gold tooth off centre, just like the Sporty Spice Girl.

'Have you got the statement sayin' that I didn't rape Mandy,' Gold countered.

'Money first,' Cahill barked, all good humour now evaporated. 'I want to see the money first.' He paused then smirked. 'Show me the money. Show me the money. Show me the money.' He held his hands wide, waiting for a reaction.

Scarlett took the cue and laughed, nudging Gold hard in the ribs. 'Very good, Mr Cahill,' she said. 'Very funny . . . Isn't it, Bruce?'

Gold stared at her, at a loss for a moment, then copped on to the *Jerry Maguire* reference. 'Oh yeah. That's a good one, Sid.' He laughed. 'Bloody funny.'

Pleased with the response, Cahill nodded. 'Yeah well. Like I said, show me the friggin' money.'

Gold bit his lip then, after a pause, dug his hand into his pocket and drew out a fat wad of fifty pound notes, tightly bound in an Ulster bank wrapper. He held out the bundle to Cahill and flipped his thumb through the notes, then drew it back and returned it to his pocket. 'I've got the money. Now what about your end of the deal? You're going to tell the truth, right? You're going to say that Mandy was lyin'?'

'I'll tell the cops as soon as you gimme the money,' Cahill said.

'Aw, come on, Sid.' Gold was getting edgier by the minute. Cahill wasn't following their prepared script and he wasn't the best at ad-libbing. 'I need more than that. How do I know you'll do it?'

Cahill shrugged. 'I'll do it.'

'Why would you when you've got what you want?' Scarlett snarled, steering the conversation back. 'You heard about Bruce's trouble fifteen years back when those people made up the story and ripped him off, and you thought you'd rip him off again. Get a piece of the action. Why should we trust you?'

Sid stared at her impassively. He knew he had the upper hand. Gold touched Scarlett's arm. 'Now let's not get excited,' he cooed. Then he sighed theatrically. 'Sid, Sid . . .' He patted him on the back. 'If you were me would you hand over ten grand without gettin' somethin' in writing?'

Cahill's face was unreadable. It struck Scarlett then that if Cahill wanted to just take the cash and throw them out onto the street, there was nothing either of them could do about it; in fact he could probably do it with one arm tied behind his back, so she was relieved when he walked over to the mantel shelf and took a piece of paper from behind a particularly ugly weeping clown figurine.

'OK,' he said. 'Just messin'.' He grinned again, flashing the gold tooth.

Gold took the paper and read it. Scarlett looked over his shoulder. The handwriting was a childish scrawl and the grammar and spelling shocking, but it covered all the relevant points, namely that Mandy had made the whole thing up.

'You haven't signed it,' Scarlett said.

'I was waitin' til I seen if yeh had the dosh,' Cahill said, taking the paper back from Gold and scribbling his name at the foot of the page. 'Now. The cash.'

Gold had edged around the room and was standing by the door. Cahill was at the other end of the room by the TV. 'No problem, Sid. I'll give it to you on the way out. You give me the paper, I'll hand over the money. Right?' He gripped Scarlett's arm and guided her firmly into the hall and down towards the front door. Cahill followed. He appeared amused by what he saw as Gold's paranoia.

'Whatever.' He was close behind with the sheet of paper in his hand. At the door Gold lingered, showing Scarlett down the path. 'Get the car started, there's a good girl.' Scarlett bristled at the words 'good girl'. He stuffed the keys into her hand. When she stopped dead, he gave her a hefty shove. 'Just do it!' he hissed urgently under his breath. Scarlett caught the imperative nature of his tone and scuttled down the path to the Beemer. She unlocked it and slid behind the wheel, secretly thrilled to be given the chance to drive it. The engine rumbled to life on the first turn of the key. Next thing Gold was legging it down the path. He jumped over the gate and ran around to the passenger side, flinging the door open and falling in. 'Go! Go! Go!' he yelled.

Scarlett hesitated just long enough to hear Cahill roar and see him make a lunge down the path. She jammed her foot to the floor and let out the clutch. With tyres screaming she achieved hyper drive seven in five seconds flat.

'What the fuck's wrong with him?' she yelled over the roar of the revving engine.

Gold dug his hand into his pocket. 'I switched the cash,' he said triumphantly. 'I gave him a duff bundle with a couple of fifties on each end and *The Daily Record* sliced up to size in the middle.' He held up the bundle of cash. 'I wasn't goin' to give that bastard ten grand. I wasn't goin' to let him get away with my bloody money.' He was high as a kite. Scarlett skidded around a corner on two wheels and the car slewed into the middle of the road. She fought with the wheel but regained control after a moment. Her blood was pumping. She was as turned on as Gold. They were both squealing and giggling like school kids after robbing an orchard. Suddenly headlights blinded her in the rear view mirror. The glam-rocker shot round in his seat and squinted against the glare, peering through the window. 'Shit, the bastard's after us in the Jeep. He's bloody comin' after us.'

'Hardly a surprise,' Scarlett yelled as she fought with the wheel.

'Shit, girl. I hope you can drive,' Gold screamed, still straining to see through the back window. 'I hope you can drive some, or we're fuckin' history.'

Chapter Sixteen

Drew scanned the line of door buzzers and selected number six. She pushed the button and waited. There was a mirror hanging directly in front of her so she tried to smooth her hair out, or at least calm it down a little. A futile task as it happened, because the misty rain had rendered it big and fluffy, heightening her resemblance to a certain ginger-coiffed fast-food front-man. When there was no reply she stabbed the button again. She had seen a light in George Fitz-Simon's second floor apartment window so she knew she was there. After a pause, when she was all but ready to give up, she heard a hesitant, disembodied voice through the speaker.

'Hello? What do you want?'

'It's me, George. Drew Looney. I wonder if I could come up? I need to have a word. I need to ask you something.'

A further pause, then she heard the door lock release. A skinny, weird-looking guy with thick glasses darted out of the lift as she reached it, giving her a start. He wore an anorak over polyester stay-pressed trousers with brown suede Hush Puppies. Drew thought that he looked like an accountant, or on second thoughts perhaps a serial killer. He stopped and turned to stare at her. She stabbed the 'doors close' button with urgency, then felt slightly foolish.

George answered her tap immediately, as if she'd been waiting behind the door. She looked flushed and on the hyper side.

'Are you OK?' Drew asked.

George snapped back, 'Of course. Why shouldn't I be? What makes you ask that?'

Drew was stunned by her abruptness. It must have shown in her face because the party organiser bit her lip and said, 'Look, sorry to be sharp. I've had a bad ... um ... a bad ... Just come in, will you.' She stood back and Drew, a tad bewildered, walked past her.

George was wearing a white towelling robe and her feet were bare. 'I didn't come at a bad time, did I?' Drew asked. George shook her head as she struggled with a lighter, trying to light a cigarette. She was having difficulty because her hands were shaking. 'I just wondered if you knew a man called Broylan Grillo?'

The lighter shot out of George's hand and skidded across the polished floor, bounced off the skirting board and finished up on the rug under the glass-topped coffee table. 'Why do you want to know? What makes you ask that?' Her face was white as a sheet and her eyes terrified.

'Um ... well ... It's to do with a story I'm working on. You see, I think he could be involved with bringing illegals into the country.' Suddenly it occurred to Drew that she was being a bit too candid. 'But I'd rather you kept that to yourself. I'm telling you this in confidence.'

George got down on all fours and retrieved the lighter from its resting place, then made a second, more successful attempt to ignite her cigarette. After inhaling deeply, she exhaled and slumped down on the sofa. 'Grillo bringing in illegals. Why doesn't that surprise me?' she said, but not to Drew. She was staring at a point about six inches above the journalist's head.

Drew noticed that her hands were still shaking, though to a lesser degree. The woman was behaving bizarrely. 'Look. Are you sure you're all right?'

George sighed. 'Not really.' She took another pull on the cigarette, then looked Drew squarely in the eye. 'You want to know about Broylan Grillo? I'll tell you about Broylan fucking Grillo. The man was a manipulating evil bastard. He dealt drugs, though he'd deny that. He'd say he was a go-between. But what's the difference? He made money out of it. He set up the deals. He was also a pimp. A sleazy fucking pimp.'

Drew was astounded. She'd had an idea he might be involved in the illegal immigrant business to some degree because of seeing him outside Iman's flat, but it had also occurred to her that he could well be just a landlord. She thought of him as a lead rather than the main party, but by the sound of things, if he was involved in drugs and prostitution, he could just as easily be involved in murder. It was only a small step. Drug dealers murdered each other all the time in the city. He could have been responsible for the killing of Nadia Iacob. This was a whole new ball game.

'But I thought he was big in the charity scene. Maddie met him through her charity stuff. She seems to think quite highly of him.'

George gave a humourless laugh. 'That's what you're supposed to think. Import–Export.' She gave an ironic laugh. 'Yeah! But, hey, what's the difference? Illegal immigrants, drugs, prostitution, I suppose that qualifies as *import–export*. It's all trading in human misery. And trust me, I should know.'

She had a point. Then George's use of the past tense dawned on Drew. 'You used the word *was*. Has he gone away or something?'

George shook her head and stubbed out the cigarette. She had smoked it down to the filter in no time flat. 'No. He's going nowhere.' She stood up. 'You want me to honour a confidence?' Drew nodded, wondering where this extraordinary behaviour was leading. George strode towards the bedroom. 'OK. Now it's your turn. You can return the favour. Come with me.'

*

They were speeding along the Crumlin Road now towards the Grand Canal. Gold was sitting with his arm over the back of the seat, keeping an eye on the Jeep which was still in hot pursuit. Every now and then the lights would pull back and let a couple of cars come between them, but just when they thought they had lost him, he'd speed up and the lights would appear once again. Scarlett's adrenaline level had dropped somewhat and the high of ten minutes previously had been replaced by a gnawing fear in the pit of her stomach. In the movies they'd have lost the bad guy by now. He'd either have run off the road in spectacular fashion or just been plain out-driven.

'Has he gone? Have we lost him yet?' she asked hopefully. She'd tilted the rear view mirror to avoid being dazzled.

''Fraid not,' came the Aussie's reply. 'Can you speed this thing up a bit?'

'I'm doin' my best,' Scarlett snapped. 'Where's the nearest Garda station?'

'I'm not goin' to the flamin' cops,' Gold sneered. 'Don't trust the bastards.'

Scarlett felt a surge of panic. 'But you've got to. It's the only way we'll shake him off.'

'Chill out, will you? We're goin' to me lawyer. Me lawyer'll handle it. He'll deal with the cops. He'll sort it. No worries.'

Scarlett felt slightly happier at this news. 'OK. So where's yer lawyer live?'

'Sandymount. Gilford Road. But we've got to shake this fella off first.'

'Like I'm not tryin'?'

They had hit the Grand Canal now and Scarlett executed a nifty right along Parnell Road, overtaking a doddery Morris Minor on the inside to avoid side swiping an oncoming Hiace van. She heard Gold take a sharp intake of breath and mutter, 'Jeez!'

She was fighting to think of a plan. Anything to lose the Jeep and the apoplectic Sid Cahill. There was no use asking Gold. He was a stranger to the city. Behind them she heard the screech of brakes. Gold held his breath as the Jeep skidded around the corner in front of an oncoming bus, missing it by inches. At Portobello Bridge the Jeep was about fifty yards behind, weaving in and out of the sparse traffic. Scarlett swerved at the last minute, slithered across the road and made a right around the corner into Rathmines Road just as the lights changed to red. She was happier now, on home territory. She had a better chance of shaking him off in a neighbourhood she was familiar with. She zoomed down Rathmines Road and took a sharp right into Leinster Road, tyres squealing, and almost immediately hung a left into Charleville Road, slowing to fifty. She cut the lights. Gold was still acting lookout. She took another left then a little wiggle around a bend to get them heading back towards Lower Rathmines Road. At the intersection she pulled into the kerb and cut the engine. There was no tell-tale sign of headlamps coming from the rear. They sat in silence. Neither was breathing. The engine made a ticking sound as it cooled. The smell of burnt rubber lingered.

After about half a minute Scarlett turned the key in the ignition. 'Get out and have a peek along the main road, will yeh? I wouldn't want to pull out there only to see him waitin' for us.'

Gold did as he was told without comment. To tell the truth he was glad to get out of the car for a minute. At this point in the proceedings he could empathise with the Pope. He too felt like kissing the ground after the last fifteen helter-skelter minutes. There was no sign of a Jeep on Lower Rathmines Road so he scuttled back to the Beemer. 'All clear. Do you know where we are, or are you just a naturally gifted Kamikaze driver?'

Scarlett laughed. 'I know where we are. This is my neck

of the woods.' She slid the car into gear. 'Gilford Road is it?'

Drew was aware that her mouth was gaping open but she was powerless to close it. Her brain refused to function. A fat, naked, hairy man, one Broylan Grillo was lying on George Fitz-Simon's Habitat rug. Apart from being physically revolting, he was very obviously dead. And he also had the tiniest penis Drew had ever seen. She couldn't take her eyes off the purple slug-like thing curled up above his groin. She forcibly dragged her eyes away. 'Can't you cover him up or something? Shouldn't you call an ambulance?' It was the best she could manage.

'Bit late for that,' George said as she pulled a lime green chenille throw from the top of a wardrobe and shook it out. Drew took the other end and between them they manoeuvred it over Grillo's body. It was not a gesture of respect, more a gesture to propriety. Grillo dead and naked was an ugly enough sight without having to look at him turning various shades of white and blue.

Drew had been totally stunned when George had walked her into the bedroom. She had given her no inkling of what to expect, so naturally it had come as a shock.

'And he just died while you were . . . well . . .'

'Just as my bra hit the floor. I had my eyes closed. I couldn't bear to look at him. Thought all the grunting was him . . . well, wanking himself off.'

'But why . . .?' Drew started, stunned. 'Why did you . . .?'

George gave the cadaver a kick. 'The bastard was blackmailing me. But not just that. It's a long story. He had some pictures of my father . . . Some compromising pictures he was going to show my mother. He said if I slept with him he'd give me the negatives and photos to destroy.'

'But why didn't you just go to the cops? Shit! The man's

a monster. You should have gone to the cops.' Drew was appalled.

George sighed. 'There's more to it than that,' she said. She lit up another cigarette. 'There are reasons I couldn't go to the cops.'

When she didn't elaborate Drew coaxed, 'Such as?'

George inhaled deeply on her cigarette then threw her head back and blew the smoke towards the ceiling. 'This is off the record?'

Drew nodded. 'Off the record.'

George stared at her for a couple of beats, trying to decide if she could trust the journalist. Bit late to worry about that, she thought. She's already seen the fucking body. She sighed in resignation and took a leap of faith. 'OK. I used to be a coke head. Grillo was my dealer, though I wasn't aware of it at the time. I'm clean now though. I was coming back from the rehab clinic that day I bumped into you at the airport. I had to get my life back. I knew I had to get my life back.' She felt the need to justify herself. She drew breath. 'Anyway, I got behind and owed money. Grillo offered me a way out. Asked me to deliver a package and he'd give me two grand.'

'Drugs?'

'Yeah. Though I didn't know it at the time.'

'Oh come on!' Drew was incredulous. 'Delivering a package for two grand. What did you think was in it?'

George felt a tinge of annoyance. 'Oh all right. So I didn't want to think about it. I needed the cash. Anyway, there was twenty grand's worth. But he'd set me up. Had one of his men mug me for the package. At least I'm sure that's what happened now. Then he said I'd have to pay for it.'

'And you did?'

'I'd no choice. I was afraid. I thought he was on the level then. You're a journalist, you know how violent the drugs world is.' She looked down at the lime green mound lying by the bed. 'Then just when I thought I was almost clear he

180

said I'd have to pay interest, and when I told him to go to hell he produced the photos.' She stared at Drew, waiting for a reaction. 'I'd no other choice. There's no way I could go to the cops. What if my mother found out about my father? It would ruin her memories. Kill her.'

Drew shook her head. 'Let me get this straight. You owed money to a drug dealer, Grillo.'

'Yes, but as I said, I didn't know he was my dealer at the time. I knew him socially, much the same way your sister-in-law-to-be knows him.'

Drew wondered if Grillo was also Maddie's dealer. 'Is he her supplier?'

'Probably,' George said. 'Though she might not be aware of the fact.'

'So you owed him money. Why did he set you up?'

George took another pull on her cigarette. 'Ego, I think. He was getting the ultimate revenge because I wouldn't sleep with him. Before that he used to give me little presents of a gram or two now and again, but then he came on to me. Big time. I thought I'd handled it well, you know, when I turned him down, but obviously not.'

'Jesus!' Drew said. 'It was a long time in the planning. What a creep. How come you didn't see through him?'

George gave a humourless laugh. 'Good question. Ain't twenty-twenty hindsight only the best thing? But you see he was so charming.'

Drew sat down next to George on the bed. 'Here, give me one of those.' George handed her the packet of Benson & Hedges and Drew lit up. 'I gave these up, but I think under the circumstances . . .'

They sat in silence, puffing away. Drew was still in a state of shock, not just at the sight of the dear, or in this case not so dear, departed, but at George's account of the appalling chain of events that had led up to it. Although it went against her nature to think ill of the dead, it was impossible to bring to mind anything good to say about Broylan Grillo.

It also put him in the frame as a possible suspect in Nadia's killing. He might not have done it himself, but she was sure he was mixed up in it in some way. It was too much of a coincidence that he was with the goons who had turned over Gregory's room. Her heart went out to George as she thought about what he had put her through. How he had manipulated her and how desperate she must have been to be driven to . . . well, to be driven to almost prostituting herself. She sighed. 'So what are you going to do?' It was some kind of perverse justice that the bastard had dropped dead before he got to violate George, but they couldn't just leave him there. Something had to be done. 'Shouldn't we call the cops or the ambulance or something? I know he's dead, but I think it's the ambulance we have to call.'

'I can't do that!' George said, horrified. 'If it gets out that he was found here, in this kind of situation, my mother will die of shame. It'll kill her. Why do you think I gave in to his blackmail in the first place?'

'But he's dead now. He's no power over you any more. Anyway, he must have the photos with him if he was going to give them back in return for, um . . . in return for . . . you know.'

'Oh I have the photos. I got them back with the negs before I let him get near me, but think about it. If this hits the papers you can imagine the inferences that people will draw?' Suddenly she looked panicky again. She grabbed Drew's arm. 'You won't print it, will you? You won't . . .'

Drew shook her head vigorously. 'No. Of course not. What do you think I am? My interest's in Grillo. I think he may well have had that Romanian girl they found by the canal today murdered.' George didn't react, as if the fact that Grillo could be capable of murder was no surprise whatsoever. Drew could see George's point about not calling the cops, but what was the alternative? Grillo was dead. There was a dead body lying next to the bed for God's sake. Soon there'd be a rotting corpse lying next to the bed. 'So what are you going to do? You can't leave him here. The cleaner's bound to notice.'

George smiled at her attempt at humour. 'We'll have to move him. Get him dressed and leave him sitting on a bench or something. The post-mortem will confirm that he died of natural causes. I didn't do anything wrong.'

Drew wasn't thrilled at her use of the plural. 'We? Did I hear you say we?'

George gave her a pleading look. 'Well I can hardly do it by myself.' She stood up and gathered Grillo's carefully folded clothes from the ottoman. 'We can put his clothes back on, then get him down to my car somehow and drive him to . . . say . . . Herbert Park and leave him on a bench. Easy peasy.' She was trying to sound up beat and positive, and succeeding to a certain degree. Drew was almost convinced. Almost, but not quite.

'I think we should go into the other room. Have a drink or a cup of coffee or something and think this through.' George opened her mouth to protest, but Drew cut her off. 'As you said, he's going nowhere.' She prodded the chenille mound with her toe, then stood up and headed for the bedroom door. 'Come on.'

After a moment's hesitation, Georgina Fitz-Simons shrugged in resignation and followed.

Mervyn Drury was around forty, about five foot ten, of slim build with a short buzz cut. He was wearing jeans, Docs and a white Billy Bragg T shirt. He looked quite different from the person that Scarlett had seen at the District Court, where he had appeared very businesslike and formal. In his civvies he looked far too groovy to be a lawyer.

'How's it going, Bruce?' he said by way of a greeting. He had a slight Cork accent which Scarlett hadn't noticed before.

'I got tapes,' Gold said excitedly. 'Tapes of Cahill admittin' that he set me up.'

Drury's eyebrows shot up. 'Are you serious?'

It crossed Scarlett's mind at that point that they hadn't checked the cassettes to see if they had recorded, their minds having been centred on surviving the psycho Cahill. She opened her coat and rummaged under her jumper. Drury eyed her suspiciously. 'What are you doing?'

'We were wired up with recordin' devices,' she said as she struggled with the micro pore. Gold was similarly struggling. He gave a little yelp as he removed a couple of strips of body hair at the same time as the device. They were standing in Drury's kitchen. The floor was littered with Lego and a small child of about two was asleep in a buggy.

'And you are?' Drury asked Scarlett as he watched the procedure with bemused interest.

'I'm Scarlett O'Hara. I work for *The Daily Record*.' She paused and shot out her hand which he shook.

'Mervyn Drury. Bruce's solicitor.'

Gold, the technophobe, had by now removed the device and was staring at it, helpless. Scarlett, who had also managed to retrieve her recorder with less physical damage than Gold, took it from his hand and hit the rewind button, first on his, then on hers. The tapes whirred back. Drury pulled out a chair from the table, removed a half eaten Mikado biscuit and sat down. 'I think you'd better start from the beginning,' he said.

The glam rocker (retired) brought his lawyer up to speed on the day's events. '. . . And I thought I'd better not tell you stuff you might not want to know about, if you know what I mean,' he finished, referring to the fact that he had visited the home of the alleged victim. He abruptly dug his hand in his pocket, removed the statement and handed it to the lawyer. 'And we got him to sign this statement.'

'So you paid him the ten grand?' Drury said, taking the crumpled piece of paper from his client and glancing at it.

'Well, not exactly,' Gold said, grinning. 'I'm not as daft

as I look. I switched it for a bundle with a couple of fifties on each end and a wad of newspaper in the middle.'

Drury nodded. 'I'd like to see his reaction when he susses that out.' Scarlett shot a look at Gold. 'OK.' The lawyer glanced at Scarlett. 'So did those yokes work?'

Scarlett hit the play button on her own device. There was a lot of rustling then she heard her own voice, tinny and high pitched.

'*Did yeh switch on yer tape?*' Then Gold's voice. '*Yeah. Done it. Ready?*'

'*As I'll ever be.*' The sound of a car door opening. '*Let's do it.*'

Footsteps as they crossed the road. The dog barking the whole nine yards. Drury listened to the tape in its entirety without comment, then carefully read the statement. After a pause, with his client and the journalist looking on, he nodded his head. 'Well, this isn't exactly an admission, but it's close enough ... The jury will have to give you the benefit of the doubt, particularly in view of this evidence. Then there's the issue of Cahill demanding money from you. That's clear enough on the tapes. We can get him for that.' He looked at Scarlett. 'So how are you mixed up in this?'

'Mr Gold came to me and told me how Cahill had asked him for money to make the case go away. And I'd found the story about his similar trouble fifteen years back in the archives, so I said I'd help him.'

'And when do you intend to run the story?'

'Monday, I should think. I want to go out there with a photographer and confront him. Why?'

'Well, running the story before the case should bring Bruce public sympathy. But I think your paper's legal people could have a problem with it at this stage.'

'Why? We have the statement, the tapes.'

'I know, but like I said, it's not exactly an outright admission. We all know what he's at, but, well, you know yourself. *The Daily Record*'s a small independent news-paper. The management's not inclined to risk expensive libel cases. But hey, give it a shot. You might catch them on a good day. In the meantime, I'll bring this stuff to the DPP and the Guards.'

Scarlett knew exactly what he was talking about. The lawyer was sure to spike it until there was some action in the courts or from the DPP. Still, not downhearted, she asked him if he'd let her have a copy of the statement, and took back the two cassette recorders, leaving Drury with Bruce's tape.

Gold was on a high, unlike Scarlett, who was already arguing with *The Record*'s lawyer in her own mind as they left Drury's house. They got into the car, Gold behind the wheel. He gave her a pat on the shoulder. 'Hey, chill out, Scarlett. We got the evidence. Even if you don't get to run the story on Monday, it'll still be your exclusive when it does go into print. No worries.'

Put that way, she pushed all negative thoughts from her mind. 'You're right. And who knows, I might be yellin' before I'm hurt. As yer man said, I might even catch the law men on a good day.'

'That's the spirit,' Gold said. 'I think it's time for a celebration drink. What d'you say?'

'Lead on, Macduff,' said the intrepid reporter.

Bruce Gold pressed the accelerator pedal and the car glided away from the kerb. Both occupants of the car were unaware of a Jeep parked in the darkness at the end of the road with Sid Cahill behind the wheel. He had been cruising around Sandymount, aware that it was Gold's neighbour-hood, and had come across the Beemer by chance. He shoved the gear lever into first and followed.

Chapter Seventeen

The buzzer sounded making them both leap sky high. 'Who's that?' Drew screeched, hand shooting to her throat.

George leapt up and ran to the hall. Drew followed and found her by a security video entry phone. A chunky man was standing looking up at the camera. 'Shit! It's Grillo's driver,' George said. 'I didn't realise he came with his driver.'

'There was no one outside when I arrived,' Drew commented. 'He must have gone away and come back again.'

'So?'

'So tell him Grillo left. Tell him Grillo had a call and left.'

'Why would he do that?'

The door buzzer buzzed again, more insistently this time. 'Just do it! Do it or he might come up.'

The threat of Grillo's driver coming up snapped George back to her senses. She picked up the phone. 'Hello?'

'Is Mr Grillo ready?' the driver asked. He was peering at his reflection in the two-way mirror, checking his nasal hair. Drew felt herself redden; she hadn't realised that there was a camera behind the mirror. 'Um . . . Oh . . . He . . . eh . . . he left about half an hour ago,' George stuttered.

'Left?'

'Yes. He, um . . . he had a call and he . . . um . . . he left.'

'Why would he do that?' the driver asked.

George looked helplessly at Drew, then pulled herself together somewhat. 'I don't know,' she snapped imperiously. 'He didn't share that information with me.'

They could almost see the cogs in the Neanderthal's brain

ticking over. He was chewing his lip and his eyebrows had knitted together over the bridge of his nose. After a pause, with George gesticulating silently at Drew and Drew doing a lot of shrugging, he finally said, 'All right so,' and walked out of the front door. Both women sighed with relief.

'Shit! I thought he was going to stay there all night,' Drew said as they made their way back into the sitting room. 'Do you think he bought it?'

'Don't see why not,' George replied, reaching for another cigarette. They had been sitting together for about half an hour, talking through the options before the driver had shown up. There were not that many. In fact, having excluded calling the emergency services, cutting up the body and disposing of it in bin liners (not a serious option) there was only the one: dress Grillo in his clothes and dump him on a park bench. They sat nursing tumblers of medicinal martini, putting off the evil hour when they would have to wrestle Grillo back into his clothes.

After a further five minutes Drew knocked back the dregs and stood up. 'Well, better get it over with I suppose.' George nodded and followed her through to the bedroom where they stood looking down at the lime green mound on the Habitat rug for a further couple of minutes. It was George who was the first to move this time. She sorted through his clothes and picked out his socks and boxer shorts. She handed a sock to Drew. 'Here. You do one. I'll do the other.'

They both knelt down and George pulled back the throw. The back of Grillo's heels had gone a mottled purpley colour but he was still warm to the touch. 'How long has he been dead?' Drew asked.

George looked at her watch. It was just after nine-thirty. 'About an hour and forty minutes. Why?'

'That purple colouring's called lividity. It's where the blood settles after death. We'll have to lay him on his back just like this when we leave him, or the cops will know he's been moved.'

'How do you know this?' George had successfully replaced the sock, having rolled it inside out first.

'I do court reports,' the journalist said as she struggled to force the other sock onto Grillo's right foot.

George reached out and picked up the boxers. 'OK. These next.'

Drew flipped back the throw and they jointly attempted to replace the underpants. It was not an easy task. In fact it was like trying to put a pair of boxer shorts onto a giant baby. Naturally, Grillo was giving them no help, so by the time they achieved their goal they were both sweating and breathless. 'Jesus! He weighs a fucking ton,' Drew gasped.

'Tell me about it!' George said. They sat on the bed to take a breather. The throw was only covering his face now, but at least the addition of the boxers made him look less vile, or maybe they were just getting desensitised.

'We'll never get him down to your car. He's too heavy,' Drew said after a while.

'I was just thinking that,' replied George gloomily. 'What'll we do?'

Drew bit her lip and thought. 'We need help,' she said. 'We need help and a wheelchair.'

Scarlett and Gold were sitting in the Waterloo House on Pembroke Road, each with a half-finished pint of Guinness in front of them. They were pretty damn pleased with themselves. Gold, because he had every confidence that he would soon be off the hook. Scarlett, because she had an exclusive on her hands. Her mobile rang. She checked to see who the call was from, and seeing Drew's name answered it. 'Hi. What are you up to?'

'Where are you?' her friend asked.

'In the Waterloo House. Why?'

'The Waterloo House? Excellent. Look, I need your help.'

'Sure. What's up?' There was a pause at the other end of the line. Scarlett mouthed '*My friend Drew*' to Gold. He nodded.

After a few seconds she heard Drew say, 'Look. I'm in George Fitz-Simons' apartment on Waterloo Road. Could you come over? I'll explain when you get here. But please come now. It's *really* urgent.'

'What's up? Has yer woman run outta vodka or somethin'?' Scarlett sniggered, remembering the gargantuan, elephant-stunning Sea Breezes that she'd made them on the night of Maddie's engagement party.

'Please. Just come. Now.' The phone went dead.

Bewildered, Scarlett dumped her mobile back in her pocket. 'D'you mind if we go over the road? Drew's got a problem. It shouldn't take long.'

Gold shrugged. 'Sure. Why not?' They knocked back their pints and headed out of the pub.

When the buzzer sounded again, Drew went out and, spying Scarlett's image on the tiny screen, pressed the door release. George was still in the bedroom. Between them they had managed to force Grillo's vest on and the left sleeve of his shirt. They found it necessary to take frequent rests as it was exhausting work. Drew waited in the hall and, as soon as she heard the lift, opened the door. She was not expecting to see Gold. 'What's he doing here?' she snapped as he stepped into the hall behind Scarlett.

Scarlett gave her a weird look. 'We were out in Ballyfingal with yer man Sid Cahill. What's your problem anyway?' She was embarrassed by Drew's rudeness. Drew hastily shut the door. She looked very agitated. Just then George came out of the bedroom. 'Who's that? What's he doing here?' She shot an accusing look in Drew's direction.

'He's Bruce Gold.'

'But what's he doing here?' Her voice was bordering on hysteria.

'We were in the pub together,' Scarlett said huffily. 'But if you're going to take that attitude we'll just fuck off again.' She turned and made a move towards the door.

'No! No! Don't go! Sorry.' Drew looked at George. 'We've no choice, George. We have to trust him.' Gold, who was still standing by the door, reached out and opened it. 'Please! We have to.'

George ran her hands through her hair. She looked truly harassed. 'Oh, all right,' she snapped.

Scarlett gave her a look that would freeze hell and continued towards the now open door. 'Well, don't friggin' put yerself out.' She sounded terminally grumpy. It was a well-known fact that Scarlett O'Hara couldn't stand rudeness.

Drew leapt forward and slammed the door shut, placing her back against it. 'Please, Scarlett. I'm sorry if George was rude. She didn't mean to be. She's under a lot of stress at the moment. Please don't go. Just listen . . . Please.'

Scarlett glanced at Gold. He shrugged. 'OK. Start talkin'.'

Scarlett was sitting on the sofa beside Drew. Gold was standing by the gas fire warming his legs. George had their undivided attention. Scarlett was staring at her open-mouthed, exhibiting much the same reaction as Drew had. Gold, on the other hand, stood impassively, his face impossible to read. Finally Scarlett shook her head and muttered, 'The bastard. The card carryin' bastard.'

'So you see, I'm in an impossible position. If this gets out it'll kill my mother, and I've done nothing wrong. It'll finish me. I can't see any other way of making it go away.'

'She's right,' Drew added. 'Damage limitation seems to be the only option.'

'But surely the cops would be discreet,' Scarlett said, not with any great conviction that this would be the case, but more in the hope that George would see sense.

Gold guffawed. 'Cops? Discreet? They don't know the meanin' of the word.'

'He's right, Scarlett. You know yourself. Stuff gets out. One word to the cops and it'll be all over next week's *Phoenix* magazine.'

Silence hung over the room for a good two minutes before George cleared her throat. 'So will you help me?'

'And he just croaked while ye were . . .?' Scarlett said, then shuddered.

'We didn't actually do it,' George said.

'But didn't yeh notice? I mean, didn't yeh even get an inklin' that he was havin' a heart attack?'

George threw a desperate look at Drew. 'George had her eyes closed. And apparently the symptoms of a heart attack are very similar to that of a man . . . Well, a man at the, shall we say, peak of excitement,' Drew said simply, casting a sly look in Gold's direction. 'I have it on good authority.'

Scarlett looked questioningly at Gold. He shrugged then said, 'Look, I know what it's like to be dropped in it by someone. Happened to me recently for the second time, and it's not nice. I know where you're comin' from. I'll help you.' He glanced at Scarlett. 'What d'you say, Scarlett? May as well be hung for a sheep as a lamb as we say in Oz.'

'We say the same in Ireland too,' commented Drew. 'Come on, Scarlett. Give it a lash. If George has to go to the cops it'll mean Grillo's really succeeded in destroying her life. It's not fair.'

Scarlett frowned. She had immense sympathy for George but the whole thing seemed a trifle dodgy, to say the least. Transporting a body to Herbert Park and leaving it by a bench. Finally she thought, Shit! What the hell. 'OK,' she said simply. 'What do yeh want us to do?'

Chapter Eighteen

They held a council of war, then Drew and Scarlett were dispatched in George's Golf to purloin a wheelchair from Vincent's Hospital A&E, and Gold helped George to finish dressing Grillo. Both tasks, on the face of it, seemed simple enough, but after struggling for ten minutes with the unwieldy corpse, Gold was beginning to wish that he had volunteered for wheelchair theft instead. 'Bleedin' nora. The bastard weighs some,' he gasped as he lifted Grillo under the armpits to enable George to slip on one sleeve of his jacket.

'Who are you telling?' she commented dryly, feeding the sleeve up his podgy arm. She straddled the body and manoeuvred the jacket around his back, then tried to bend the left arm at the elbow in order to slip it on. Not a chance. The arm wouldn't budge. 'What's the matter with him?' she muttered, trying again.

'Fuck! Rigor mortis is settin' in,' Gold said. 'We'll have to move sharpish or he'll soon be completely rigid.'

'Rigor mortis! How do you know?'

Gold let go of the body and it thudded back like a sack of spuds to the rug. 'I worked as a mortuary attendant when I left school. Before me glam rock days.'

'So what does that mean? Rigid?'

'Means that inside of an hour he'll probably be a stone stiffie. Won't bend until the rigor wears off.'

'Shit! How long will that take?'

Gold shrugged. 'How long's he been dead?'

George glanced at her watch. 'Just over three hours. Why?'

Gold's invisible eyebrows took a hike up his forehead. 'Three hours. Hmmm.' Then he nodded. 'Well, that would be about right. Usually takes up to four, but of course he was, shall we say, *engaged in physical activity* at the time of death. Happens quicker then. Somethin' to do with the muscles bein' deprived of oxygen.' He was standing, apparently unconcerned, gazing down at the body.

George could feel the panic rising. 'So what are you saying exactly? How long before the rigor whatsit wears off?'

'About thirty-six hours. As soon as the muscles start to decompose.'

George's lip did an involuntary curl of disgust at the mention of decomposition.

Gold crouched down on his hunkers. 'What I'm sayin', love, is he's goin' to be one difficult sod to move.' He hooked his forearms under Grillo's armpits once more and heaved. 'Here, gimme a hand.'

'What are you doing?' There was a note of hysteria in her tone.

'Take his ankles. We've got to get him sittin' in a chair. Rigor works its way down the body. He's got to be sittin' down before his legs go stiff or we'll never get him into the flippin' car.'

George, on auto pilot, did as she was told. In her mind she had disassociated the cadaver from the living Grillo. It was the only way she could cope. Pretend you're moving a piece of furniture she told herself. Pretend it's a sofa.

Drew and Scarlett pulled up in the car park of Vincent's Hospital. 'OK,' Drew said, taking control. 'I'll run in and grab a chair. If anyone stops me I'll say I've someone in the car who can't walk. OK?'

'OK,' Scarlett agreed. 'I'll keep the engine runnin' in case we need to make a quick getaway.' She was well pumped again sitting behind the wheel of the sporty Golf. It wasn't as good as Gold's top of the range Beemer, but the engine had a lovely throaty growl nonetheless. She watched her friend trot away in the darkness towards the A&E.

As she neared the entrance, the surreal nature of the situation dawned on Drew and her heart started to beat wildly. She stopped to steady herself. *What the hell am I doing? Jesus! Am I right in the head? Shit! I'm helping a comparative stranger to dispose of a fucking dead body.* She felt light-headed now and slightly nauseous, not for the first time that day. *Calm down,* her alter ego soothed. *Calm down. It's natural justice. Grillo was bad news. Anyway, George didn't do anything wrong. The rat died of natural causes. Just like him to cause the maximum amount of trouble.* Yes, but it's breaking the law. *What law?* her alter ego countered. *Who says it's against the law to move someone who's died of natural causes?* She didn't dwell too deeply on that. She looked over at the Golf and saw Scarlett gesticulating wildly, telling her to get on with it. All right for her.

Drew took a few deep breaths. *I've come this far. No turning back now,* she told herself in a burst of bravado. She walked to the doors and waited for them to open. Nothing happened. She hesitated, and just before her courage left her the doors slid apart. She walked in. As is the norm on a Friday night around pub chucking out time the place was a hive of activity, which suited Drew's purpose. She scanned the reception area and the corridor beyond for a vacant wheelchair. Most of the chairs in the waiting area were occupied and the walls of the main corridor were lined with people on trolleys waiting to be admitted. The woman behind reception was talking to a drunk who was holding a big wad of what looked like T shirt to a cut on his head which appeared to be pumping blood. She was trying to take his details with some difficulty, as his friend kept interjecting, making smart remarks and roaring with laughter as only a drunk can. The receptionist had a bored look on her face and spoke very slowly and deliberately, ignoring matey as she asked the patient various relevant questions.

Drew sidled through the swing doors marked *no entry* and looked around for a wheelchair. There were none in sight. She was frustrated. She'd expected the place to be littered with the things. Compared to the waiting room, this area was relatively calm. It was lined with curtained-off cubicles and she could hear the rumble of conversation. Then a curtain swished back and a nurse stepped into the corridor. She stopped when she saw Drew. 'Are you looking for someone?' she asked.

'Um . . . my friend's in the car. She's hurt her ankle and she can't walk. I was looking for a wheelchair to bring her in.'

'Right,' the nurse said. 'I'll fetch a porter.'

Panic. 'No need! I can do it!' Before the words were out of her mouth a young man appeared wheeling an empty chair. 'Oh, Larry. Go out to the car park with this woman, will you? Her friend has a hurt ankle and needs a wheelchair.'

'No problemo,' the young man said, grinning at Drew. 'Lead the way.'

Drew only just managed to hold back an involuntary whimper. She walked meekly back through the swing doors and headed for the exit, Larry close behind. She contemplated taking off at a belt and jumping into the car, but what was the point in that? She might as well have a notice pinned to her back reading 'Acting suspiciously. Please call cops'. She could see Scarlett sitting behind the wheel. The engine was still running. As they approached, Scarlett cut it. Larry wheeled the chair round to the driver's side and opened the door. 'How'd you manage to drive with a bad ankle?'

'With difficulty,' Scarlett said tartly, glaring at Drew behind his back as he helped her into the chair. The three

196

set off towards A&E together. 'How'd you do it?' Larry asked.

'Parachute jump,' Scarlett said, giving him a dazzling smile. 'Hit the ground at a wallop.'

'No kidding?'

It was Drew's turn to glare at her friend behind the porter's back. Larry wheeled them into reception. The drunk was still giving the receptionist grief. Larry told Scarlett to hand in her details, and that he was off the following day if she'd like to go for a drink. She told him she'd see him before she left and blew him a kiss as he went off about his business.

'What'll we do now?' Drew hissed.

'Just wheel me back to the fucking car,' Scarlett hissed back.

Trying to look casual, but failing miserably, Drew wheeled Scarlett towards the exit. She felt thoroughly self-conscious and she had the sensation of walking through a bath of tar.

'Get a bleedin' move on,' Scarlett muttered. 'Get me outta here.'

With effort, Drew co-ordinated her limbs and managed to quicken her pace without falling over. She heaved a sigh of relief when they were once again outside. She sped across the car park. There was a further nerve-shredding glitch as they tried to figure out how to fold up the chair, but the technically minded Scarlett cracked the code after about thirty seconds and then dumped it in the back of the Golf. No one had taken any notice. Behind the wheel once again, Scarlett gunned the engine and they headed for Waterloo Road. Drew was having strong misgivings again. If pinching a wheelchair had caused her such stress, how was she going to cope with dumping a body in Herbert Park?

'Well, that was a piece of cake,' Scarlett said as they pulled out into the flow of traffic. Drew made no comment.

They found George and Gold in the sitting room drinking beer. Drew accepted George's offer of a drink, but asked if there was any chance of a vodka shot instead. Scarlett requested the same. George returned moments later with four shot glasses and a bottle of Absolut. It looked as if it was Dutch courage all round.

'Did you manage to dress him?' Drew asked after she had knocked back her second shot.

George nodded. 'With difficulty. Rigor mortis was setting in, so Bruce suggested we sit him on a chair before his legs stiffened up.'

'But you can't do that!' Drew protested. 'We have to put him lying down or the cops'll know he's been moved. We have to leave him lying down.' The panic was back.

'But if we hadn't bent his legs we'd never get him into the car,' George wailed.

'But the cops will know. They'll know he's been moved.'

'What are ye on about?' Scarlett snapped. She was getting edgy herself now. The vodka was having the effect of neutralising the adrenaline and she was in a better frame of mind when pumped with adrenaline. Suddenly all three women were talking at once, no one listening to the others. The overall feeling was of growing hysteria.

'GIRLS! GIRLS!' Gold roared. 'SHUT THE FUCK UP.' Then in a normal voice, having gained their attention, 'This isn't helpin'.'

The three women stared at him, silenced by the sheer volume.

'That's better,' he said. 'You can't lose it now. There's a dead body in there.' He inclined his head towards the bedroom. As if they needed reminding. 'We've got to stay calm, George did nothin' wrong. We're doin' nothin' wrong. We're merely relocatin' him. Even if the cops do suss he's been moved, so what? The autopsy will tell them that the sleazoid died of natural causes, and no one can point the finger at George, can they?' He picked up the bottle of

Absolut. 'Now how about one for the road.' He looked at his watch 'It's almost eleven-thirty. I reckon we should give it another hour, then get him down to the car and do the business. What do you say?'

Chapter Nineteen

Sid Cahill was nothing if not persistent. Slow at school, he had eventually mastered reading by sheer tenacity and bloody mindedness. The Christian Brothers might argue the point, citing the lash of the birch as the incentive, but this was not the case. By the age of seven the young Sid Cahill was immune to violence. His father, a truculent drunk, routinely battered his wife and children on his return from the pub. Feigned sleep was no deterrent. Sid Cahill senior would drag them all out of bed and stand them shivering in a row in the kitchen, asking unanswerable questions. Anything to provoke a fight. Any excuse to slide the belt from the loops of his trousers, wind it around his gnarly hand and swing his arm back as far as it would go.

At first he had been unable to believe his eyes. The audacity of the man, switching the cash for a couple of measly fifties and a chunk of cut up paper. In a way he had to admire the Aussie, but he was angry with himself for under-estimating him so badly. He didn't think the wanker had it in him. But he'd be sorry, that was a given. No one messed with Sid Cahill and got away with it. He was sitting behind the wheel of the Jeep in the shadows across the street. The Beemer was in plain view, parked at the front of the building. He would wait as long as it took. When the girl had come out and driven off in the Golf with the other one, he had wondered if Gold would be there for the night. He had thought that he was supposed to be shagging her, and if so, where was she going? Then it occurred to him that perhaps she *was* just an assistant and Gold was riding a classier bit of stuff in one of the apartments. It made sense. Yer woman was skinny as a rake with no tits to speak of. Why would a man like Gold, with all that dosh, ride a flat-chested, mouthy piece like that?

When the two had returned later and gone back in, he had cheered up. If she was back, then maybe Gold was going to make a move soon. He hoped so. He was bored. The anger had worn off, and now all he was left with was the need to teach Gold a lesson he wouldn't forget. And get his ten grand, of course. Mustn't forget the ten grand. It was a matter of principle. A deal was a deal. The poxy statement would do Gold no good, and that was all he had. He'd dictated the words to Clint, his ten year old, himself. His brief would get that thrown out before it was even presented in evidence if the wanker went to the cops with it. He laughed out loud and pressed the play button on the CD player. The heater was on and he was comfortable. He would wait for as long as it took. Soon Celine Dion's voice filled the Jeep and Cahill leaned back in his seat, folded his arms and closed his eyes.

Getting Grillo into the wheelchair wasn't easy. The advancing rigor mortis was holding his left arm about ten inches out from his side and it kept getting in the way of the arm rests, until Scarlett had the sense to realise that the arms of the chair were removable. There was much heaving and pulling. All four had now disassociated the body from the living version. For Gold it was easier than it was for the others as he had never seen Grillo alive, and anyway he was used to corpses. Eventually the cadaver was sitting in the chair. His eyes were open and had, by this time, gone cloudy. The former mortuary attendant pointed out that this was a normal state of affairs and launched into the science, but the women shut him up. It was more information than they needed.

They all stood back, a little breathless, and studied their

handiwork. Grillo's head was lying to one side, unmovable due to the rigor, and there was still the problem of his left arm. It looked unnatural sticking out like that. George planted a baseball cap on his head and pulled the peak down low. It was an improvement as it covered the staring eyes, but he looked silly in his shirt sleeves, and the jacket wasn't an option. Scarlett folded the throw and placed it over his knees, tucking it in, then George unearthed a magenta Pashmina and wrapped it around his shoulders. The effect was somewhat startling, but beggars can't be choosers; the lime green throw and other accessories were all they had available.

'His shoes! Don't forget his shoes!' Drew pointed at the Argyle-stockinged feet poking out from under the rug. 'It'll look iffy if he's found without his shoes.'

George guffawed. 'It was iffy long before the shoes, sunshine,' she said, which lightened the charged atmosphere a tad.

At last they were ready. Gold pushed the chair out into the hall and George, carrying Grillo's jacket, peeked out to make sure the coast was clear. The lift doors were open so she scuttled over and held them. Then Gold made his way across the hallway, followed by Drew and Scarlett. The wheelchair, George and Gold filled the lift to capacity, so the other two took the stairs at a gallop. As Drew pushed open the door leading to the lobby from the stairwell, to her horror she saw the weird guy she'd bumped into earlier waiting for the lift. She gave Scarlett a desperate look. They could hear the lift rumbling down.

As the doors opened, George and Gold were greeted by the sight of Drew, with her hands firmly clamped to the cheeks of a skinny guy in an anorak and stay-pressed strides. She was kissing him passionately on the mouth, while he stood rigid and obviously in shock. Gold zoomed the chair out of the lift and, popping a wheelie, hung a sharp right towards the front door. George was close behind. Scarlett, who was as stunned as everyone else, except perhaps for the anorak guy who would soon be suffering the effects of post traumatic stress disorder, waited a beat then raced after them.

When Drew heard the front door swing closed, she pushed anorak guy hard in the chest. 'Get your filthy hands off me,' she snarled, then high-tailed it after the others. When she reached them they were man-handling Grillo into the back of Gold's car. George was kneeling on the back seat pulling, whilst Gold and Scarlett were lifting and shoving. Drew picked up the throw from the driveway where it had fallen, then folded the Pashmina and placed them on the front seat. With Grillo installed, George and Drew got into the back beside him, but as far away as possible, which wasn't that far due to the stiff left arm which was wedged hard against the door. Gold was behind the wheel with Scarlett riding shotgun.

There was a silence whilst they all took half a minute to get their heads together, then Gold exhaled loudly. 'Right,' he said. 'Let's get this show on the road. Where are we takin' him?'

'You drive, I'll navigate,' said his de-facto personal assistant.

Sid Cahill jerked awake as his head dropped forward onto his chest. He was disorientated and groggy from the heat and the sleep. Celine was still singing her little French Canadian heart out. He smiled as he listened to her telling him that love would survive, then his eye caught the dashboard clock and he immediately jolted fully awake. 'Fuck!' It was nearly twenty to one. He shot his head around and peered at the car park, just in time to see Gold's Beemer turning left, heading towards Morehampton Road. The car was full. As far as he could tell there were three in the back and Gold and the mouthy one in the front. He decided to follow in the hope that Gold would eventually dump the others, then he could get him on his own, liberate the cash if he still had it on him, and give him a beating he wouldn't forget in a hurry. He did a U-turn and followed.

Unaware that they had company, Gold drove to the end of Waterloo Road and turned left again, as directed by Scarlett. The traffic was sparse. That was when he spotted the headlamps in the rear view mirror. At first he wasn't too worried and slowed to let the car pass, but he became edgy when the other driver slowed too. He pressed the accelerator and speeded up. The car behind speeded up. Scarlett gave him a quizzical glance, then noticing him clocking the rear view mirror, turned in her seat and peered through the back window. Another glance confirmed that the vehicle in pursuit was a Jeep. She groaned. 'Oh no. I think it's Sid Cahill.'

'What! Who's Sid Cahill? What are you talking about?' More than a touch of agitation had returned to George's voice.

Drew wasn't too happy either. 'I thought you were finished with him. What's he doing here?' she demanded.

'He's after his money,' Gold said. 'I switched the cash for a dud pile and he must have come lookin' for me.'

'But how? How did he know where to find you?'

'Beats me,' Gold said, pressing the accelerator pedal to the floor. The car surged forward. All bar Grillo and Gold were staring through the back window now, watching the headlamps in pursuit.

'Turn here! . . . Here!' Scarlett yelled, and Gold did a screeching left into Herbert Park. 'Cut the lights! Cut the lights!'

Gold got the message and he cut the lights.

'Do you think he saw us putting Grillo in the car?' George asked, still on the edge of panic.

'Dunno,' Gold said. 'I doubt it. He wasn't in the car park, I'm sure of that, so he must've been parked on the road, and we loaded laddo there on his blind side.'

'God, I hope so,' George muttered.

There were almost through Herbert Park by this time, doing close to eighty-five, with the Jeep still in touch. Though Gold had cut the headlamps he couldn't do anything about the brake lights.

Drew said, 'We'll have to change the plan. We can't leave him here with Cahill up our bum.'

'Well, quick thinking Batman,' George snapped. 'How did you work that one out?' Drew glared at her in the darkness.

'We'll have to take him to the Phoenix Park. It's darker there and it'll be easier to lose Cahill on the way,' Scarlett said to Gold, ignoring George's sarcasm. 'Take the next left and head across town. We might lose him at a red light.'

'But Phoenix Park's on the North Side,' George protested, but no one was listening as Gold executed a textbook, rubber burning handbrake turn when they reached the Merrion Road. Drew was too busy trying to stop the cadaver from falling against her as the car swayed and yawed violently at every turn, and Scarlett was frantically trying to think of the most direct route to Europe's largest park.

Gold sped on up towards the city centre. Through the back window the headlights were still very much in evidence.

'Take a left. Take a left,' Scarlett screeched almost immediately, but the BMW was going too fast and instead of shooting up Elgin Road, the car skidded. By the time Gold had regained control they were halfway along Northumberland Road.

'Gimme more notice, will you?' Gold yelled, fighting with the steering. George was still peering out of the back window, her eyes on the Jeep. 'Shit! What are we going to do? What the fuck are we going to do?' she wailed. 'We can't drive round the city centre with a fucking dead body in the car. What if we're stopped by the cops?'

'Chill out, love,' Gold whooped. He was enjoying himself. He hadn't experienced a high like this since his last fix at the end of the eighties.

'Left, left, left!' Scarlett shouted as they reached Haddington Road. The car swerved violently but Gold got control again and soon Scarlett was yelling for him to make a right onto Upper Leeson Street. 'Now go right down past the Green and hang another left when I tell you. We'll lose him in the Liberties.'

About twenty yards from the junction of Leeson Street and St Stephen's Green they could see that the lights were on amber. Gold put his foot down and closed his eyes. As they shot through on the red, he suddenly swerved right.

'What the fuck are you doing? This is one way,' Scarlett roared. 'I said straight on. Straight on!'

'You said *right* past the Green, lady. Make up your fucking mind.' All this whilst he was grappling with the wheel and avoiding the oncoming traffic.

'I said right *past* the green, yeh eejit. I meant straight on.'

Oblivious of the hassle going on in the front, Drew and George were trying to push Grillo upright again. As Gold had swerved on two wheels against the one-way traffic flow, the body had chosen that moment to keel over as a result of the centrifugal force brought about by the hyper speed turn, and he was lying across their knees, his left arm sticking up in the air.

'Get him *off* me.' George grunted with the effort and between them they heaved him a little way up, then, as luck would have it, the next left finished the job and flung him back against the door. There was much hooting of horns and flashing of headlamps from the oncoming traffic. 'Keep going straight then take a left into Cuffe Street, then a right into George's Street,' Scarlett yelled over the roar of the engine as she knelt up in her seat and searched for the Jeep. Through the back window she saw it skid and slew sideways, smashing into a cab at the taxi rank. The queue leapt back en masse and she gave a hearty 'Eeeee-haaaa.'

Gold swerved across the end of the Green, cutting up a new Hyundai, then made a little jink into Cuffe Street. 'Where now? Where now?' His adrenaline level was through the roof, as was Scarlett's.

'I said right! RIGHT!' Scarlett yelled, struggling with the safety belt as she turned back to face the front. As Gold took a sharp right into George's Street, Grillo was thrown back on top of George and Drew.

'Fuck! Give us a hand, Scarlett,' Drew gasped. 'He weighs a bloody ton.'

Scarlett wasn't listening; she was once again concentrating on their route. Gold darted a look in the rear view mirror, and seeing no sign of the Jeep slowed to a reasonable speed.

'Take the next right and we'll stop for a bit in the Liberties,' Scarlett said. She needed time to think. She needed a breather. Gold did as he was told and after doing a few random lefts and rights cruised to a halt in a quiet side street. He switched off the engine.

The silence was deafening as they sat there catching their collective breath. 'What now?' Gold said after a moment.

'Um . . . could someone get this bastard off us?' pleaded George from the back. 'He's a fucking dead weight.'

After a ten-minute respite, Gold started the car and they drove sedately across the city to the North Side, travelling along the quays and crossing the Liffey at Heuston Bridge. Phoenix Park was deserted and Scarlett directed Gold past the zoological gardens towards the Papal cross, turning off the main thoroughfare where there was a convenient clump of trees.

'Wouldn't it be better if we found a bench?' George said. 'I thought the idea was to leave him sitting on a bench.'

'Can you *see* a friggin' bench?' Scarlett asked testily. The hormone high had waned by now and she was feeling exhausted. She just wanted to dump the body and get as far away from it as possible.

'She's right, George. Let's just get shot of him. It's equal now anyway. Let's just leave him here,' Drew said. She was in the same frame of mind as her friend, and was close to wondering why she had ever agreed to help in the first place. As there was a general murmur of agreement from the front of the car, George gave in gracefully.

It was a far easier task to get him out of the car than it had been to load him up. In fact, he almost fell out when Gold opened the door. Drew helped him to manoeuvre the body by guiding the legs. They lowered him to the ground and left him lying on his back with his knees in the air, looking up at the stars through milky eyes.

George couldn't face going home. It was too soon. The image of Grillo lying on her Habitat rug was still fresh in her mind. Sensing that this might be the case, Drew suggested that she spend the night at her place. George was relieved and didn't need any persuasion. They dropped Scarlett off in Rathmines first. She was still a little worried about Cahill. 'D'you think yeh should be going back to your place?' she said to Gold. 'What if Cahill catches up with yeh?'

Gold shook his head. 'I can handle him.' This was pure bravado on his part. He was well aware that Cahill could probably beat him to a pulp, but was counting on the hope that the big bruiser didn't know where he lived.

Scarlett was dubious. 'Well . . . if yeh say so.'

'Thanks for the vote of confidence,' the Aussie replied, grinning. 'Anyway, when Mervyn takes that stuff to the Guards tomorrow they'll probably arrest him.'

Scarlett gave him a peck on the cheek then got out of the car. 'Well, if yeh see him hangin' around, call the Guards, OK?'

'OK,' the glam rocker agreed, and drove off towards Sandymount.

Chapter Twenty

The alarm woke Drew at eight. She was still groggy. It had been after four by the time she and George had wound down enough to sleep, despite the fact that they had both been thoroughly wrung out like dishcloths by the events of the previous few hours. She snapped on the radio to listen to the news. There was no mention of a body being found in Phoenix Park. She wasn't sure if she was pleased or not. In one sense she hoped that he would never be found at all, which was an unlikely scenario seeing as they had dumped him only a couple of yards from the road, but on the other hand she wished the whole sorry business would just go away. It was only then that the seriousness of the situation fully struck her. What kind of an eejit was she, helping to dump a dead body in the middle of the Phoenix Park? That made her an accessory. But an accessory to what? She only had George's word for it that Grillo had died of natural causes. What if she had actually murdered him? Drew couldn't blame her if she had, but nonetheless that would make her an accessory to murder, a scary, not to say appalling thought. She gave herself a mental shake and told herself not to be so stupid. Of course he'd died of natural causes. It was a heart attack. There were no signs of violence on the body, and anyway, although he was short, the man was stocky and far stronger than George. She'd have had no chance of overpowering him without some sign of injury to herself. This thought calmed her and the panic receded, then she heard the last news item in the bulletin.

'The 1970s Australian glam rock star, Bruce Gold, was

found badly beaten near his sister's home on Park Avenue, Sandymount, early this morning. He was taken to St Vincent's Hospital and is in a serious but stable condition. Mr Gold is currently on bail, awaiting trial on a charge brought under the sexual offences act. The Gardai are following a definite line of enquiry.'

The phone rang. Drew snatched it up. 'Did yeh hear the news?' Scarlett's voice at the other end of the line. 'Cahill got Bruce. It must've been Cahill. We should tell the Guards.'

'Tell them what?' Drew was horrified by the concept. 'That we were with Gold, driving round the city with a dead body in the back of the car and Cahill was following us?'

'Don't be an eejit. I mean, tell them about Cahill blackmailin' Bruce and about Bruce switchin' the money. I've got the tape. I can prove it's true. And he *was* followin' us. An' he must've followed us to have found us at George's place, right?'

Put like that it seemed eminently sensible. Drew relaxed. 'Sorry. I'm a bit wound up about the other business. It only just dawned on me that it was probably not the most sensible thing I ever did in my life.'

She heard Scarlett exhale. 'Yeah. I know what yeh mean. I think I must've still been on a high from the sting on Cahill. I mean, the whole thing was unreal, what? Mind you, I *was* sorry for her, and I wouldn't shed any tears for the likes of that shit head. Even if she had done him in, it was better than he deserved.' She paused. 'Anyway, I'm goin' to call Vinnie and tell him about Cahill.'

'On the news it said the cops were following a definite line of enquiry,' Drew said. 'Do you think they suspect Cahill anyway?'

'Dunno,' Scarlett replied. 'But they will by the time I'm finished.'

'OK. See you later so,' Drew said and hung up the phone.

She heard George moving about and found her in the kitchen, hunting in the cupboards.

'Hope you don't mind. I was looking for some coffee,' she said. She looked awful, haggard, as if she hadn't closed an eye at all.

'They haven't found Grillo yet,' Drew said. 'At least, it wasn't on the news, but Bruce Gold was badly beaten up. He's in hospital.'

George gaped at her. 'The Cahill guy?'

'Most probably. Scarlett's going to call her cousin, he's a cop, and tell him that Cahill was following us last night.'

George visibly paled. 'You can't be serious?'

'Chill out. She'll only give him the abridged version. She'll omit the part about us and Grillo.'

George sat down at the kitchen table. She was white as a sheet now and her hands were shaking violently. 'I'm sorry,' she gulped, then started to sob. Drew felt awkward. It embarrassed her when people cried. She never knew what to do. She gingerly placed her hand on George's shoulder. 'Hey, it'll be OK,' she murmured. 'It'll be fine.'

'Fine? How the hell can it be fine? We dumped a dead body in the park last night, for God's sake! What if the cops trace him back to me? What if his driver or someone tells them he was at my place?'

'So what? You just tell the cops the same story as you told the driver. Someone called Grillo and he left. You don't know where he went. He didn't say. What's wrong with that?' She paused, then added, 'Of course, you'll have to say he left quite early. Say about ten minutes after he arrived, because of the time of death.'

'But what about Cahill? Suppose he saw us with Grillo?'

Drew bit her lip. She had a point, but it was time to be pragmatic. She pulled out a chair and sat at the table. 'Look, George. It's pointless theorising. Stick to the story. *Believe* the story. If Cahill did see anything, he saw us wheeling a disabled figure to the car. The baseball cap was hiding Grillo's face. In fact, with the Pashmina and the throw over his knees, he looked for all the world like a little old woman. I vote you just deny it. Swear till you're blue in the face that he's talking bollox.' The kettle clicked off so she stood up and set about making a pot of tea.

'But . . .'

'But nothing. Anyway, it's hardly in Cahill's interests to admit he was within a hundred miles of Bruce Gold last night, is it?'

George shrugged. 'I suppose not.'

'There you are then. You're in the clear.' Brave words, as much for her own benefit as they were for George's. She carried the pot over to the table and then got out cups, milk and the sugar bowl. 'Fancy some toast?'

George wasn't listening. 'Will you come back with me?'

'What?'

'To the apartment. Will you come back with me? I can't face it on my own.'

'Um . . . I suppose so,' she said reluctantly, wishing she had work as an excuse. Wishing that it wasn't her day off.

George chose to ignore the unwilling undertones. 'Thanks. You're a star.' She stood up abruptly. 'I'll go and get dressed.'

Drew sat at the table over her cup of tea, recalling the events of the previous twenty-four hours. She agreed with Scarlett. None of it seemed real. In all the excitement, for a while, Nadia Iacob had slipped from her thoughts, but the fact remained that she was dead, and Broylan Grillo, lately deceased, was probably responsible. Sadly, the fact that said Mr Grillo was now of the deceased persuasion meant that her chief lead was now also dead.

Vinnie listened to Scarlett's story and, after she had finished, dropped the tape into a cassette recorder and punched the play button. He listened to the tape in its entirety. 'And we gave the other copy to Bruce's solicitor, Mervyn Drury, along with the signed statement,' she said as the cassette clicked off. She retrieved it and put it in her bag. 'He's handin' his copy over to you lot today.'

'And he really switched the bundle of cash for a dud one?' Vinnie said with half a smirk on his face. 'He did a switch on the likes of Sid Cahill? Does he *have* a death wish?'

'Yeh never said Cahill was a bleedin' psycho.'

'I did. I said he was violent.'

'But not a friggin' psycho. If ye'd been a bit more up front, Bruce wouldn't be lyin' in Vincent's now.' She was annoyed by his flippancy. More than that she was feeling guilt-ridden for going along with Gold's plan for the sting, despite Vinnie's information about Cahill's past. But then he'd never specifically *said* that Cahill was a psycho. Subconsciously she wondered if she'd used selective hearing and ignored the implications, but that was something she refused to confront. The truth was, she felt seriously culpable, wondering if she should have tipped the guards off about the sting. About Cahill's extortion attempt. She had refused to admit to herself that they might be out of their depth. She thought that they could handle any situation that might come up. She wondered what Joe Mulloy would say. Probably nothing as long as she put in good copy.

'You should have told us,' Vinnie said. 'Barging in there like that. It was stupid and dangerous going in on your own.' He was agitated now. She was being thoroughly hypocritical. If Gold was lying in the hospital he'd help put himself there. 'Anyway,' he continued. 'That's all academic now. And if Cahill beat up Bruce Gold he's bound to bear a few marks, on his hands if nowhere else. We'll pick him up.'

'Great. When?'

Vinnie frowned. 'Why?'

Scarlett grinned at him. 'So I can get Lenny down here,'

she said. 'Everyone knows a good news story needs pictures.'

The apartment was exactly as they had left it. The four shot glasses were still on the coffee table along with the remains of the bottle of Absolut, and the ashtray still needed to be emptied. Drew walked over and picked up the glasses along with the vodka and took them into the kitchen. George followed her and got a fresh bottle out of the freezer. 'Fancy a martini?'

'Bit early for me,' Drew said.

George stared at her for a beat then shrugged and set about mixing a jugful. 'Suit yourself.'

Drew left her to it and wandered into the bedroom. The bed was rumpled, the sheets half hanging on the floor, the rug askew. She bent down and straightened it. Other than that there was no sign that a man had died there. She heard movement behind her and turned to see George with a tumbler of martini in one hand and a black bin liner in the other. She put the glass down and proceeded to drag the linen off the bed.

'Where are the clean ones?' Drew asked, and George directed her to the airing cupboard. When she returned, George had stuffed the sheets, pillow cases and duvet cover in the bin liner. The duvet was lying in a heap by the door. Drew wondered if that was for the chop too. She wouldn't be surprised. Nothing would get her to sleep on those sheets, let alone in the bed. She dropped the linen on the mattress and sat down. 'What are you going to do now?' she asked.

George took a long gulp of her cocktail and sat down next to her. 'Get my life back together, I suppose. At least I can concentrate on my business now I don't have Grillo to worry about.'

'How much did he take you for?' Drew asked.

'Altogether? Upwards of twenty grand, not counting the fortune I threw away on my habit, perhaps another thirty over two years,' George said matter of factly, and Drew gasped.

'Jesus! I didn't think it was that much. How much were you doing?'

George gave her a weary look. 'A lot.'

In the cold light of day Drew felt a tad less understanding. 'You should have cut your losses and gone to the cops.'

She got George's back up. 'What do you know? I was afraid of him. He was blackmailing me. He physically threatened me. He had me attacked by one of his heavies. I'd no choice.'

'You could have gone to the cops,' Drew persisted.

'Yeah. Right! Excuse me Mr Policeman, but this horrid man's threatening me because I lost half a K of charlie I was delivering for him . . . Get real.' She took another gulp of her drink. 'I tell you, you never know how far you'll go. You never know what lengths you'll go to in the cause of self-preservation. Believe me. Been there, done that.' She drained the glass. 'Bought the frigging T shirt.'

It was easy to be sanctimonious, to humph and say, Well I'd never do that, but George had it right. What did she know? She'd never been that desperate. They sat side by side on the end of the bed, George trying to think up a game plan to get the business up and running again, Drew wondering what to do next as far as the refugee story was concerned. But sitting there in the bedroom, Grillo kept impinging on their thoughts. Everywhere they looked in the room it reminded them that not twelve hours before he was lying dead on the rug beside the bed.

'Was it hard?' Drew asked.

'What?'

'The thought of going to bed with him?'

'What do you think?' George's tone was somewhat jaundiced. It bothered her to feel judged and put her on the defensive. 'Hey, we've all slept with a few frogs.'

They lapsed into silence, each lost in their own thoughts

again. After a moment Drew asked, 'Was it really awful . . . you know . . . Grillo . . .'

George took a slug of her drink. 'Grossville.' She shuddered then broke a grin. 'Still, I suppose I was saved by the bell so to speak. Ironic or what?'

Drew laughed despite her disgust. 'What do you know about him?' she asked after a pause.

'Such as?'

Drew shrugged. 'Well, like where did he live? Did he have an office? Any partners, anything like that?'

George rocked her head from side to side as she thought about it. 'Come to think of it, I know very little. I don't know where he lives . . . lived . . . I was never at his house, and I know nothing about his business, his legitimate business that is. He made vague references to import–export and the travel industry, but that's it.'

Drew gave a mirthless laugh. 'Travel and import–export seem close enough.'

'He does have a villa somewhere on the Adriatic though. He asked me out there for a weekend once. That's when I knocked him back, so I suppose that's when . . .' She paused, remembering. Wondering if things would have turned out differently if she'd slept with him then.

Drew was staring at her, expecting her to go on. When she didn't the journalist said, 'Are you sure you can't think of anyone he had business dealings with? Anyone I could talk to, to get background on him?'

George had only been half listening. Her mind was taken up with *what ifs*. What if she *had* started a relationship with him? What if she had seen through his evil game plan? What if she had refused to deliver the package that night? What if she'd cut her losses, sold up, bolted to New York or London and started over? She looked up, aware that Drew was waiting for an answer. 'Sorry?'

'Grillo. Do you know anyone I could talk to, who could give me some background?' When George continued to stare at her with a vague look on her face, she said, 'I know he's involved in this refugee thing. The illegal immigrants. I think he had one of them killed. I want to follow it up.'

'Refugee thing?'

It was exasperating. 'I told you last night. I think Grillo's bringing illegals into the country and then exploiting them in sweat shops.'

George didn't care a jot about refugees or illegal immigrants, she just wanted Drew to go now. She was weary. The alcohol had relaxed her to a degree and she had a strong wish to finish the jug and take a long hot bath and a handful of sleeping tablets. To get into bed, pull the covers over her head and forget about her problems for a while. Most of all she wanted to forget about Broylan Grillo. 'Ummm . . . I'll think about it and get back to you, OK?' She stood up and walked towards the hall. An unspoken invitation for Drew to leave.

Drew hesitated for a second then followed, irritated that George seemed to be so disinterested. 'Please, George. Help me here. You knew him. You must be able to think of someone.'

But George still wasn't listening. She had stopped abruptly in the hall and was staring at the hall stand, her lips slightly parted. 'The briefcase,' she said. 'That's his briefcase.' She tapped her toe against the old-fashioned brown cowhide briefcase sitting on the floor under the beech hall stand. It was battered and well worn. 'We forgot the briefcase.'

A rush of adrenaline surged through Drew's veins. She knelt down and tried to open it, but the spring catch was locked.

'What are you doing?'

'Have you got a knife or something? I need to force the lock.' George was standing stock still, pale as a ghost and shaking again. Drew raised her voice. 'George! Get a grip. Now isn't the time to lose it! We need to see what's in here.'

'No! We should just dump it! Take it and chuck it in the

Liffey,' she said. 'We should get rid of it. What if the cops . . .'

'George! Get real. What if there's something about you in here? What if he kept photos or something back? We have to look inside.' In truth, she was clutching at straws in an attempt to get George back on side. She was obviously on the point of falling apart, but Drew's main concern at this point wasn't George's welfare. She wanted to open the case. She needed to see if there was anything inside that would give her a lead on the illegals. An address, names, anything.

The mention of the photos did it. Without a word George rushed to the kitchen and after a bit of crashing and banging, returned a minute later with a handful of knives. Drew selected one and tried to force the lock, but she had no experience with locks and it wouldn't budge. George was fidgety. When she could no longer stand the suspense of watching Drew fiddle unsuccessfully, she picked up a large carving knife and shoved Drew to one side. 'Here, let me.' She proceeded to saw through the leather flap, then wrenched the case open.

Drew reached over her shoulder, pulled out a large brown envelope and opened it. She could see a bunch of 8x10 glossy photos and a strip of negatives. Without looking at them, she handed the envelope to George. 'I think these could be yours,' she said. George snatched the envelope and ripped it open. Meanwhile, Drew grabbed a sheaf of papers and sat back on her heels to read them. She was vaguely aware of George cursing as she tore the pictures to shreds, muttering, 'The bastard! The fucking lying bastard.'

The papers appeared to be invoices, but there were no details other than code numbers, the initials GJ and the words 'Cash owing'. She flipped through them and made a mental calculation. The figures added up to about three-and-a-half thousand. She wondered what they were for. Did Grillo owe this money to a third party, or were they his, ready for distribution and collection? She searched for an address, letter head, phone number, anything, but Grillo was obviously a careful man. Then, beside her, she was aware of George's sharp intake of breath. She glanced round and saw that she had a huge wad of cash in her hands. It was larger than a brick, twice as thick in fact.

'Good grief!'

George was staring at the cash as if unaware of what it was. A second later she snapped out of it and flipped her thumb through the end. It was made up of fifties and twenties.

'How much do you think's there?' Drew asked, mesmerised. She had never seen that much cash in a lump.

George shook her head. 'Only one way to find out.' She flipped off the rubber band and broke the bundle in two, handing half to Drew. 'Here, get counting.'

Chapter Twenty-One

Sid Cahill was feeling lousy. His head was banging where Gold had caught him with an unexpected wallop to the left temple. He peered at himself in the mirror. A tell-tale purple and faintly green ring was inching its way under his eye and it was tender to the touch. He patted it gingerly with his fingertips. It had been a sucker punch. He hadn't seen it coming, but then neither had Gold when he'd clattered him with his laced fists from behind as he got out of the car. He'd gone down like a ton of bricks and he'd heard all the air expel from his lungs. Cahill had walked round and lifted him up by the front of his jacket. He could see by his eyes that he was dazed. Dazed, fighting for air and disorientated. Hadn't seen it coming, stupid fucker. Did he really think that he could just walk away? Did he seriously think that he could screw Sid Cahill? He'd pulled his fist back and aimed at Gold's nose. There was a satisfying crunch as his knuckles connected with the cartilage and bone, and he felt his hand wet and warm from the gush of blood. He could smell the blood and it made him happy. He knew that he had hurt the bastard. Gold had his hands to his face and was groaning and staggering, so he'd grabbed him by the jacket again and drawn back his arm to take another swing. The Aussie had ducked and the wild punch had caused Cahill to lose his balance momentarily, then Gold bobbed up and head butted him. He'd seen stars and his ears rang, then he saw red. The anger exploded and he'd gone in fists flying, beating Gold mercilessly to the ground, then going in with his feet, kicking and pummelling.

After the red mist of rage had worn off he had slumped exhausted against the car, fighting for his breath, his heart beating wildly in his rib cage. He dropped down on his hunkers, balanced himself and, placing his hands on his knees, dropped his head. It took him a couple of minutes to recover his breath and for his heartbeat to get back to normal. Gold was lying in the shadow of the car, face down in the dirt of a flower bed. Sid heaved himself up and stood over the Australian, looking down, trying to gauge if he was conscious or not. Then the inert Gold gave a little groan, so Cahill drew back his leg and kicked him hard in the side. Gold gave an oofing sound then was silent. Cahill stood over him for another two minutes, waiting to see if he moved again, then crouched down, searched his pockets and liberated the cash. He grinned and his teeth shone white in the darkness. 'Thank you, Bruce,' he said, patting him on the shoulder. 'Thanks a bundle.'

He'd made the news, not Cahill, but Gold. Stable, the report had stated. In a serious condition but stable. He hadn't meant it to go that far. He'd thought a bit of a smack would be enough. Gold would hand over the cash without a murmur and he'd have been taught a lesson, an expensive one because he'd have to get the nose fixed, but experience is costly, it was a known fact. And at the end of it Gold would have learned that it wasn't nice to renege on a deal. Still, he felt vaguely apprehensive. He'd lost it when the Aussie had head butted him. Completely lost his rag. But it wouldn't do if Gold made a complaint. He'd have to do something about that. There was no way he was going to do time for that washed-up moron. He wasn't going to do time for anyone. Not when he had spent most of his forty-three years carefully avoiding what was, in his line of work, an occupational hazard. Something would have to be done about Gold's mouth, he decided, then sniggered when he recalled the crunch as his fist had connected with yer man's front teeth. He looked down at his bruised knuckles. Good job yer man went down so quick. He'd done most of the damage with his feet. He'd been a bit peeved after the event that he hadn't been wearing the Docs with the steel toe caps. The toe caps would have ensured that Gold kept his mouth shut. Permanently. As it was he'd had to dump the blood-spattered trainers. Pity. They were brand new.

He grinned at his reflection. He felt tough, a hard man. Sid Cahill, the hard man. He bent his arms at the elbow and tensed his biceps and pecs, admiring the image in the mirror. Then he patted his belly. It was flat and hard. Hard like him. Everyone knew he was hard. He felt aroused with thoughts of silencing Gold permanently. No bother to him. Those thoughts always left him feeling empowered. Empowered by the choice of life over death. Last night he'd had the power. He could have finished Gold off if he'd felt like it. But he hadn't. Now he wondered if he'd made a mistake. Gold wasn't one of *them*. Not an ordinary decent criminal. He would blab when he came round. Blab and whinge like there was no tomorrow. He didn't understand the code. You pay your debts. You show respect or you pay the consequences, but above all, you keep your mouth shut. You take the beating and you keep your lip buttoned. That was the code.

He felt someone's eyes on him and he jerked his head around towards the bathroom door. Mandy was standing there in her nightdress and slippers, her hair every which way. 'What happened to you?' she asked.

'Nothin',' he growled. 'Mind yer business.'

'Pardon me for askin',' she said, throwing her eyes to the ceiling. 'You know yer man got smacked last night.'

Sid grinned. 'Yeah.'

'Good enough for him,' Mandy pouted. 'You gonna be long?'

Sid Cahill took a last look at his eye then parted his lips and examined his teeth for damage. Satisfied that they were all intact he stood back and stretched his arms above his head. His right shoulder was on the stiff side, but a run and an hour or so at the gym would take care of that, then maybe he'd do a hospital visit.

Scarlett called Lenny and they drove over to Ballyfingal to get a quote from Cahill and some pictures. She felt safe enough with Lenny in tow, but by the time they made it out to the house, Vinnie and a couple of uniforms were there but there was no sign of Sid. Mrs Cahill, a brittle-looking blonde with roots, an older version of Mandy, was shouting insults at them as they left the house, evidently after searching the place. Scarlett walked up the path. The motor of Lenny's Nikon was whirring, the shutter clicking away, and as Ma Cahill caught sight of him, she let off a roar of invective that made even the veteran photographer blush. They could hear the tirade even after she had stomped inside and slammed the door shut. Scarlett saw an upstairs curtain twitch and caught a glimpse of Mandy's sulky face. The girl gave her the finger then disappeared.

'No luck then,' she said to Vinnie. 'No sign?'

Vinnie shook his head. 'Didn't think he'd be here, but we had to try.' He strode back to his car and gave her a 'See you,' as he got in.

Scarlett and Lenny headed back towards town. 'Will we go to Vincent's?' Lenny suggested. 'Might get a piece of our Bruce wired up to the machines.'

'You're all heart, Lenny,' Scarlett commented. 'But I do want to go there. He might be up to talkin'. And anyway, I want to see how the poor bugger is.'

She heard Lenny mutter, 'Friggin' perv,' under his breath.

'No he isn't. He was set up. I told yeh. Sid Cahill set him up.'

Lenny managed to smirk and curl his lip in disgust at the same time, not an easy task but it spoke volumes as to how the photographer felt about Bruce Gold.

*

Twenty-eight thousand pounds. They had laid it out on the floor of the hall in twenty-eight piles of one thousand each. Both women were kneeling on the floor staring at it. Drew was surprised that there was so much. She had imagined that sort of a sum would have a larger volume. 'It just goes to show,' she said.

'To show what?'

Drew sniffed then shrugged. 'Well, I didn't think there'd be that much in it. It wasn't that big a bundle.'

George leaned over and scooped up a wad of cash. 'You know, by rights this is mine. The bastard stole this from me.' She was holding the cash to her chest, defensive, expecting Drew to make some protest.

Drew just nodded. 'Whatever. He probably suckered some other poor sod out of that lot.' She pushed herself up onto her knees and dragged the briefcase over to her. George, surprised by the journalist's attitude, hesitated for a second, then began collecting the rest of the money. Her money.

Drew didn't protest because she didn't care, wasn't interested in Grillo's money. She pulled the briefcase open wide and looked inside. Apart from the invoices, his mobile phone and the cash, now all on the floor, it was empty. She was disappointed. What now? Then she noticed a protruding zipped compartment and her heart lifted with hope. She whipped it open, slid her hand inside and drew out a green leather-bound Filofax. It was well worn like the briefcase. Well worn and bulging with information. George was still collecting the cash together. Drew left her to it and went through to the sitting room.

When George had gathered the money, she put it in the drawer of her bedside table. She was in good spirits. Grillo, by default, had switched on the light at the end of the tunnel, and it was a monster light, a regular Super Trooper. With the money she would be able to get her life back. Pay off the mortgage arrears, the car payments and all the other bills. Eight-and-a-half grand should sort all that out, so that left almost twenty in reserve. Twenty grand to shore her up. To give her a breathing space to get the business back on line.

Or not.

Now, she realised, she had choices. Real choices. There was nothing to stop her selling up and moving right away. Selling the apartment would give her another big lump of equity. She had bought before the boom and property prices went through the roof. For the first time in almost a year George Fitz-Simons felt exhilarated, hopeful, enthusiastic. Grillo was out of her life for good. How ironic that he should have supplied the means of her liberation. The Broylan Grillo savings scheme. She smiled. She couldn't help it. She wanted to sing. She was free.

Drew, meanwhile, was trawling through Grillo's Filofax. She flipped backwards through the diary first. His writing was spidery and quite difficult to read, but she persevered. The entry for the previous day simply read, GF. 7.30., but he had circled the date in red. The day before that was blank, but the day preceding that had a scrawled note: GJ Rathmines 8 p.m. She recalled that that was the night she had seen him outside Iman's flat with the two heavies. The night that Gregory's room had been turned over. The night Nadia Iacob had failed to show up for their meeting. The night Nadia Iacob was murdered and dumped by the canal. Was that only forty-eight hours ago? God! It seemed like an age. As she flipped the pages she noted that all of the entries were brief and gave her little information. She was back to September now. She flipped another page and found a phone number scrawled on the tenth. It was a Dublin number with the initials GJ under it. She scribbled the number in her notebook and carried on her search. The initials GJ came up repeatedly which suggested that he was important. The August 7th entry had a mobile number but no name. She made a note of that also, then dug her mobile out of her bag and dialled. The call was diverted to voicemail. 'You have reached the voicemail of,' there was a pause and a heavily accented voice said, 'Goran Jovanovic.' The recorded voice then requested that she leave a message after the tone. She terminated the call.

Goran Jovanovic. GJ. She heard George pottering around in the kitchen. The radio was on and she was singing to herself. She called out, 'Does the name Goran Jovanovic mean anything to you?'

The singing ceased. Then George padded into the sitting room. She was in a towelling robe and her hair was damp. 'Sorry, what did you say?'

'Does the name Goran Jovanovic mean anything to you?'

'No. Who is he?'

'Don't know, but he figures heavily in Grillo's diary. My guess is he's one of the heavies I saw Grillo with the other night.' George looked at her blankly. Drew had forgotten that she wasn't party to any of that. 'I saw Grillo the other night,' she explained. 'He had these heavies with him. I think that's when they murdered the girl.'

George nodded, but just as Drew had no interest in what she did with the money, George had little interest in Grillo or his associates. Grillo was history. He was out of the picture and she had stuff of her own to deal with. 'No, sorry, never heard of him.' She stood for a moment, then the microwave pinged and she turned abruptly and trotted back to the kitchen and began to sing along to 'American Pie' with Madonna.

Drew went back to the Filofax. There were more meetings with Goran Jovanovic; in fact Grillo seemed to see him regularly, three or four times a week. Drew wondered if GJ was an employee, an associate or what. Apart from obvious social entries like 'Charity ball', or more specifically 'Ethiopian famine banquet' (a surreal concept), or further back 'Special Olympics', the notes were succinct and mostly made up of initials, the odd location and a time, so it was hard to make any kind of sense of it, although there did seem to be a certain pattern. Grillo met GJ mostly in Rathmines and mostly in the evening, which suggested to Drew that maybe GJ did something else during the day. She turned to the address file and looked under the Js on the off-chance that Grillo had listed Goran Jovanovic's address. For some reason she wasn't expecting it to be there, but to her surprise, it was. With hindsight she realised there was no reason for Grillo not to have listed it. The man, by George's telling of it, was an arrogant sod. He obviously thought he was invincible. Goran Jovanovic had a flat on the North Circular Road, Phibsborough end by the postal district number. She checked the phone number. It differed from the one scribbled on the diary page.

She made a note of the address and the phone number, then got out her mobile again and dialled the number that Grillo had scribbled in the diary under Jovanovic's name. She got an answering machine. 'Leatherland is closed for the weekend. Please leave a message after the tone and we'll get back to you.' Obviously a business of some sort, perhaps a factory? It was unlikely to be a shop if it was closed on a Saturday. The sweat shop? She made a further note, with a reminder to look Leatherland up in the phone directory. She flicked through the other addresses. Maddie Reibheinn's was listed, both at home in Foxrock and in Justin's Temple Bar penthouse. George of course was listed. So were a number of politicians and many of Dublin's so-called Glitterati. Broylan Grillo was well connected. There were a number of business cards tucked into a pocket in the front of the leather book. As she was picking them out she heard a yelp from the kitchen. She turned abruptly in her seat. George was standing in the doorway. All her jauntiness had disappeared and she had that haunted look again. 'They found him. It's just been on the news. They found him.'

It took a moment for Drew to cop on. Although Grillo was very much on her mind with the excitement of finding a good solid lead, she had almost forgotten that he was dead. 'But they were bound to find him. We knew they'd find him,' she said, though she felt her stomach immediately contract at the news and she had to fight the urge to panic. It was easy to say that they were bound to find him and so on, but now it was a reality. 'What did the report say?' she asked, trying to keep her voice even.

'It said that a Dublin businessman had been found dead in suspicious circumstances in Phoenix Park. They said suspicious, Drew. *Suspicious*.' She was wringing her hands and her face was pinched.

Drew laughed. Not out of any sense of amusement but at the madness of the situation. 'Of course it was suspicious. He was lying on his back with his knees in the air for God's sake. What did you think they'd say?'

'But I thought . . .'

The laughter had calmed Drew's initial anxiety. She got up and walked over to where George was clinging to the door frame. 'Listen. The autopsy will show that he died as the result of a heart attack. He died of natural causes, George. You didn't do anything wrong . . . except perhaps dump him in the park, but they can't link you to that. They've no reason to suspect you had anything to do with it.' Or me for that matter she added mentally, crossing her fingers.

'I suppose you're right,' George conceded and gave Drew a weak smile. She felt foolish almost losing it like that. Of course they were bound to find Grillo. There was no way that they could miss him. The visual image of Grillo lying as if on an upturned chair that flashed across her consciousness caused her to giggle with tension. Then she pulled herself together. 'Right. You're right. They were bound to find him. We've nothing to worry about. Absolutely nothing.'

Chapter Twenty-Two

Goran Jovanovic was frustrated. He'd been waiting at the factory for forty minutes now and there was still no sign of Grillo. It was unlike the Pole so it bothered him. It also bothered him because Grillo had the money and he needed it. He needed it now. Twenty eight grand, of which he owed sixteen to the Chechens. For no discernible reason he had a bad feeling about it. He had never had any occasion to doubt Grillo before; in fact things had gone remarkably smoothly until now. Until the girl had run off. Bad enough that she had gone, but she was a good worker, one of the best on the machines. Still, that was sorted and it was a lesson to the others, so maybe it was for the best. But it left them one experienced machinist down and they were short as it was. The interior of the car was getting oppressive so he lowered the window and inclined his head towards the air, then glanced at his watch again. Almost eleven. Dudayev was bringing in another six tonight. The Chechen would be expecting his money. He had a lot to do. He took out his mobile and dialled Grillo's number.

When the phone rang Drew froze, then grabbed it and peered at the screen. On the illuminated display she saw the initials GJ. On an impulse she hit the yes button and held the phone to her ear.

'Where the fuck are you? I've been waiting at the factory for the last forty minutes.' The voice was thick and accented and she recognised it as that of Goran Jovanovic. Her hands were shaking so much she almost dropped the phone. He barked, 'Grillo?' She broke the connection.

George was staring at her, horrified. 'Why didn't you just let it ring? Why did you answer it?' Her voice was hoarse and up a couple of octaves again.

'I don't know.' She held the phone in her hand, staring at the screen, then it rang again, an insistent tinny version of a well-known classical piece that Drew couldn't put a name to, but was now more commonly known as a phone jingle. GJ was on the screen again. She let it ring until the message minder picked up the call and the phone was silent. When she looked up, George had left the room, but she could hear her banging about in the bedroom. She sat for a moment gathering her thoughts.

Fact: Grillo and Jovanovic were bringing illegals into the country to work, probably with the promise of good money. But, according to Iman and Gregory, once here they were held and made to work like slaves, ostensibly to pay off their travel debts.

Fact: the factory. Jovanovic said he was at the factory. Grillo and Jovanovic must be tied up with the factory in some way, or why else would Jovanovic be waiting there for Grillo?

Fact: Nadia was dead because she ran away and Grillo and Jovanovic needed to silence her, ergo, Grillo and Jovanovic were probably responsible.

It crossed her mind that she should go to Vinnie with this, but what if he asked her where she had gleaned the information from? She could hardly say that she'd found Jovanovic's address whilst trawling through one Broylan Grillo's Filofax after dumping his body in Phoenix Park. She could hardly mention Nadia; the moment for that had well passed. And she had made a promise to Iman and Co. that she'd keep them out of it. There was always the old chestnut of confidential sources, of course. She decided to wait and use that when she had a bit more to tell. Until she could identify

Goran Jovanovic and maybe discover the whereabouts of the factory. That way she could just point Vinnie in the right direction, stand back, light the blue touch-paper and follow closely with Lenny and Nikon in tow.

She gathered up the receipts and the Filofax and stuffed them into her bag. Then, as an after thought, she picked up Grillo's mobile and dialled up his voicemail to check his messages. He had only the one from Jovanovic, his voice sounding even more ratty that it had only moments before. She hung up and dropped Grillo's phone back in her bag. The empty briefcase was lying on its side on the floor next to the coffee table. In a fit of paranoia she hurried to the kitchen and grabbed a tea towel, then wiped the case thoroughly to remove her fingerprints. She felt a tad stupid, but when paranoia strikes there's little else you can do but go with it.

At the front door she stopped and called to George, 'I'm off, George. I'll drop round later and maybe we'll go out for a drink or something.' She didn't wait for a reply, just slammed the door after her.

When the lift doors opened the weird guy was there in front of her. His eyes took on the look of a bunny caught in the headlamps as soon as he caught sight of her. Drew wasn't sure what to do. Should she give him a cheery 'Hello!' as if nothing had happened? Last night's smacker on the lips was probably the nearest the poor sod had ever got to sex, at least to sex where another person was involved. Should she pretend she had never laid eyes on him before? As she stepped forward into the lift, Thumper leapt aside and bolted past her towards the sanctuary of his apartment. As the doors slid shut, Drew saw him on his knees, fumbling with his keys. All the time his frightened eyes never left her. She smiled to herself and promptly forgot about him. She had plans. Plans that required the use of a car.

*

Maddie was sitting up against the pile of pillows. The look of pale fragility had been replaced by one of abject boredom, a testament to which was the vase of naked stems left over after a petal-picking fest. Drew handed over a box of hand-made chocolates and a bundle of glossy magazines, along with the statutory air kiss. 'How are you *feeling*?' she asked with all the sympathy she could muster.

'Fed up. Fed up and miserable,' she bleated. 'I've been here on my own all morning. Not a soul has come near me. I'm *soooo* miserable.'

'Oh poor you,' Drew said, giving her a hug. 'When are they discharging you?'

Maddie gave a pitiful sigh. 'Not until tomorrow. And Justin's coming home today. I *soooo* wanted to be home before him.'

'Oh, I'm sure he'll understand,' Drew said, trying to coax her into a happier frame of mind. 'He's probably worried about you. Probably well pleased that you're in here being looked after.'

Maddie frowned, then bit her lip. 'Well, the thing is . . . I was wondering . . .'

'What?' Drew asked, still with the cardboard smile pasted to her face.

'I was wondering, well . . . do you think you could do me a teensy weensie favour?' She held her thumb and index finger half a centimetre apart and her voice developed that wheedling quality that drove Drew mad when she heard her future out-law use it on Justin. He was a sucker for it and got taken every time. 'The thing is,' she continued, raising her shoulders and cocking her head to one side, little girlie fashion, 'as you know, I had to leave the penthouse in rather a hurry, and I was wondering if you could . . . um . . . tidy up a bit. Especially the um . . . *bathroom*?' She put heavy stress on the word bathroom, and as she said it cast her eyes down to the bed cover. Drew got the picture immediately.

'The bathroom?' Drew said innocently. 'But I thought you had a cleaner?'

'Well, yes,' Maddie whined. 'But there are *certain things* one wouldn't want the help to see, if you get my drift.' She tapped the side of her nose, which Drew thought an appropriate gesture considering the nature of the *certain things* she didn't want the help to see . . . or Justin come to that. She didn't make it easy for Maddie though. It was pure bloody mindedness on her part, but it was also fun to see the fiancée from hell squirming for a change. She stared, apparently uncomprehending, at Maddie, who was getting increasingly uncomfortable. 'Um, the *charlie*.' She whispered the word. 'I need you to tidy *charlie* away.'

Drew stifled a smirk. 'Oh. *Charlie*.' She tapped the side of her nose to show that she understood. 'Don't worry. Give me your keys and I'll sort out *charlie*. When did you say the cleaner's coming?'

Maddie visibly relaxed. 'Not sure.' She leaned over to her locker and took out her keys. 'Here you are. You're soooo good to do this, Drew. I really appreciate it. I owe you one.'

'Two,' Drew replied, smiling sweetly. 'I think you owe me two now.' She took the keys from Maddie. 'By the way, where's your car?'

'My car? Why?'

'Better check the car too, just in case.' She did the nose tapping thing again and Maddie copped on straight away.

'Oh God! You're so right. Please, *please, do* check the glove compartment won't you? It's in the underground garage. The code's one-one-four.'

'No problem,' Drew said, almost skipping towards the door, mission accomplished. 'I mean, you wouldn't want the hired help to go rummaging in your glove box, would you?'

Scarlett was shocked by the sight of Bruce Gold. He was bandaged almost from head to foot, both legs in traction and wired up to a bunch of machines all bleeping away. He was like something out of a spoof horror movie. She met Maisy in the corridor outside intensive care where she was leaning against the wall drinking from a can of Pepsi. She was solemn but unemotional. 'He's doing OK,' she said. 'Took an awful beating though. I didn't hear a thing. If it wasn't for next door's dog sniffing around and raising the alarm he'd be in a worse way. The doc said he was lucky.'

He didn't look very lucky. Scarlett introduced Lenny, who was trying to look inconspicuous, his camera still in the bag. 'What's the damage?' she asked.

Maisy counted off on her fingers. 'Both legs broken. Collar bone. Right arm in a couple of places. Left wrist, half a dozen busted ribs. Broken nose and right cheek bone, and a few teeth kicked out. Yes . . . he was lucky all right.'

'Lucky?'

Maisy shrugged. 'Lucky he's got such a thick bloody skull. Only got concussion. No skull fractures or, God forbid, brain damage. On the face of it it's all superficial. No vital organs damaged.' She blessed herself, then leaned forward towards Scarlett. 'Listen, I've been picking up the pieces for Bruce for as long as I can remember. He was always in scrapes as a kid. Accident prone, he was. This isn't the first beating he's taken. But he's as tough as nails, he'll get over this, mark my words. That fella has the luck of the devil.'

'Oh right,' Scarlett said. Bad luck was obviously a matter of degree as far as Maisy was concerned. 'Has he said anything yet? Did he say who it was?'

Maisy shook her head. 'They sedated him. Thank God he's not in a coma or anything, but they gave him pain killers. So he's saying nothing at the minute. Me, I think it was that Cahill fella you both went to see last night. Bruce said he was going to switch the cash, so I guess he wasn't too rapt about that. Am I right?'

'You could say that,' Scarlett said. 'I told the cops about

Cahill. They're following it up. They're looking for him to bring him in for questioning.'

Maisy made a humphing sound. 'Bloody cops.' She obviously shared her brother's opinion of the police. Not surprising considering Bruce's experience. 'Couldn't organise a piss up in a bloody brewery.'

Lenny coughed. 'Uh . . . would it be OK to take a photo?' he asked Maisy. 'So the public can see what a terrible state he's in?'

Gold's sister nodded and gestured towards the door. 'Fire away, love, whilst there's no nurses about. That ward sister's a bloody dragon.' Lenny didn't wait for a second invitation and they both watched as the photographer shot off a dozen frames from various angles. Then Scarlett said, 'Tell him I was asking for him when you talk to him, will you? And tell him I went to the cops about Cahill and the story should be in on Monday.'

Maisy smiled. 'Thanks, love. You're one of the few who believed him. I know he didn't do those things, and I know he's grateful that you're helping him. Not many people stand up to be counted over something like this, you know. And believe me, I know from the last time. The Press bloody crucified him. Nailed him to the bloody barn door.'

Scarlett blushed. She was embarrassed that Maisy and Bruce thought her so noble when her chief motivation was the story. 'No problem,' she said, lamely fighting the urge to turn and flee. 'No problem at all.'

He recognised the girl. The skinny, flat-chested piece. From the end of the corridor he saw her talking to an auld wan outside the intensive care unit. He ducked back around the corner and, as he did so, two uniformed cops walked by. They were talking together and didn't give him a second look. 'Fuck it!' he thought. 'They've got a guard on him.' Sid Cahill was downhearted by this development, though not defeated. He knew time was on his side. Gold was unconscious but stable. He'd lied on the phone and told the nurse he was Gold's cousin, and although she had sounded sceptical, she'd given him the up-to-date bulletin.

Earlier, after Angie had phoned him at the gym and told him the cops had raided the house, he was livid. He'd taken it out on the punch ball, nearly sending it into orbit, then after he'd calmed down he had thought the problem through. Pragmatism was the word. It was a particular favourite of his. He'd always had a fondness for it, ever since he had heard John Bowman, or one of those political bods on the telly who did *Prime Time*, use it. He'd looked it up in the dictionary and immediately decided that the word summed him up to a tee. Pragmatic. That was Sid Cahill. It was time to be a pragmatist. If the cops were coming back, that meant they'd been away. He looked at his watch. Shift change. All he had to do was go away until the next shift change, slip in and do the business. Was that being pragmatic or what? Pleased with himself, he headed back towards the lift with a spring in his step.

Drew met the cleaner outside the door of the penthouse on her way in. She introduced herself and told her about Maddie – the official version, that is. The cleaner, a young woman of about twenty or so, nodded, showing appropriate sympathy, but Drew could tell that her heart wasn't in it, and felt sure she detected a faint smirk after she had finished the telling. She could understand why, having been witness to Maddie's abysmal social skills. It was only as she opened the bedroom door and caught the overwhelming stench of stale vomit that she remembered the soiled bed cover. She hurried over to open the window, then retreated to the bathroom. All she needed to do there was remove Maddie's snorting tube and empty the remains of her stash down the loo. She hid the little ziplock bag in the bottom of the waste bin. Then she took a towel and wiped any powdery residue that was left off the unit. She briefly wondered why she was aiding and abetting her future sister-in-law. It was a question for which she had no answer, other than she hoped that Maddie might have learned a lesson, so what was the point in causing a fuss and alienating Justin to boot? In the *who would he believe* stakes it was a one-horse race.

'Jeasus!' The cleaner had entered the bedroom.

Drew poked her head out of the bathroom door. 'Sorry. Forgot to say. She was sick on the bed cover.'

The cleaner, with mouth contorted in disgust, rolled the cover into a ball and dumped it on the floor. Drew checked the rest of the bathroom drawers for drugs then, satisfied that it was fine, left the cleaner spraying air freshener with gay abandon. On balance, in Drew's opinion, the stale vomit odour was marginally less awful than the air freshener.

Maddie's red BMW Z3 was in her parking bay in the underground car park. Drew slid in behind the wheel, then leaned over and popped the glove box. Another ziplock, with a hefty load of white powder nestled amongst the flotsam. Drew was taken aback. Though she didn't use drugs of any kind, she wasn't naïve, and the amount shocked her. It implied that Maddie was a serious user. She wondered if Justin had any idea. Surely he couldn't fail to notice. But if he did know, why was Maddie so anxious for her to remove any traces from the penthouse? She wished that she hadn't found it. She didn't want to be involved in what could only, for her, be a no win situation. She stuffed the bag in her pocket with a view to dumping it later and reversed out of the parking bay.

Chapter Twenty-Three

The RTE mid-day news gave Broylan Grillo's name as the businessman found dead in the early hours of that morning in Phoenix Park in suspicious circumstances. Goran Jovanovic heard the news whilst driving along Dame Street and almost crashed his Toyota into the back of a bus. The newscaster added that after the state pathologist had visited the scene, the body had been removed to the city morgue for autopsy. Jovanovic drove on past Dublin Castle, up to Lord Edward Street, then when the traffic allowed, pulled into the side of the road. He needed to think. The uneasy feeling of earlier was now full-blown anxiety. Who had killed Grillo, and why? Jovanovic was aware that Grillo had many varied business interests, both legit and otherwise. His fat fingers poked many pies and he was bound to have made enemies by the very nature of the game. It would be hard to know where to start. It could be one of many.

Then, more worryingly, he wondered, did Grillo have the cash with him at the time? Was it a simple opportunist robbery, or something more sinister? Was it one of the Romanians, in retaliation for the girl? No. He discounted that. They were too afraid. Then it hit him like a ton of bricks. Someone had answered Grillo's phone long after he was dead. Who had Grillo's phone, and if they had his phone, did they have the money? He racked his brain trying to work out what to do. Their meeting had originally been planned for last night so Grillo could well have withdrawn the money from his account, but then he had rescheduled. Jovanovic had been irritated by this. He didn't like it when plans changed at the last minute. He was a cautious man. Grillo had placated him. It was his birthday, he had said, and he was going to have the woman. He was almost rubbing his hands with glee when he'd explained. Jovanovic thought he was pathetic. Letting a woman get to him like that. And this one had got to him big time. He was obsessed. To the Serb it showed weakness, and in his book weakness was dangerous, but conversely he was well aware that another's weakness could also be used as a weapon. He had filed the notion away for future reference.

No use now, Grillo was dead. Maybe the woman was the key. The Pole had been with her. He started the engine and drove up to Christchurch Place, then took a right at the lights and headed for the Quays. He had the number of Grillo's driver, Tommy Walsh. The driver would give him the woman's address. He would start with the woman.

George was feeling drained. She had thought that once the Grillo problem had been solved she'd be on top of the world, but right now she felt exhausted beyond belief. If she had stopped to think about it she would have realised that the exhaustion was a reaction to the constant stress of the past few months; her body's way of making her rest and recuperate, or conversely a reaction to the sudden absence of adrenaline that her bloodstream had become accustomed to. Then again it could have been due to the crying jag she had succumbed to shortly after Drew had left. She had been feeling fine until she heard the news that Grillo had been found. Then the euphoria of earlier, when she had found the money, had suddenly vanished, to be replaced by a deep feeling of hopelessness and she had sunk down on the kitchen floor and sobbed. Not flimsy little girlie sobs but big gusty ones that racked her entire body.

The crying had lasted a good hour and now her eyes were puffy, her head ached and she had this overwhelming fatigue. She heaved herself up with the aid of the draining board and splashed her face with cold water. Drink. That's what she needed. A stiff martini. No, a vodka shot. Maybe several. She needed a speedy hit. She half regretted the fact that she had no drugs. Then it struck her. There should be the remains of a wrap of coke in her bedside table. One hit couldn't do any harm. She needed it. She'd been through a lot in the past twenty-four hours. She hurried to the bedroom and pulled out the drawer with such force that it slipped off the runners and fell to the floor, scattering bank notes everywhere. In her distressed state it took her a moment to remember that she had stashed the money there. She gathered it up into a bundle. Her hands were shaking now so she had some difficulty. After a minute she gave up and stuffed it under the mattress out of the way, and then searched the drawer to see if there was even half a wrap lurking in the back. No such luck. Frustrated, she flung the drawer across the room. She was on the verge of tears again. She was shaking and anxious.

'Get a grip,' she said aloud. 'Get a grip!' She breathed deeply. Yoga breathing, the way the therapist had coached her at the clinic. After half a minute she felt calmer. 'Don't lose it now, girl,' she reproved herself. 'Keep it together.' Talking to herself helped. She practised her yoga breathing some more and, when she felt able, went back to the kitchen to find the vodka.

Scarlett's Bruce Gold story was shaping up well. Conscious of Mervyn Drury's comment about *The Record*'s lawyers, she had written two versions of the blackmail story, one naming Cahill, along with the cropped photo of Sid, and the second without naming him. She also wrote a separate piece about Gold's assault. Nudge, nudge, wink, wink. Which version of the blackmail story would run depended on the lawyers and whether the cops managed to get their act together and nab Cahill or not. As she was polishing the assault story, Lenny wandered in. He had the prints of Gold lying in his hospital bed, and the ones of the ranting Mrs Cahill and a particularly jaded-looking Vinnie. He dropped them on her desk. 'I'll be off so,' he said. 'Goin' to the rugby.'

'Thanks, Lenny. Isn't it happy for yeh.'

Lenny yawned and stretched, then adopted a pseudo weary expression. 'Ah, sure it's a dirty job but some poor bugger has to do it.' Having said that, he shambled off. At the door of the newsroom he passed Drew on the way in. 'Have the two of ye no homes to go to?'

Drew stopped. 'Where are you off to?'

'The rugby,' he said. He nodded towards the newsroom. 'Herself is inside.'

Drew found Scarlett at her desk perusing Lenny's photographic handy work. She pulled up a chair. 'So how's your mate Bruce?'

Scarlett dropped the photos. 'He's a mess, but he'll live.' She lowered her voice, even though the newsroom was empty. A daily paper, *The Record* only rostered a skeleton staff on Saturdays. 'I suppose yeh heard they found yeh man in the park.'

Drew nodded. 'They were bound to.' She picked up the snapshot of Cahill and his son. 'Who's this? Cahill?'

'The very man,' Scarlett said, then handed her Lenny's photo of Mrs Cahill berating Vinnie. 'His auld wan's a hard-lookin' piece.'

Drew laughed. 'Vinnie doesn't look the best either.' She dropped the snapshot back on the pile. 'I got Maddie's car.'

'She gave yeh the car?' Scarlett couldn't hide her incredulity. 'The Z3? Feck! How'd yeh do that?'

'I did her a favour. I cleaned up her act so to speak.' When Scarlett's expression told her that she hadn't the slightest comprehension, she added, 'I got rid of *charlie*'s remains from the penthouse.'

Scarlett got her drift and laughed. 'Jeasus! Burke and Hare have nothin' on you.'

'So what are you up to?'

Scarlett clicked the save icon on her computer screen. 'Just finishin' up. Why?'

'I wondered if you fancied a drive. I've a lead I need to follow up on the refugee story that involves a bit of driving and I could do with company.'

Scarlett pushed back her chair. 'Sorry, love to have a spin in yer woman's Z3, but I want to go see if Bruce's conscious yet. I need a quote to finish off the assault story.'

Drew was disappointed but understood. She too pushed back her chair. 'OK. Whatever. Might catch up with you later?'

Scarlett grinned. 'Listen, after last night I intend to go on the tare. Are yeh up for it?'

'Count me in,' Drew said, without the slightest need of persuasion.

The phone was ringing when Goran Jovanovic turned the key in the front door. He hurried himself so as not to miss the call.

'How are you doin', Goran?' It was Sid Cahill.

Jovanovic didn't want to talk to Sid Cahill. He had more important things on his mind, like twenty-eight grand for instance. 'What do you want, Cahill?'

'Who rattled your bleedin' cage?' came the reply.

The Serb felt a surge of annoyance. 'What do you want, Cahill? I'm busy.'

'We had a meetin'. Where were yeh?'

Goran Jovanovic cursed silently. In his anxiety about Grillo the meeting with Cahill had slipped his mind. 'Oh. Yes. My apologies. Something came up,' he replied in a placatory tone. 'We should reschedule.'

'Re-bleedin'-schedule my arse. You owe me, Jovanovic. I want me money. I done the job and I want me money.'

Jovanovic drummed his fingers on the hall table. He was anxious to be rid of Cahill. He considered the man something of a loose cannon. He was too volatile, too unpredictable. It had been Grillo's decision to use him. 'He's cheap and he'll get the job done,' he'd said. Jovanovic didn't agree that cheap was necessarily a valid criterion, but as time had been of the essence – the girl had needed to be made an example of – he'd had no choice but to agree, albeit against his better judgment.

'OK. Meet me up at the factory in Inchicore in about half an hour. You know where it is?' Jovanovic said. He knew he had two grand in the safe at the factory.

'Oh I do, Goran. I do,' Cahill said. 'It's nice doin' business with yeh.'

After Cahill's call he hunted for Tommy Walsh's number and dialled

Drew parked a little way down the road on the opposite side, where she had a clear view of the house. It was a two-storey mid-terrace divided into flats, on the Phibsborough end of the North Circular Road. From her vantage point she could make out only two door bells, which suggested that the house was split into only two flats. Jovanovic's was number two, therefore Drew deduced it was probably on the first floor. She squinted at the front upper bay window and wondered if he was even there, then had a brainwave and pulled out Grillo's Filofax, found Jovanovic's address and dialled the number. The phone rang half a dozen times before it was picked up.

'Jovanovic.'

She broke the connection, her heart thumping. After a brief interval Goran Jovanovic strode out of the house. He was tall and wiry with skin like a pineapple. His hair was fairish, thinning at the hairline, oiled and pulled back in a skinny, greasy ponytail. He wore a dark overcoat. He got into a newish metallic grey Toyota and drove off. Drew waited until he was ten yards down the road then followed. She kept a couple of cars between herself and Jovanovic.

She'd seen it done enough times on *The Bill* and other cop shows to know that that was the way to do it. She got edgy a couple of times when she missed the lights, but caught up with him at the next set. Anxious that she might lose him on the Quays, she overtook the car in front leaving only an acid green Nissan Micra between them. He crossed the river at the Four Courts and headed towards Heuston Station, along St Johns Road onto Concolbert Road. The traffic was steady so she allowed an Opal Vectra to overtake her. Ahead of her she saw his indicator flashing amber. She changed lanes and took the left into Inchicore Road. Ahead his indicator was flashing again. Right this time. She slowed, feeling conspicuous in the bright red sports car, then as soon as he had made the turn, put her foot down and sped after him. The flow of traffic on Sarsfield Road impeded her at this point and by the time she made the right turn, the Toyota was nowhere in sight. Frustrated, she put her foot down again, but fifty yards further on there was still no sign of Jovanovic. She was frustrated and angry. Where the hell was he? She pulled into the side of the road and stopped the car. The man couldn't have vanished into thin air. He couldn't have turned off, there was nowhere to go. Then, as she was sitting there considering her options, the Toyota with Jovanovic at the wheel sped past. It took her only an instant to recognise him. She had no idea how she had managed to overtake him, but didn't waste time on speculation. Having no intention of losing him again, she shoved the Z3 into gear and took off after him.

Chapter Twenty-Four

The cop on guard outside ICU told Scarlett that Bruce Gold was conscious, but still in no state to talk to anyone. She knew him vaguely from seeing him at the District Court.

'Oh, is it yourself,' he'd said by way of a greeting. 'How's things down at *The Record*?' Scarlett smiled and humoured him with a bit of small talk before he gave her the info. She would have preferred to have found it out for herself, but there wasn't a hope in hell that she would be allowed in to see Gold, not being a close relative. She was therefore relieved to see Maisy and collared her as she came out of the ward.

'How is he?'

'Getting there,' she said. 'They're movin' him to a regular ward tomorrow. He's breathin' on his own now. I just came out for a break whilst they're fixin' him up.'

'Did he say anything? Did he say who beat him up?'

Maisy shook her head. 'No. He's flyin' somewhere up in the stratosphere on the pain killers so he's not makin' much sense. But you and I know who it was. It was that Cahill guy.'

'The cops are lookin' for him,' Scarlett said. 'They'll get him. It's only a matter of time.'

Maisy glanced over at the uniform who was leaning against the wall surreptitiously picking his nose and guffawed. 'Phwah!'

Scarlett touched her arm. 'They will, really, Maisy. They'll get him.' Maisy didn't look convinced. 'Is there any chance yeh could get me in to see him?' Scarlett asked under her breath, casting a wary glance at the Guard, still studiously excavating his proboscis. 'Maybe if he sees me it'll get his head together. I need a quote for the story. I need to hear him say it was Cahill.'

Maisy shrugged. 'I could say you were me niece, I suppose.'

'Would you?'

After about fifteen minutes a nurse came out of the ward and smiled at Maisy. 'You can go in again. He's comfortable now.'

'Thanks nurse.' They watched her walk away then Maisy grabbed Scarlett's arm. 'Come on, love. Let's go in and see your *Uncle* Bruce.'

Scarlett shot a guilty look in the cop's direction, but he was more intent on watching the nurse's bottom as she walked away.

Bruce attempted to smile when he recognised her, then winced with the effort. He looked terrible. *Comfortable* was obviously a comparative term. 'Does it hurt?' she asked gently, cringing as the words left her mouth. Stupid question. Up close he looked even worse than the view through the glass. Both eyes were blackened, the right closed entirely. His face was the size of a balloon, his nose resembled an aubergine and his front teeth were missing.

'Only hurts when I laugh,' he whispered. She had to bend forward to hear him as his voice was rasping and the missing teeth caused him to lisp.

'Who did it, Bruce?' she asked, anxious to get to the nitty gritty in case he dropped off to sleep again. 'Was it Sid Cahill?'

Gold gave a weak nod.

'Good one, Bruce. That's a quote, right?'

Gold gave another brave nod, but he was fading fast. His eyelids fluttered as the morphine took a hold and he was sucked up into the stratosphere again.

*

246

The building looked unused. It was a two-storey boxy structure that had seen better days. Weeds grew up through the cracked concrete forecourt and a couple of windows were boarded up. Jovanovic's car was parked near a set of grimy glass doors over which hung a faded sign: *Leatherland*. An old and warped *Beware of the Dog* sign sagged drunkenly from the chain link perimeter fence.

Drew had parked across the road but she was uncomfortable about it. In this area, a car of the calibre of Maddie's stuck out like a librarian in a brothel. She noticed a few gurriers between the ages of about six and ten quietly circling, eyeing it up. She had no doubts that they'd be capable of removing the wheels and stripping the engine while she was still sitting in it. A pet lover, she generally liked dogs, nice lollopy Labradors or cute Yorkies, but as she made a point of avoiding the vicious salivating variety she decided to take her chances with the gurriers. She kept one weather eye on them and the other on the Toyota in front of the factory. As she was considering what to do next, a Jeep drove past and swung into the factory yard. She watched with interest as the driver got out. He stretched then readjusted himself in his jeans before making for the glass doors. Drew strained her eyes, questioning what she saw, then reached for her mobile.

Jovanovic had the cash ready. He saw Cahill arrive. Not that he was looking out for him, he was more intent on the red BMW Z3 that he'd spotted in the wing mirror on Phibsborough Road, once on Quays, then on Concolbert Road. He'd pulled into a service station just to make sure, convinced that it was merely paranoia, but then he caught up with her again, passing her at the side of the road.

Cahill came straight up to the office and barged in. 'How's it goin'?' He pulled out a chair from behind the desk and sat down, resting his feet on the desk top. Jovanovic was still watching the car. He could see the woman behind the wheel. It occurred to him that maybe it was Grillo's woman, but what was she doing following him? Had Grillo been shooting his mouth off to her? What did she know?

'What's up with you?' Cahill was staring at him now.

Jovanovic turned from the window. 'Do you know a woman with a red BMW Z3 by any chance?'

Cahill shrugged and shook his head. 'No? But if you're lookin' for one I'm sure I could fix you up,' he leered. The Serb stared at him. He decided that he disliked this man more every time he saw him. When the hit-man got no response from his contractor he shrugged. 'Suit yerself.' He swung his feet to the floor and stood up. 'Show me the money,' he said. 'Show me the money.' He was grinning like a madman and shouting, 'Show me the bleedin' money.'

Jovanovic gave a curt nod. 'OK, OK.' He walked to the desk, pulled open the top drawer and took out an envelope. 'Here.' He handed the envelope to Cahill. Cahill took it and stuffed it in his pocket. 'Aren't you going to count it?'

Cahill shook his head. 'I know where you live,' he said, still grinning. He thrust his hand forward. Jovanovic hesitated then shook it. 'Good to do business with you,' Cahill said. 'If you ever need any more clearing up done gimme a call.'

Jovanovic walked back to the window as soon as Cahill left the room. Stocky as he was, the man was light on his feet and barely made a sound as he hurried down the stairs. Jovanovic watched as he climed into the Jeep. The Z3 was still there. A decision needed to be made. After a moment's thought he had it, and he smiled to himself. It had to be the woman. He would drive to her apartment in Balls-bridge. Turn the tables so to speak. He was still smiling as he locked the factory door behind him and headed to his car. He tried to imagine how she would feel when she realised where he was leading her. He slid behind the wheel and started the engine. At the gate he paused, glancing to the right to give her plenty of time to follow, but the red BMW Z3 had gone.

At first Drew thought that Cahill was heading for Ballyfingal, but then he started to drift steadily east. She tried to reach Scarlett on her mobile again but the call was diverted straight to her message minder. She cursed silently in frustration. What was the point of having a mobile if you never switched the damn thing on? She was finding it hard to keep up with Cahill. He was a maniac driver. In desperation she tried Vinnie. He answered on the third ring.

'Vinnie, it's Drew.' She didn't give him a chance to say anything, thrashing straight on. 'Vinnie, I'm in Maddie Reibheinn's car following Sid Cahill.'

'Cahill? Why the hell are you following him?'

'Because he nearly killed Bruce Gold, you eejit. I thought you were looking for him. I thought you wanted to pick him up for questioning.'

Vinnie's reply was a tad strained. 'Yeah we are, but what the fuck are you doing chasing a psycho like Cahill? Where the fuck are you?'

Drew looked about for a landmark. 'Um . . . I'm not sure. We're heading east.' Then she saw a sign. 'I'm on Crumlin Road. Crumlin Road . . . Hang on, he's turning right into . . .' She strained her eyes, searching for a road sign, then dropped the phone onto her lap as she made the turn. She heard Vinnie's distant frantic voice. 'Drew? Are you still there?'

On the straight once again, she picked up the phone. 'Yes, I'm still here.' A road sign flashed past. 'I'm on Bangor Road. Can't you put out a call or something? I'm afraid I'll lose him, he drives like a fucking mad man.'

'He *is* a fucking mad man. Don't get too close. Keep your distance and keep the line open till I get some back-up sorted out.'

Drew dropped the phone again as a roundabout loomed up, and fought with the wheel, but couldn't get into the inside lane to follow Cahill as he sped off at the first exit. With screeching tyres she hung another circuit and swerved in front of a people carrier to make the exit second time round. She winced at the chorus of hooting and scorching tyres. There was no sign of Cahill's Jeep ahead of her. She overtook a couple of cars but it was hopeless. He was miles ahead. She picked up the phone from her lap. 'Vinnie?' She could hear him speaking urgently to someone in the background, then he came back on the line. 'Drew? Where are you now?'

She looked around. She hadn't a clue. 'We turned left at a roundabout and I'm driving past a park now.'

'A park? OK, I think I know where you are. Are you still with Cahill?'

Drew peered into the distance. 'No. I think I've lost him.'

'Don't worry about it. Are you OK?'

'I'm fine. I'll just motor along here and if I see him again I'll call you.' Suddenly she saw a familiar landmark. 'Hang on. I know where I am. I think I'm coming up to Rathgar.'

'Yeah. That's right. Why don't you go home now and leave this to the professionals?' Patronising bastard.

'I'll go home when I'm good and bloody ready,' she snarled. 'And whilst you're at it you might want to check out a factory called Leatherland and a man called Goran Jovanovic.'

'What are you talking about?'

'Nadia Iacob. Jovanovic is running a factory with illegal immigrants in Inchicore. Check it out. I think Jovanovic and a man called Broylan Grillo probably murdered Nadia because she ran away.' At the mention of Grillo she cringed. Anger always made her run off at the mouth, it was one of her failings. She could have bitten her tongue off. Grillo was the last name she wanted to be associated with.

'How do you know this? Why didn't you say anything yesterday at the murder scene?' He sounded livid.

'Now is not the time, Vinnie. Just check it out. Leatherland. Inchicore.' She broke the connection and threw the phone on the seat next to her. It rang almost immediately, but she ignored it, letting her voicemail pick up the call. Arrogant fucking bastard, she fumed. To think Scarlett even considered that we'd be good together.

Goran Jovanovic kept an eye on the rear view mirror all the way across town to Ballsbridge, but caught not a glimpse of the red BMW. At first he thought that maybe she had driven the car out of sight, unaware that she'd already been spotted, with a view to following him again. But why? When there was no sign of her it made sense that she had followed Cahill. But he couldn't figure out why the woman would follow Cahill. He would have had less problem with it if he had not been aware that she had followed *him* to the factory. It worried him. What did she know? What had Grillo told her? But most of all, why? What was the point? What was she after?

He was on Waterloo Road now. He slowed and looked at the numbers. Walsh had given him little or no information about Grillo's movements of the previous night, other than the fact that when he'd called the woman's apartment to collect him as arranged, she'd told him that Grillo had left suddenly. Jovanovic had asked the driver where Grillo had gone and with whom. The driver said he hadn't a clue, that the woman had said that Mr Grillo hadn't shared that information with her. It just didn't scan. Why would Grillo, a careful man, go off without his driver, especially if he was carrying twenty-eight grand about his person? And he knew that for a fact now. Walsh had told him that Grillo called at the bank late that afternoon. You don't hire protection then go off without it.

Yes, something was definitely wrong. Things were beginning to unravel.

He pulled into the car park and drove around to the back of the building out of sight of the road. It occurred to him then, as he sat there waiting for the red Z3 to show up, that maybe she hadn't followed Cahill at all. Perhaps she had just lost courage and driven off somewhere. Logically, there was no reason why she should follow Cahill. This thought made him feel a little better. More in control. If that was the case she could be dealt with. He preferred to be in control. He didn't like dealing with the unexpected, the unplanned. But he knew with certainty that if the girl did have the cash, was responsible in some way for Grillo's death, he would be well able to deal with her. He would have no problem getting the money back. Then maybe he'd call on Cahill again. Much as he disliked the man, he had carried out the contract on the girl promptly and efficiently. He could tidy up the loose ends. It also crossed his mind that in one way, whoever had killed Grillo had done him a favour. Grillo's share of the factory, and the loan that had enabled Jovanovic to buy a share, died with him. In reality, the factory was now his. He was the sole owner. It was a cheering thought. And if things did go seriously pear-shaped for any reason, he would just take the twenty-eight grand and disappear again. The Serb was in the habit of always keeping a back door in view and he was a survivor because of this philosophy. He always made sure that he had a contingency plan worked out. But now he decided it was time to be proactive.

Goran Jovanovic got out of the car and walked round to the front door. There he waited in the lobby in the hope that one of the residents would either come in or out. When neither happened, he rang all the door bells. There was a clamour as three or four voices simultaneously crackled over the speaker but, inevitably, someone hit the door release and Jovanovic pushed the security door and made for the lift.

He had no trouble with the lock of the girl's flat. Although there was a mortise lock in evidence it was not engaged so he only had a simple Yale to deal with. He closed the door quietly and had a look around. In front of him the sitting room door was wide open and immediately his eye fell on the briefcase lying on its side on the coffee table. He had a sudden surge of hope as he strode over to it, which faded as soon as he saw that the lock had been forced. He wrenched it open and was unsurprised to find it empty.

Chapter Twenty-Five

When Scarlett and Maisy went down to the cafeteria to get a bite to eat, Scarlett checked her messages, then immediately called Drew back. 'Where are yeh?'

'Where the hell are you? I've been ringing you for ages.'

'I had to switch the phone off. I'm still at the hospital. Did yeh call the cops? Did yeh call Vinnie? Are yeh still followin' Cahill?'

'I lost him, the man drives like a lunatic, but Vinnie's on the case. How's Gold?'

Scarlett sighed. 'He's a feckin' mess, but he told me Cahill attacked him, so at least I can use the quote. He on heavy pain killers right now, so I was lucky to catch him between shots.'

'Look, I'm quite close by, would you like a lift into town?'

'In the Z3, are yeh jokin' me!'

Drew laughed. She was well aware of Scarlett's love affair with fast cars. 'I'll even let you drive.'

As soon as Drew killed the call her phone rang again. The caller display told her it was Vinnie. She let it ring out, then changed her mind and called him back. He might have an update on Cahill.

'Vinnie?'

'Tell me what you know about Nadia Iacob,' he said without preamble.

His tone should have angered her, but she thought, what the hell, I can't put this off any longer. She drove into a vacant space in St Vincent's Hospital car park and cut the engine. 'OK,' she said, 'here's what I know.'

Cahill made his way up to intensive care, keeping an eye out for cops. He didn't expect any trouble. He knew for sure that they'd only have the one on duty; Gold was hardly a priority and the shift was due to change shortly. He scanned the doors as he strolled along. Cahill never hurried anywhere unless on four wheels. He had learned that running or moving at speed when on foot only drew attention, and he confined himself to running only on a treadmill at the gym, or as a last resort when in flight. Ahead of him, two young doctors in white coats walked out of a door marked *Staff*. He let them walk on a bit, then ducked inside the room. He was prepared in case there was anyone inside, he'd ask directions to X-Ray or something, but the small staff room was empty. After a brief search he found what he was looking for, a white lab coat thrown across the back of a chair, so he picked it up and tried it for size. Best to look inconspicuous. Best to blend in. Witnesses would only see the coat. 'He was a doctor, Sergeant. He had a white coat.'

It was a tad tight around the chest but if he left it open it looked OK. He viewed himself in the mirror, then picked up a stethoscope that someone had left on the sofa and slung it around his neck. George Clooney, eat your bleedin' heart out, he thought. Angela would love him in this. Maybe he'd hold on to the outfit for later after the pub. He turned from side to side, admiring his reflection. Not bad for forty-odd, he thought to himself. He sucked in his stomach and tensed his pecs. Not bad at all. Just then the door opened and a young Asian man walked in. Embarrassed, Cahill pretended to fix his lab coat. 'Well, things to do,' he said lamely and sauntered casually out.

From the end of the corridor he could see the uniform leaning against the wall chatting to a nurse. He was a fat, lazy looking bastard. Cahill walked over to a notice board and feigned interest. The cop was still talking. Cahill looked at his watch, it was just going on two. Any minute now, he thought. As the words were forming in his head, the cop looked at his watch, then glanced up and down the corridor. Cahill surreptitiously did the same. There was no sign of the cop's relief. He was hoping that the fat bastard would just go, he looked the type who would say *feck it* and leave, but he didn't. He leaned against the wall again, arms folded. Cahill was getting agitated. After a couple of minutes, Fat Bastard looked at his watch again. As he did so a young cop hurried past Cahill, and Fat Bastard, spotting his relief, heaved himself off the wall. Cahill read his lips. 'Where the feck were you?'

They chatted for a minute or so, then Fat Bastard strode down the corridor towards the lift. No danger of him taking the stairs. Cahill ducked his head away, but Fat Bastard didn't give him a second glance. The relief cop was younger. Thin but tall. Cahill watched as he peeked in at Gold through the window of ICU, then walked over to the window on the corridor and looked out. A nurse went into Gold's room and came out a couple of minutes later. The young cop said something to her and she laughed. They stood talking for a couple of minutes, bantering. Cahill was past agitated now, he was edgy. Very edgy. He was mentally kicking himself for not finishing the job last night. The last thing he needed was for a ponce like Gold to grass him up for GBH – attempted murder even, if the cops got heavy. He was angry with himself for losing it in the first place, and for what? He could have taken the cash from the Aussie no problem. Now he had to shut the whinging bastard up.

The nurse moved on and the cop resumed his post outside Gold's door. Cahill racked his brains, trying to think of a plan. He had to get the cop away from Gold's door, but how? Just then fortune smiled on Sid Cahill. He saw the young cop glance up and down the corridor, then make a bee-line for the Gents. Cahill didn't waste any time. He strode purposefully up the corridor towards Gold's room.

Vinnie Hogan knew that the name Broylan Grillo rang a bell, and it took only moments to recall that one Broylan Grillo had been found dead that morning in the Phoenix Park. Not his case, but ten to one it was the same guy. How many people by the name of Broylan Grillo lived in Dublin? He had called a friend at Garda headquarters and learned that, although the circumstances surrounding the death were initially suspicious, the autopsy had revealed that the man had died of natural causes, namely a heart attack. That there were no signs of violence on the body and it had been moved post-mortem. The man had American citizenship and was resident in Dublin. Enquiries were ongoing.

Drew had given him the address of the Leatherland factory as well as Goran Jovanovic's address on North Circular Road. She had refused to elaborate on her sources, saying only that they were reliable, were not involved in any crime and that she had promised not to drag them into it. He knew it was useless attempting to persuade her. She was a journalist. He also knew her well enough to have no doubt that the information would have some substance. He suspected that maybe the source or sources were illegals themselves, even though Drew had sworn that they were not, but he didn't labour the point. He glanced at his watch. Just after two. He should have been going off shift now, but instead he set about organising search warrants.

Drew found Scarlett and Maisy in the cafeteria sitting over half finished cups of tea. There was the remains of a chocolate muffin on Scarlett's plate, which Drew eyed up hungrily. Her stomach reminded her that she hadn't eaten anything since the night before, so she reached over and popped it into her mouth.

'Any news on Sid Cahill?' Scarlett asked.

Drew, mouth full, shook her head then swallowed. 'But it's only a matter of time. How big is Dublin? Where can he go?'

'What about the other thing? The refugees?'

'I filled Vinnie in on that too. I found the factory. I'm heading back out there to have a snoop in a while, after I've called in on George. She wasn't too good this morning. I want to make sure she's OK. Then maybe I'll swing by Jovanovic's flat and doorstep him. Depending on how fast the cops move, I should have cracking copy for Monday's first edition.'

Scarlett pushed her chair back and stood up. 'Are you fit then? I'm headin' back to the office.' She gathered her coat and bag, then frowned. 'Shit! I left me cassette in the ward. We'll walk up with yeh, Maisy.'

It was Scarlett who noticed that there was no guard outside Gold's ward, but she said nothing to the others, just quickened her pace. As she reached the door she felt a further twitch of anxiety. The blinds were drawn and the door closed. A couple of paces ahead of the other two, she cupped her hand to the glass and peered into the room. She relaxed somewhat when she saw a white-coated figure standing beside Gold's bed, until her eyes became accustomed to the dimness and she realised that the figure was holding a pillow over the Australian's face. Afterwards she couldn't remember wrenching the door open or reaching the bed. All she remembered was jumping on Cahill's back and gouging at his eyes with her fingers. Drew and Maisy, who had no idea what was going down, heard the hullabaloo and a string of expletives from Cahill as he backed out of the room thrashing his arms, trying vainly to dislodge Scarlett, who was hanging on like a limpet. The ensuing commotion, Drew and Maisy screaming and yelling at Cahill, and Maisy battering him with her handbag, brought the Guard hurtling from the Gents, zipping his flies as he hurtled. He joined the melee, baton drawn. A crowd had gathered by this time. Cahill managed to dislodge Scarlett by backing into the wall with some force. Drew heard her grunt as all the air was knocked out of her lungs and she slid to the floor. It took the cop, two orderlies, a porter and the young Asian doctor whom he had encountered in the staff room to subdue Cahill. Drew helped Scarlett to her feet. She was white-faced and gasping but livid and pumped for action. As Cahill lay face down on the floor being cuffed by the shamefaced cop, she aimed a hefty kick at his side. 'Bastard!'

'I'll pretend I didn't see that,' the cop muttered.

Meanwhile, Maisy and a nurse were checking Gold out. Thankfully he was fine, unaware of the drama, blissfully floating on his morphine cloud. Just like buses, none when you need one, then four come along together, the place was swarming with cops within ten minutes and Cahill was carted off into custody. Scarlett had regained some colour by this time, but was still high as a kite, as were Drew and Maisy. After a while, when they stopped babbling and came down a couple of notches, Maisy said, 'Well, I think I'll go home for a while now the excitement's over.' She reached out and squeezed Scarlett's hand. 'Thanks again, love. We appreciate your help, me and Bruce.'

They parted in the car park and Drew let Scarlett drive into town, switching places outside *The Daily Record* office on Abbey Street.

'I'll call yeh later and we'll go out on the tare,' Scarlett said as Drew slid across into the driver's seat.

'Count on it,' Drew replied.

George opened her eyes, immediately regretting it as a pain shot through her head like a javelin. Her mouth was dry and her stomach nauseous. Perhaps the guts of half a bottle of vodka in the space of fifteen minutes wasn't the most sensible breakfast she reflected as she squinted at the clock. Two thirty-five. She'd been asleep for over three hours.

Asleep? Passed out more like. But strangely, although feeling like death, mentally she felt better. Calmer. She had cried all the tension out of her system. She rolled over and sat up. The pain in her head increased in waves in tune with her heartbeat. She closed her eyes and rested her head in her hands until the thumping subsided, then tentatively stood up. A rush of dizziness overcame her and she steadied herself against the bed. Then the phone rang. She winced as the noise assaulted her, then made a grab for the receiver to make it cease.

'George Fitz-Simons.'

'Are you OK?' Drew's voice. 'You sound terrible.'

George sat down on the side of the bed again. 'I'm fine. I just woke up. I was asleep. What's up?'

'Hey, listen, all kinds of shit's been going down. I was on my way over to Inchicore, but I'll drop by on the way and fill you in.'

In her present delicate condition, George found Drew's enthusiasm both irritating and exhausting. 'What stuff? What are you talking about?'

'Stuff to do with Grillo and the illegals he was bringing in. Anyway, I'm in traffic so I'll see you in a bit.'

Before she could put her off, Drew hung up. George groaned. The last thing she felt like was talking to anyone, let alone about Grillo, and she didn't give a shit about illegals.

She was still muttering to herself as she heard the bedroom door open.

Goran Jovanovic had been sitting on the sofa, a crystal tumbler of vodka in his hand, waiting. He had found the Absolut in the freezer, only about an inch in the bottom of the bottle, but enough to pour over ice. He looked at his watch. He had been in the apartment almost half an hour and there was still no sign of the woman. Grillo's briefcase sat on the sofa beside him. When the phone rang he sat staring at it. He had no intention of answering, then it stopped ringing and he heard a muffled voice coming from the bedroom. It gave him a jolt. He had assumed that the apartment was empty because the woman's car wasn't outside. It hadn't struck him to check it out. He rose from the sofa, walked softly towards the bedroom door and opened it. She was sitting on the bed. Blonde and beautiful.

'Who the fuck are you?'

'Who the fuck are you?' he countered.

He was an ugly man with horribly pock-marked skin and greasy hair dragged back in an elastic band. His accent was thick and foreign sounding but she wasn't afraid. The vodka and the roller-coaster that she had ridden over the past twenty-four hours had dulled her emotions. Paralysed them even. She just wanted him to leave, whoever he was. She stood up. 'Get out of my apartment.'

He was still standing in the doorway. 'Where's the woman? Where's Grillo's woman?'

That caught her attention, the mention of Grillo, and her heart started to pound in her chest again. 'What are you talking about?' It came out in a squeak.

He bounded across the room and grabbed her wrists. 'The woman in the red BMW. Grillo's woman. Where is she?'

He was hurting her. 'I don't know what you're talking about. I don't know anyone called Grillo.' She struggled to free herself and in desperation bit his hand hard.

He screamed and jumped back, then swiped her across the face with the back of his hand. 'Liar! Bitch! His briefcase is out there.' He indicated the sitting room with a jerk of his head, then put his hand to his mouth and sucked at the wound. 'His driver said he was here. I know he was here. Where is his woman? Where is the money?'

The slap and mention of the money set George's resolve. There was no way she was going to hand over that money. It was hers. Rightfully hers. It was her future. She put her hand to the side of her face. She could feel it was hot and it stung. 'I don't know what you're talking about. What briefcase? What money?'

Jovanovic grabbed a handful of her hair and dragged her towards the door.

She staggered after him, holding her head to lessen the pain. 'You're hurting me! ... Let go you bastard! ... I don't know what you're talking about. Who are you? What briefcase?' Like a child caught out in a lie, she continued with the fruitless denial. On reaching the sitting room he gave her a shove towards the sofa.

'*That* briefcase.'

She tripped and fell, landing on her knees, her face inches away from the leather case. 'That's not mine.' She grasped at a straw. 'It's ... um ... it's my flatmate's.' She crawled away from him and stood up, keeping the sofa between them. 'And I don't know anyone called Grillo.'

'He was here. His driver told me he was here last night. Don't lie.' He took a step towards her and she flinched.

'There you are then. I wasn't here last night. My flatmate said she wanted the place to herself. I was out. I wasn't even here.'

He stared at her, trying to decide if she was telling the truth. It was possible. The woman in the BMW must be Grillo's woman, or why would she have followed him?

George searched his face for some sign that he was buying into it. 'Honestly. I was out. She said she wanted the place to herself. I don't know this Grillo person.'

She saw Jovanovic's shoulders relax and she too relaxed a little. Maybe he would go now. Maybe he'd leave her alone. He motioned to the armchair. 'Sit,' he said. 'We will wait for the woman together.'

Chapter Twenty-Six

Drew got a parking space right by the front door. She was still high on adrenaline and on the prospect of an exclusive. It had been a long time since she had had the chance to ferret out a piece of good hard news. She had all but forgotten the buzz. Eat your heart out, Brendan Kerrigan. Vinnie's call had been as difficult as she had expected and she wasn't sure how seriously he would take it. Still, that was his problem. She had given him all the information she had, well, almost all; she had omitted any further reference to Grillo, making the excuse that his was just a name she had been given.

Stay-pressed polyester man was coming through the security door as she approached. She faltered, wondering what his reaction would be. Malevolently she gave him a beaming smile and a chirpy, 'Hello, gorgeous,' and was unsurprised when he froze for an instant before galloping past her out of the front door without looking back. Drew caught the security door before it swung shut.

George was growing steadily more anxious. When she had blurted out the lie about a flatmate it had slipped her mind that Drew was due any minute. She wondered who Jovanovic was talking about when he had referred to Grillo's woman in the red BMW. If Grillo was involved with someone else, well that was good. She could shift the blame onto her. But then of course there was the problem of the briefcase. How could she explain that away? She cursed herself for not getting rid of it, but she'd been in no state to

263

think clearly. Besides, how was she to know that this bastard would come looking for it? Would he really think that Drew was Grillo's girlfriend? Surely not. She was hardly the type the vile little man would go for, not in the wildest stretches of the imagination. But then if Jovanovic didn't come to that conclusion, would she have a sudden attack of conscience and tell the truth? No, she was a journalist and everyone knew journalists didn't have consciences. More likely the threat of physical violence would cause her to blab, and George was now under no illusion that Jovanovic would resort to physical violence in order to get his sticky hands on the money. She wondered if he was aware of how much Grillo had had with him. She had to work on the assumption that he did. Still, Drew didn't know where she had hidden the cash, so she would just continue to deny any knowledge and, hopefully, would strenuously deny that she was the girlfriend. The flaw in the plan: how would they explain away the frigging briefcase?

A tap on the door made Jovanovic rise from his seat and he grabbed George by the arm. 'Get rid of them.'

'But what if it's my flatmate?'

'She has no key?'

George cringed. He pushed her in the back, propelling her towards the door. She peeped through the spy hole. 'It's Drew,' she hissed. 'It's my flatmate.' Whatever the consequences of having Drew blab, she decided that she had a better chance of coming out of the situation unscathed if she had company. If she wasn't alone with this creep. He'd have a hard time handling two of them. She opened the door. Drew stood grinning in the doorway.

'Hi. You won't believe the morning I've had.'

As soon as she walked through the door, Jovanovic slammed it behind her. Drew spun around. She smelt him before she saw him. A sickly sweet smell of aftershave or cologne or something. It reminded her of Brendan Kerrigan. She recognised him immediately. George had been hoping that Jovanovic would realise that Drew was not the woman he was looking for now, but was shocked when he grabbed her by the arm and pushed her roughly against the wall. 'Where is it? Where's the money, bitch?'

They went through the same *What money? I don't know anyone called Grillo* routine as George had not fifteen minutes previously. Then George was further stunned when Jovanovic said, 'Why were you following me? That was you in the red BMW. I recognise you. Why did you follow me?'

Drew shot a look at George. Her mouth was hanging open and her eyes were panicky, darting every which way as if looking for a way out, so she was no help. She took a deep breath. 'My name is Drew Looney and I'm a journalist with *The Daily Record*. I was following you, Mr Jovanovic, because I believe you are importing illegal immigrants into this country and exploiting them in your factory, Leatherland. That's why I was following you. My editor knows where I am at this moment, and I have also passed on all the information I have to the Gardai.'

'You are not Grillo's woman?' He stared at her through narrowed eyes, struggling with the information she had just given him. It occurred to him then that the other one must be lying. He spun around and grabbed George by the arm. 'Liar! Fucking liar. You *are* his woman. Where is the money?'

'Mr Jovanovic,' Drew's voice was full of authority, but she was quaking in her boots. He ignored her. She raised her voice. 'Mr Jovanovic, could I have a comment on the allegations concerning the traffic in illegal immigrants, please? And I warn you, if you don't let go of Ms Fitz-Simons, I'll have no alternative but to call the Guards.'

The Serb pushed George hard and she stumbled against the wall, cracking her head. In an instant he had Drew in a head lock, a long bladed knife at her throat. Even in her slightly disoriented, fuzzy state George couldn't believe what a prat Drew was to try and face off this mad man. Jovanovic's eyes were wild. 'Give me the money or I cut her throat,' he yelled at George. Drew was clawing at the Serb's hands, trying to loosen his hold. He was choking her.

'I don't know what you're talking about,' George wailed. 'I don't *have* any money.'

Drew felt a warm trickle on her neck, but felt no pain. She knew that he had cut her, but wondered why it hadn't hurt at all. She could see George staring, horrified. Jovanovic tightened his grip until she thought that she was going to pass out. 'The money,' he yelled again. Drew looked down and saw the red drips on her jacket. Fuck, he's going to kill me, she thought. She couldn't speak because of Jovanovic's arm squeezing the life out of her. She knew that if something didn't happen soon he'd either choke her or cut her throat. She struggled, trying to loosen his grip, then thankfully George screamed, 'OK. OK. Let her go. I'll get the fucking money.'

It seemed like a lifetime before Jovanovic released his grip. Drew, gasping, sucked air into her lungs. She put her hand to her throat. It came away red. 'I need a towel,' she said. Jovanovic looked around then grabbed the magenta Pashmina off the hall stand and thrust it towards Drew. She hesitated, not because she was reluctant to get blood on the cashmere wrap, but because it was the one that had been around Grillo's shoulders the previous night.

'Take it!' he barked. She did as she was told. 'The money.' He gripped Drew's arm again. He still had the knife in his other hand. Drew saw that it was a switch blade, thin and about seven inches long. A couple of drops of her blood stained the sharp edge of the steel.

George led him towards the bedroom then pointed at the bed. 'It's under the mattress.'

'Get the case,' he ordered. 'I will slit her throat if you try anything.' Neither woman doubted him. George returned a moment later with Grillo's briefcase. 'Put the money in the bag,' he ordered. He pushed Drew forward. 'You. Help her.'

George lifted the edge of the mattress revealing the loose bank notes. Heaps of them. It looked so much more now they were out of the wrappers. They began lifting handfuls and stuffing them in the case. Jovanovic stood by watching, his face more passive now. Obviously the sight of all that money had a palliative effect on him. When they had gathered up all the cash Jovanovic walked round behind them and lifted the mattress higher, checking to see that they had it all. As he was doing this Drew reached into her pocket and withdrew Maddie's ziplock bag of cocaine and slipped it into the side pocket of the briefcase. She wasn't altogether sure why she was doing it. Somewhere in the back of her mind she hoped that if the cops did catch up with him and Jovanovic tried to wriggle out of it, the discovery of the coke would be enough to hold him, charge him even. George saw her and her eyes became huge, her brain registering that there must be at least five grams in the bag. Drew gave an imperceptible shake of her head, and George looked away. Satisfied that he had all the cash, Jovanovic let the mattress fall back on the bed.

'You'll go now?' George said. 'We won't tell anyone.'

Jovanovic ignored her. He spoke to Drew. 'You have the BMW?'

Drew nodded and fished the keys out of her pocket. 'Take it. It's parked outside the front door.'

'No,' he said. 'You will drive me. We will go together.'

'There's no need for that.' George's panicky voice high as a Smurf's.

Jovanovic gave a crooked smile. Drew noticed that his teeth were yellow, the front incisor discoloured brown. 'You have a choice,' he said. 'I cut your throats to keep you silent, or you come with me until I decide what I will do.'

No contest.

Chapter Twenty-Seven

Drew was happier driving than she would have been sitting in the back. She could see George through the rear view mirror. Jovanovic was crunched up next to her holding the open blade in his hand. 'Drive,' he barked. 'To my flat. North Circular. You know where it is.'

Drew reversed out of the parking space and turned right onto Waterloo Road, irritated that he appeared to know that she had followed him from his flat. So much for the usefulness of the surveillance techniques learned from *The Bill*. Her brain was working overtime. Through the rear view mirror Jovanovic looked tense. He had his right arm around George now, and she was cringing away from him. It was a toss up as to whether her reasons were fear, disgust or his overuse of men's toiletries.

'Don't try to be smart,' he growled. 'I stick the bitch if you try to be smart.'

Drew believed him and tossed the plan that had just formed in her head of rear ending the first cop car she came across. It was a vain hope anyway. Even driving past Pearse Street Garda Station there wasn't one Garda car, motor cycle or even cop in evidence. She crossed the Liffey at the Four Courts, still without encountering the long arm of the law, and was at a loss as to what to do. Sure, she could jam on the brakes, open the driver's door and make a run for it, but what about George? What if he panicked and stabbed George? She was trapped in the back of a two-door sports car. No, she decided, best to wait until they were out of the car. Better chance for both of them to avoid injury if away from the confines of the car.

She felt a sudden surge of hope as ahead of them outside the Law Society on Blackhall Place she spied a Garda checkpoint. She glanced in the rear view. Jovanovic was looking out through the rear window and hadn't seen it yet. There were three cars ahead of her. The Guard pulled the first one in and his partner glanced at the tax and insurance disks on the next and waved him on. Drew glanced in the rear view again. Jovanovic was still peering out of the back window. She edged the car forward, contemplating what to do. Her options were limited. Accelerate then jam on the brakes. Odds on Jovanovic would be taken off guard and would be flung forward in the seat, maybe knocked senseless as he wasn't strapped in. But then neither was George. What if she whacked her head on the back of the driver's seat? Broke her neck even. The other option was to attract the cops' attention. But how?

'Don't even think about it,' Jovanovic snarled from the back seat and Drew's heart fell. To add insult to injury, the cop didn't catch her eye, even though her face was going through a full range of expressions. He just glanced at the tax and insurance disks and waved her on, more interested in the flash car than the occupants.

'Move, move!' Jovanovic hissed. 'Get moving. Go! Go! Go!'

Drew put her foot on the floor and surged away, tyres screeching. Jovanovic and George were both thrown back in their seats. She heard Jovanovic grunt and George yelp. Through the wing mirror she saw with mounting frustration that the cops didn't react. Not even a turned head.

Sod's law.

Jovanovic was still grunting and cursing but George was silent. Drew snuck a quick look over her shoulder and saw that she was sitting back in her seat, bolt upright, in the furthest corner away from Jovanovic, her face the colour of uncooked pastry. Jovanovic was bending over, scrabbling about on the floor. It was only then that she realised, too late, as he picked up the knife, that he had dropped it as she accelerated and he was flung back. He seemed unaware that the move had been deliberate. 'Take it easy,' he shouted. 'Slow down.'

Drew throttled back a bit. She was coming into heavy traffic anyway, so her progress was impeded. She took a left onto the North Circular Road off Phibsborough Road and carried on until she was in sight of Jovanovic's flat.

'Drive past.' He said from the back seat. 'Drive past and stop when I tell you.'

Drew took another look in the rear view mirror and saw that once again he had an arm around George and was holding the blade to her side. She followed his instructions to the letter.

Vinnie had been fortunate to catch District Justice Wise as he got back home from his usual Saturday round of golf, so the search warrants had been obtained relatively speedily. He was standing in the sitting room of Jovanovic's first-floor flat looking out of the window. The search had unearthed nothing of an incriminating nature so far and he was disappointed. They needed a lead on the Nadia Iacob case. So far they had nothing. None of the girls working the Canal knew her, which suggested that she probably wasn't a hooker. No one else had come forward, not surprising considering she was an illegal so those who did know her were likely to be illegals themselves, and there were no witnesses.

'Got his passport,' Jack Hartigan said. Vinnie turned back from the window. 'Goran Jovanovic.' He mispronounced the J and the C of the last name, hardening them. 'He's Serbian. Stamped entering France, but no Irish visa.'

He handed the passport to Vinnie then continued to look through the documents in the sideboard drawer. Vinnie took it, thumbed through the pages then turned back to the window. Jovanovic was also an illegal. But where did the man Grillo come into it? Drew had named him specifically. Was it co-incidence that he was also dead? He was legal and by all accounts a respectable businessman, though he'd been unable to establish from where the man derived his sizeable income as yet. The only information he had been able to glean from Garda Headquarters was that he had died of natural causes, he held an American passport, had no next of kin and lived in a large apartment on Shrewsbury Road. The only iffy thing about it was that the body had been moved after death. Why?

These thoughts were milling through his mind when below him a red BMW Z3 cruised by. He snapped to attention as he saw the driver looking up at him. It was clearly Drew, driving Maddie Reibheinn's car. She was staring directly at him but didn't acknowledge him. He also made out two figures in the back: a woman and a man. As they were level with the house she suddenly accelerated past so he didn't get a good look at the passengers.

'Drive to the factory,' Jovanovic snapped. He sounded even more edgy. He couldn't fail to notice the white Garda car parked half on the pavement outside the flat. Apart from the blue and yellow dayglo stripe along the side, the flashing blue lights on the roof were a dead giveaway. Drew had recognized Vinnie's more subtle Renault and had seen him standing in the upstairs window. She was unsure if he had seen her, but at least it showed that he had taken heed of the information she had given him. Hopefully there would be more cops at the factory. As she drove along the North Circular towards Infirmary Road heading for Conyngham Road, she made up her mind that come hell or high water, she would do whatever it took to get the cops' attention. There was no way she was going to drive past the factory, whatever Jovanovic said. There were too many secluded factory sites in the area. It was too dangerous. No telling what Jovanovic would do given an isolated spot. She hoped that the cops would be a tad more discreet this time, perhaps parking around the back, which would improve the odds of George and herself coming away in one piece. She sent telepathic messages to Vinnie, willing him to have seen her. She didn't hold out much hope.

Then she had a brainwave. Her mobile was in her pocket. Casually, with one eye on Jovanovic in the rear view mirror, she slid her hand into the pocket and fished it out, dropping it onto her lap. Jovanovic had relaxed a little and had let go of George. She had scooted as far away from him as she could. All of four inches away. Drew reached over and switched on the radio, flipping the volume control upwards to cover the bleeping sound of her phone. She scoured her memory. She was certain that Vinnie was the last person she had called. As Boyzone blared out of the speakers she punched *redial*.

'Put it off!' Jovanovic barked. 'Put it off. Do nothing unless I tell you!'

Drew reduced the volume. 'I thought there might be news,' she said.

'Put it off!' Jovanovic yelled, reaching forward over the seat. Drew snapped it off quickly, afraid that if he leaned fully over the seat he'd see her mobile lying on her lap. The car was instantly silent. Jovanovic settled back in his seat. The purr of the engine only just covered the sound of Vinnie's phone ringing.

When Vinnie saw Drew's number on the display he hit the yes button. 'Drew?'

All he heard in reply was a fit of coughing, then Drew's distant but insistent voice. 'Where did you say you wanted me to take you, *Mr Jovanovic*? The factory in *Inchicore* was it?'

*

272

The factory appeared to be deserted when they reached it. Jovanovic ordered her to drive in and park around the back. Immediately Drew regretted her hope that the cops might employ some subtlety, and was relieved when there were no patrol cars lurking in the shadow of an overflowing skip.

'What now, *Mr Jovanovic*?' Drew's voice had increased in decibel terms, but Jovanovic seemed not to notice. She turned in her seat. George was staring at her as if she was mad.

'Get out,' Jovanovic said.

Drew undid her seatbelt and used the opportunity to slip her phone back in her pocket. She opened the door and slid out, then lifted the seat forward. Jovanovic shoved George out ahead of him. She stumbled, but Drew caught her. Then the Serb handed Drew a bunch of keys.

'Round to the front. Open the door.' He grabbed George roughly by the arm and pushed her ahead of him. He was still using the threat of the blade, which he held within a couple of inches of George's kidneys. She complied without struggling, not wishing to have any class of amateur 'ectomy'.

Drew's hands shook as she struggled with the lock and Jovanovic was showing signs of impatience. She shot a look at George whose expression was hard to read; somewhere between terrified and down right pissed off. It was hard to tell.

The inside of the building was as dilapidated as the exterior. A panel sagged from the suspended ceiling and one of the fluorescent fittings dangled by a wire. Through a cruddy glass panel, Drew saw a large empty space with a concrete floor. Ahead of them was a staircase and Jovanovic hustled them up to a landing.

'The door at the end,' he said, encouraging George with a poke in the back.

'Don't do that!' she snapped. 'I'm going. I'm fucking going.'

As they walked along the corridor Drew lagged behind a little and glanced through an open door. It was a long room, the length of the corridor in fact, about fifteen feet. She saw two rows of industrial sewing machines, eight in all. There were finished leather jackets in pastel shades, Gucci knock offs hanging up on a rail and the component parts and half finished garments in boxes scattered around.

'Get a move on,' Jovanovic barked. He reached back and grabbed her arm.

Drew scowled at him and shook his hand off. 'Chill out will you, Jovanovic.' Then at a zillion decibels, 'IS THAT WHERE THE ILLEGALS WORK? IN THERE IS IT, MR JOVANOVIC, ON THOSE MACHINES?'

He looked startled by her attitude and the volume, and for an instant she thought that he might hit her, but he didn't. He paused for a beat then said, 'Mind your business.' He tapped the side of his nose, which brought Maddie to mind. At the end of the corridor he kicked a door open and the two women walked ahead of him into a small office. Unlike the rest of the building it was clean and bright, if sparsely furnished. Only a desk with a phone/fax and an answering machine, an electric typewriter, two chairs and, incongruously, a vile bronze desk lamp in the shape of a leaping salmon. There was also a filing cabinet and a hefty old-fashioned safe about three feet by two. Drew stifled an hysterical snigger. It had the look of something out of an old Western movie, out of *Butch Cassidy and the Sundance Kid*.

'You can let us go, you know. We won't say anything,' George said, in her most charming tone. Jovanovic ignored her and spoke to Drew.

'Open the safe. You have the key. It's the big one.'

She still had the keys in her hand. She fumbled, selecting the right one, then bent down and unlocked the safe. Jovanovic shoved her roughly out of the way then and pushed a brass handle to one side. There was a satisfying clunk then he swung the door open.

For some reason Drew had been expecting it to be full of bank notes, old-fashioned dollar bills, but then she *was* under a lot of stress. Jovanovic reached in and pulled out a bundle of passports secured by a thick elastic band.

'Do those passports belong to the illegal immigrants you're bringing in, Mr Jovanovic?' the journalist asked, still enunciating as if she was reading the news for the deaf. Conscious of the open phone line in her pocket, she was speaking very loudly and slowly so as to increase the chances of Vinnie hearing what was going down. Jovanovic was staring at her again as if she was some kind of lunatic, as was George.

'Have you got Nadia Iacob's passport too? Did you kill Nadia Iacob, Mr Jovanovic? Did you have her killed because she ran away and was going to expose your racket?'

Suddenly Jovanovic snapped and sprang forward, walloping Drew with his closed fist. 'Shut the fuck up!' He caught her full in the face and catapulted her back through the door of the office into the corridor. The blow was ferocious. 'Shut the fuck up! Shut the fuck up!' He was ranting out of control. Drew was knocked dizzy by the blow, but was still conscious. Jovanovic was coming at her again. She shuffled back on her bum, trying to get away from him, not wanting to take another blow. She saw him draw his leg back as if preparing to give her a kick and she pulled her knees in to her chest and wrapped her arms around her head, rolling to the side in the foetal position, waiting for the attack. Suddenly there was an almighty crunch and Jovanovic bellowed like a wounded rhino, then another crunch and a thud, followed by a thump. Jovanovic was screaming, then after the last thump he was silent. Drew opened her eyes to see George standing over Jovanovic with the bronze leaping salmon in her hand. There was blood everywhere. It was at that point that Drew's entire face began to scream with pain and they heard the distant wail of sirens.

Epilogue

Like Bruce Gold, Jovanovic also had a thick skull. He was concussed, had a broken collar bone where George had misjudged the last wallop with the leaping salmon, and was under guard in Saint James's Hospital.

Vinnie had arrived with the cavalry two minutes too late, but was nonetheless a welcome sight to George. Drew, by that time, had passed out with the pain of her broken nose and jaw. He was horrified at the sight of her lying motionless in a tangled heap, at first fearing that she was dead. She was whisked off to James's, also under police escort, which left George to drive the Z3 back to Maddie's garage.

After the pain killers kicked in and Drew's nose had been set and her jaw wired, the following day, though somewhat groggy, she insisted that Scarlett find a laptop somewhere so she could write her copy for Monday's first edition. There was no way she was going to let a broken jaw and mangled nose come between her and the best copy she had ever written. The euphoria and adrenaline rush sustained her until it was finished, then she called for more pain relief and passed out peacefully for two days. Vinnie spent every free hour sitting by her bed waiting for her to come round. Seeing her lying in the factory limp and lifeless, covered in blood, had almost caused him heart failure.

In light of the circumstances and tapes, the DPP dropped the charges against Bruce Gold. Scarlett wrote her piece relating Sid Cahill's blackmail plot and his attempt to murder the glam rocker. It made riveting reading, particularly with the tape transcripts, but Joe Mulloy was a tad pissed off that both stories had made the one edition. He felt it would have been better for circulation if they'd been spaced a couple of days apart. But then good news was like the bus thing. Nothing happening for weeks, then it all goes down at once.

Vinnie found Nadia Iacob's passport among the documents belonging to the illegal factory workers and questioned Jovanovic about it. After staring at the wall for twenty-four hours he eventually caved and passed the buck, claiming that Nadia Iacob's murder was nothing to do with him. He piled the blame onto Grillo and Sid Cahill, which was a turn up for the books. It certainly ensured that if convicted, Sid wouldn't see the light of day for a long time.

Sid in turn pointed the finger firmly back at Jovanovic, so the cops threw a conspiracy charge at the two of them for good measure. The other documentation at the factory confirmed that Jovanovic and Grillo were producing counterfeit Gucci leather jackets using illegal labour. A Chechen national, one Igor Dudayev, was arrested at Dublin Port with five Romanian nationals in the back of his container lorry. Nadia Iacob's fellow workers were arrested in a house in Finglas and all immediately applied for political asylum.

The police never figured out who had moved Broylan Grillo's body after his death.

On the third day, Iman Dirie visited Drew in hospital with the news that she was going to visit Nicolae Illescu in Paris. She thanked Drew for taking an interest and apologised for refusing to get involved. It was a one-sided conversation however, because Drew's jaw was still wired up.

As Iman was leaving Vinnie arrived. It was the first time Drew had seen him since she had spied him in the window of Jovanovic's flat and she felt a worrying flush of pleasure at the sight of him. The nurses had told her of his vigil at her bedside. He took the opportunity, whilst her jaw was wired, to suggest that perhaps Scarlett had the right idea and they should give it another shot. Drew would have grinned had she been able. She was secretly chuffed seeing as he was asking her out even though she had withheld information, even though at that moment she bore a startling resemblance to Hannibal Lector. Maybe Scarlett *was* right after all. Maybe he did fancy her.

Barbara Looney was flushed, basking in Drew's reflected glory, and the women at her bridge circle were duly impressed by the gory details of the exploits of Drew Looney, serious journalist (my daughter you know). Maddie was a touch annoyed that Drew had borrowed her car, until Scarlett gently reminded her that she owed her sister-in-law-to-be her life, not to mention the fact that Drew hadn't grassed her up about the drugs overdose to Justin. Maddie suddenly became all sweetness and light, largely because Scarlett implied a threat to bubble her if she wasn't nicer to Drew.

George Fitz-Simons got her life back on track with the aid of the twenty-eight grand she just happened to *find* in the briefcase in the back of Maddie's car. She felt no sense of guilt. The money was hers by rights. Grillo had stolen it from her. That apart, she felt it was little enough pay back for the ordeal of seeing him naked. As she was emptying it onto the bed to sort it into manageable bundles she came across the ziplock bag of cocaine nestling in the side pocket. She picked it out, opened it, poked her finger in and rubbed it on her gums. Then in a fit of bravado she went straight to the bathroom and emptied it down the loo. She felt a pang of regret as the swirling water washed it away, but deep down knew she was doing the right thing.